Gary Hocking

The Debt Collectors
of Auschwitz

Disclaimer

This novel is entirely a work of fiction. The names of characters, the characters themselves and the incidents written in this story are the work of the author's imagination. Any resemblance to any person is entirely coincidental.

Historical Note

This is historical fiction. It is based in World War Two and attempts to make references to historical places and events with well researched accuracy.

Note to the reader

Some of my family were in German prisoner of war camps. I grew up with people around me constantly talking about the war. When I was four years old Holocaust survivors became my neighbors. I played with their kids, I ate meals with them and I knew they were a lot different to my parents. My mother taught them English as much as she could and as I got older she told me about their experiences as she had been told about them.

As a voracious reader I read a ton of books about the Holocaust and the two world wars. I studied three languages at University as well as history. I taught literature for a living for a lot of years.

As I grew up I toured the camps and as a German speaker I interviewed and had conversations with many people from both sides of that major war. I always wanted to find out how they felt about it and what made them participate in it. Mostly I travelled alone but sometimes I took my family through these dreadful camps. My most memorable conversations were with the many Holocaust survivors that I met along the way.

A great deal of people today do not know much about the camps or the people who survived them. So in this book I wanted to not write a thriller that emphasized the horror of war but to show people what it was like to have this imposed on you and your family. What happened before, during and after the Holocaust. I have lived with this theme for most of my life and my hope is that I have succeeded in writing an exciting story that will teach as well as be of interest.

1

You Are Standing On My Grave

Auschwitz-Birkenau 1970

My hands were shaking again.

I stood at the edge of the crematorium ruins, watching twenty three Polish schoolchildren hurry back to their bus through the February cold. They hadn't asked the usual questions today. No raised hands wanting to know about numbers, about methods, about how it felt to work here. Just notebooks hastily scribbled in, cameras clicking, eyes averted from mine.

They could sense it, I suppose. The way I'd been coming apart at the seams these past months.

Dr. David Rose, they'd introduced me. Oxford University. As if the title still meant something, as if I hadn't abandoned my perfectly respectable career in Holocaust Studies to take this job that made no rational sense. My colleagues thought I'd lost my mind. Margaret and Harold, safe in their Sussex cottage, had stopped asking when I'd be coming home.

I couldn't explain to them what I couldn't explain to myself. Why I'd felt compelled to come here, to this place that haunted my sleep. Why standing among these ruins felt more like coming home than anywhere I'd ever lived.

The nightmares had started eighteen months ago. Always the same fragments. A woman's voice singing in a language I didn't recognize but somehow understood. The smell of carbolic soap mixed with terror. Small hands reaching through wire, always just out of reach. I'd wake gasping, tears on my cheeks, my body remembering something my mind refused to acknowledge.

The mist was rising from the cold ground now, thick as a burial shroud. I should have been walking back to the main gate, should have been heading home to my cramped flat in *Oświęcim*. Instead, I found myself moving deeper into the camp, past the familiar paths where I led my tours, toward the far corner where the preservation work hadn't yet reached.

My breath came in sharp puffs that clouded the air. The fog was thickening, muffling the distant rumble of the school bus pulling away, the last sound of the living world. Here, in this forgotten corner where the broken bricks lay scattered like discarded bones, the silence felt absolute.

I bent to pick up a fragment of weathered stone, and the moment my fingers closed around it, the world tilted sideways.

"You are standing on my grave."

The voice cut through me like a blade made of memory. I spun around, the brick tumbling from my nerveless fingers, my heart hammering against my ribs.

Nothing. Only mist and the weight of watching eyes.

"I'm losing my mind," I whispered to the fog. The breakdown I'd been fighting for months had finally arrived. This was how it ended, not with a bang but with hallucinations in a Polish death camp.

"You are not mad, child." The voice was closer now, gentle but commanding. "You are drowning in secrets that were never yours to carry."

A scent drifted through the fog, pipe tobacco and old cologne, faded but unmistakable. My knees nearly buckled. That smell had been threading through my nightmares for months, always just out of reach, always accompanied by a melody I couldn't place.

"I am Jacob, your grandfather." The words wrapped around me like an embrace. "I have come to you, my beloved David, because you are dying inside, and I cannot bear to watch you suffer alone."

"This isn't real." I pressed my palms against my temples, but the voice continued.

"You have carried a burden too heavy for any soul to bear. Your past has been stolen from you, but it calls to you still. That is why you came here, why you cannot stay away."

The fog swirled, and for a heartbeat I seemed to see him. Tall, stooped shoulders, kind eyes behind wire-rimmed spectacles. A face that belonged in my dreams, in the spaces between sleeping and waking where truth lived.

"Wait." I reached toward the shape in the mist, but my hand closed on empty air. "I need to understand. Why can't I remember? Why do I feel like I'm dying inside?"

"Because you are, child. The truth has been buried so deep it's poisoning you from within." The voice was fading now, carried away in the wind. "Find Miriam Weiss. She holds your past, David. She is the key to your survival."

"Where? How do I find her?"

"She lives still. In New York. Find her before it's too late."

A lullaby drifted through the air, the same melody that had been haunting my sleep. Now, instead of filling me with dread, it wrapped around me like a mother's arms. The tune I'd been humming unconsciously for months, the song that made me weep without knowing why.

Then silence.

I stood frozen in the thickening fog, my breath visible in sharp bursts. The scent of tobacco lingered for another moment before the wind carried it away, leaving only the smell of old stone and winter earth.

When I finally moved, my legs felt unsteady. I made my way back through the ruins, past the memorial plaques and preserved barracks, toward the car park where my rented Škoda waited alone. The caretaker would be arriving soon to lock the gates.

As I fumbled with the keys, my hands still trembling, something shifted inside my chest. For the first time since the nightmares began, I felt the crushing weight of isolation lift slightly. Not the careful, puzzled affection Margaret and Harold had always shown their strange, damaged adopted son, but something fierce and unconditional. The kind of love that reaches across death itself.

Jacob. My grandfather.

The fragments in my mind began shifting, trying to form a picture I'd never been allowed to see. A grandfather I'd never known but somehow recognized. A woman named Miriam who held the keys to everything I'd lost. Parents who had died somewhere, somehow, leaving me with nothing but nightmares and an inexplicable pull toward this cursed place.

I sat in the car as darkness fell around Auschwitz-Birkenau, the engine running but my hands still gripping the wheel. New York. Miriam Weiss was in New York, an ocean away from where I sat.

I couldn't wait until tomorrow. I couldn't spend another night drowning in fragments and half-remembered terrors. Tonight I would drive to Kraków, catch the first flight to London, then onward to New York. Tonight I would begin the search for the woman who held the keys to my survival.

For the first time in my life, I had a name to call the voice that sang in my dreams.

For the first time in months, I had hope.

2

The Berlin Interpreter

Miriam Weiss knew six ways to say "peace" in different languages, but in the spring of 1935, none of them meant a goddamn thing anymore.

She stood in Humboldt University's grand foyer, her stomach twisting tighter with every passing minute. The Italians had arrived late, after their taxi got lost. They came in laughing, shoulders loose, as though the delay was part of some running joke. The British clustered near the refreshments, their voices lowered as though speaking too loudly might violate some unspoken rule of diplomacy. The Americans filled the marble space with noisy ease, their words bouncing like loose coins against the high ceilings.

Miriam often found herself wondering how entire nations came to wear these temperaments like second skins. Was it the climate? History? Chance? Why should Italians sparkle where Germans stiffened? If character could be shaped by culture, what was Berlin shaping now? What was Germany becoming?

The swastikas rising along that wonderful street in Berlin, Unter den Linden, offered one answer. But perhaps not the only one.

The Germans moved differently. Quieter, but not quiet. Like they owned the place. Which, of course, they did.

Her navy dress chafed at her neck. The perfect translator was supposed to be invisible. Hard to be invisible when you cannot breathe properly.

"*Buongiorno, signori. Sono Miriam Weiss, la vostra interprete per la conferenza.*" (Good morning, gentlemen. I am Miriam Weiss, your interpreter for the conference.) A simple introduction, but the Italian delegation's relief showed in the softening of shoulders and nods.

Twenty minutes until this circus began. International trade agreements, for God's sake. Like rearranging deck chairs while the ship quietly shifted course toward jagged rocks. But pretense ruled Berlin now. Pretense that the new flags weren't heavy with swastikas. Pretense that words could still paper over what everyone already sensed.

As she moved through the hall, sunlight caught on something across the street: a fresh poster slapped onto a wall. Even from this distance, she recognized the caricature, nose exaggerated, eyes narrowed, as another layer added to Berlin's growing ugliness. Her smile didn't falter.

"Fräulein Weiss."

Professor Webber. Fifty-something, beard trimmed with military precision. Two years ago, he'd recommended her for her first major assignment. These days, his eyes rarely held hers for long.

He had a French diplomat in tow, short, balding, nervous.

"Our guest has concerns about the translation arrangements," Webber said stiffly, his words clipped in that careful way so many now adopted. As if speaking for audiences they couldn't see.

Miriam switched easily to French, watching the diplomat's shoulders ease as her words landed. Webber gave a tight nod and turned away.

"Show Monsieur Rousseau to the preparation room."

Across the foyer, a young man watched her. Tall, broad-shouldered, with the kind of profile that belonged on a statue rather than a university campus. He held a copy of Faust in one hand. His gaze was steady, lacking the flicker of nervousness so common in Berlin these days. Something about him seemed familiar, though she couldn't place where she might have seen him.

Later, in the quiet of an empty corridor, she leaned against the wall and closed her eyes. Ten seconds to herself. Nine. Eight.

"It must be exhausting."

Her eyes snapped open. The young man stood a few feet away, studying her with Baltic-blue eyes. Up close, she noticed a thin scar tracing along his jawline, not the clean line of a dueling scar, but something jagged, accidental.

"I beg your pardon?"

16

"Being inside so many minds at once. French, Italian. That's three languages already this morning. It must feel like weaving between worlds."

There was no condescension in his tone, only curiosity. She found herself answering honestly.

"Each language has its own rhythm. Its own logic."

"And which logic do you call home?"

Her spine stiffened. Was this a test? "German, of course."

He smiled faintly. "Forgive the obvious question." He extended a hand. "Dieter Ecker. Final-year law student."

The name clicked. "Ecker. You're Professor Ecker's son."

His face tightened almost imperceptibly. "You know my father?"

She did. Heinrich Ecker, who'd taught constitutional law until his dismissal last year. Officially for "restructuring." Unofficially for his vocal opposition to certain legal reforms. The kind of professor who'd once filled lecture halls, now persona non grata.

"I know of him," she said carefully.

"Then you understand why I find bridges between worlds so fascinating these days." His voice carried a weight that made her reassess everything about this conversation. "Translation isn't just about words, is it? It's about finding ways to say what needs to be said when the old words have been... redefined."

Now she understood his interest. And why he'd approached her despite the risks.

"Miriam Weiss," she said, completing their introduction.

"I know. Your reputation precedes you. The linguist who never falters."

"You make me sound like a magician."

"Isn't that what we need now? People who can make impossible things possible?"

The corridor felt smaller. Not with flirtation, but with shared understanding. Two people whose fathers had built careers on words, watching those words lose their meaning.

"I should return to the auditorium."

"Of course." He stepped aside. "Perhaps we might continue this conversation another time? The university café?"

She studied his face. Heinrich Ecker's son, carrying his father's intellectual courage and his father's dangerous principles. Someone who understood exactly what she was risking by simply being here.

"Perhaps," she said. "If our paths cross again."

"I've found paths have a way of crossing, if one pays attention," he replied, holding up his Faust before turning away.

The conference proceeded without incident, which in 1935 Berlin counted as its own small victory. By late afternoon, her head ached, not from translation itself, but from resisting the urge to smooth over the German trade minister's increasingly nationalistic tone. Each aggressive phrase she faithfully rendered felt like another small betrayal of the room's stated purpose.

Outside, Berlin greeted her with long shadows. She chose a detour through the Tiergarten, sparing herself from another walk past the posters and banners that multiplied daily.

The park still held remnants of the old Berlin. The same paths her father had walked as a boy. But even here, change whispered through the trees, fewer people lingering on benches, more hurried footsteps on the gravel paths.

"Fräulein Weiss!"

Dieter jogged toward her, slightly breathless, hair mussed, tie loosened.

"Are you following me, Herr Ecker?" she asked, more curious than alarmed.

He flushed. "I saw you enter the park. I thought fate might be offering that continuation of our conversation. Though I admit I walked faster than usual to catch up."

"Most women would find that concerning rather than charming."

"Are you concerned?"

She studied him. In the dappled evening light, his face appeared younger, the scar more pronounced. There was an earnestness to him that felt oddly misplaced in 1935 Berlin, or perhaps it was exactly what Berlin needed.

"No," she admitted. "Though perhaps I should be. These days, even coincidences require careful consideration."

"These days," he echoed quietly, acknowledging everything they couldn't say directly.

They walked in silence until reaching the western edge of the park.

"This is where I leave you, as promised," he said.

"You never fully explained your interest in translation."

He looked past her toward the city. "My father used to say that law was about finding the right words to protect what mattered. But what happens when the words themselves become weapons? When 'legal' and 'right' no longer mean the same thing?"

The question hung between them, dangerous and necessary.

"Translators," he continued, "still work with pure meaning. Word to word, thought to thought. No matter what's happening outside, in that moment of translation, truth still exists."

The sincerity in his voice struck something inside her. Here was someone who saw her work not as mechanical but as a kind of resistance.

"The university café," she said, surprising herself. "Tomorrow at four, if you're still interested."

His smile transformed his serious face. "I will be there."

The Weiss apartment smelled of roasting chicken and her mother's anxiety. Hannah Weiss looked up from her book as Miriam entered, but her eyes held that particular tightness that had become familiar over the past year.

"Your father's not back yet," she said without preamble. "The faculty meeting was supposed to end at three."

Miriam checked the clock. Past seven. Her stomach tightened.

"Perhaps it ran long."

"Perhaps." Hannah's fingers worried the edge of her bookmark. "Professor Kellner stopped by this afternoon. He wanted to discuss your father's course on Romantic poetry. Said there were 'concerns' about the reading list."

Miriam sat heavily in the chair opposite her mother. Professor Kellner, who'd once been her father's closest friend. Who'd celebrated every one of Solomon's promotions, every published paper.

"What kind of concerns?"

"Heinrich Heine, for one. Too much emphasis on Jewish contributions to German literature, apparently." Hannah's voice carried a bitterness Miriam rarely heard. "As if Heine wasn't one of Germany's greatest poets. As if your father hasn't spent twenty years proving that Jewish scholars can love German culture as deeply as anyone."

The front door opened with Solomon's familiar double-turn of the key. But his footsteps in the hallway sounded heavier than usual.

He appeared in the doorway, still wearing his coat, his face gray with exhaustion.

"Papa?" Miriam rose.

"Sit, both of you. Please." He remained standing, hands clasped behind his back in his lecturing pose, though tonight it looked more like a man bracing himself.

"They've asked me to take a leave of absence. Effective immediately."

The words landed like stones in still water. Hannah's book slipped to the floor.

"On what grounds?" Miriam's voice came out steadier than she felt.

"Restructuring. Budget concerns. The usual euphemisms." Solomon's mouth twisted. "Twenty-three years of service. Students who still write to thank me for opening their minds to Goethe's genius. But apparently, my particular insights are no longer... valuable."

Hannah stood slowly, crossed to her husband, and took his coat with the kind of deliberate care that held grief at bay.

"We'll manage," she said simply.

"Will we?" Solomon's voice cracked slightly. "Hannah, they're taking everything we built. Everything we believed in. The Germany we thought we knew..." His voice trailed off.

"It Is still here," Miriam interrupted, surprising them both. "In this room. In your books. In the students who still remember what you taught them."

20

Her father looked at her with something like wonder. "When did you become so wise, my child?"

She thought of Dieter Ecker, of his father's dismissal, of their conversation about finding new words for old truths.

"Someone reminded me today that truth exists in translation. Even when everything else changes, the moment of carrying meaning from one place to another, that stays clean."

Solomon studied her face. "You sound like you've been thinking about something more than trade agreements."

"Perhaps I have."

From the piano, Hannah began to play, not one of her own compositions this time, but Bach. Something structured and mathematical and utterly reliable. The notes filled the apartment like a promise: that some things endure, even when the world shifts beneath them.

Tomorrow, Miriam would meet Dieter Ecker at the university café. Tomorrow, she would continue learning what it meant to build bridges when the ground kept moving beneath them.

But tonight, she sat with her parents in their shrinking world, and helped them remember who they were when the lights went out.

3

Love and Betrayal

Four Thursdays had passed since their first meeting at the café, and Miriam was beginning to understand the rules of a game she hadn't known she was playing.

Each conversation with Dieter stretched longer, each debate more carefully weighted. She watched him test the boundaries of acceptable criticism, probing how far he could push before retreating to safer ground. A law student learning to navigate shifting legal terrain.

"The law is supposed to protect people," Dieter said, tapping a newspaper article about the latest civil restrictions. His voice carried frustration, but she noticed he glanced around the café first.

"And when the lawmakers are the ones you need protection from?" Miriam asked.

His gray eyes met hers. "That's when reasonable people work from inside the system."

"'Special legal measures' instead of persecution," she said quietly. "'Protective custody' instead of imprisonment."

"Exactly. Words matter. The right ones in the right place can change minds."

Miriam nodded, but something cold was forming in her chest. She was beginning to see the pattern: Dieter criticized the methods while accepting the premise. He questioned the execution while embracing the system.

Four Thursdays of watching him practice this delicate balance. Four Thursdays of realizing that even the best Germans were learning to accommodate rather than resist.

"That day at the reception," Dieter said, his voice softening as it often did when he shifted from politics to personal matters, "I couldn't focus on anything else. Three languages flowing from your mouth like you were born speaking all of them."

Heat crept up her neck, but she studied his face carefully. The admiration was genuine, but there was something else there. A fascination with her foreignness, her difference, that felt dangerous.

"It's just a skill," she replied.

"No." His hand moved across the table, covering hers briefly. "It was beautiful. You were beautiful."

The compliment should have pleased her. Instead, she found herself cataloging it as evidence. Evidence of what, she wasn't yet sure.

Outside, darkness had swallowed Unter den Linden. Dieter walked beside her, close enough that their arms brushed with each step.

"Tell me something nobody knows about you," he said.

"I learned Russian from Anna Karenina and a battered dictionary when I was fourteen."

He laughed, delighted. "Of course you did. Meanwhile, I still mangle 'Bonjour' after six years of French."

"I could teach you," she said, the offer opening a door to a future she was increasingly certain would never exist.

At their usual parting corner, instead of their customary formal nod, Dieter took her hand. Before she could prepare herself, he leaned down and kissed her. A brief, soft press of lips that felt like a question.

"Been wanting to do that since I heard you speak Italian," he said.

"Your timing needs work. I was speaking French today."

His smile transformed his serious face. "Saturday, then?"

The pattern established itself through spring into early summer. Debates over coffee that grew more cautious each week. Cultural events where Dieter's choices seemed increasingly calculated. Walks through the Tiergarten where their conversations danced around topics that had once been simple.

At the Mendelssohn concert, Dieter had deliberately left the program open, the Jewish composer's name visible to anyone who cared to look. When an older couple noticed the program and began muttering about "degenerate music," he wrapped his arm around her shoulders. Not hiding. Claiming.

Later, in the Tiergarten's darkness, their kisses deepened into something that felt like hunger. Between embraces, they whispered about impossible futures.

"Switzerland," he said against her hair. "After I finish my degree. A practice in Zurich."

"We could build something there," she replied, allowing herself the fantasy. "Your legal mind, my languages. Somewhere this madness hasn't reached."

But even as she spoke the words, Miriam was calculating. How long before the madness did reach Switzerland? How long before there was nowhere left to run?

The fantasy sustained her through increasingly troubling signs at home. Her father's colleagues had become unavailable for dinner. Her mother's piano students were canceling lessons with flimsy excuses. The translation work that had once come easily was drying up, one rejection letter at a time.

Dieter became her talisman against the growing certainty that their world was shrinking daily. But even that comfort was complicated by her growing awareness of how carefully he managed their relationship. Public enough to seem defiant, private enough to remain deniable.

On a rain-soaked Thursday in late May, Miriam arrived at their usual café to find Dieter already seated, his untouched coffee growing cold. His face had a stillness that sent warning signals through her body.

"What's wrong?" she asked, settling into the chair across from him.

He scanned the nearly empty café before answering. "I've been offered a position. Junior clerk at the Ministry of Justice. Working under Reichskommissar Koch on civil code reform."

Koch. One of the legal architects of the new racial laws. Miriam kept her expression neutral while her mind raced through implications.

"That's quite prestigious," she said carefully.

"It comes with certain requirements." His fingers drummed against the table. "Party membership being the primary one."

"I see."

"Miriam, think about this strategically. The Party isn't monolithic. There are different voices, people working from inside who can moderate the worst impulses."

She watched him construct his rationalization in real time, each word carefully chosen to make collaboration sound like resistance.

"And you would be one of those moderating influences?"

"I could try to be. Koch respects intelligent analysis. If reasonable voices abandon the system entirely, who's left to guide it?"

The logic was seductive and utterly wrong. Miriam realized she was watching someone she cared about disappear before her eyes, replaced by someone who spoke the same words but meant different things.

"My father believed that once," she said quietly. "That reasonable minds would prevail."

"Your father was removed because he refused to adapt," Dieter replied, then immediately looked stricken by his own words. "I'm sorry. I didn't mean..."

"You did mean it," she said, studying his face. "You meant exactly that."

The silence stretched between them until Dieter leaned forward, his voice dropping to barely above a whisper.

"What about us, Miriam?"

She had been expecting this question and dreading it in equal measure.

"What about us?"

"The position comes with scrutiny. Koch made it clear that certain associations would be... problematic for someone in my role."

"Certain associations." Her voice remained level. "You mean Jews."

"Anyone whose background might raise questions about my commitment to current policy." He reached across the table as if to take her hand, then stopped. "At least publicly."

There it was. The offer of secrecy, of relegation to shadows and careful meetings and the slow death of anything real between them.

"What about our plans? Switzerland?"

Pain flickered across his face, quickly replaced by something harder. "Miriam, be realistic. My career will be in Germany. I need to establish my position now, while opportunities still exist."

The calculation in his voice struck her like cold water. He wasn't choosing between love and career. He was choosing between two versions of himself, and the version aligned with power was winning.

"I understand," she said, withdrawing her hands to her lap. "You've made your choice."

"It's not that simple..."

"It's exactly that simple." She stood, reaching for her coat. "You've decided what kind of man you want to be, Dieter. Now I need to decide what kind of woman I'm going to become."

"Miriam, wait. We could still see each other. Carefully. Privately."

She paused in putting on her coat, studying his face. Even now, he didn't understand what he was asking. What he was offering her.

"No," she said, the firmness in her own voice surprising her. "We can't."

She walked into the rain without looking back, her mind already moving beyond grief toward something colder and more useful. If Dieter Ecker, who had kissed her beneath Mendelssohn's forbidden melodies, could be seduced by a party pin and career advancement, then accommodation was not the answer.

If reasonable Germans would choose comfort over conscience, then being reasonable was a luxury she could no longer afford.

That night, listening to rain against her window, Miriam replayed the café scene with the detached interest of a chess player analyzing a completed game. Where she had expected to feel pain, she found something sharper and more clarifying.

Dieter's betrayal had revealed the essential truth: in this new Germany, being Miriam Weiss was becoming a liability that no amount of skill or charm could overcome. The game had changed, and she needed new pieces to play it.

Three weeks later, leaving the library where she had been researching emigration procedures that seemed increasingly futile, she spotted Dieter emerging from a government building across the street. The transformation was remarkable. His student slouch had been replaced by a crisp suit and confident stride. A small red-and-black pin gleamed on his lapel.

He was flanked by two men in Party uniforms, laughing at something one of them had said. His posture was straighter, his gestures more expansive. The earnest law student had been expertly erased.

His eyes found hers across the busy street. For one heartbeat, something like regret crossed his face. Then one of his companions said something, and Dieter turned away, continuing down the street without acknowledgment.

The casual erasure was more effective than any deliberate cruelty could have been. It showed her exactly how completely someone could disappear while remaining visible.

That evening, when her father mentioned new registration requirements for Jewish businesses, Miriam listened with the focused attention of someone gathering intelligence. She found herself studying her parents with new eyes, seeing their visibility, their stubborn insistence on remaining themselves, as strategic errors in a game they refused to acknowledge they were playing.

Her father still believed in the power of reason and scholarship. Her mother still played Chopin in their front parlor where neighbors could hear. They remained themselves with a kind of magnificent defiance that was going to get them killed.

Miriam loved them for their integrity and knew she could not afford to follow their example.

Across Berlin, in his new government apartment, Dieter Ecker reviewed legal briefs that would further restrict Jewish participation in German economic life. His work had earned early praise from Reichskommissar Koch. The party membership had proven easier than expected.

Only occasionally did doubt surface, usually in the quiet hours before dawn when Miriam's face would appear in his mind. But those moments grew less frequent. There was important work to do, and his position allowed him to influence policy in small but meaningful ways.

When reviewing residence registrations later that week, he paused at a familiar Charlottenburg address. The Weiss family. Their religious designation was clearly noted in red ink.

He hesitated, pen hovering over the file. Then he marked it for expedited review, telling himself it was merely procedural efficiency. Nothing personal. Simply his duty as a responsible civil servant in the new Germany.

The file moved to the priority stack, and Dieter returned to his other work, already forgetting the decision that would bring the Gestapo to the Weiss apartment within days.

Meanwhile, in her bedroom, Miriam sat before her mirror studying her reflection with the calculating gaze of someone planning a complex deception. Dark hair, serious eyes, features that marked her as Jewish to anyone looking for such markers.

Soon, she decided. Very soon, Miriam Weiss would need to disappear entirely. And someone else, someone who could navigate this new world with perfect invisibility, would need to take her place.

The transformation had already begun in her mind. The physical change would follow.

She was done being a piece in someone else's game. It was time to become a player.

4

Becoming Layla

Miriam's dismissal letter arrived on Reich Ministry letterhead, the words inside as bland as unsalted bread.

> *We regret to inform you that your services for the*
> *upcoming trade delegation to Brussels will no longer*
> *be required...*

No explanation. None needed. The third letter in two months. Her translation work was being systematically eliminated.

On the bed lay yesterday's newspaper, folded to page four where a small article announced Professor Solomon Weiss had been placed on "indefinite leave" from Humboldt University. The article cited "curriculum reorganization." Another bloodless phrase disguising uglier truth.

Miriam stared at her reflection in the bedroom mirror. Dark curls framed features that had become increasingly dangerous. The thought that had been growing for weeks surfaced again: perhaps Miriam Weiss needed to disappear.

A sharp knock interrupted her thoughts. Not the tentative knock of a neighbor but the authoritative rap that had become too familiar in their building. Three families had already vanished from the fourth floor this month.

She smoothed her skirt, arranged her face into neutral politeness, and opened the door. The smell of wet wool and leather struck her first.

"Yes?"

The older of two men consulted a small notebook. Heavyset, forty-something, with the face of a bank clerk in another life. "Fräulein Miriam Weiss?"

"Yes."

"Gestapo. May we come in?"

She stepped aside, mind racing. The officers entered with practiced efficiency. The older one took the lead while the younger, barely twenty with acne-spotted cheeks, remained by the door.

"Is your father home?"

"Yes. In his study. Shall I fetch him?"

"Not yet." The officer's gaze swept the apartment, cataloging the piano, bookshelves, tasteful artwork. "We have questions about your activities."

Her activities. Which ones? The translation work? The philosophical salon? Or somehow Dieter?

"Of course," she said, translator's training keeping her voice steady despite the fear coursing through her veins. "Please, sit."

He declined with a curt shake. "We've received reports about political discussions at a bookshop in Kreuzberg. Oranienstrasse."

The Thursday evening salon. Those discussions that had once seemed so innocent.

"I attend literary talks there," she replied carefully. "The owner hosts readings. Philosophical discussions. Nothing political."

"Discussions of Nietzsche and Marx are inherently political. Especially when attended by Jews and known dissidents."

The bluntness hit like a physical blow. Her face betrayed nothing.

"I'm a professional translator," she said evenly. "I have scholarly interest in philosophical terminology across languages."

The officer consulted his notebook again. "And your relationship with Dieter Ecker? Also scholarly?"

There it was. Dieter's name in a Gestapo file.

"Herr Ecker was a student when my father taught at Humboldt. We shared intellectual interests."

"Present tense. 'Share,' not 'shared.' You maintain this intellectual relationship?"

Before she could respond, the study door opened. Solomon Weiss emerged, his tall frame slightly stooped from recent events, but his bearing still dignified.

"Lehmann," Solomon said, recognition flickering. "I thought I recognized your voice."

The Gestapo officer stiffened almost imperceptibly. "Professor Weiss."

"Not anymore, it seems." Solomon moved beside Miriam. "To what do we owe this visit?"

"Routine inquiries about your daughter's associations."

"I see." Solomon's voice carried the measured tone Miriam remembered from his lectures. "Have these inquiries yielded evidence of wrongdoing?"

Lehmann's expression hardened. "Your daughter frequents a known gathering place for subversive elements and maintains an inappropriate relationship with an Aryan man. Neither is technically illegal at present, but both demonstrate questionable judgment."

"My daughter's judgment has always been excellent," Solomon replied quietly. "As you might recall from your time in my advanced seminar. Your essays on ethical judgment were rather less nuanced, as I remember."

Dangerous words. Embarrassment flickered across Lehmann's face, followed by anger, then settled back into official blankness.

"Consider this a warning, Professor. Your family is under observation. Given your classification, it would be advisable to ensure your behavior is beyond reproach." His gaze shifted to Miriam. "All of you."

They left with the same efficiency they'd arrived. No dramatic threats, no physical intimidation. Just the implied menace of observation.

When the door closed, Solomon's shoulders sagged. Miriam guided him to a chair.

"I'm sorry, Papa. I've been careless."

He waved her apology away. "You've done nothing wrong."

"I should have been more discreet about the bookshop. About Dieter."

"They would have found another excuse." Solomon rubbed his temples. "That's how it works now."

"They know about Dieter," she said quietly.

"You need to end that association. Not because there's anything wrong with it, but because it places you both in danger."

"I already have." She paused, studying her father's worn face. "Papa, I need to speak with Mama's friend Rachel. The one who works in theater."

Solomon looked puzzled. "Rachel Goldmann? Why?"

"Because I think it's time for Miriam Weiss to disappear."

Rachel Goldmann's apartment occupied the top floor of a building that had seen better decades. Twenty years as a costume designer and makeup artist for Berlin's theaters had taught her to see past surfaces to possibilities beneath.

"*Liebling*," she said, embracing Miriam at the door. "Your mother said you might visit, but not why."

Rachel was small, fifties, with sharp eyes that missed nothing and hands that moved with the precision of someone who had spent decades transforming actors into other people.

"I need your help with something unusual," Miriam said, settling into the cluttered sitting room. Every surface was covered with sketches, fabric samples, photographs of theatrical productions.

"How unusual?"

"I need to become someone else. Completely. A German someone."

Rachel's expression didn't change, but her hands stilled on the teacup she was pouring. "I see. This someone would need to pass close inspection?"

"The closest."

Rachel set down the teapot and studied Miriam's face with professional intensity. "Hair, obviously. But that's the least of it. You move like a Jew, *liebling*. You hold yourself like someone asking permission to exist."

"Can you teach me not to?"

"I can try." Rachel moved to a cabinet filled with theatrical supplies. "But first, let me tell you what you're really asking. Hair lightening isn't like rouge or powder. It's dangerous chemistry that will burn your scalp and need constant maintenance. Miss one touch-up, let your roots show, and you're dead."

The bluntness was oddly comforting. Someone who understood the stakes.

"I'm ready."

"No, you're not. But we'll make you ready." Rachel pulled out a small bottle of clear liquid. "This is what we use for blonde ingénues. Mostly ammonia and hydrogen peroxide. It will hurt, and the smell will make you sick. But it works."

She lined up several more bottles, each labeled in precise handwriting. "Root touch-up formula. Hair rinse to maintain color. Emergency coverage for uneven fading. Every three weeks, exactly. No exceptions."

Miriam took notes, her hands steady despite the magnitude of what she was planning.

"You'll need a story for where you get supplies. Theater people can buy these without suspicion. A secretary in Charlottenburg cannot."

"What do you suggest?"

"A cousin who works in film. Lives in Munich, sends packages. I'll arrange shipments, but you pay for everything. This isn't charity, *liebling*. It's survival."

They spent an hour on chemistry, timing, techniques for even application. Rachel's instructions were precise and unforgiving.

"Now," Rachel said, "we practice being German."

She stood and transformed before Miriam's eyes. Posture straightened, chin lifted, gaze became direct and challenging. She crossed the room with a stride that radiated entitlement.

"Twenty years watching them in opera houses," Rachel said, dropping the pose. "Men in their boxes, women in their furs. I know how they move, how they think, how they see the world."

For two hours, Rachel drilled Miriam on posture, gesture, the way confidence manifested in physical space. How to enter a room as if you owned it. How to make eye contact that judged rather than pleaded. How to carry yourself like someone who had never questioned their right to exist.

"Good," Rachel said finally. "Now the harder part. How to think like them."

They worked on expressions, subtle facial movements that conveyed moral superiority. How to look at Jews on the street with proper disgust and indifference. How to discuss Nazi policy with genuine-sounding enthusiasm.

"It's acting, *liebling*," Rachel explained. "The deepest kind. You must believe the character while never forgetting who you really are. Lose either piece, and you're lost entirely."

As evening approached, Rachel retrieved the lightening solution. "Are you ready?"

Miriam nodded, though her stomach churned.

"Then sit. Remember, once we start this, there's no going back. Miriam Weiss will be gone forever."

The chemical smell was overwhelming, burning her nostrils as Rachel applied the mixture with practiced efficiency. Miriam gripped the chair arms as the solution began working, her scalp tingling, then burning.

"Ten minutes," Rachel said, watching the color change. "No more, or you'll have chemical burns."

They sat in tense silence, an ammonia smell filling the small bathroom. Miriam's eyes watered, and she fought the urge to scratch her burning scalp.

"Time," Rachel said, guiding her to the sink.

Cold water was a relief, washing away chemicals and revealing transformation. Miriam's dark curls were gone, replaced by bright blonde hair that changed her entire face structure.

"My God," she whispered at her reflection.

"We're not finished," Rachel said. "Sit."

She worked another hour, trimming and styling the newly blonde hair, then applying makeup with master artist skill. Foundation to lighten Miriam's complexion. Powder to set everything. Subtle adjustments to eyebrows and lips that somehow made her features look sharper, more Aryan.

When Rachel finally turned her toward the mirror, Miriam barely recognized herself.

"The clothes," Rachel said, producing a canvas bag. "Borrowed from the theater's contemporary collection."

A tailored gray suit with white blouse. Black leather shoes. A small silver brooch shaped like an eagle.

"Turn around," Rachel instructed when Miriam had changed. "Walk to the window and back."

Miriam followed instructions, conscious of how differently the clothes felt, how they changed her posture automatically.

"Better," Rachel observed. "But you still move like someone asking permission. Again. This time, remember you're better than everyone else in the room."

They practiced until Miriam's neck ached, until she could cross a room with confidence of someone who had never questioned their place in the world.

"Now," Rachel said, "the most important part."

From a small box, she removed a gold cross on a delicate chain. "Your confirmation gift. You wear this always."

Miriam's hands shook as she fastened it around her neck. The weight felt alien against her skin.

"And this," Rachel said, producing another box. Inside, nestled on black velvet, was a Nazi Party badge.

Miriam stared at it, unable to speak.

"I know," Rachel said softly. "But without this, nothing else matters."

With trembling fingers, Miriam pinned the badge to her lapel. The metal felt cold, malevolent.

"Look in the mirror," Rachel said.

The woman looking back was a stranger. Blonde, confident, wearing the symbols of the Reich with apparent pride.

"I feel sick," Miriam whispered.

"Good," Rachel replied. "If you ever stop feeling sick, you've lost yourself entirely."

Rachel opened another drawer, retrieving a small card. "Josef Kleinman. He'll give you the papers to make this real."

The tobacco shop in Moabit was narrow, cramped, smelling of Virginia leaf and stale beer. Miriam followed the shopkeeper's directions through a curtained doorway to a back room where a man sat reading behind a small desk.

Josef Kleinman was younger than she'd expected, perhaps forty, with the solid build of someone who had once been athletic. His eyes seemed to absorb light rather than reflect it.

"Fräulein Weiss," he said without preamble. "Sit."

As her eyes adjusted to the dim light, she could make out more of his features. A thin white scar along his right cheekbone. Hands that remained perfectly still.

"You're Kleinman."

"For this conversation, yes." His voice was surprisingly cultured. "I'm told you need new papers."

"Yes."

"Why?"

The directness caught her off guard. "Because Miriam Weiss can't survive in Berlin anymore."

"Many leave. Easier than what you're attempting."

"I'm not leaving."

"No, you're not." He leaned forward slightly. "You want to work for the people who want to destroy you."

The words hung in the air. How did he know?

"Your transformation is excellent," he continued, studying her appearance. "Professional quality. Rachel's work?"

She nodded, startled.

"Good. She understands what's required." He opened a drawer, removing blank paper. "Most people want to become invisible. You want to hide in plain sight. In the most dangerous place possible."

"Yes."

36

"Why?"

"Because that's where the information is. Where I might actually do some good."

Kleinman smiled, the expression transforming his severe face. "Very good. Now, who exactly are you becoming?"

For the next hour, they constructed Layla Brandt piece by piece. Birthplace: Dresden. Education: University of Munich. Family background: father a professor, mother a pianist, both killed in a car accident five years earlier.

"Religious affiliation?"

"Protestant. Lutheran."

"Political development?"

"A gradual convert. Someone who saw the economic improvements and became convinced."

Kleinman tested her knowledge of Nazi ideology, correcting gaps, explaining how a true believer would think and speak.

"The documents will take one week," he said finally. "They'll be perfect, or as close as human skill can achieve. Some will even exist in official records."

"The cost?"

"Your services, occasionally. I'll need translations. Documents from various countries that require a skilled eye." His smile held no warmth. "Consider it an ongoing arrangement."

"For how long?"

"Until I say otherwise."

The binding nature was clear. Miriam nodded acceptance.

"Bring me a photograph when you return," he said. "Professional quality. Layla Brandt as she wishes to be seen by the world."

A week later, Miriam returned carrying a portrait taken at a studio in Charlottenburg. The photographer had captured the cool confidence she and Rachel had worked to achieve.

Kleinman examined the photograph, then opened a leather portfolio. Inside were documents that would give Layla Brandt complete existence.

Birth certificate. School records. University diploma. Letters of reference. Identity card. Work permits. Religious documentation. Each document perfectly aged, expertly forged.

"The birth certificate is registered in Dresden," Kleinman explained. "Should anyone check city records, they'll find it properly entered."

The final document was a certificate of Aryan ancestry, tracing Layla Brandt's bloodline back four generations.

"Memorize every name, every date," he said. "Your life depends on them."

As Miriam prepared to leave, Kleinman stood and extended his hand. "You have courage, Fräulein Brandt. You'll need it."

His handshake was firm, his eyes holding hers for a moment longer than necessary. "We'll meet again under different circumstances."

That night, Miriam held the gold cross in her palm, studying it in dim light. Tomorrow she would find an apartment in a suitable neighborhood. By week's end, Layla Brandt would be established in Berlin, ready to offer her services to the Reich.

She fastened the cross around her neck, feeling its weight against her skin. No longer completely alien, but not yet familiar. Like Layla herself, a presence taking form within her.

In the mirror, she practiced the expression Rachel had taught her. Cool confidence edged with moral superiority. The look of someone who had never questioned their place in the world.

"Layla Brandt," she said aloud, testing the sound.

The name felt strange on her tongue, but she would make it real through repetition, through performance, through the absolute necessity of survival.

Miriam Weiss was gone. Layla Brandt had arrived.

And Berlin would never see her coming.

5

Layla Emerges

The apartment in Charlottenburg came furnished with everything Layla Brandt needed: respectability, the right address, and neighbors who wouldn't ask uncomfortable questions. Miriam paid three month's rent in advance, her new papers passing their first real test with the landlord's perfunctory inspection.

"Fräulein Brandt," Herr Mueller said, returning her identity documents. "Your references from Dresden are excellent. The apartment is yours."

She signed the lease with steady hands, her signature practiced until it looked natural. Layla's signature, not Miriam's careful script.

The morning after moving in, she stood before her new mirror, applying makeup with the precision Rachel had taught her. The reflection showed a confident German woman preparing for an important interview, but beneath the surface, something else watched from behind blue eyes that had once been brown.

She fastened the gold cross around her neck, its weight a daily reminder of what she was pretending to be. The Nazi pin felt heavier still when she attached it to her lapel. Each morning, these rituals of transformation grew slightly easier, and that ease terrified her more than the initial revulsion had.

The Reich Ministry of Propaganda occupied an imposing building on Wilhelmstrasse, its Nazi flags hanging motionless in the still air. Layla approached the entrance with measured steps, her leather briefcase containing her immaculate credentials and the buried knowledge that she was walking into the heart of the machine designed to destroy her.

Inside, the marble halls echoed with the sounds of efficiency: typewriters, telephones, the sharp click of heels on stone.

Everything was designed to intimidate, to remind visitors of the Reich's power and reach. A bronze eagle perched above the reception desk, its wings spread in eternal dominion.

"Fräulein Brandt?" A secretary looked up from her desk, her hair styled in the approved fashion, her expression professionally neutral. "Herr Direktor Weber will see you now."

Weber's office was spacious but not ostentatious, dominated by a large desk and the obligatory portrait of the Führer. The man behind the desk was younger than Miriam had expected, perhaps forty, with the lean build of someone who took physical fitness seriously.

"Please, sit," Weber said, gesturing to a chair opposite his desk. "Your application is quite impressive."

"Thank you, Herr Direktor."

"University of Munich, languages department. Top honors." He consulted her file. "Your professors speak very highly of your linguistic abilities."

Miriam nodded, projecting quiet confidence while her mind catalogued every detail that might expose her. Kleinman's work was holding up perfectly, but she felt the constant weight of maintaining the performance.

"We have a particular need for someone with your language combination," Weber continued. "English and French, especially. Our correspondence with diplomatic missions requires absolute precision."

"I understand completely, Herr Direktor. Nuance in translation can affect international relationships."

"Exactly." Weber leaned back in his chair, studying her with the calculating gaze of someone accustomed to evaluating loyalty. "Tell me, Fräulein Brandt, what drew you to Berlin? You could have found translation work in Munich."

The question she had prepared for, but his intensity made her pulse quicken. "I wanted to be part of Germany's renewal, Herr Direktor. To contribute to our nation's resurgence on the world stage."

"And your political development? When did you first embrace our cause?"

"Two years ago," she replied smoothly. "After seeing the remarkable improvements in our economic situation. I attended a rally and heard the Führer speak about Germany's destiny." The lie tasted like ashes, but her voice remained steady.

Weber nodded approvingly. "Many of our best people came to the cause through practical observation rather than early ideology. It shows good judgment." He paused, pen hovering over her file. "Tell me about your family background. Your parents died in an automobile accident, I see."

"Yes, Herr Direktor. Five years ago." The fictional tragedy felt like a knife twisting in her chest. "They would have been proud to see me serving the Reich."

"I'm sure they would." His gaze lingered on her face. "You have excellent German features. Very Aryan. Your ancestry documentation is complete?"

"Of course, Herr Direktor. Four generations, as required."

The interview continued for another twenty minutes, Weber testing her language skills with sample documents, her knowledge of diplomatic protocols, and her understanding of the Reich's international objectives. Each question felt like walking across thin ice, any crack threatening to plunge her into freezing darkness.

"Excellent," Weber said finally. "We'll start you in the translation pool, working on routine diplomatic correspondence. Assuming your references check out completely, you can begin Monday."

"Thank you, Herr Direktor. I won't disappoint you."

"I'm sure you won't." He stood, extending his hand. "Welcome to the Ministry, Fräulein Brandt."

Walking back through the marble halls, Layla felt a strange mixture of triumph and self-loathing. She had succeeded. Miriam Weiss, who couldn't get work translating trade documents, had been buried so completely that Layla Brandt could walk into the heart of the Nazi propaganda machine and be welcomed with open arms.

The thought should have felt like victory. Instead, it felt like the first spadeful of dirt on her own grave.

That evening, Layla walked through the Tiergarten, following a route Rachel had taught her. At the third bench past the memorial, she sat and opened a book of German poetry, appearing to read while actually scanning for surveillance.

Satisfied she was alone, she made her way to Friedrichstrasse, to a small music shop she had located during her reconnaissance. The sign read "Hoffman's Music" in elegant script, with a display of instruments and sheet music in the window.

Inside, the shop smelled of paper and wood polish. The elderly proprietor looked up from organizing violin strings, his expression carefully neutral.

"Good evening," she said. "I'm looking for recordings of classical German composers. I've just moved to the neighborhood."

"Of course, Fräulein. We have an excellent selection." His eyes flickered to her Nazi pin, cataloguing, evaluating. "Might I suggest our Bach collection? Very popular with young people these days."

She browsed the records while he served other customers, studying the layout, the staff, and the rhythm of the shop. When they were finally alone, she approached the counter with a Mozart symphony.

"I wonder," she said quietly, "if you might know of a way to send musical gifts to friends who've moved away. Perhaps through other music lovers who share similar interests."

The old man's hands stilled on his ledger. For a long moment, he studied her face. "Musical appreciation takes many forms," he said finally. "Sometimes the most beautiful melodies reach those who need them most, even across great distances."

"I would be very grateful for such a service," she replied. "My friends mean everything to me."

He nodded slowly. "Return Thursday afternoon. Browse the classical section. If you find something particularly moving, you might leave it for someone else to discover."

Thursday afternoon, she stood in the classical section of Hoffman's shop, her hands shaking as she slipped a note between the pages of a Bach cantata score. The message was brief, coded in references to philosophical terms her father would recognize:

> The dialectic proceeds. Your student applies Kantian principles to practical ethics. The categorical imperative now requires new premises. Please confirm your continued interest in metaphysical discussions. — Your devoted pupil

She left the shop without purchasing anything, her heart hammering against her ribs. The first thread connecting Layla to Miriam's past had been spun.

Monday morning arrived gray and cold. Layla's first day at the Ministry began with orientation in a sterile conference room where new employees learned the protocols of serving the Reich. She sat among a dozen other fresh-faced Germans, all radiating the eager competence of people grateful for the opportunity to advance the Fatherland's interests.

"The work you'll be doing shapes how the world sees Germany," explained Frau Kellner, a thin woman in her forties who spoke with the precision of someone who had never made an error. "Every document that passes through our translation department represents the Reich's voice to foreign nations."

Layla nodded with appropriate enthusiasm while nausea churned in her stomach. She would be helping Nazi Germany speak to the world. The bitter irony was almost unbearable.

After orientation, Frau Kellner led her to a large room filled with translators, each working at neat desks arranged in precise rows. The space hummed with quiet efficiency, dozens of voices serving the Reich's international ambitions.

"You'll start with routine correspondence," Frau Kellner explained, placing a stack of documents on Layla's assigned desk. "Letters from our embassy in Paris, responses to diplomatic inquiries. Nothing classified yet, but everything is important."

The work was familiar. The content was poisonous.

Her first assignment was a letter from the German ambassador in Paris, reporting on French reactions to recent legislation restricting Jewish participation in universities. The ambassador's tone was matter-of-fact, discussing the systematic removal of rights as if it were a technical matter requiring diplomatic finesse.

Layla read the German text, understanding every word, every implication. Then she began translating it into English, her professional skills intact despite her moral revulsion. Each sentence felt like a betrayal of everything she had once been.

"The French academic establishment has expressed some concern regarding our recent educational reforms," she typed, the euphemism for persecution flowing from her fingers like blood from a wound. "However, our embassy believes these concerns can be managed through appropriate diplomatic channels."

By lunch, she had translated three such documents. Each one advanced the Reich's narrative, normalized the persecution, made the unthinkable sound reasonable. Her hands remained steady, her translations flawless, but inside she felt pieces of herself dying with each completed page.

"Excellent work," Frau Kellner said, reviewing her translations that afternoon. "Your English is flawless. You understand the nuances we need. We'll have more challenging assignments for you soon."

That evening, Layla attended her first Nazi Party meeting in the local district office. The room was crowded with true believers, their faces animated with fervor as they discussed the Reich's latest achievements. She took a seat in the middle rows, visible but not prominent, as Kleinman had advised.

"Comrades," the district leader announced, "tonight we celebrate our Führer's latest diplomatic triumph. Austria has seen the wisdom of reunification with the Fatherland."

Applause filled the room. Layla clapped with appropriate enthusiasm, her expression reflecting the satisfaction expected of a loyal Party member. Inside, she thought of Austrian Jews she had met at university conferences, wondering which of them were already dead.

The speaker continued, outlining the Reich's bright future, the destiny of the German people, and the necessity of racial purity. Layla nodded at the right moments, made the proper responses, became part of the collective voice affirming the Reich's righteousness.

As the meeting progressed, she found herself studying the faces around her. Some showed the glazed fervor of true believers. Others wore expressions of careful attention that might have concealed doubt. How many were performing, like her? How many had buried their true selves so deep they could no longer find them?

"The Jewish question requires a final solution," the speaker declared. "Through our vigilance and dedication, Germany will be cleansed of this contamination."

More applause. Layla's hands came together mechanically while her mind recoiled from the words. Final solution. She filed the phrase away, another piece of intelligence about the Reich's intentions.

After the meeting, several members approached her. New faces were always noticed in the close-knit community of Party faithful.

"I don't think we've met," said a woman in her fifties, her gray hair pulled into a severe bun. "I'm Frau Richter."

"Layla Brandt," she replied, offering her hand. "I'm new to the district. Just moved from Dresden."

"Wonderful! We always welcome dedicated Party members. What brings you to Berlin?"

"Work," Layla replied. "I've just taken a position with the Ministry of Propaganda."

Frau Richter's eyes lit up with approval. "How exciting! Important work, serving the Reich directly."

"I'm honored to contribute," Layla said, the words feeling like broken glass in her mouth.

The conversation continued, Frau Richter introducing her to other members, establishing her place in the social hierarchy of committed Nazis. By the end of the evening, Layla Brandt was no longer a stranger but a welcomed addition to the community.

Walking home through the darkened streets, she passed a Jewish bakery, its windows now covered with anti-Semitic graffiti. The Star of David painted on the door had been defaced, turned into a twisted symbol of hatred. A year ago, she might have bought bread there as Miriam Weiss.

She stopped walking. Without thinking, her hand rose to touch the window where the graffiti spelled out "*Juden raus*" (Jews out) in crude red letters. For one unguarded moment, grief cracked through Layla's facade.

A group of *SA* (Storm Detachment) men rounded the corner, their voices loud with beer and bravado. Layla quickly dropped her hand and continued walking, but not before one of them noticed her standing before the Jewish shop.

"Something wrong, Fräulein?" he called out.

Her blood froze, but Layla's training held. "Just checking to make sure nothing was damaged," she replied coolly. "These shops should be properly boarded up, not left to attract vandals."

The *SA* man grinned. "You're right. Can't have the neighborhood looking shabby." He looked her up and down approvingly. "Good German instincts."

As they walked away, Layla realized how close she had come to exposure. One moment of letting Miriam surface, one instant of unguarded emotion, had nearly destroyed everything.

She could not afford to feel. Not grief, not rage, not the human responses that marked her as different from the monsters she lived among. Survival required perfect performance, and perfect performance demanded the death of everything authentic within her.

Her second week at the Ministry brought the promotion she had been hoping for and dreading in equal measure. Frau Kellner called her into the supervisor's office on Friday afternoon.

"Your work has been exemplary," she said. "Herr Direktor Weber wants to expand your responsibilities."

Weber's office felt more familiar now, though no less threatening. She sat in the same chair, her posture confident but respectful.

"Your translations have impressed several departments," Weber began. "We're assigning you to more sensitive material. Cultural outreach programs, correspondence with sympathetic intellectuals abroad, university liaison work."

"I'm honored by your confidence, Herr Direktor."

"This work requires absolute discretion," he continued. "You'll be handling communications that shape international opinion about our Jewish policies. The Reich's reputation depends on how these matters are presented to foreign audiences."

The assignment was both an opportunity and a trap. More sensitive work meant greater access to information, but also greater scrutiny. And she would be directly involved in crafting the propaganda that made genocide palatable to the world.

"I understand the responsibility," she said.

"Excellent. You'll be working directly with Herr Zimmermann in Cultural Affairs. He'll brief you on the specific requirements."

As she left Weber's office, Layla felt the weight of her double existence crushing down on her. She was succeeding as a Nazi functionary, earning trust and advancing within the system she despised. Each success as Layla felt like another betrayal of everyone she had once been.

But it also meant she was exactly where she needed to be: inside the machine, trusted with its secrets, positioned to learn what the Reich was planning for the future.

That evening, she returned to Hoffman's music shop. In the window, a violin stood propped against a stack of Wagner records, with a small porcelain conductor figure beside it. The signal that a message waited.

She browsed the classical section until other customers left, then found the Bach cantata where she had left her first note. Between the pages was a folded paper in her father's handwriting:

Metaphysical discussions continue despite changed circumstances. Original premises remain sound though external conditions deteriorate. New regulations affect academic positions. Practical applications of theoretical principles become more pressing daily. Your former professor values continued correspondence. — S.W.

Her parents were still alive, still in Berlin, but her father's careful phrasing told her their situation was becoming desperate. New regulations. Academic positions. They were being systematically isolated, prepared for whatever final solution the Reich had planned.

She left her own message, hidden in the score of a Mozart requiem:

Practical ethics demands immediate application of survival principles. Theoretical discussions should relocate to more favorable academic environments. Resources available for research sabbaticals. Consider visiting scholarly institutions elsewhere. Time becomes a factor in all philosophical investigations. — Your concerned student

Walking home, she realized she was crying. The tears came without warning, silent streams down her carefully made-up cheeks. She wiped them away quickly, looking around to make sure no one had seen.

Layla Brandt did not cry for Jewish families facing deportation. Layla Brandt celebrated the Reich's efficiency in handling the Jewish question.

But buried beneath Layla's perfect performance, Miriam Weiss was dying a little more each day, grieving for parents she could not openly love and a world she could not openly mourn.

In her apartment, she stood before the mirror, studying the stranger who looked back at her. Blonde hair, cold blue eyes, the Nazi pin gleaming on her lapel. Every day, this woman became more real while Miriam faded deeper into memory.

Soon, she feared, the performance would become the only reality. Soon, she might forget she had ever been anyone else.

The thought terrified her more than any threat the Reich could make.

But she straightened her shoulders, checked her appearance one final time, and prepared for another day of serving the machine that sought to destroy everything she had once loved.

The balance was delicate, dangerous, and growing more precarious with each passing day. But she would maintain it, whatever the cost to her soul. Because inside the heart of the Reich's machinery, she might find ways to throw sand in the gears, to slow the destruction, to save lives.

It was a small hope, built on the grave of everything she had once been. But it was enough to keep both Layla and Miriam alive in the same body, walking the same dangerous path toward an uncertain future where one of them might not survive.

6

The Severing of Ties

Three weeks after beginning at the Ministry

Layla Brandt woke before her alarm clock rang. She always did. The overcast Berlin morning filtered through thin curtains as she swung her feet to the cold floor.

In the mirror, a stranger looked back at her. Blonde hair fell in flawless waves around a face scrubbed of any softness. Three weeks ago, her dark curls had framed the gentler features of Miriam Weiss. That woman existed now only in the dangerous corners of Layla's mind, corners she visited less frequently with each passing day.

She applied her makeup with mechanical precision. Rouge on high cheekbones. Lipstick the color of fresh blood. Eyes lined to appear wider, bluer, colder. The transformation required no thought anymore.

The radio crackled with morning news. Victories on the Eastern Front. The Führer's latest speech. She listened carefully, memorizing details she might need to reference in conversation. Knowledge was survival.

"Germany will be cleansed," the announcer declared. Layla repeated the words under her breath, practicing the conviction of someone born into this belief.

Outside, Berlin had transformed as thoroughly as she had. Swastika flags fluttered from every building. German soldiers strutted down the streets, their boots striking the pavement in rhythm. Women with blonde children smiled at them.

Layla walked toward Friedrichstrasse, her heels clicking with purpose. She glanced at shop windows with casual interest until she reached Hoffman's Music, her gaze moving across the display without slowing.

A violin stood propped against a stack of Wagner records. Beside it, a small porcelain figure of a conductor.

The signal.

Her pulse quickened, but her face revealed nothing. She continued walking for another block before circling back, pausing to check her reflection in another shop window.

The bell above Hoffman's door jingled as she entered. The shop smelled of paper and wood polish. Herr Hoffman stood behind the counter, his thin frame bent over a ledger. He glanced up, recognition flickering briefly before vanishing beneath professional courtesy.

"Guten Morgen" (Good morning), Fräulein Brandt."

"Herr Hoffman." Layla nodded with the exact degree of politeness one showed shopkeepers. "I've come for the Beethoven recordings we discussed."

"Of course." He gestured toward the back wall. "Jakob has just organized that section this morning."

The boy appeared from behind sheet music. No more than twelve, with blonde hair and a Hitler Youth uniform beneath his shop apron. His gaze held the innocent eagerness of a child who had known only the Reich.

"Can I help you find something, Fräulein?"

"I'll browse, thank you," Layla replied, moving toward the classical section.

The door jingled again. A Wehrmacht officer entered, his medals catching the light. Layla felt him study her as she bent toward the lower shelves.

Behind the records filed under "B," she found what she sought. The sleeve looked identical to the others, but felt heavier. Something hidden within.

She took the record to the listening booth and slipped it onto the turntable. Under cover of Beethoven's Ninth Symphony, she extracted a folded paper from between record and cover.

50

Her fingers remained steady. Trembling belonged to Miriam. Layla was steady as winter.

The Wehrmacht officer lingered near the front, discussing martial music with Herr Hoffman. She forced herself to listen to a full movement before emerging, record in hand.

"I'll take this one," she told Hoffman.

"An excellent choice, Fräulein." His attention never strayed to the slight bulge in her handbag where the note now rested. "Will there be anything else?"

"Not today."

She paid and left, passing the officer with a polite nod.

The park bench was isolated enough for privacy yet public enough to avoid suspicion. Layla opened her compact mirror, checking for followers while pretending to powder her nose. Satisfied she was alone, she unfolded the note.

Two messages. One in her father's careful handwriting, one in an unfamiliar script that could only be Dieter's.

Her father's words first: We cannot abandon our home. What would we take with us? Where would we go? Your mother believes we can wait out this madness. I have seen the cycle of history. This too shall pass.

Stubborn old man. Miriam had inherited his stubbornness, but Layla had discarded it.

The second message was worse.

Treblinka is not a labor camp. No one works there. No one returns. Trains leave weekly from Berlin Grunewald station. The next major transport is scheduled three days from now. All Jewish names are collected for processing. S & H on the list. This is my last message. Moving east. Burn this.

Layla read it twice, then tore it into pieces and scattered them in different waste bins throughout the park.

In her apartment, she composed her response. The code system was based on her father's philosophical writings, innocent references that would mean nothing to censors.

Dearest Father, You once wrote that the greatest act of courage is surrender to necessity. Remember your Kant: "When the end is required, the means to it are also required." Mother's music will find new audiences elsewhere. Her hands can play on any piano. The child who disagreed with your third thesis now understands your wisdom but insists that adaptation preserves the core. The books you value can be rewritten from memory on safer shores. Do not delay. Do not pack sentimentally. Do not trust anyone else. Remember me through Bach. Your loving daughter

She sealed it in an envelope and slipped it into the sleeve of a Bach cantata record.

The next morning, she returned to Hoffman's, carrying the record.

"Not to your liking, Fräulein Brandt?" Herr Hoffman asked.

"The recording quality was poor," she replied. "Perhaps Jakob could check the others to ensure they aren't similarly flawed."

The boy stepped forward. "I'll check them right away, Fräulein."

"Thank you, Jakob. You're very helpful."

As she turned to leave, a woman entered the shop. Layla's composure nearly cracked. Professor Adelstein from the university, her father's former colleague. The woman who had attended Shabbat dinner at their home twice a month for years.

Layla turned toward a display of flutes, angling her face away. Professor Adelstein walked past, close enough that Layla could smell her familiar lavender perfume. The scent triggered unbidden memories: Friday evenings, challah bread cooling on the kitchen counter, her mother lighting candles while Professor Adelstein discussed philosophy with her father. For a moment, the flood of remembrance threatened to crack Layla's carefully constructed shell.

But Miriam was dead. Layla stood rigid, forcing her breathing to remain steady, until the professor moved to the classical section. Only then did she slip out without looking back.

Her hands trembled as she walked down the street. She stopped in an alley and pressed her palms against the cold brick wall until the shaking stopped. Such reactions belonged to a ghost. Layla Brandt had no memories of Shabbat dinners or lavender perfume.

Three days passed. Layla went through her routines. Applied for advancement within the Ministry that would put her closer to sensitive information. Practiced her German accent. Read approved literature. But underneath her perfect performance, Miriam's buried heart counted the hours, knowing that somewhere in Berlin, her parents faced their final moments.

On the fourth day, the signal appeared in Hoffman's window. Not the violin and conductor, but a metronome placed directly in the center of the display. The emergency signal.

She entered the shop with the same measured steps, but Herr Hoffman's face told her everything before he spoke.

"Fräulein Brandt, I'm afraid that the Bach cantata series has been discontinued," Herr Hoffman said.

The words cut through her facade like a blade. She knew the code: They have been taken.

"That's unfortunate," she replied, her voice steady though her chest felt hollow. "Was there no warning?"

"None. The decision came suddenly." His fingers tapped twice on the counter. Two days ago.

"I see." Layla kept her tone neutral while something inside her crumbled to ash.

Jakob watched from behind a shelf, oblivious to the real conversation.

"Was a shipment sent out before the cancellation?" Did they try to escape?

"Yes, but it was returned," Hoffman replied quietly. They were caught.

"And the next series?" Where are they now?

Hoffman's gaze flickered. "Eastbound, I believe." On the trains to Treblinka.

"Thank you for the information." Layla's voice didn't break. Layla's voice couldn't break because Layla had never had parents named Solomon and Hannah Weiss. That had been Miriam, and Miriam was dead.

She purchased a recording of Wagner's "Ride of the Valkyries" and left.

That evening, as she sat numbly in her apartment, a final message arrived, delivered by a postal worker. Inside the envelope was a folded note and a ticket stub for the Eastern Front train.

The information is confirmed. I go where I might be useful or where I might find absolution. You were right to end what couldn't continue. Live, Layla Brandt. Someone must witness. Know that what we had was real, even if we cannot be. I will remember Miriam's laugh when I have forgotten everything else.

The handwriting belonged to a man she had once loved, a man named Dieter who had loved a woman named Miriam. Neither of them existed anymore.

She read the note three times, her throat constricting with each word. I will remember Miriam's laugh. He had loved Miriam truly, and now he was walking toward almost certain death believing she was someone worth remembering. The knowledge that she had been loved, genuinely loved, felt like both a gift and a dagger twisting in her chest.

She burned the note in her sink, watching the flames consume his elegant handwriting. When it was ash, she washed it down the drain.

From beneath her mattress, she withdrew the final photograph of Solomon and Hannah Weiss. Her father behind wire-rimmed glasses, the same ones she had inherited before changing her eye color. Her mother's hands resting on her shoulders, the pianist's fingers that had taught Miriam to love Bach. Miriam between them, smiling. A family that no longer existed.

She held the photograph for a long time, studying their faces. Her father's kind eyes, the way they crinkled when he laughed at his own philosophical jokes. Her mother's gentle mouth, always ready with encouragement when Miriam struggled with difficult passages. The three of them together, unaware that this moment would be their last.

She struck a match and held it to the corner. The flames consumed their faces slowly, her father disappearing first, then her mother's hands, finally Miriam's young, hopeful smile. She held it until the heat touched her fingers, then dropped the remnant into the sink with the other ashes.

The night stretched endlessly. She lay in bed staring at the ceiling, practicing her German accent in whispers, conjugating verbs, reciting Nazi slogans until the words became meaningless sounds that filled the silence where grief threatened to surface. When dawn finally came, her eyes were dry and her voice was steady.

The next morning, Layla Brandt submitted her application for advancement to the senior translation department within the Ministry. Her credentials were impeccable. Her references spoke highly of her character and loyalty.

In her small apartment, she adjusted her uniform before the mirror. The stranger looked back, blonde and cold and seamless. Behind those blue depths, something else lived, something that remembered the sound of her mother's piano and her father's voice reading philosophy by lamplight, something that treasured the memory of Dieter's love even as it buried it forever.

But that something was buried so deep that no one would ever find it. Not the Reich. Not her coworkers. Not even Layla herself on most days.

She straightened her jacket, checked her seams, and stepped out into the Berlin morning. The sun shone on the swastika flags. German soldiers marched down the street. Layla Brandt walked among them, belonging seamlessly to this world that had devoured the one before it.

Behind her, she left nothing but ashes in a drain and a ghost named Miriam that no one would ever see again.

7

The Perfect German

April 12, 1942 - Three months after joining the Ministry

The red folder crashed onto Layla's desk. Brenner hovered above, morning light catching his spectacles. Not a smile, not a frown. Just cold efficiency.

"Congratulations, Fräulein Brandt. Three months in, and already another promotion."

She concealed her fear with practiced calm. Enough pleased surprise, not enough to draw scrutiny.

"Thank you, Herr Brenner."

Oberführer (Senior Leader) Becker noticed your Polish translations. He wants you in his section." Brenner's gaze narrowed. "Security level three. Unusual for someone so new."

Was it too fast? She scanned his face for suspicion but found only the irritation of losing a useful subordinate.

"I'll do my best to meet his expectations."

"Room 417, fourth floor. Someone will bring your files." Brenner paused at the door. "Enhanced rations come with the position. Forms are in the folder."

She kept her expression neutral despite the reminder of her new privilege in a system built to destroy her people.

After he left, she opened the folder. An eagle and swastika waited for her signature. Miriam Weiss would have burned it. Layla Brandt signed.

The fourth floor corridor smelled of beeswax polish and stale cigars. Her heels clicked against marble, each step echoing.

"Room 417, Fräulein." The secretary pointed to a brass-plaqued door. "Oberführer Becker's office is at the end. Always knock three times."

The space was triple the size of her old desk area, with a window overlooking Wilhelmstrasse and an oak desk instead of utilitarian metal.

When the secretary closed the door, Layla pressed her palm against the wood. Three months ago, she entered this building certain her disguise would fail. Now she had an office where men planned her people's destruction.

A sharp knock. Hilde Müller stepped in without waiting, her pale gaze immediately taking inventory.

"Moving up." Her tone slid between admiration and suspicion. "The pool can't stop talking. Nobody advances this quickly."

Layla smoothed her skirt. "The Oberführer values Polish fluency, apparently."

"Watch yourself up here." Hilde leaned closer, cigarette breath mingling with expensive perfume. "These aren't paper pushers. They make decisions. They watch everyone."

"I appreciate the warning."

Hilde lingered, assessing. "Where did you study languages again?"

"Munich University." A lie worn smooth from repetition. "Professor Hauser's program."

"Ah." A flicker in Hilde's expression. "We should have lunch sometime."

After Hilde left, Layla wondered if the woman suspected something or just resented her success. Either way, danger.

She unpacked her belongings: a framed photo of Dresden purchased after creating her identity, a desk calendar, a fountain pen that had been her father's sixteenth birthday gift. The pen, the only real piece of Miriam Weiss in this office.

She traced its worn silver cap. Grief surfaced briefly. She tucked the pen away. Such feelings couldn't exist in room 417. Here, she was Layla Brandt, loyal German.

"Tell me about the Zwinger." The question dropped into mindless weather chatter. Torsten Hoffmann from Propaganda fixed her with sudden intensity. "I visited Dresden last spring."

A trap. Her pulse remained steady despite her fear. She had prepared for this.

"Which part impressed you?" She stirred sugar into coffee, spoon clinking against china. "The Crown Gate with the gold work, or the galleries? I walked through the porcelain collection with my father after church on Sundays." She let nostalgia creep into her tone. "He loved the Japanese pieces."

Details flowed: baroque architecture, gardens, the north wing restoration from '37. Information absorbed during months of desperate study, delivered like childhood memories.

Hoffmann's suspicion faded. "You know your hometown well. Too many Germans neglect our cultural heritage."

Back in her office, she added this to her catalog of tests passed. Her fictional Dresden father joined her shadow family: the strict mother, childhood friends, university classmates. Each lie required supporting details.

The lies came easier now. That terrified her more than any Nazi interrogation.

At her kitchen table on Lietzenburger Straße, Layla altered her handwriting to create a masculine scrawl. The apartment, an upgrade from her previous lodging, featured thin walls suitable for overhearing neighbors.

"My dearest Layla," she wrote, making it rougher than her father's elegant Viennese script. "Lublin remains challenging but we progress. Local elements resist natural order, but they'll learn discipline or face consequences."

She filled the page with romantic platitudes and veiled SS activities. Her fictional lover, SS Hauptsturmführer (Captain) Heinrich Vogel, existed only in these carefully crafted letters.

She sealed the envelope, adding a stolen postmark. Tomorrow she would "receive" it at breakfast where her landlady would notice. By afternoon, the building would know about her SS boyfriend.

The fiction started by accident. A clerk asked her to dinner; she mentioned an SS boyfriend to discourage him. Too effective. Others treated her differently afterward, creating useful distance.

From her drawer she removed a framed photograph of a blond officer, handsome in the generic Aryan way. Cut from a propaganda magazine. Heinrich Vogel watched over her bedside table, her fictional protector.

Which scared her more? How easily the lies came, or how convincingly she played their flawless German?

The meeting hall reeked of cigarettes, cheap cologne, and fear. Rows of chairs faced a swastika-draped podium. Hitler's portrait tracked Layla as she found a seat near the back.

Her Nazi pin, now worn smooth from months of daily use, caught the light as she adjusted her jacket. The small symbol had become as natural as breathing.

"First local meeting?" The woman beside her wore lipstool too red against pale skin. "Greta Fuchs, Labor Administration."

"Layla Brandt, Foreign Ministry." She summoned her mother's customer service warmth. "Transferred from Dresden recently."

"You'll enjoy the Berlin meetings. Kreisleiter Wagner (District Leader) actually holds your attention." Greta lowered her tone. "Handsome too, for his age."

Kreisleiter Wagner, red-faced with receding hairline but a powerful presence, led them through the anthem. Layla mouthed words she had forced herself to memorize. Then Wagner launched into his speech about "purifying" German society.

"We continue strengthening the Volk by removing harmful elements," he declared, fist striking the podium. "Last week, our Moabit district efforts identified six Jewish households hiding their status." His smile stretched wide. "These vermin have been relocated."

Relocated. Layla kept her face neutral while cataloging details. Moabit raids. Six families.

"Now we focus on Charlottenburg," Wagner continued. "Intelligence suggests similar problems there. Volunteers for Tuesday's verification sweep?"

Hands rose. Eager citizens volunteering to hunt Jews. When Greta glanced expectantly, she raised her hand too. Charlottenburg, where other families like hers might still hide. She needed to know their methods.

Wagner nodded approval. "Excellent. Now, suggestions to improve identification methods? Our enemies grow cleverer in their deceptions."

Silence. Then Layla heard herself speak.

"If I may, Kreisleiter."

Every gaze turned to her. Voice steady despite her racing heart.

"Documents can be falsified. Cultural knowledge can't. Perhaps questioning suspects about local traditions, regional history, and religious practices would expose artificial backgrounds."

She had just detailed how she herself might be caught.

Wagner pointed at her, expression bright. "Excellent suggestion from our dedicated member. Your name?"

"Layla Brandt, Foreign Ministry translation division."

"Fräulein Brandt shows the intelligence we need. Cultural verification." Sharp nod. "We implement it immediately."

After the meeting, Wagner sought her out personally. She answered his questions with a confident smile while self-loathing twisted her insides.

Sleep fled that night. Faces without names haunted her, people who would be caught because of her suggestion. But silence itself drew suspicion in a regime demanding constant loyalty demonstrations.

"The Oberführer will see you now."

The secretary's words pulled Layla from Polish military dispatches. After three months, she had earned a reputation for finding subtleties others missed.

Oberführer Becker's office: massive desk, leather chairs, map-lined walls. Red pins clustered east, marking German advances.

Becker stood silhouetted against gray April light. He turned as she entered, everything the regime considered ideal. Strong jaw, arctic stare, blond hair graying at temples.

"Fräulein Brandt. Your work impresses." His aristocratic Prussian accent spoke of private schools and old money. "Sit."

She took the chair, spine straight, hands folded.

"Your Warsaw dispatch translations revealed patterns my previous translators missed." He tapped a folder. "Resistance activities are cleverly hidden in agricultural reports."

"Thank you, Oberführer." She kept her tone humble.

He studied her like a specimen. "Where did you learn to read between lines?"

Rehearsed answer: "My father worked in international banking. He taught me language conceals as much as it reveals."

"Valuable lesson." Becker produced a black-bordered folder, the highest security classification. "Special assignment requiring your talents."

He slid it across. "Warsaw Jewish district communications. The ghetto. I need translation and analysis. What are they hiding? What are they planning?"

Layla accepted with steady hands. Inside: possibly information about families she knew, streets where she had played during childhood visits to relatives.

"I'm honored by your trust."

"With honor comes privilege." Another paper. "Category One rations. Better housing available next week. The Party rewards value."

"Germany has been generous."

"Germany rewards loyal children." Cold smile. "Friday. My desk."

Alone with the documents, she forced professional detachment while translating reports about the ghetto where her parents had spent their final months. Clinical descriptions of overcrowding, disease, starvation.

"I've heard excellent things about Munich University's linguistics program." Klaus Weber raised his brandy at the Austrian Embassy reception. "When did you complete your studies there?"

Layla wore dark blue that highlighted her blonde hair without frivolity. Nazi pin positioned precisely on her lapel.

Weber's question carried unmistakable weight.

"I finished in '38," she said, sipping champagne. "Professor Hauser's comparative linguistics program."

"Hauser?" Weber's brow furrowed. "The name isn't familiar."

"Austrian born. Eastern European languages specialist." She smiled at invented memories. "His Slavic root structure lectures packed the hall, though his exams terrorized us."

She described details researched months ago: the western reading room, specific campus buildings, student gathering places. She had never visited Munich, but spoke of it like home.

"The university has certainly expanded since my time," Weber mused. "Different professors, different programs."

"Education evolves constantly," Layla agreed. "The Reich demands excellence in all fields."

Weber's suspicion seemed to fade, replaced by professional courtesy. When he later introduced her as "a fellow linguistics graduate," she felt the familiar double edge of her performance. Each successful deception preserved her safety while binding her tighter to her fiction.

Later, a ministry car delivered her to her new Kurfürstendamm building. Marble lobby. Uniformed elevator operator. Neighbors included a Gestapo colonel and an aircraft manufacturer's wife.

In her apartment, she removed her Nazi pin, placing it in its velvet box. The empty floorboard space where her parents' photograph once lay felt like an open wound. She pressed her palm against the hollow wood, remembering their faces before the flames consumed them.

This emptiness justified everything: the meetings, the constant lies, the nauseating complicity. Tomorrow: more translations, more deceptions, more navigating the heart of the regime that murdered her family.

Spring brought unexpected warmth to Berlin. In her office, Layla worked through intercepted communications between Warsaw and neutral embassies. Her security clearance now granted access to diplomatic pouches, censored letters, and monitored phone call transcripts.

The intercom's buzz jolted her. "Fräulein Brandt, bring the Lodz analysis immediately." Becker's tone crackled with tension.

She gathered the documents and hurried down the hall. Becker wasn't alone. A tall SS officer studied the map wall, red pins in hand. Standartenführer (Colonel) collar insignia.

"Fräulein Brandt, Standartenführer (Colonel) Vogel from Eastern Security Administration." Becker gestured toward his desk. "He has questions about your Lodz ghetto resistance assessment."

Vogel. Her fictional boyfriend's surname. Coincidence sent ice through her veins, but she maintained her composure.

"Standartenführer" she acknowledged with a slight head bow.

Vogel turned from the map, cold stare assessing her. "Your analysis predicted Sector Four resistance weeks before our intelligence confirmed it."

"The correspondence patterns suggested organization there, sir."

"Your work saved German lives, Fräulein." Vogel stepped closer. "Seventeen saboteurs executed based on your intelligence."

Horror flooded her. Seventeen people died because of her translations.

"I'm pleased to serve the Reich," she said, words burning her throat.

Oberst Hartmann's Grunewald villa dinner party represented Layla's infiltration pinnacle. Military and Party officials mingled with allied diplomats despite wartime austerity.

Four months after starting at the ministry, Layla navigated this world confidently. Her blue silk dress, purchased with enhanced ration coupons, marked her new status.

"Fräulein Brandt translates for Oberführer Becker," her hostess told an Italian attaché. "Quite indispensable, I hear."

During dinner, conversation turned to the "Jewish question." Layla maintained her pleasant expression while Oberst Hartmann described "resettlement" with bureaucratic satisfaction.

"Eastern territories will soon be completely cleansed," he announced. "Necessary, if sometimes unpleasant."

"A burden Germany bears for Europe's future," a Luftwaffe colonel agreed, raising his glass. "To the final solution architects."

Glasses clinked. Layla raised hers mechanically, wine bitter as poison.

After dinner, she excused herself to find the powder room, then took a calculated wrong turn toward the study. The door slightly ajar, conversations and cigar smoke escaping.

"Warsaw emptied by August," Hartmann was saying. "Treblinka's increased capacity will handle the volume."

"Same in Lodz," another added. "Chelmno processes them efficiently now."

"The Reichsführer wants accelerated timetables," a third stated. "No half measures."

She steadied herself against the wall, committing every word to memory. Warsaw emptied by August. Accelerated timetable.

When the evening ended, Hartmann helped with her coat, hands lingering on her shoulders.

"Join us again, Fräulein Brandt. Refreshing to have intelligent young people at these gatherings."

In the ministry car returning home, Layla watched Berlin's darkened streets pass. Her performance had succeeded beyond any expectation. She now accessed information that might save lives, if she could find a way to use it.

In her apartment, she hung the blue silk dress carefully. From the empty hiding place beneath her floorboard, she felt only hollow wood where her parents' photograph once rested.

"I'll make it mean something," she whispered to their memory, touching the space where their faces had smiled before the flames took them.

Midnight approached. In hours, she would return to the ministry, pin on her swastika, and translate documents detailing her people's destruction. She would smile at colleagues planning genocide.

And beneath that performance, Miriam Weiss would gather information, search for patterns, seek ways to use her position before more lives were lost.

Even if it cost her own.

8

Layla's Discovery

Standartenführer Vogel sat directly across from her, his notepad angled exactly on the polished conference table. Ten minutes into the briefing, Layla noticed his gaze lingering on her whenever she spoke. Not the usual male assessment she'd grown accustomed to deflecting, but something colder, more analytical.

"Fräulein Brandt," *Oberführer* (Senior Colonel) Becker questioned, tapping the Warsaw report she'd translated. "Your analysis of sector seven communications suggests organized resistance forming. Explain your conclusions."

She kept her voice steady, professional. "The language patterns shifted in March. References to 'weather conditions' increased threefold but actual meteorological terminology decreased. Classic substitution coding."

Vogel's pen stopped moving. "Impressive pattern recognition for someone with academic language training."

"My father taught me to read between lines in his banking correspondence. Words conceal as much as they reveal."

"Indeed." Vogel's smile never reached his stare. "Speaking of family connections, your boyfriend Heinrich Vogel. Related to me perhaps?"

The question was delivered with deliberate casualness. Layla maintained her pleasant expression while ice flooded her veins.

"I wouldn't presume, *Standartenführer*. Germany has many Vogels."

"True. Yet few in the SS near Lublin. I know most officers there personally."

She navigated the moment with practiced ease. "Perhaps I've misunderstood his exact posting. Security limits what he shares in letters."

"Naturally." Vogel closed his notebook with careful precision. "Security concerns us all."

After the meeting, Becker held her back with a slight gesture. "The *Standartenführer* requested your personnel file this morning."

"Is something wrong, sir?"

"Routine verification. Excellence attracts attention, Fräulein Brandt. Your work impresses important people." His icy stare assessed her. "A promising development for your career."

She recognized the warning beneath his words. Attention meant scrutiny. Scrutiny meant danger.

Back in her office, Layla locked the door and leaned against the cool window. Ten seconds of weakness before Layla Brandt reasserted control. But the damage was done. They were investigating.

The next few days brought subtle signs of surveillance. A man in a gray hat who appeared on her morning commute three days running. Her apartment showed microscopic evidence of search: slight displacements in her dresser contents, a different fold in her bedsheets, the photograph of her "parents" moved two centimeters from its usual position.

They had been inside, looking for evidence of Miriam Weiss. Her secret floorboard compartment remained undisturbed, but that could mean they were watching to see what she did next.

Sleep abandoned her. She lay in darkness, reviewing her options while knowing the walls were closing in. The emergency plan had always included possible escape routes, false papers for another identity, hidden funds. But implementing it now would confirm their suspicions.

And what of the other Jewish families hiding in Berlin? Her ministry position had provided intelligence that helped warn several households before raids. Abandoning her post meant abandoning them too.

When morning came, it brought no clarity, only the certainty that Layla Brandt's carefully constructed existence hung by an increasingly fraying thread.

"Fräulein Brandt! What a delightful surprise."

Kreisleiter Wagner spotted her across the ministry canteen, waving her to his table where Hilde Müller and two SS officers sat. She composed her features into pleased recognition.

"*Kreisleiter*. An honor."

"Join us. We were just discussing your cultural verification proposal." Wagner's face beamed with satisfaction. "So effective we've implemented it across three districts."

Cold dread filled her. Her suggestion at the party meeting now actively hunting Jews.

"Gratifying to hear, *Kreisleiter*."

"The Charlottenburg verification sweep identified twelve families with suspicious documentation but flawless local knowledge." Wagner cut his schnitzel with measured movements. "Your approach finds the cleverer ones hiding behind paperwork."

Twelve families. Because of her suggestion.

"Your method exposes deeper deceptions," the younger SS officer added. "Jews who study German customs, memorize city details. Surface-level disguises."

"The true German knows things that cannot be studied," Wagner declared. "Childhood traditions, local expressions, proper social behaviors."

Hilde Müller watched her throughout this exchange, pale gaze narrowed with something that might have been suspicion or simple envy.

That afternoon brought the phone call she had been dreading.

"Fräulein Brandt, your presence is requested at tonight's district party meeting." *Kreisleiter* Wagner's voice boomed with enthusiasm. "We'd like you to present your cultural verification method to regional leadership."

"Tonight? I'm flattered, but perhaps someone with more experience would be better suited."

"Nonsense! Your insights impressed *Standartenführer* Vogel himself. He specifically requested your participation."

Her pulse faltered. "The *Standartenführer* will attend?"

"Indeed. Along with representatives from Security Administration. Your work has attracted significant attention."

A trap, disguised as recognition. They would never arrest her at the ministry where her exemplary work earned respect. Better to expose her before party zealots eager to witness another enemy unmasked.

"I would be honored, *Kreisleiter*."

"Excellent. Albrecht Hall, eight o'clock. Wear something appropriate for addressing leadership."

The Albrecht Hall gleamed with polished wood and Nazi banners. Party officials and their wives filled rows of chairs, an audience of predators in evening wear. *Standartenführer* Vogel stood near the podium conversing with *Oberführer* Becker. Both men observed her entrance with careful attention.

Layla wore navy blue, modest yet professional, blonde hair swept into a simple knot. The ideal German civil servant, possibly for the last time.

"Fräulein Brandt." *Kreisleiter* Wagner guided her toward the front row. "We've allocated fifteen minutes for your presentation, followed by questions."

"Questions?"

"Certainly. Regional security leaders have significant interest in refining your method."

She scanned the audience, identifying four Gestapo officers, several SS commanders, and ministry officials. In the back corner stood two men with the unmistakable stillness of security personnel monitoring exits.

No escape. Only performance remained.

Wagner's introduction passed in a blur of patriotic platitudes. Then she stood at the podium, faces turned expectantly toward her.

"Cultural verification identifies enemies of the Reich who have mastered documentary deception," she began, voice steady despite her racing pulse. "False papers can be created, but true German cultural knowledge cannot be falsified."

For twelve minutes she outlined her methodology, explaining how childhood experiences, local traditions, and regional vocabularies formed identity markers impossible to counterfeit convincingly. The systematic explanation of how she herself might be caught.

"Most effective are unexpected questions about childhood experiences," she concluded. "Religious holidays, school traditions, neighborhood landmarks. Emotional memory creates authentic responses genuine Germans provide instantly."

Applause followed. Then *Standartenführer* Vogel stood, and she knew her time had ended.

"Fascinating methodology, Fräulein Brandt. Perhaps a demonstration would be instructive."

"Of course, *Standartenführer*."

"You've explained how to identify Jewish imposters. Given your Dresden background, what specific cultural questions would you ask someone claiming Dresden origins?"

She drew from her exhaustive study of the city. "Dresden children sing a specific Advent carol with distinctive regional verses. I might ask which verse mentions the Frauenkirche bells."

Vogel nodded approvingly. "And school traditions?"

"Dresden Gymnasium students participated in Elbe Day swimming competitions each May. The traditional route passed under four bridges."

"Excellent examples." Vogel paced slowly before her. "Now, an interesting question. What if we apply your methodology to ministry personnel? Security requires constant vigilance, even among ourselves."

The audience murmured approval. This was why they had come.

"As you suggested, unexpected questions reveal the truth." Vogel's tone hardened. "Tell us about Professor Hauser's distinctive lecture style at Munich University."

The room fell silent. The trap revealed itself completely.

"He favored etymological diagrams on blackboards," she answered, maintaining eye contact. "Often taught while walking through student desks."

"Curious." Vogel produced a document from his jacket. "Munich University has no record of Professor Hauser in their linguistics department during your attendance years."

"The February bombing damaged the eastern campus archives," she replied, though her prepared explanation now felt hollow.

"We checked faculty directories published annually. No Hauser listed from 1935 through 1938." Vogel's voice cut through the hall like a blade. "We also verified your father's position at Sächsische Landesbank. No Brandt worked in foreign accounts during the period you claim."

The audience shifted, sensing blood. Her carefully constructed identity crumbled with bureaucratic precision.

"Most revealing was your translation of the Warsaw ghetto report." Vogel withdrew a familiar page from his pocket. "Our document specialists identified this margin notation as Yiddish script, partially erased."

He held the page for the audience to see. Gasps and murmurs rippled through the room.

"When applying your cultural verification method to yourself, Fräulein Brandt, several inconsistencies emerge."

A screen lowered, and a projector clicked on. Her university identification photograph appeared, but not of Layla Brandt. Miriam Weiss stared back at her, younger, dark-haired, unmistakably herself.

"Warsaw University, 1935. Miriam Weiss, linguistics department, Jewish student. Identified by former classmates now working for the Reich relocation administration."

The whispers turned hostile. Wagner's face contorted with betrayed fury. The assembled officials leaned forward like spectators at a gladiatorial match.

"Additional evidence includes falsified Dresden documentation, nonexistent SS officer Heinrich Vogel, and specialized knowledge of Warsaw Jewish quarter streets not included on German maps."

Vogel's methodical presentation stripped away every layer of her performance, each revelation met with fresh murmurs from the audience. The perfect German secretary was revealed as the enemy hiding among them.

"Miriam Weiss," Vogel addressed her directly, abandoning all pretense. "You have infiltrated the Reich Foreign Ministry, accessed classified documents, and falsified your racial identity. These acts constitute high treason against the German state."

70

Two security officers moved toward her. *Oberführer* Becker observed with unreadable expression, perhaps calculating what secrets she had accessed in his department.

She straightened her spine, finding unexpected calm in the moment of complete exposure.

"My name is Miriam Weiss," she acknowledged, voice carrying through the suddenly silent hall. "I am a German Jew born in Berlin, and I have served the Foreign Ministry with greater loyalty than it deserved."

The security officers seized her arms. She didn't resist.

"Take her to headquarters for processing," Vogel ordered. "Full interrogation protocols."

As they escorted her through the parting crowd, faces regarded her with fascination and disgust. She kept her head high, refusing to grant them the satisfaction of seeing her fear.

Outside, a black car waited. April night air carried the scent of linden trees, perhaps the last breath of Berlin she would ever draw as a free woman.

The interrogation stretched across three days. Not physical torture, her value as a skilled linguist meant damaged hands would reduce her usefulness. Instead, they used sleep deprivation, endless standing, thirst, and relentless psychological pressure.

"Who received your intelligence?" "What documents did you copy?" "Which other Jews work within the ministry?"

Through it all, Layla Brandt faded like morning mist, leaving only Miriam Weiss facing her captors with stubborn silence.

On the third day, *Standartenführer* Vogel returned, carrying a file that would determine her fate.

"Your situation has been evaluated at the highest levels." He placed the documents before her. "Your language skills remain valuable despite your deception."

"I won't translate documents that harm my people."

"Your cooperation isn't requested, merely your capability." Vogel's tone held no cruelty, only bureaucratic finality. "You're being transferred to Auschwitz-Birkenau. Their administration requires multilingual processors for incoming transports from various European territories."

The words hit her with physical force. Birkenau. The camp whose reports she had translated, whose true purpose she understood completely.

"When?"

"Transport leaves tomorrow morning. Special compartment, given your skills."

She studied his face, searching for any crack in his professional composure. "You know what happens at Birkenau. You've read the same reports I've translated."

"I know the Reich processes security threats according to established protocols."

"You know they're killing us by the thousands. You've seen the logistics yourself."

Vogel gathered his papers without responding. At the door, he paused, and for a moment his mask slipped slightly.

"For what it's worth, Fräulein Weiss, your work at the ministry was exceptional. Had circumstances been different..."

"Had I not been Jewish," she said flatly.

"Had priorities been different," he corrected, his voice carrying the faintest note of something that might have been regret. "The Reich values skills like yours, but ideology supersedes individual utility."

After he left, Miriam sat in the harsh light, accepting what would come. Not the quick death she had feared, but something potentially worse. Survival through complicity in her people's destruction.

Morning arrived with a plain dress, worn shoes, a thin jacket. Two guards escorted her from headquarters to Anhalter Bahnhof where a passenger train waited. Unlike the cattle cars she had read about in transport reports, she boarded a third-class passenger compartment guarded by two SS men.

Privilege, of sorts. Private transport to hell.

Through the window, Berlin receded into morning mist. The city where she was born, where she had created Layla Brandt, where she had failed to save her parents but perhaps helped other families escape a similar fate.

The train gathered speed, rocking gently as it carried her east. Toward Poland. Toward Birkenau. Toward whatever remained of life for Miriam Weiss after the death of Layla Brandt.

The guards discussed her in low voices, thinking she couldn't hear.

"Speaks seven languages. Will work translating for new arrivals."

"Impressive deception. Months at the Foreign Ministry without detection."

"Shows what they're capable of. Clever and dangerous."

Miriam closed her eyes, not to sleep but to think. For nearly two years, she had survived as Layla by becoming someone else entirely. Now she would have to survive as Miriam in Birkenau by remembering who she had been before all this began.

The translator who moved between worlds. The daughter who failed to save her parents. The woman who had once believed identity was something you chose rather than something imposed upon you by forces beyond control.

As the train crossed into Poland, she felt Layla Brandt die completely, leaving only Miriam Weiss facing whatever horrors waited ahead. She had lost everything except the most dangerous possession of all: knowledge of what awaited at the journey's end, and the fierce determination to survive it.

The ideal German was gone. The Jewish daughter remained.

9

Arrival in Birkenau

The train shuddered to a halt with the screech of metal on metal. Through the small window, Miriam glimpsed watchtowers silhouetted against an overcast sky, searchlights sweeping the ground in mechanical arcs. The guards who had accompanied her stepped onto the platform first, their boots clattering against concrete.

"*Raus!* (Out!) Everyone out!"

Unlike the chaos she had read about in ministry reports of cattle car arrivals, her small group of specialized prisoners was processed with clinical efficiency. No dogs, no immediate violence, just the methodical stripping away of humanity disguised as administrative procedure.

Twenty women stood naked in a concrete room that reeked of disinfectant and something else. Fear, perhaps, or despair absorbed into the walls themselves. The commands came in rapid German from a female guard whose face remained as expressionless as if she were directing the unloading of furniture.

"Arms up! Turn! Bend! Spread your legs!"

Miriam complied automatically, her mind retreating to the same detached space that had protected her during Gestapo interrogations. Her body was just an object now, something to be examined, catalogued, processed. She had translated the forms that created this procedure. Now she experienced it.

When rough hands grabbed her hair (the blonde locks that had helped make Layla Brandt credible), yanking her head back for the electric clippers, something inside her finally flinched. Her languages might save her life, but they couldn't save this: the carefully maintained disguise that had been her mother's pride before it became dark waves.

The clippers buzzed against her scalp. Cold metal vibrated against bone as her hair fell in clumps to join the growing pile on the concrete floor. Each pass revealed more of the skull beneath, the universal vulnerability that no identity could disguise.

"Next! Move!"

A prisoner in striped uniform shoved a bundle into her arms. Rough fabric, wooden clogs that didn't fit, before pushing her toward another station. Unlike the other new arrivals being processed in the main camp, Miriam and several other women had been separated for the translation section.

The tattooing station made everything final. The needle bit into her forearm with mechanical precision: A-7291. The digits that would now represent her entire identity, burned into flesh like a brand on livestock.

"Translation division," the prisoner murmured in Polish as she worked, her eyes never rising to meet Miriam's. "Administrative Block 7."

The words carried the faintest undertone of something. Resentment? Warning? Already the divisions of the camp hierarchy were becoming clear.

They were herded through the remaining intake procedures with ruthless speed. Delousing powder showered over newly shaved heads, cursory medical examinations, forms filled out by clerks who recorded language capabilities with far more care than they did names.

"Russian, you claimed?" An SS officer with wire-rimmed glasses looked up from his clipboard, studying Miriam with the interest of someone evaluating a useful tool.

"Yes, sir." She replied in Russian, intentionally simplifying her grammar to suggest competence without complete mastery. Better to exceed expectations than fail to meet them. A lesson learned in the ministry that applied here with deadlier stakes.

He switched to French, firing rapid questions about her background. She answered with a perfect Parisian accent, then demonstrated the English that had once impressed British diplomats at embassy receptions. German went without saying. Polish was tested last, her fluency immediately apparent.

The officer made final notations, then stamped her file with a thud that echoed in the small room. "Primary assignment: Polish section. Report to Block 7 for housing."

She was given no time to rest. A female guard escorted her and several other women across a section of the camp that seemed almost separate from the main facility. The barracks here were still crude, but marginally better maintained. Less overcrowded. Functional rather than purely punitive.

"Administrative section," the guard announced as they walked. "Block 7 handles translation and documentation. You eat, sleep, and work there unless specifically directed elsewhere. Attempting to contact general prisoners is forbidden. Sharing information about your work is forbidden. Failing to meet translation quotas is forbidden." Her mouth twisted into a thin smile. "Everything is forbidden except what is explicitly permitted."

Block 7 sat between buildings marked "Records" and "Communications." Through the windows, Miriam glimpsed typewriters, filing cabinets, the bureaucratic machinery that kept this place functioning. Unlike the overcrowded barracks visible in the main camp, Administrative Block 7 was divided into dormitory sections with actual beds. Three-tiered wooden bunks with thin mattresses and blankets that, while inadequate, were cleaner than anything she had seen since her arrest.

Inside, prisoners were being assigned bunks by a hollow-eyed woman with a supervisor's armband. Miriam found herself directed to a lower bunk in the corner, where a thin woman with closely-shorn dark hair was already sitting.

"Rivka," the woman said simply, moving slightly to make room on the thin mattress. No surname, no additional information. Just a name, offered as the barest acknowledgment of shared humanity.

"Miriam," she replied, using her real name aloud for the first time in nearly two years.

Rivka nodded and they sat in silence while Miriam observed their surroundings. The barracks housed perhaps forty women, all with the same shaved heads and hollow expressions, the uniform look of systematic starvation. Some were already lying on their bunks, staring blankly at the wooden slats above. Others moved with the careful conservation of energy that marked those who understood survival depended on rationing every resource.

"You are new," Rivka finally said, her voice low enough that it wouldn't carry. Something in her tone suggested experience with being careful, with knowing when to speak and when to remain silent. "Today's transport?"

"Yes."

"Languages?"

"German, Polish, Yiddish, English, French, some Russian."

Rivka's eyes showed a flicker of something that might have been approval. "Good combination. Polish section most likely. High demand these days."

"You've been here long?"

"Six months. Warsaw, among other things." She paused, and in that silence Miriam sensed layers of story deliberately left untold. "Privileged prisoner. Better to die quickly than live long in this place."

The starkness of the statement settled between them. Miriam understood it not as despair but as brutal honesty, the kind of clear-eyed assessment necessary for survival here. There was something in Rivka's manner that spoke of authority, of someone accustomed to making hard decisions. No false hopes, no comforting illusions.

A whistle blew, and women began moving toward the door with practiced efficiency. Rivka stood, gesturing for Miriam to follow. "Evening rations. Take whatever they give. Eat slowly."

The food was marginally better than what Miriam had expected from ministry reports. A watery soup with actual vegetables visible, a piece of dark bread, a small scraping of what might have been margarine. She ate at a measured pace while observing the unwritten choreography of the mess hall. Who sat where. Who spoke to whom. Which prisoners were treated with deference by others.

Rivka moved through the space with quiet confidence, acknowledging certain women with subtle nods. Others seemed to defer to her slightly, nothing obvious enough to draw guard attention, but clear to someone watching carefully. Whatever her background, she had found ways to navigate this place that kept her alive and granted her a measure of respect.

After the meal, they returned to the barracks as darkness fell over the camp. Through the small windows, floodlights created a perpetual twilight, a constant reminder that true privacy, true rest, true darkness were luxuries not permitted here.

"They will separate us by language groups tomorrow," Rivka said as they lay side by side in the narrow bunk. "Polish speakers are in highest demand. Many records to process."

"From the new territories?" Miriam asked.

"No." Rivka's voice held the flat effect of someone stating facts rather than describing mass murder. But underneath, Miriam detected something else. A pain held under careful control. "From those who will never leave this place. Death certificates. Property inventories. Transport records. The administration of disappearance requires extensive documentation."

The bitter irony struck Miriam with physical force. She had seen these mechanisms from the ministry side, translating the administrative communications that flowed between Berlin and the occupied territories. Now she would see them from the inside, as both processor and potential subject of the same system.

"Sleep," Rivka advised, her voice carrying the authority of someone accustomed to giving guidance. "Tomorrow will require all your strength."

But sleep proved elusive despite overwhelming exhaustion. The barracks filled with the sounds of women coping with trauma. Soft weeping, occasional cries from nightmares, the restless shifting of bodies on inadequate pallets. Through the thin walls came the distant sounds of the camp: guard dogs barking, searchlights humming, the mechanical sounds of a place that never truly slept.

In this half-light, lying beside a stranger whose breathing carried its own stories of loss, Miriam conducted a ruthless inventory of her situation. Her parents were almost certainly dead, processed through the same transportation system she had once helped administer from Berlin. Her own survival through the initial selection had been secured only through her language skills. A temporary reprieve rather than genuine safety.

And whatever work she would be assigned tomorrow would directly support the very machinery designed to process and eliminate her people. The same translation skills that had elevated her, then helped her survive as Layla Brandt, now kept her from immediate death while maintaining the system designed for her destruction.

Such hopelessness might have crushed someone less accustomed to adaptation, to finding paths through impossible situations. But Miriam had already survived the destruction of her life as a respected translator, the creation and maintenance of Layla Schmidt, the interrogation rooms, the systematic unraveling of her performance. Each transformation had required abandoning what came before, assessing new realities with clear-eyed precision.

Birkenau would require the same, but with even narrower margins for error, even fewer resources, and more dire consequences for miscalculation.

Beside her, Rivka shifted slightly, and Miriam caught a whispered word in Polish. A name, perhaps. Or a prayer. Something private and precious guarded even in sleep.

As she finally drifted toward uneasy sleep, Miriam found her thoughts turning to the ministry documents she had translated, the names and faces of those who had created this system. *Standartenführer* Vogel with his bureaucratic precision. *Oberführer* Becker with his cold efficiency. The dinner party guests who toasted the "final solution" while cutting their schnitzel.

In those drowsy moments between consciousness and sleep, a cold certainty formed: if she survived this place, there would be a reckoning for those who had built it, those who ran it, those who turned the great machinery of bureaucratic murder with such professional dedication.

And she would be part of that reckoning, if she lived. Not just for herself, but for her parents, for all those being processed through the Reich's system of erasure. For the children whose names Rivka whispered in her sleep.

The thought followed her into dreams where forms and documents and tattooed numbers swirled together in an endless bureaucratic nightmare, a cold flame of purpose burning beneath the shock and horror of her first day in hell. Somewhere in those dreams, she heard a voice that might have been her own, or her mother's, or Rivka's, promising that memory would survive this place, that witnesses would remain to tell what happened here.

Even if survival came at the cost of everything else they once were.

10

The Second Day

Morning arrived with the siren at 4:30, followed by shouts from prisoner functionaries. "*Aufstehen!* (Get up!) Roll call! Move!"

Miriam and Rivka rose with the immediate responsiveness of those who understand that hesitation could be fatal. Around them, the other translators straightened inadequate bedding, adjusted ill-fitting uniforms, prepared to face whatever this new day would bring.

Outside, dawn lightened the eastern sky as prisoners assembled in rows before the barracks. Guards moved among them, counting, occasionally pulling someone from the ranks for perceived infractions of rules never explicitly stated but enforced with immediate violence.

"Translator section will report to the administration block after breakfast," announced a prisoner functionary wearing the same striped uniform but with an armband marking her as a kapo. "New arrivals will be assessed for assignments."

Breakfast meant thin gruel and ersatz coffee distributed after roll call. Miriam ate mechanically, recognizing that nutrition now represented survival rather than sustenance. Around her, other women did the same, some struggling to keep down even these minimal rations.

As they shuffled toward the administration block, their wooden clogs clicking against the ground, Rivka provided hurried orientation in the same flat voice she had used the night before.

"Administration is divided by function. Records. Communications. Special projects. Each has language sections." Her words came in short bursts between shallow breaths. "Polish and Yiddish most in demand. Then Hungarian. Russian for eastern operations."

"And the work itself?" Miriam asked, keeping her voice equally low.

"Documentation," Rivka replied. "Always documenting. The living. The dead. Those in between."

The administration block was a substantial building near the camp entrance. Two stories of brick and concrete housing the camp's extensive bureaucracy. Inside, the contrast with the primitive barracks was stark: polished floors, proper electric lighting, desks and filing cabinets and typewriters creating an almost normal office atmosphere.

German officers in immaculate uniforms moved through the spaces with brisk efficiency, occasionally pausing to issue instructions to prisoner workers who received them with perfect deference.

The new translator group was led to a large room on the ground floor and directed to sit on benches along one wall. A German officer entered with a clipboard. Thin-faced, spectacled, with the distracted air of an academic rather than a military man. He began calling numbers. Not names. The women had ceased to have names the moment their tattoos dried.

"A-7291," he called.

Miriam rose, the number still unfamiliar enough that she hesitated before recognizing it as her own.

"Languages?" the officer asked without looking up.

"German, Polish, Yiddish, English, French, some Russian," she replied.

The officer made a notation. "Polish section. Room 12. Report immediately."

Each woman was assigned to language sections based on their reported abilities, distributed with the same efficiency as everything else in this place where accuracy was applied to destruction.

Room 12 was filled with desks where a dozen women were already working, each with stacks of documents. A German sergeant looked up as Miriam entered.

"New translator?" he asked, his tone suggesting she was an expected delivery rather than a person.

"Yes, *Herr Feldwebel* (Sergeant). A-7291. Polish section."

He consulted a list, found her number, and made a check mark. "Desk seven. Report to Prisoner 82944 for assignment."

Desk seven was occupied by a hollow-eyed woman whose prisoner uniform hung loosely on her frame. Despite this, she had the alert gaze of someone whose mind remained sharp.

"New?" the woman asked. "Polish section?"

"Yes. A-7291."

"Sit." She gestured to the empty chair. "I am Anna, 82944. You will translate these." She indicated handwritten forms. "Into these." She pointed to typed forms with carbon copies. "Prisoner intake records. Handwritten by kapos during processing. Must be properly entered into official files."

Miriam picked up the first form. Her hands trembled slightly as she read the handwritten Polish: Name: Sarah Kowalczyk. Age: 6. Origin: Warsaw. Parents: Deceased. Assigned to: Children's Block 31.

Six years old. A child who should be playing with dolls, learning to read, safe in her mother's arms.

"Be exact," Anna advised, watching Miriam's face carefully. "Errors mean punishment. Never falsify, they check randomly. Begin with this stack, I will review the first ten. Questions?"

"The children," Miriam's voice came out hoarse. "Block 31..."

Anna's expression hardened. "You translate. Nothing more. Their fate is not your concern if you want to survive."

Miriam forced herself to begin typing. Sarah Kowalczyk became another entry in the administrative machinery, her six-year existence reduced to carbon paper and filing categories. Each keystroke felt like a betrayal, but stopping would mean her own death, and dead translators helped no one.

The second form was worse: Mordechai Goldstein, 43, Warsaw. Profession: Doctor. Family status: Widow. Three children, ages 8, 10, 12. All assigned to Children's Block 31.

By the fourth form, Miriam's vision blurred. She was processing the intake records for an entire transport from Warsaw, families torn apart, children separated from parents, all documented with bureaucratic precision. The same cold efficiency she had once admired in the Foreign Ministry. Now she understood what that efficiency had actually served.

"Focus," Anna whispered sharply. "Emotional responses draw attention."

She was absorbed in forcing her fingers to type mechanically when the office door opened and a new officer entered. The momentary stillness of the other women alerted her. A collective tension that rippled through the room like a held breath.

Looking up, she saw a tall SS officer in his late thirties, his uniform immaculate, his bearing suggesting both authority and awareness of it. He spoke quietly with the sergeant, reviewing documents with focused attention.

"*Untersturmführer* (Second Lieutenant) Drexler," Anna whispered, barely moving her lips. "New head of records section. From Berlin's central administration. Dangerous. Very correct. He notices everything."

Berlin. Central administration. The words registered with particular weight. This officer had potentially been part of the same ministry apparatus where Layla Brandt had worked.

Miriam studied him as he moved through the office, occasionally stopping to review work at various desks. His inspection was thorough, his comments to prisoners precise and technically focused rather than abusive. A different kind of danger from the shouting guards, but equally lethal for those who failed to meet his standards.

When he reached the desk beside theirs, Miriam kept her eyes lowered while being acutely aware of his presence. She could hear him examining another translator's work, his questions sharp and specific. The proximity of authority made her skin crawl, memories of Gestapo interrogations flooding back unbidden.

"This transliteration is inconsistent," he said to the woman at desk six. "Polish surnames require standardized German phonetics. Redo this entire batch."

The woman nodded frantically. "Yes, *Herr Untersturmführer*. Immediately."

Then he was at desk seven. Miriam forced herself to continue typing while he picked up several of her completed forms, examining them with the critical eye of someone who understood proper documentation.

"These are unusually precise," he commented to Anna. "New translator?"

"Yes, *Herr Untersturmführer*. Arrived yesterday. A-7291."

"Previous experience?" Drexler asked, the question directed at Miriam.

She looked up, meeting his gaze directly but briefly. "Translation work in commercial documents, *Herr Untersturmführer*." The partial truth came automatically.

"Origin?"

"Berlin, *Herr Untersturmführer*."

Something flickered in his expression. Not recognition, but sharp interest. He picked up another of her forms, studying not just the translation but her handwriting, her formatting choices. The scrutiny reminded her uncomfortably of Gestapo officers examining her false papers.

"Berlin. I was stationed there before my transfer here." His voice carried casual authority, but his eyes remained calculating. "Where in Berlin?"

"Charlottenburg, *Herr Untersturmführer*."

He nodded slowly, making a notation on his clipboard. "Your technical accuracy is noted, A-7291. However," he picked up the form she was currently working on, "I see you've hesitated on this entry. The child's assignment shows no completion time."

Miriam's pulse quickened. She had indeed stopped typing while reading about another six-year-old, thinking of the countless children who had passed through the ministry's deportation orders she had once translated so efficiently. "I was ensuring accuracy of the Polish spelling, *Herr Untersturmführer*."

"Accuracy is essential," Drexler agreed, his tone deceptively mild. "But efficiency is equally important. These records serve crucial administrative functions. Delays in processing can create significant complications."

The threat was clear beneath the bureaucratic language. Miriam nodded. "Understood, *Herr Untersturmführer*."

"Good." He set the form down precisely where he had found it. "Your Berlin background suggests familiarity with proper administrative procedures. I trust that will prove valuable here."

As he moved on, Miriam kept her expression neutral despite the cold fear crawling up her spine. Karl Drexler. Berlin's central administration, now transferred to Birkenau's records section. A man who valued accuracy, who noticed details, who maintained professional correctness even in this place designed for murder.

And now he was specifically interested in her.

"Careful," Anna breathed once Drexler had moved to the far side of the room. "He's marked you as potentially useful. That can be good or very bad."

Miriam returned to her typing, but her mind raced. Drexler's questions had been too specific, too focused. Did he suspect something about her background? Had her hesitation over the children's records revealed too much?

The rest of the morning passed in tense concentration. Form after form, prisoner after prisoner. Each document represented a human life reduced to administrative data, each carbon copy another link in the chain of bureaucratic murder.

When the lunch whistle blew, Miriam had processed thirty-seven intake records. Thirty-seven people, including twelve children, all catalogued with the same mechanical precision she had once applied to diplomatic correspondence.

"You did well for the first day," Anna said as they prepared to leave. "But be careful with Drexler. Men like him don't forget faces or names. Especially not faces like yours."

"What do you mean?"

Anna glanced around, ensuring they weren't overheard. "You don't look like what you are. That made you valuable as a translator, but it also makes you memorable. And memorable can be dangerous."

That evening, as the translator group shuffled back to their barracks, Miriam observed Drexler crossing the yard toward the SS quarters. His posture remained perfect, his movements efficient, his manner suggesting complete comfort with his role in this machinery of death.

Watching him disappear into the officers' building, something crystallized within her. A purpose more specific than mere survival, more focused than general thoughts of future reckoning.

If she survived Birkenau, men like Karl Drexler would face consequences for their "correct" administration of murder. Not just the shouting guards with their overt brutality, but the clipboard-carrying officers who documented death with professional detachment.

She would remember his name. His face. His manner. His Berlin background. His interest in her precision and origins. Would catalog this information just as she had once catalogued details from ministry documents.

Not for now. Now was for survival, for navigating the day-to-day realities of Birkenau, for maintaining whatever narrow margin separated life from death.

But for later. For after. For the time that would come if she endured.

The cold determination that had begun her first night found specific focus in Karl Drexler's professional assessment of her translation work. Not rage or hatred, but something more dangerous because more sustained. The absolute certainty that precision could serve justice as readily as it now served murder.

As she entered the translator barracks, returning to the crowded bunk she shared with Rivka, Miriam carried this new certainty within her. A private truth hidden beneath her prisoner's uniform and shaved head and tattooed number.

The machinery that had processed her into this hell had also created the conditions for its own eventual reckoning. And she would be part of that reckoning, beginning with Karl Drexler, late of Berlin, now serving the Reich's purposes at Birkenau with such professional dedication.

The thought accompanied her into another night of fitful sleep, a cold comfort in a place designed to strip away all comfort, all hope, all possibility beyond the next roll call, the next meal, the next day's work of recording the living and the dead with equal thoroughness.

But now that work had a face. And that face would not be forgotten.

11

The Wolf

Berlin, 1938

It was the watch that sealed the deal.

Yakov Feldman studied the gold timepiece as afternoon light caught its surface: a Patek Philippe Calatrava with a cream dial that whispered wealth without shouting it. It had belonged to a textile merchant from Frankfurt who had believed in Yakov's fictional shipping company. By the time the merchant realized his investment had vanished, Yakov was already in Berlin, wearing a new name as naturally as he wore the man's watch.

They called him Wolf. The name had stuck after his third score in Hamburg when a mark had said he moved like a predator, circling before the strike. The comparison pleased him. Wolves survived by reading weakness, exploiting opportunity, adapting to whatever environment would keep them fed.

He adjusted his tie in the Hotel Adlon's bathroom mirror. The lights were merciless, revealing every line. Not that Wolf had many imperfections. His reflection stared back: blond hair swept with careful carelessness, blue eyes that could manufacture concern or delight on command, a face that made Nazis see their ideal, never suspecting the Jewish blood beneath the performance.

The irony never lost its bitter edge: how easily they embraced him, this perfect specimen with a circumcision scar and memories of Shabbat candles he'd worked hard to forget.

He smoothed a wrinkle from his tailored suit jacket, another "donation" from a previous mark. The clothes, the watch, the precisely calibrated German accent with its Swiss inflection were his tools, as essential as a scalpel to a surgeon.

A soft knock on the bathroom door.

"Herr Richter?" A woman's voice, hesitant but warm. "Are you nearly ready? The opera begins at eight."

Wolf's face transformed as warmth replaced calculation in his eyes, the smile he'd spent years perfecting in mirrors across Europe.

"Just a moment, my dear Hildegard," he called.

He opened the door to find Hildegard von Kleist waiting, her face brightening. Forty-two years old, widow of a factory owner who had died conveniently early, leaving her with more money than sense and a desperate need for validation. Three weeks of orchestrated "chance" meetings had led to tonight, when "Heinrich Richter," Swiss businessman, would suggest a partnership requiring significant financial commitment.

It was nothing personal. Just business. Sentiment was a luxury predators couldn't afford.

"You're exquisite tonight," he said, brushing his lips against her gloved knuckles.

She touched her neck. "Heinrich, you'll make me self-conscious."

"Good," he said, watching her pupils dilate. "Then we match."

The lie settled between them, cloaked in flattery. Wolf had learned early that people believed what they wanted to believe. And what Hildegard von Kleist wanted was that a handsome, younger man found her irresistible, not that he had targeted her after reading about her husband's death in the financial pages.

They were halfway to the revolving doors when Wolf saw him.

A man in a crisp SS uniform, dark hair slicked back, eyes sharp and predatory: *Sturmbannführer* (Major) Werner Schneider. They had crossed paths two years earlier in Munich, when Wolf was operating under a different name. Wolf had escaped, leaving Schneider humiliated and thirty thousand Reichsmarks poorer.

Schneider had been different then, a young officer with ambition but little power. Now he wore the uniform of a man who had found another path to advancement, one that required no subtlety.

Wolf turned his face away, guiding Hildegard toward a side exit. "The night is too beautiful for the main doors," he explained. "Let's step out through the garden."

Too late. Recognition settled over him like a death sentence.

"Feldman!" The name, his real name, rang out across the marble floor. "Yakov Feldman!"

Hildegard looked up at him, confusion clouding her features. "Heinrich?"

Wolf's mind raced through possibilities, discarding each as rapidly as it formed. Side exit: twenty paces. Front doors: fifty. Schneider: moving closer, hand at his hip.

"I'm afraid there's been a misunderstanding," Wolf said to Hildegard.

"There's no misunderstanding, Jew," Schneider spat, close enough now that others in the lobby were turning to watch. "Did you think I would forget your face?"

Wolf released Hildegard's arm. "Run," he whispered.

"What is happening?" she demanded.

"This man is a criminal," Schneider announced loudly. "A Jewish thief hiding among decent Germans."

The lobby went silent. Wolf could feel dozens of eyes on him, see disgust forming on faces that moments ago would have nodded respectfully. His Aryan appearance meant nothing the moment the word "Jew" was attached to it.

"Is this true?" Hildegard whispered, stepping away. Her eyes, which had looked at him with such warmth, now held nothing but fear and revulsion. "Are you?"

Wolf didn't answer. There was nothing to say. He analyzed the distance to the side exit, tensed to run.

Pain exploded in the back of his skull. He hadn't seen the second officer approaching. Wolf fell to his knees, the marble floor rushing up. He caught a glimpse of polished boots before another blow sent him sprawling.

Through blurring vision, he saw Hildegard backed against a pillar, one hand covering her mouth. Not just horror at his treatment, but at her own proximity to someone like him.

"I trusted you," she said, barely audible.

Wolf might have laughed if he could have drawn breath. Trust, as if her interest hadn't been as transactional as his own. She wanted validation; he wanted money. Neither had offered anything real.

Rough hands dragged him to his feet. Blood trickled down his neck, warm and sticky. His mouth filled with the metallic tang of his own blood.

"Yakov Feldman," Schneider said, close enough that Wolf could smell coffee and schnapps on his breath, "you're under arrest for fraud, theft, and contaminating Aryan bloodlines."

As they dragged him out, Wolf caught a last glimpse of the hotel lobby: the glittering chandeliers, the fine marble, the world he had convinced himself he could navigate indefinitely. The game had finally ended, but not because he'd made a mistake. Because the rules had changed around him.

Leipzig, 1924

The transformation had begun years earlier, with a single moment of clarity.

Fourteen-year-old Yakov stood in the doorway of his father's study, watching Rabbi Isaac Feldman organize papers for the community relief fund. Outside, voices carried from the street, growing louder, more aggressive.

"Jews out! Jews out!"

His father continued working, pen scratching across donation records with steady concentration. As if the chanting beyond their windows was merely weather.

"Father," Yakov said. "Shouldn't we..."

"Lock the door? Hide?" Rabbi Feldman didn't look up. "They want us to be afraid. Fear is what they feed on."

The chanting grew closer. Then came the crash of breaking glass from the bakery next door, followed by laughter. Mrs. Goldstein's terrified screaming.

Yakov ran to the window. Three young men in brown shirts were methodically destroying the bakery's front window while a crowd watched. Some cheered. Others simply observed with the detached interest of spectators at a show.

"They're destroying everything," Yakov said, his voice cracking. "Mrs. Goldstein is seventy years old."

His father finally looked up. "And what would you have me do? Fight them with my fists? That would give them an excuse to burn down the synagogue."

"But we can't just..."

"We endure," his father said firmly. "As we have always endured. This madness will pass."

Yakov stared at him. This man who commanded such respect in their community, whose wisdom guided so many families, whose learning was vast and deep. At that moment, he looked small. Helpless. Naive.

The next morning, Yakov walked past the bakery's ruins. Mrs. Goldstein sat amid the wreckage, weeping quietly while neighbors whispered their sympathy and offered what little help they dared.

That afternoon, he followed the brown shirts to a beer hall where they celebrated their victory with cheap alcohol and loud boasting. He observed from across the street, noting their swagger, their confidence, their absolute certainty that strength was the only currency that mattered.

Two weeks later, he stole forty marks from the synagogue charity box.

Not because he was hungry. Not because his family lacked necessities. But because something inside him had shifted, realigning toward a new understanding of how the world actually worked.

His father's books spoke of justice, of divine providence, of the arc of history bending toward righteousness. But Yakov had seen the arc of history that afternoon: it bent toward whoever was willing to use force while others offered prayers.

He used the stolen money to buy clothes that didn't mark him as a rabbi's son. A jacket that let him walk through Leipzig's central district without drawing stares. Shoes that didn't whisper "Jew" with every step.

The theft was easier than he'd expected. No lightning strikes, no immediate divine retribution. Just forty marks that bought him access to spaces previously forbidden.

With his new clothes and his mother's Aryan features reflected in his own face, Yakov discovered he could go anywhere, speak to anyone, be anyone. The revelation was intoxicating.

"Where were you this afternoon?" his father asked one evening.

"Studying," Yakov lied smoothly. He had been at a café in the university district, listening to students debate politics, learning to mimic their accents and attitudes.

His father studied him with troubled eyes. "You've been distant lately. Distracted."

"I'm fine, Father."

"Your Hebrew is suffering. Rabbi Stern mentioned your lack of preparation for yesterday's discussion."

Because Yakov had been learning more useful lessons elsewhere. How to read people's desires and weaknesses. How to project confidence and belonging. How to become whoever the situation required.

"The world is changing, Yakov," his father continued. "Perhaps more rapidly than I initially believed. But our traditions, our faith... These are what will preserve us."

Yakov nodded dutifully while thinking: Traditions preserve nothing. Faith preserves nothing. Only adaptation preserves anything.

By his sixteenth birthday, Yakov had become expert at reading the desires behind people's expressions, the insecurities that drove their choices, the precise words needed to make them believe whatever served his purposes.

His father never discovered the theft. Never learned about his son's afternoon expeditions beyond the Jewish quarter. Never suspected that the boy who sat respectfully through religious instruction was systematically teaching himself to prey on human weakness.

The last conversation between father and son came on a gray October morning in 1926.

"I've arranged an interview for you at the seminary in Frankfurt," Rabbi Feldman announced over breakfast. "Your learning, when you apply yourself, shows real promise."

Yakov set down his coffee cup. "I'm not going to seminary, Father."

"It's time you consider your future seriously. The community needs educated young men who..."

"The community needs young men who understand reality," Yakov interrupted. "Seminary won't teach me that."

His father's face went pale. "What are you saying?"

"I'm saying your way doesn't work. Prayer doesn't stop brown shirts. Tradition doesn't prevent broken windows. Faith doesn't put food on tables or safety in homes."

"You're speaking of sacred things as if they were mere..." Rabbi Feldman struggled for words. "As if they had no meaning beyond immediate utility."

"Meaning is a luxury," Yakov said, standing. "Survival isn't."

He left Leipzig that afternoon with everything he owned in a single suitcase. He never saw his father again.

By 1928, Yakov Feldman had become Wolf, moving through Germany's cities like his namesake: patient, observant, striking when opportunity presented itself. His father's books had taught him to read; his own experiences taught him to read people. Both skills proved profitable.

Sachsenhausen, 1940

The razor scraped his scalp raw, blonde waves hitting the floor as guards shouted orders. Then the stripping, fine wool and silk exchanged for striped rags that reeked of the previous wearer's fate.

The shock wasn't the brutality. Wolf had expected that. The shock was how quickly his carefully constructed identity dissolved. All the clothes, mannerisms, accents that had protected him for over a decade, stripped away in minutes.

"Name?" A clerk sat behind a desk, not bothering to look up.

"Heinrich Rich..." Wolf began automatically, then stopped. The lie would do him no good here. "Yakov Feldman."

The clerk's eyes narrowed at his face, lingering on the blue irises, the straight nose. "Nature's deception," he muttered, stamping the form with unnecessary force.

Wolf said nothing. It was a reaction he'd encountered before, that superstitious discomfort when Jewish features didn't match Nazi propaganda.

The processing continued with mechanical efficiency. Then came the number, needle biting into his forearm, driving ink beneath his skin with each painful jab. Wolf watched, detached, as the digits appeared. No longer Yakov Feldman. No longer even Wolf. Just a number in a vast accounting system.

In the barracks that first night, Wolf catalogued his new environment with the same systematic attention he'd once applied to potential marks. Guard rotations. Prisoner hierarchies. The small opportunities for advantage that existed even here.

A skeletal man sidled up to him, eyeing him with sharp assessment. "You're strong," he observed quietly. "That's good. They need workers in the quarry. Ask for that assignment if you can."

Wolf studied the man, noting how he held himself, not broken, not yet. A survivor. "Why the quarry?"

"More food. Hard work, but if you're strong..." The man shrugged. His eyes were deeply sunken but alert, intelligent. "I'm Abram. Professor of mathematics, University of Berlin. Until they decided Jews couldn't teach Aryan children."

Wolf assessed him more carefully. Education meant intelligence. Intelligence could be useful. "And now?"

"Now I count stones and calculate survival probabilities." A ghost of a smile flickered across Abram's cracked lips. "What did you do, before?"

"Businessman," Wolf replied, which was true enough.

"What kind of business?"

Wolf met his gaze directly. "The profitable kind."

Abram's laugh turned into a cough. When it subsided, he said, "Here, we're all in the same business now. Staying alive."

Over the following months, Wolf learned the intricate economy of camp survival. Information was currency. Skills were capital. Relationships were investments that might pay dividends in bread, protection, or advance warning of selections.

He volunteered for the quarry detail, where exhausting labor was offset by marginally better rations. His Aryan appearance made some guards treat him with less immediate hostility, an advantage he exploited carefully.

But it was his talent for reading people that proved most valuable. Wolf could identify which kapos might be bribed, which guards had weaknesses to exploit, which prisoners could be trusted with small confidences.

"You adapt quickly," Abram observed one evening as they shared their meager soup. Six months had passed, and both men had learned to eat slowly, making each spoonful last.

"Adaptation is survival," Wolf replied. "Everything else is luxury."

"Even conscience?"

Wolf considered the question. In his pre-war life, conscience had been an obstacle to overcome. Here, it could be lethal. "Especially conscience."

Abram nodded slowly. "I told myself the same thing at first. But be careful, my friend. Lose too much of yourself, and survival becomes meaningless."

"Meaning is luxury too," Wolf said.

But late at night, lying on his narrow bunk, Wolf sometimes wondered if Abram was right. What would be left of him when this ended? What pieces of Yakov, of Wolf, of whatever he was becoming would remain?

He pushed such thoughts away. Philosophy was another luxury he couldn't afford.

By 1943, Wolf had carved out a precarious but sustainable existence at Sachsenhausen. He worked the quarry during the day, traded information and small favors in the evening, and slept the careful sleep of someone who understood that vigilance was the price of another dawn.

When the transport orders came, he wasn't surprised. The war was going badly for Germany. Camps were being consolidated, populations transferred, the machinery of murder growing more efficient.

"Birkenau," Abram said quietly as they waited in the formation for transport. "I've heard things."

"What kind of things?"

"Bad things. Worse than here."

Wolf studied his friend's face. Three years had aged Abram decades, but his intelligence remained sharp. If he was frightened, there was a reason.

"Then we adapt again," Wolf said simply.

"And if adaptation isn't enough?"

Wolf met his gaze. "Then we find another way to survive."

Birkenau, 1943

Wolf stepped off the transport train at Birkenau and into an entirely different category of hell.

The journey from Sachsenhausen had taken three days in a sealed cattle car packed so tightly that men had died standing up. When the doors finally opened, the light sliced into his eyes like razors.

The air carried smoke and something else, something sweet and terrible that caught in his throat, coating his tongue with the taste of other men's endings.

The selection process was swift and decisive. Officers pointed left or right as each prisoner passed. Wolf had heard rumors about this procedure: left meant death, right meant work.

As he approached an officer, Wolf instinctively straightened his posture, making himself look strong despite the hollowness in his cheeks. The familiar instinct of self-preservation, refined over years of reading what people wanted to see.

The officer barely glanced at him before pointing right.

Relief flooded through him, followed immediately by the recognition that gratitude for hard labor rather than immediate death marked how far his standards had fallen.

Abram appeared beside him in the group directed right, his friend having made the same journey from Sachsenhausen. The professor looked even more skeletal than before, but that same intelligence still burned in his eyes.

"Welcome to the end of the line," muttered another prisoner nearby.

Wolf said nothing. He had learned that silence was safety, that drawing attention meant danger. But his eyes never stopped moving, cataloguing the layout, the routines, the hierarchies visible even from this distance.

Processing at Birkenau was more efficient than Sachsenhausen, more mechanized. Every step designed for maximum throughput with minimum waste of German resources.

When it was over, Wolf stood in a new uniform, with an additional number tattooed on his arm, waiting for assignment to barracks and work detail.

A prisoner wearing an armband that marked him as a block elder moved among the new arrivals, assessing them with the detached eye of a farmer sorting livestock.

"You," he said, stopping in front of Wolf. "Previous camp?"

"Sachsenhausen," Wolf replied, keeping his voice neutral. "Quarry detail."

The block elder nodded, making a note on his clipboard. "Strong back. Good. We need those." He studied Wolf's face with the same uncomfortable attention Wolf had grown accustomed to. "You don't look like one of us."

"He's with me," Abram said, stepping forward. "Records warehouse. We need someone who can lift crates."

The block elder's mouth twitched, almost a smile. "Your little kingdom of paper, Professor?" He shrugged. "Fine. Building 4. Both of you."

As the block elder moved on, Abram moved closer to Wolf. "Records warehouse. Indoor work. Away from the elements. Better than most alternatives here." Abram glanced around the processing area. "I've heard things about this place from transfers. If we can get a warehouse assignment, it's our best chance."

"Why help me?" Wolf asked.

Abram's gaze was direct. "Because you're a survivor, like me. And because the few of us who've made it this far need to watch out for each other."

That night, in the crowded barracks, Wolf lay on his narrow bunk and thought about the long journey that had brought him here. From the rabbi's son who'd stolen from charity boxes to the con man who'd preyed on human weakness to the camp prisoner who calculated survival in increments of bread and information.

Each transformation had required abandoning previous versions of himself, adapting to new realities, becoming whatever circumstances demanded. The process had kept him alive, but at what cost?

Beside him, men wept or prayed or lay in stunned silence. Wolf did none of these things. Instead, he began to plan. Tomorrow would bring new challenges, new systems to understand, new angles to identify.

The game continued, perhaps more desperately than ever. And Wolf intended to win it, whatever winning meant in a place designed to ensure that no one won at all.

But for the first time since leaving Leipzig, he wondered if Abram was right. Could someone lose so much of themselves in the service of survival that survival itself became meaningless?

The question followed him into an uneasy sleep, where he dreamed of his father's study, of brown shirts laughing over broken glass, of hotel lobbies and gold watches and the faces of marks who'd believed his lies because they needed to believe them.

In his dreams, all the versions of himself stood in judgment of each other, and none could claim innocence.

12

Rivka's Journey

Pre-War Krakow

Rivka's boots echoed through the station corridors. Even after nearly a decade on Krakow's force, the sound still turned heads. She caught herself in the window: uniform crisp, hair pulled back tight, thirty-five years of living etched only at the corners of her eyes.

"Lieberman!" Marek's meaty hand waved a folder from the records room doorway. His voice dropped to a conspiratorial growl. "Chief's been throwing everyone else's statements in the bin. Says yours is the only one worth a damn."

Rivka's mouth twitched. She'd worked harder than any man on the force to earn that respect. Perfect arrests, watertight cases, never giving anyone an excuse to question her competence.

"Tell him an hour. Maybe less."

As she passed the bullpen, colleagues nodded. Not friends, but men who'd learned that respect wasn't optional. She'd earned it by being twice as good for half the credit, by solving cases others couldn't crack.

The awareness hit her before she heard him. Kowalski. Standing in the doorway like he'd been there all along, watching her with something new in his eyes. Something that hadn't been there yesterday.

"Something I can help you with, Kowalski?" She kept working, voice neutral.

Seven years they'd worked together. Sharing coffee on stakeouts. That time he'd carried her home drunk from the department celebration, never mentioning it again. Partners in everything but name.

His silence stretched until she had to look up. When he spoke, his words carried the weight of stones.

"My brother says we need to cleanse Poland of foreign influences. Says your people have taken too many positions that should belong to true Poles."

Her pencil stilled. Foreign influences. Your people. As if nine years of service, of bleeding for this job, meant nothing.

"I'm sorry to hear that," she said quietly.

He shrugged. "Times are changing. People should know where they stand." He walked away without waiting for her response.

Fear settled beneath her ribs as she left the station. Everything looked different now. German newspapers where Polish ones had been. Conversations dying as she passed. Goldstein's bookshop window with its new sign: "Under New Management."

She stopped cold. Around the corner from her apartment, yellow paint defaced the Abramowitz family door. Last week, the Felds. Week before, the Steins. Crude stars had appeared overnight, marking Jewish homes like a hunter's trail.

Lieberman. The name her father had spoken with pride now felt dangerous in her mouth.

The apartment on Józefa Street carried the scent of chicken soup and fear, though only she could detect the latter. The door had barely closed when Sarah launched herself forward.

"Mama's home!" Her daughter's curls tumbled wild, untamable as her spirit. Six years old and already sent home twice for arguing with her teacher about whether girls could be doctors.

David crashed into her legs a moment later, face smeared with something sticky and purple. "I made a boat, Mama! A real one!" His voice dropped to a whisper. "It only sank once."

She knelt, breathing them in. Soap and dirt and that indefinable scent that was purely her children. These two lives she'd created with Jakob, before consumption took him three years ago.

"This miracle boat requires my inspection, obviously."

Erika sat at the kitchen table, steam rising between her and Rivka like unspoken words. Jakob's mother had moved in after his death, claiming the children needed a grandmother's guidance. Really, they all needed each other.

"You look worn through," Erika said. Never one to soften a truth.

"Bad day." The tea scalded her tongue. She welcomed the pain.

Erika's knuckles went white around her cup. "The Wassersteins left for America. Sold everything. Three tickets west."

Rivka set her cup down. "They've been threatening that since '35."

"This time they're gone. Rachel says I should talk to you again. About the children."

"No." The word cracked between them.

Erika's eyes flashed. "Listen to me, Rivka. Even your uniform won't protect you if things get worse. Jakob would..."

"Don't." Rivka's voice broke. "Not him."

A widow for three years and Jakob's name still drove air from her lungs. She remembered him with his quiet laugh and steady hands, Jakob who'd died before David could remember his face.

"He'd want his children safe," Erika said, stubborn as her son had been. "He'd want you safe."

The tea had gone cold. Rivka couldn't look up. "This is our home. My job is here. The children's school, their friends. Where would we even go?"

"My cousin in Palestine..."

"With what money? On what papers?" The questions hung between them. "It's too late for that, Erika."

But late at night, listening to her children breathe from the bedroom, Rivka pulled out maps. Traced routes west, calculated distances, estimated costs. Her police training kicked in automatically. Assess the situation. Plan for contingencies. Always have an escape route.

The German Occupation

German troops marched into Krakow on a gray Tuesday morning. Rivka watched from her window as tanks gouged the cobblestones, leaving scars in stone that had stood for centuries. The children pressed against her legs, feeling the tremor she couldn't hide.

"Are those our soldiers, Mama?" David's eyes were wide, confused.

"No, *kochanie* (beloved)." She stroked his hair, each strand fine as silk. "They're visiting. It won't be for long."

The lie burned her throat. She'd read the intelligence reports, heard the radio broadcasts before they went silent. This wasn't a visit.

She reported to work the next day, uniform immaculate as always. The station had transformed overnight. German notices were plastered where Polish ones had hung. An SS officer at the front desk, watching Polish officers with cold, reptilian eyes.

Rivka assessed the situation with professional instincts. New power structure. Different rules. Her years of reading criminals' faces served her well here, recognizing predators in different uniforms.

Chief Wojcik intercepted her in the hallway, his face the color of dirty snow. "Lieberman. My office."

She followed him, feeling the stares. Yesterday's colleagues looked through her or at the floor. Some watched with something like accusation, as if she'd brought this on them all.

Wojcik closed the door. For once, he didn't sit behind his desk but leaned against it, suddenly small in his own office.

"They're taking inventory of all Jewish officers," he said without preamble. "You need to go home."

"Sir, I can still..."

"No, Rivka, you can't." Her first name, after all these years of "Lieberman." "This isn't a request. It's for your own safety."

"And if I refuse?"

His face hardened. "Then you're a fool. Some of the men have already..." He trailed off, but she understood. Someone had identified her to the Germans.

"Kowalski," she said.

Wojcik didn't deny it. "Take your family and go somewhere. Anywhere but here."

She thought of Erika's cousin in Palestine, of the Wassersteins with their American tickets. Options that no longer existed.

"Thank you, sir." She extended her hand.

He hesitated, then took it firmly. "You were a good officer, Lieberman."

Were. Past tense. A career erased with a single word.

The restrictions descended like hammer strikes. No trams, no parks. Armbands mandatory. Businesses seized, radios confiscated, curfews enforced by rifle butts and boot heels. Each morning brought new ways to be erased.

Rivka adapted. Her police training served her now in different ways. She found hidden routes between buildings to avoid German patrols. Memorized guard rotations and shift changes. Sewed yellow stars while the children slept, her fingers remembering the precise stitches Jakob's mother had taught her.

She traded her mother's silver candlesticks for potatoes and flour when rations dwindled to nothing. Moved the children's beds away from windows after bullets shattered glass in the apartment above.

"It's only temporary," she told Erika, told herself. "We just need to survive until the British and French push them back."

But her police instincts read the signs differently. The systematic nature of it all. The paperwork, the lists, the careful documentation. This wasn't chaos or opportunistic violence. This was a plan being implemented with Germanic efficiency.

She began hiding things. Small amounts of money sewn into coat linings. Documents buried in the courtyard. A knife wrapped in cloth behind the loose brick by the stove. Preparations for something she couldn't name but felt approaching.

The day she found their names on a posted list of "relocated" apartments, Rivka knew their time had shrunk from weeks to days. That evening, she watched as three families were marched from their building, disappearing into military trucks that reeked of diesel and despair.

"We have days, not weeks," she told Erika that night, after the children were asleep.

Erika nodded. Three months of gradual strangulation had aged her years. "What do we do?"

"We run."

"Where?"

Rivka had no answer. Her maps and plans assumed time to prepare, money to spend, papers that would be accepted. None of that existed now.

"I don't know. But we can't stay."

The Separation

They came for her on a Tuesday morning. Three sharp knocks, then the door exploded inward in a shower of splinters. Two German soldiers and behind them, Kowalski in his Polish uniform. His face blank, eyes lifeless as stone.

"Rivka Lieberman?" One soldier stepped forward, checking a list. "Former police officer?"

"Yes." Her voice remained level while her heart hammered against her ribs. Training kicked in. Stay calm. Assess. Look for opportunities.

"You and your family will come for processing."

Sarah appeared in the bedroom doorway, sleep-rumpled and confused. "Mama?"

"It's all right, Sarah." Rivka forced her face to soften. "We're just going to register with the new authorities. Go help Grandma get David ready."

"All Jews must register," the soldier recited, bored already. "Bring only essential items. One bag per person."

Rivka looked at Kowalski, searching for any remnant of the man who'd carried her home that night, drunk and laughing. "My children are very young. Is this really necessary?"

Something flickered behind his eyes, quickly buried. "Orders, Lieberman. Just following orders."

She'd heard those words from criminals before. The last refuge of men who'd abandoned their conscience.

They were marched through streets becoming foreign under her feet. German signs, German uniforms, German words crushing the Krakow she'd protected for nearly a decade. Rivka's police training made her catalog details automatically. Routes, personnel, procedures. Information that might matter later.

Other families joined them, a stream of confused, frightened people converging on a school gymnasium now transformed with German efficiency.

Inside, chaos wore the mask of order. Tables where documents were checked and stamped. Lines dividing men from women, young from old. The sharp scent of fear beneath antiseptic and sweat.

Erika held David against her chest, her lined face a mask above his curls. Sarah stood beside Rivka, small fingers digging half-moons into her mother's palm.

"Name?" A clerk barely glanced up.

"Lieberman. Rivka, Sarah, David, and Erika."

The man made notations. "Occupation?"

"Police sergeant," Rivka said, the last time she would claim it.

That made him look up, eyebrows raised. He said something in German to the guard beside him, who laughed.

"Former police," the clerk corrected, his accent thick. "Now, unemployed."

They were photographed, documented, their few possessions logged in ledgers. At the next station, a woman in a gray uniform held out her hand. "Jewelry. All of it."

Rivka removed her wedding ring without expression. The gold band Jakob had placed on her finger eight years ago. Erika did the same, mouth tight with fury.

Sarah's hand flew to her throat, where Jakob's last gift hung. A small Star of David on a thin chain. "No, Mama. Papa gave it to me."

"I know, *neshomeleh* (little soul)." Rivka knelt, keeping her voice low and steady. "But we must do as they say right now."

"It's mine." Sarah's chin lifted, so like her father it hurt to see. "He said always to wear it."

The guard stepped forward, impatient. "The necklace. Now."

"Please," Rivka said. "It has no value. It's just..."

The slap caught her across the cheekbone, snapping her head sideways. She heard Sarah's scream like it came from underwater.

"Mama!"

Rivka straightened, touching her split lip. Training took over. Don't escalate. Protect the children. Survive this moment to reach the next.

"It's all right," she began, but two more guards appeared, pulling Sarah away from her.

"No!" Rivka lunged forward. "Sarah!"

Something cracked against her skull. She stumbled, the room spinning. When it steadied, Erika was fighting as they tore David from her arms.

"The children go to the youth section," someone said. "For their own good."

"I am their mother." Rivka fought with everything she had, using every technique from years of subduing criminals. Nothing worked against these men with their empty stares. "Sarah! David!"

Sarah's face disappeared behind the closing door, mouth stretched in a scream Rivka could no longer hear. One small hand reaching, fingers grasping at nothing. Then gone. Both her children, gone.

"I will find you!" Rivka's words sprayed blood from her split lip. "I swear it, Sarah! I'll find you both!"

But her voice echoed in a room that didn't care, swallowed by a machine too vast and merciless to fight alone.

Later, in the women's section of a cattle car bound for places whose names meant nothing yet, Rivka sat in darkness and felt pieces of herself break away. The police sergeant who'd earned respect through competence. The mother who'd promised to keep her children safe. The woman who'd believed civilization had rules that couldn't be broken.

All of it stripped away, leaving only the animal core of survival.

But even in that darkness, as the train carried her toward an unknown hell, Rivka held onto one thing: the promise she'd made. Sarah and David were alive somewhere in this system. And she would find them, or die trying.

The woman who emerged from that cattle car would be different from the one who'd entered it. Harder. More ruthless. Someone who understood that in a world without rules, survival required abandoning everything except the will to continue.

But she would remember. She would remember two small faces, two voices calling for their mama. And that memory would be both her torment and her strength, driving her forward through whatever came next.

The oath she'd taken as a police officer had been to protect and serve. That oath was gone now, along with everything else. But the new oath she made in that cattle car, whispered to herself in the darkness, was simpler and more absolute:

Find them. No matter what it cost. No matter who she had to become.

Find them.

13

The Broken Bread

The crust of bread hit the mud with a wet slap. Wolf watched it fall: the kapo's thick fingers opening, the small piece tumbling through the gray afternoon air and landing in the thin winter slush beside the laundry barracks. The kapo hadn't noticed, continuing his patrol along the line of prisoners waiting for the afternoon work detail to form up.

No one moved at first. In Birkenau, sudden movements drew attention, and attention meant death. The guards counted heads twice daily, but they watched for motion constantly, like cats tracking mice.

Wolf's eyes moved between the bread, the guard twenty meters away lighting his cigarette, and the kapo now thirty paces down the line, barking orders at a group of new arrivals. Five meters to salvation, one wrong step to a beating or worse. Other prisoners had seen the fallen crust too. He felt their hunger like heat radiating from their bodies, but months of camp life had made them cautious. Hesitation kept you alive, but it also kept you hungry.

All except one man who moved the same instant Wolf did.

A slight, wiry figure broke from the opposite line of prisoners waiting for kitchen duty. Wire-rimmed glasses clung to his gaunt skull, somehow unbroken despite everything this place did to destroy what people brought with them. They converged on the fallen crust like two compass needles drawn to the same magnetic point.

Wolf reached it first, his longer stride and broader frame giving him the advantage, but as his fingers closed around the sodden prize, a bony hand clamped over his. He looked up into the face of his competitor.

Behind those smudged lenses, dark eyes held Wolf's gaze with something he hadn't seen in months. Intelligence, yes, but also resilience. And beneath the layer of camp grime and exhaustion, something that looked almost like humor. As if this man understood the absurdity of two human beings fighting over a piece of bread smaller than a child's fist.

Neither spoke. What was there to say in Birkenau? Hunger had its own language, and they both spoke it fluently. Wolf outweighed the other man by at least twenty kilos, even in his current state. The struggle would be brief and decisive.

The smaller man lunged forward, trying to break Wolf's grip with a sudden twist. Wolf shifted his weight, using the man's momentum against him the way he'd learned in a dozen street fights before the camps. They tumbled into the mud, breath steaming in the cold air.

Around them, prisoners shifted almost imperceptibly, creating a loose circle. Not close enough to be considered participants if the guards noticed, just near enough to witness whatever would unfold. Wolf caught glimpses of their faces: hollow cheeks, sunken eyes, but something alive flickering behind the exhaustion. As if watching two men fight over bread was better entertainment than they'd had in months.

They grappled in near silence, only the sound of fabric tearing and boots scrabbling for purchase in the slush. The man's strength surprised Wolf. Not physical strength, that had been burned away by months of starvation, but the kind born of absolute necessity. The strength of someone who refused to give up, even here.

Wolf had lived by his muscles before the camps. Enough remained to matter. He gained the upper hand gradually, pinning the smaller man beneath him, the bread clutched in his fist above the mud. Victory, such as it was: triumph over another starving prisoner for a morsel that would barely ease hunger for an hour.

The man beneath him went still. Not surrendering, just stopping. He looked up at Wolf with steady dignity, chest rising and falling with controlled breaths. No pleading, no anger, just acceptance of whatever would come next.

Those eyes.

Wolf saw something in them that stopped him cold. The same quiet refusal to let Birkenau define what remained of his humanity. This man had been stripped of everything, reduced to fighting in mud for scraps, but something essential remained intact. Something Wolf recognized because he'd been systematically destroying it in himself for months.

His mother's voice echoed across twenty years: "Yakov, we break bread together because we are family. Because sharing makes us human."

Wolf's grip loosened on the crust. Something shifted in his chest, like a frozen lock suddenly forced open by unexpected warmth. He pushed himself up from the mud and extended his hand, the bread resting in his palm.

"Take it," he said, his voice rough from disuse.

The smaller man sat up slowly, suspicion plain on his face. Around them, the circle of witnesses stirred. Kindness was rare enough in Birkenau to be dangerous, often just cruelty wearing a different mask. Or worse, a sign of mental breakdown that would bring unwanted attention from the guards.

The man adjusted his glasses with careful fingers, somehow still delicate despite months of brutal labor. He studied Wolf with the methodical assessment of someone who had learned to trust nothing at face value.

"Why?" he asked. His voice carried the faint accent of educated German, the kind that belonged in university lecture halls rather than concentration camps.

Wolf had no answer that made sense, even to himself. A month ago, a week ago, he would have kept the bread without hesitation. Survival meant taking what you could, when you could, from whoever was too weak to stop you. That was the lesson Birkenau taught every day, reinforced by hunger and brutality and the constant presence of death.

But something had changed in him when he looked into this stranger's eyes. Like recognizing like. Two men who had somehow maintained a core of themselves despite everything designed to strip it away.

"Just take it," Wolf said again.

With movements that spoke of ingrained courtesy, the man reached out and accepted the crust. His fingers brushed Wolf's palm for just an instant, the brief contact of warm flesh almost shocking in a place where human touch usually meant violence.

110

Then, without hesitation, he broke the bread in half and offered one piece back to Wolf.

The gesture stopped Wolf cold. In a place where men killed each other over potato peels, where survival had reduced most prisoners to their most primitive instincts, this stranger had divided what little he had been given. The act was so unexpected, so fundamentally decent, that for a moment Wolf forgot where he was.

"Together," the man said simply.

Wolf stared at the offered half, his mind struggling to process what was happening. He couldn't remember the last time another person had shared anything with him without expecting something in return. Couldn't remember the last time he had been touched without cruelty or been treated as if his life had value.

Slowly, he took the piece of bread.

They ate in silence, making the small morsels last, chewing slowly to extract every bit of nourishment and flavor. The bread was coarse and stale, but Wolf found himself savoring it in a way he hadn't experienced since childhood. Not just the food, but the sharing of it. The quiet communion of two human beings acknowledging each other's worth.

Around them, the other prisoners began to drift away as whistles blew and guards shouted orders for work details to form up. But a few lingered, watching this small miracle with something like wonder. As if they needed to witness proof that decency could still exist in this place designed to destroy it.

Wolf wiped his hands on his striped uniform and extended one toward the smaller man.

"They call me Wolf," he said.

The man regarded the offered hand for a moment, then took it in a grip that was firmer than his frame suggested.

"Daniel Kraus," he replied. "Originally from Frankfurt."

Their hands remained clasped a moment longer than necessary, both men recognizing that something unprecedented had occurred. A human connection forged despite Birkenau's systematic efforts to reduce them to animals competing for scraps.

"*Juden!* Jews! Back in line! Move!" A guard's shout scattered the remaining onlookers like startled birds. Wolf and Daniel released their handshake and stepped away from each other, heads bowed, resuming the protective posture that kept camp inmates invisible to casual observation.

But as they shuffled to their respective places in the forming work details, Wolf found himself glancing back at Daniel's receding figure. The man moved with purpose despite his obvious exhaustion, spine straight despite months of labor designed to break bodies and spirits.

A tailor, Wolf would learn later during one of their careful conversations. Before the camps, Daniel had run a shop in Frankfurt that dressed German businessmen who would eventually turn on him with the rest of the country. His hands, now calloused from hauling laundry bundles and scrubbing floors, had once created elegant suits with mathematical precision.

That night, lying on his wooden bunk in Barracks 23, Wolf thought about the bread they had shared. The half-crust was nothing, barely enough to register in his empty stomach. But the choice to share it changed everything. It felt like the first truly human interaction he'd experienced since his arrest, the first moment when someone had treated him as if his life mattered.

Daniel, somehow, made him remember who he might become after this, if there was an after. Made him wonder if survival was worth anything if it meant losing everything that made survival meaningful.

Three days later, Wolf spotted Daniel across the morning roll call assembly. They stood in different blocks, separated by fifty meters of muddy ground and the watchful eyes of guards who shot prisoners for infractions as minor as talking during count. But Wolf recognized those wire-rimmed glasses immediately.

Daniel must have felt his gaze. He looked up, meeting Wolf's stare across the distance with a slight nod of acknowledgment. Nothing more could be risked under the constant surveillance, but the brief contact was enough. A reminder that in this place designed to isolate and dehumanize, connections could still be forged.

That afternoon, Wolf made sure his document delivery route passed near Block 17, where he had observed Daniel standing that morning. He carried a stack of inventory forms between buildings, one of the privileged assignments that came with his work in the records warehouse. As he rounded the corner of the kitchen barracks, a familiar voice spoke from the shadows.

"You're still alive, then."

Wolf paused without turning his head, adjusting his stance to block any observer's view of the shadowed alcove where Daniel waited.

"So far," Wolf replied quietly. "You?"

Daniel stepped partially into view, keeping his back to the brick wall. Up close, Wolf could see the toll three days had taken: deeper hollows beneath those prominent cheekbones, new lines around his eyes. The camp consumed everyone at its own pace, but determination still burned behind those wire-rimmed lenses.

"More or less," Daniel answered with what might have been dry humor. "Work detail?"

"Records," Wolf said, glancing around to ensure no guards were watching their position. "Document delivery between buildings."

Understanding flickered in Daniel's expression. Document delivery meant mobility, access to different areas of the camp, opportunities to observe and gather information. In Birkenau, knowledge was currency almost as valuable as food.

"Useful," Daniel commented.

Wolf nodded slightly. "I have some flexibility in my routes."

The word hung between them, heavy with possibility. Flexibility meant chances to meet, to share information, to maintain the human connection they had discovered over shared bread.

A door slammed somewhere behind the kitchen barracks. Both men tensed, ready to move apart if guards appeared.

"Block 17, bunk 22," Daniel said quickly. "If you have reason to pass by during evening distribution."

Wolf gave an almost imperceptible nod. "I might find reasons."

They separated without another word, Wolf continuing on his assigned path while Daniel melted back into the shadows. To any casual observer, the exchange would have appeared meaningless. Two prisoners briefly occupying the same space, nothing more.

But as Wolf delivered his forms to Administration Building 3, he felt a fundamental shift in his perception of the camp. Before meeting Daniel, he had seen Birkenau as a maze to be navigated alone, every other prisoner a potential threat or obstacle to his own survival. Now there was Daniel, another fixed point in the chaos, another reason to remain alert and alive.

That evening, as the translator group shuffled back to their barracks after the day's work, Wolf found his route naturally taking him past Block 17. The evening meal distribution was underway, prisoners lined up with their dented metal bowls to receive the day's second portion of watery soup.

He spotted Daniel near the end of the line, those distinctive glasses catching the fading light. As Wolf passed behind the laundry detail, Daniel turned slightly, their eyes meeting for just an instant. No words exchanged, but the brief contact carried weight. Acknowledgment. Continuity. The promise that their connection would endure despite everything designed to prevent it.

In his bunk that night, Wolf lay awake longer than usual, thinking about Daniel Kraus from Frankfurt. About wire-rimmed glasses and steady hands that had broken bread to share with a stranger. About the strange, fragile web of humanity that persisted even in a place specifically engineered to destroy it.

In his previous life, Wolf had been a predator by choice and necessity, forming connections only to exploit them. Here, connections meant vulnerability and risk, but also, perhaps, the difference between surviving and remaining human.

As sleep finally claimed him, Wolf wondered if there were others like Daniel scattered throughout the camp. People who had managed to retain their essential nature despite everything taken from them. People who might, together, find ways to resist that had nothing to do with weapons or escape attempts, and everything to do with maintaining dignity in a place designed to strip it away.

For the first time since his arrival at Birkenau, Wolf fell asleep thinking not just of his own survival, but of what survival might mean if shared with others. The Wolf who had stalked through Berlin's elegant hotels, preying on human weakness, would have dismissed such thoughts as dangerous sentimentality.

But that version of himself was fading. In its place, something different was emerging. A man who understood that in Birkenau, true strength might lie not in taking from others, but in what little remained possible to share.

The bread Daniel had offered back to him had been more than food. It had been an invitation to remember what it meant to be human. And Wolf found himself, against all odds and expectations, ready to accept that invitation.

14

The Healer (1938-1941)

The Surgeon's Hands

Berlin, November 1938

The overhead lights of Charité Hospital's operating theater cast harsh shadows across the exposed brain tissue of the sixteen-year-old girl. Sophie Adler, daughter of Judge Heinrich Adler, lay draped beneath blue surgical cloths. Three other surgeons had pronounced the case hopeless. A tumor wrapped around her optic nerve, they'd said. Blindness was certain; death, probable.

Levi didn't believe in hopeless cases.

Every eye in the room tracked his movements as he worked with the rhythm of twenty years' practice. His scalpel moved with delicate precision, separating malignant tissue from healthy matter one millimeter at a time.

"Suction," he murmured.

Dr. Klaus Fischer, his assistant for seven years, moved instantly. No one spoke. Even breathing seemed intrusive in the focused silence.

"Impossible," whispered a visiting surgeon from Munich, forgetting professional decorum.

Levi didn't acknowledge the comment. He had stopped believing in impossibility the first time he'd watched his father extract a bullet using kitchen tweezers and a shot of schnapps for anesthesia.

Three hours later, Levi stepped back from the table and peeled off his gloves.

"Close for me," he told Fischer. "The nerve is intact. She'll keep her sight."

The room exhaled collectively. Levi noted the admiration in their eyes, but also something else: a flicker of discomfort, as if his skill made his Jewishness even more inconvenient.

In the scrub room, Dr. Wagner, the hospital director, cornered him. Wagner was overweight with thinning blond hair and ambitious eyes. The Party pin on his lapel gleamed under the harsh light, new enough that Wagner still unconsciously touched it several times an hour.

"Remarkable work, Blum," Wagner said, clapping him on the shoulder. "Simply remarkable. You've saved the judge's daughter. He won't forget this."

Levi dried his hands methodically. "The girl will recover. That's all that matters."

Wagner lowered his voice. "You must join us for dinner next week with the new Minister of Health. He should meet Berlin's finest surgeon."

Something flickered in Wagner's eyes, perhaps regret at extending an invitation that would complicate his political standing.

"Of course," Levi replied, though they both understood the invitation might evaporate.

Wagner hesitated, glancing at the empty corridor before leaning closer. "These are unusual times, Blum. Your skill is valuable to the hospital. Very valuable."

"Thank you," Levi said, understanding the unspoken message. Your skill makes you temporarily useful despite your blood.

"Just, perhaps consider keeping a lower profile. The judge's daughter, perhaps it would be best if Fischer took credit for the procedure."

Levi looked at Wagner for a long moment. "The girl's name is Sophie. She likes to paint. Her tumor would have blinded her within weeks. I didn't save her so Fischer could build his reputation."

Wagner's face reddened. "It was merely a suggestion."

"Of course," Levi replied. "And I appreciate your concern."

That evening, home was a spacious apartment in Charlottenburg, filled with books and the lingering scent of Ruth's perfume: jasmine and something darker, like saffron. Ruth had already set the table when he arrived, candles lit despite the early hour.

Levi paused in the doorway, watching his wife arrange silverware with deliberate movements. At thirty-eight, Ruth remained as striking as when they'd met during his residency. Her dark eyes were quick and intelligent, her movements precise, like his own. A professor's daughter with a mathematician's mind, she had the unsettling ability to see patterns before they fully emerged.

"You're staring," she said without looking up.

"A husband's privilege."

She smiled, but the smile didn't reach her eyes. "I heard about your surgery. The judge's daughter."

Levi went to the sink, washing his hands with the thoroughness ingrained after decades of medical practice. The water ran hot enough to sting.

"News travels quickly."

"Fischer's wife told me. She called to cancel our theater plans." Ruth's voice remained neutral, but Levi caught the subtle tension in her shoulders. "Apparently they received a last-minute invitation to dine with her parents."

The same Fischer who had assisted him for seven years. The same Fischer whose son Levi had treated for pneumonia last winter, refusing payment when he learned of their financial difficulties.

"Wagner invited me to dinner with the Minister of Health," Levi said.

Ruth placed the final fork precisely aligned with the table's edge. "Did he? How many hours before it's canceled this time? The last one vanished from his calendar an hour after a visit from the local Party official."

"Ruth..."

"When is this grand dinner?"

"Next week."

"Shall I wager how many days before it's canceled?" She turned to face him, her expression softening at whatever she saw in his face. "I'm sorry. That's unfair."

Levi dried his hands, uncomfortable with her apology. Ruth had been right about everything so far. Three years ago, she had suggested they consider leaving Germany. Two years ago, she had insisted they should. One year ago, she had begun making concrete plans that Levi had gently dismissed.

"Wagner suggested Fischer should take credit for the surgery," he admitted.

Ruth went very still. "And what did you say?"

"I reminded him of the patient's name."

A knock at the door interrupted Ruth's response. Their dinner guests had arrived, Friedrich Klein and his wife Helga, friends for fifteen years. Friedrich greeted him with the same bear hug he'd used since their student days, though his round face had hollowed, the jovial flush faded to nervous pallor.

"The hospital is buzzing about your surgery," Friedrich said as they settled in the sitting room with glasses of schnapps. "They're calling it impossible."

"Nothing is impossible with the right approach," Levi replied.

The conversation flowed easily at first: medical cases, mutual colleagues, music. But when Ruth mentioned a cousin who had emigrated to Palestine, a subtle shift occurred. Friedrich cleared his throat, Helga examined her fingernails with sudden interest, and the topic drifted to the weather with the deliberate speed of those avoiding quicksand.

Later, as coffee was served, Friedrich mentioned the new regulations at the hospital.

"Mere bureaucracy," he said, not meeting Levi's eyes. "Nothing to concern yourself with, of course."

"Of course," Levi echoed, watching his friend's discomfort.

When their guests had gone, Ruth stood at the window, looking down at the darkened street. Below, automobiles glided past, their headlights cutting through the November fog. Somewhere, a radio played a Wagner piece, the notes drifting up like smoke.

"They're good people," Levi said quietly.

"Yes," she agreed. "And that's what terrifies me."

She turned from the window. "Good people who will stand aside while evil unfolds before them, telling themselves there's nothing they can do. Friedrich couldn't even look at you when he mentioned those 'new regulations.'"

"He's afraid."

"We should all be afraid, Levi. That's my point."

The First Fractures

December 1938

Each week, fewer patients filled his waiting room chairs. By December, the space echoed with absence. Levi noted but did not comment on the dwindling number of non-Jewish patients. Those who remained were the loyal ones: elderly professors who had known him for decades, patients whose lives he had saved, those who came after dark with apologies about "the current climate" whispered like a diagnosis too terrible to name aloud.

From his office window, Levi could see a new medical clinic that had opened across the street, its fresh paint and swastika flag vibrant against the gray December sky. GERMAN DOCTORS FOR GERMAN PEOPLE, the sign proclaimed in bold Gothic lettering. Three of his former colleagues had joined its staff, men who had once asked his advice on difficult cases.

The nurse knocked softly before entering with patient files. Fräulein Müller had been with him since he opened his practice. At fifty-two, her iron-gray hair and unsmiling efficiency disguised a compassionate heart.

"You have five cancellations today," she said without preamble. "I've tried to reschedule."

"Thank you," Levi replied, understanding what remained unsaid. No one was rescheduling anymore.

Fräulein Müller hesitated at the door. "Dr. Blum, my nephew works at the Ministry of Health. He says there are new regulations coming. About Jewish doctors."

Levi acknowledged her words with a slight nod. "I appreciate your concern."

"My sister's family is in Switzerland. They say..."

"Fräulein Müller," Levi interrupted gently. "It would be best if you didn't share such information with me. For your sake."

She straightened her uniform. "I've worked for you for seventeen years, Dr. Blum. I'll decide what's best for my sake."

That evening, Ruth greeted him with travel brochures spread across his desk. Bold lettering promised NEW BEGINNINGS IN AMERICA. OPPORTUNITIES IN PALESTINE. MEDICAL POSITIONS IN PARIS.

"My sister's family is already in Paris," she said without preamble. "Jacob has connections. He can find you a position at a hospital there."

Levi looked up from his medical journal. "And abandon my patients?"

"Your patients are abandoning you," Ruth said, her voice tight with frustration. "Please, Levi. Look around you."

She gestured toward the window. Outside, painted across the elegant façade of their building, someone had scrawled *JUDEN* - Jews in dripping red letters. The building manager had promised to remove it, but a week had passed. The slur remained, the red now faded to rust-brown.

"This will pass," he insisted. "Germany is a civilized nation. This madness can't last."

Ruth's laugh held no humor. "A civilized nation where synagogues burn? Where old men are beaten in the streets? Where did you practice medicine the night of November 9th, Levi? Remind me."

The memory surfaced unwillingly: glass shards embedded in flesh, broken bones, terrified eyes. Kristallnacht. He had treated seventeen patients in his home that night, while outside, the mob howled for Jewish blood. His surgical instruments laid out on the dining room table, Ruth boiling water in the kitchen, torn sheets for bandages.

"You can't save everyone," Ruth said more softly.

"I'm not trying to save everyone," Levi answered. "Just those I can reach."

Their arguments grew more frequent, more heated. Ruth packed and unpacked her suitcase several times before finally making her decision.

"I've booked passage to Paris," she announced one morning over breakfast. "Next Thursday."

Levi looked up from his coffee. "I see."

"Come with me," she pleaded, reaching for his hand across the table. "We can start again."

"This is my home, Ruth. My patients need me. My place is here."

"And my place is with you," she whispered, "but I cannot stay and watch this happen. I cannot pretend we have a future here."

"Do we have a future apart?"

The question hung between them like fragile glass. Ruth withdrew her hand.

"That depends on you," she said finally.

The night before her departure, they held each other in silence. No more arguments, no more persuasion. Just the quiet acknowledgment of two paths diverging.

At the station, her hand lingered on his face, tracing the line of his jaw as if memorizing it. The platform thronged with travelers, many with the same hunted look, the same desperate determination.

"I'll write when I arrive," Ruth said. "Join me, Levi. Promise you'll consider it."

"I promise," he said, knowing it was only half-true.

He watched until the train disappeared, swallowed by distance and winter fog. The platform emptied gradually, leaving him alone with porters and the occasional police officer who studied his features with pointed interest.

The apartment felt cavernous without her. Levi worked longer hours, returning home only to sleep and read her letters, each one urging him to follow.

One evening, as Levi was locking his office, Friedrich appeared in the doorway. His friend's face had grown gaunt in recent months, the jovial roundness replaced by sharp angles.

"Walk with me," Friedrich said.

They strolled through the hospital garden, barren in the January chill. Friedrich spoke of inconsequential things until they reached a secluded bench.

"I've been instructed to reduce my association with Jewish colleagues," Friedrich said finally, his voice barely audible. "Wagner has a list. Your name is on it."

Levi inclined his head slightly.

"They're monitoring who speaks to you, who consults with you. Last week, Schmidt was questioned about why he referred a patient to you."

"Schmidt has referred patients to me for fifteen years."

"Fifteen years means nothing now," Friedrich said, his voice cracking. "You should go, Levi. Go to your wife. Soon, we won't be able to pretend you belong here."

"This is my country, Friedrich. Where else would I belong?"

His friend's pitying glance was answer enough.

Friedrich reached into his coat, withdrawing a small package wrapped in brown paper. "Medical journals," he said loudly. "You asked to borrow them."

Later, alone in his study, Levi unwrapped it to find no journals, but instead a letter describing the new restrictions being drafted against Jewish doctors. Along with it, Friedrich had included two hundred Swiss francs and a name, someone who could help arrange passage out of Germany.

A Country No Longer His

April 1939

The letter arrived on official stationery, its language coldly bureaucratic. Dr. Levi Blum's medical license was revoked, effective immediately. The reason given was a "failure to meet new professional standards for medical practitioners."

Levi remembered the day he'd received his license, twenty years earlier. His father had framed it, displaying it prominently in the family home in Bavaria. "This," his father had said, "is what they can never take from you. Knowledge. Skill. The ability to heal."

Twenty years of medicine condensed to a single sheet of paper. Revoked.

Levi folded the letter precisely and placed it in his desk drawer, alongside the growing collection of official notices: his removal from the hospital board, his disbarment from the medical society, the cancellation of his university teaching position.

That evening, he removed the brass nameplate from his office door. LEVI BLUM, M.D. - NEUROLOGICAL SURGERY. The nameplate came off easily, just two screws. Twenty years of work, reputation, identity. Gone with two turns of a screwdriver.

Word spread quietly through the Jewish community of Berlin. Patients began arriving at his apartment: children with fevers, elderly with chronic conditions, a woman in early labor. Levi treated them in his study, converted now to a makeshift examination room. Payment came in the form of food, used books, sometimes nothing at all.

"You should charge something," said Mrs. Abramson, an elderly neighbor who had appointed herself his secretary. Mrs. Abramson had lost her husband two years earlier to heart failure. Levi had treated him in his final months, ensuring comfort when cure was impossible. Now she stationed herself in his sitting room each day at precisely eight o'clock, notebook in hand.

"I have enough," Levi replied, though his savings were dwindling. Ruth sent what she could from Paris, but currency restrictions made transfers difficult.

"Enough for now," Mrs. Abramson said with the bluntness of the very old. "But later? What happens when you have nothing? What happens to all of them?" She gestured toward the small crowd in his waiting room.

The question haunted his nights. What would happen to them? To his patients, to his neighbors, to the entire community slowly being strangled by regulations and restrictions.

Each night, Levi read Ruth's most recent letter by lamplight. The paper had grown thin from handling.

"My dearest Levi, Yesterday I walked along the Seine and thought of our summers in Bavaria. Paris grows more crowded each day with people like us, hoping to outlast the storm in Germany. Jacob has secured an apartment for you near the hospital. The chief surgeon is eager to meet you. Please, my love. There is nothing left for you there. Come while you still can. I wait for you, always. Ruth"

The knock came at midnight, urgent but hushed. Levi, still dressed despite the late hour, opened the door to find Elias Rosen, once a wealthy department store owner, now haggard and thin.

"My wife," Elias whispered. "The baby is coming early. She's bleeding heavily. The midwife won't come."

Levi reached for his medical bag without hesitation.

"Dr. Blum," Elias said, his voice shaking, "they are watching our building. If you're seen..."

The unfinished sentence hung between them. If you're seen.

Levi paused, his hand on the worn leather of the bag Ruth had given him on their tenth anniversary. Inside were instruments that had saved countless lives, instruments he was now forbidden to use.

Through the window, he could see the first pink smear of dawn touching the Berlin skyline.

"Wait five minutes," Levi said finally. "Then leave. I'll follow a different route."

As Elias disappeared down the darkened stairwell, Levi returned to his desk and wrote a quick note.

"My Ruth, You were right. I will come. Wait for me. Levi"

He sealed the envelope and placed it on the table for posting in the morning. Then, taking his medical bag, he slipped out into the Berlin dawn, a healer in a country that no longer wanted his healing.

Elias's apartment building stood on a narrow street in what had once been a fashionable district. Now, Jewish families crowded into subdivided spaces as restrictions tightened.

He entered through the service entrance, climbing five flights of narrow stairs. In the cramped bedroom at the top, Golda Rosen lay in a spreading pool of blood, her face gray with pain and fear.

"Doctor," she whispered, recognition and relief flooding her features. "You came."

"Of course I came," Levi said, setting down his bag and rolling up his sleeves. "Now, let's meet this child of yours."

Outside, Berlin awakened for another day. But in this small room, a doctor's hands, skilled, steady, and defiant, prepared to welcome new life into a world grown dark.

15

The Healer - The Numbered Days

Birkenau, March 1942

The first month passed in hunger and exhaustion. Morning roll calls in the freezing dark, standing at attention for hours while guards counted and recounted, prisoners sometimes dropping dead where they stood. Then the march to labor sites: construction, digging, hauling stones, work designed to extract the last measure of strength.

Levi was assigned to a construction kommando, building new barracks for the expanding camp. The work was crushing, especially for hands trained for delicacy rather than brute force. His palms split open, bled, became infected, healed partially, split again. Each evening he would examine them in the dim barracks light, these hands that had once performed surgeries now barely capable of grasping a spoon.

"You won't last two months in construction," Daniel the tailor told him one night. Their ribs pressed together on the narrow bunk that somehow held six men. The straw beneath them had long since compressed to nothing. "You need to find different work."

"How?" Levi's voice scraped out, his throat parched despite the watery soup they'd been given hours earlier.

"There's a selection coming. For the camp hospital." Daniel's words came in measured bursts, conserving energy. "They need orderlies. Not doctors, they have those, but men to carry bodies, clean waste."

"How do you know this?"

Daniel's lips twitched, not quite a smile. "I take in the kapo's uniform when he loses weight. Amazing how talkative men become when you're on your knees with pins near their testicles."

The camp hospital was a misleading name for the low barracks where the ill were housed, not to heal but to die away from the sight of healthy workers. Still, it was indoor work, marginally warmer, less physically demanding. And perhaps, Levi thought, a place where his medical knowledge might prove useful.

The selection came two days later. Prisoners were lined up outside the hospital barracks, examined for strength and health, a perverse inversion of normal medical screening.

The SS doctor, a young man with wire-framed glasses and a perpetual sneer, moved down the line, asking each prisoner his former occupation. When he reached Levi, Daniel's advice echoed in his mind.

"Occupation?" the doctor asked in bored German.

"Butcher," Levi replied.

The doctor's gaze lingered on Levi's hands, still bearing construction scars but retaining their essentially educated shape. "A butcher with a gentleman's hands?"

"My father owned the shop," Levi said. The lie came easier than expected. "I did the cutting, but not the heavy work."

For a moment, the doctor's gaze met Levi's, clinical, assessing, not quite believing. Then he nodded. "Hospital duty. Next!"

The camp hospital consisted of three long barracks, each packed with wooden bunks stacked three high. The stench was overwhelming: infected wounds, dysentery, gangrene, and death. Prisoners lay two or three to a bunk, often soiled in their own waste, some unconscious, others moaning in pain or delirium.

Kapo Franz, a German criminal prisoner with a green triangle on his uniform and a face scarred by violence, explained Levi's duties with cruel efficiency.

"You clean," he said, gesturing to the filth-covered floor. "You carry out the dead. You help the doctors when ordered, which means holding patients down for procedures. You do not speak unless spoken to. You do not steal medications or food. Breaking these rules means joining them." He nodded toward the patients. "Understand?"

126

"Yes, Kapo," Levi replied.

Franz smiled, revealing several missing teeth. "Good. Begin with him." He pointed to a body on a bottom bunk, already stiff with rigor mortis. "Take him to the mortuary. Then come back for the others."

The work was grim beyond imagination. Each day Levi carried fifteen to twenty corpses to the small building behind the hospital where they awaited transport to the crematoria. He cleaned excrement and vomit from floors and bunks. He held down screaming men while doctors performed crude surgeries without anesthesia.

But in the quiet moments, when the SS doctors were absent and only prisoner doctors remained, Levi began to reveal his knowledge.

It started with a simple suggestion to Dr. Pachter, a Polish Jewish physician who had somehow maintained his humanity despite the horror surrounding them.

"The man in bunk seventeen," Levi murmured as they changed filthy straw. "His symptoms suggest typhus, not dysentery."

Dr. Pachter glanced at him sharply. "And how would you know this, orderly?"

"I worked as an assistant to a doctor before the war." It wasn't quite a lie, but not the full truth either.

Pachter studied him for a long moment, then nodded almost imperceptibly. From that day, a cautious alliance formed between them. Levi would quietly observe patients, passing his assessments to Pachter in whispered exchanges. Occasionally, when no SS guards were present, Pachter allowed him to examine patients directly.

"You have a surgeon's touch," Pachter remarked one night as they worked late, lancing boils on a patient's back. "Where did you train?"

Levi hesitated, cleaning his hands with the rough soap they'd been given. The question carried risk. Too much knowledge, too much education, and he might find himself marked for selection.

"Berlin," he admitted finally, after ensuring they were alone. "Charité Hospital."

"You're that Blum? The neurosurgeon?"

"You've heard of me?"

"I attended a conference where you presented. 1937, I think. A paper on optic nerve tumors." Pachter shook his head in wonder. "And now you're carrying corpses."

"We're all reduced," Levi said simply.

"Not entirely." Pachter passed him a scalpel. "Finish this procedure. I'll watch the door."

Slowly, carefully, Levi reclaimed small pieces of his identity as a healer. Always in secret, always at risk of discovery, he began treating patients under Pachter's protection. The work gave him purpose beyond mere survival, though survival remained a daily battle against starvation, disease, and despair.

At night, lying in his bunk staring into darkness, Levi would often think of Ruth. Not as she had been in those final days in Berlin, anxious, pleading with him to leave, but as she had been in happier times. Ruth reading by lamplight, her profile sharp against the glow. Ruth laughing as they walked along the Spree on summer evenings.

Wait for me, he had written in that final letter. How naive he had been, how blind to the gathering darkness. She had seen it coming, and had tried to warn him. Now he clung to one hope: that her foresight had saved her, that she had fled Paris before the occupation.

Three months after his arrival, a new transport brought prisoners from France. Among them was a professor of literature from the Sorbonne, a man named Léon Bernard who had once visited their home in Berlin for a dinner party in 1935. Levi recognized him immediately, though the elegant intellectual had been reduced to a skeletal figure.

"Professor Bernard," Levi said, helping the man onto a hospital bunk. "Do you remember me? Levi Blum. You came to our home in Berlin."

Bernard stared at him blankly, then recognition dawned slowly.

"Dr. Blum? Ruth's husband?"

"Yes," Levi replied, his voice suddenly tight with hope. "Have you seen her? In Paris?"

Bernard's face clouded. He looked away, then back at Levi with obvious reluctance.

"She was taken in the roundup. July 1942. The Vélodrome d'Hiver."

The words struck Levi like a physical blow. Ruth. Taken. The hope he'd carried for months crumbled instantly.

"Where?" he managed to ask through a throat that felt suddenly constricted. "Where did they send her?"

"East," Bernard replied, the single word carrying the weight of a death sentence. "I'm sorry."

Levi stood frozen beside the bunk, unable to process what he'd heard. Ruth, who had been so careful, so prescient about the danger. Ruth, who had escaped Germany while there was still time. She had been caught anyway.

That night, Levi lay rigid on his bunk, eyes open, feeling nothing except the empty space where his heart had been. Ruth might be in this very camp. She might already be ash climbing from those chimneys. The not knowing had been torture, but this half-knowing was worse.

In the following days, he moved through his duties like an automaton, barely registering the filth, the corpses, or the suffering around him. He performed his tasks mechanically: lifting bodies, cleaning floors, holding down patients for procedures. But the spark that had begun to rekindle in him went dark.

Dr. Pachter noticed after three days. He pulled Levi aside one evening as they finished their rounds.

"You're going to die if you continue like this," he said bluntly. "I've seen it before. Men who give up."

"My wife," Levi said, the words like stones in his mouth. "She was sent east. From Paris."

Understanding dawned in Pachter's eyes. He had seen this grief too many times to require explanation.

"I'm sorry." He hesitated, then added, "But you must live, Blum. To bear witness. To remember her."

"Remember?" Levi gave a bitter laugh. "Who will be left to hear our memories, Pachter? Who will believe what happened here?"

"Someone will survive," Pachter insisted. "Someone must tell the world. Why not you?"

Levi wanted to argue, to surrender to the despair that felt more honest than hope. But something in Pachter's voice, the quiet certainty, made him pause.

"What's the point of surviving if she's gone?"

"Because she loved you," Pachter said simply. "And love doesn't end with death. It transforms into obligation."

The question lingered in Levi's mind as he returned to his duties. Why not him? What made his grief more special than that of thousands of others in this place? What gave him the right to surrender when others fought on despite similar losses?

Two days later, as he helped distribute the thin soup that passed for dinner, Levi came to a patient he had been avoiding. A young boy, perhaps fourteen, with an infected leg wound that would likely require amputation. The boy reminded him painfully of a patient he had treated in Berlin, a child who had recovered completely under his care.

"Are you a real doctor?" the boy asked suddenly as Levi held the bowl to his cracked lips.

Levi hesitated, glancing around to ensure no guards were listening, then nodded. "I was. Before."

"My father was a doctor too," the boy said. "In Kraków." His voice, cracked from thirst, somehow still held the simple confidence of youth. "He said doctors don't get to choose who lives."

Levi carefully rewrapped the leg, noting how the infection had spread. "Your father was right."

"Then you can't not be a doctor," the boy said with the logic only children possessed. "Not even here."

The words hung in the air between them. Levi finished the bandaging in silence, but something had shifted inside him. The boy was right. Ruth was right. Pachter was right.

Later that night, Levi sought out Dr. Pachter. "The boy in bunk twenty-two," he said. "We can save his leg."

Pachter looked skeptical. "Gangrene is setting in. The SS doctor has already scheduled an amputation for tomorrow."

"I've seen this infection before," Levi insisted, his voice growing stronger with each word. "If we can drain it properly, apply the right mixture of sulfa powder..."

"We don't have enough sulfa."

"I can get it," Levi answered, his mind already formulating a plan. "The kapo in Block 4 has an infected tooth. I'll make a trade."

Pachter studied him for a long moment, noting the change in his posture, the return of purpose to his voice.

"Welcome back, Dr. Blum."

The next morning, Levi negotiated with the kapo, trading his bread ration for three days in exchange for a small packet of sulfa powder. It wasn't much, but combined with proper drainage and careful wound management, it might be enough.

The procedure had to be performed in secret, during the brief window when the SS doctors were absent. Working by touch more than sight in the dim barracks, Levi reopened the wound, drained the infection, and applied the sulfa with careful precision. The boy gritted his teeth but didn't cry out.

"Will it work?" the boy whispered.

"We'll know in a few days," Levi replied. "But your father would be proud of your courage."

Three days later, the infection had receded. The angry red streaks that had been climbing toward the boy's hip had faded. The wound was healing cleanly.

When the SS doctor arrived for his scheduled amputation, he found a patient with a leg worth saving. Annoyed but unable to justify the surgery, he moved on to other cases.

"You did it," Pachter murmured to Levi as they watched the boy take his first tentative steps a week later.

Levi nodded, feeling something he had thought lost forever: the satisfaction of healing, the purpose that had driven him since his first day of medical school.

That evening, as Levi carried another corpse to the mortuary, he found himself looking up at the vast sky stretching above the camp. Winter was yielding to spring, patches of muddy ground appearing between melting snowdrifts. In Berlin, the first crocuses would be pushing through the soil in the Tiergarten. Ruth had loved those early flowers, their stubborn insistence on life after the long darkness of winter.

Her voice, whether memory or imagination, seemed to whisper: You have always been stubborn, my love. Now be stubborn about surviving.

He would live to see the end of this place. He would bear witness. He would remember, not just Ruth, but all of them. The living and the dead. The boy whose leg he had saved. Professor Bernard, who had brought him the terrible news about Ruth but had also, somehow, brought him back to himself.

Number 73829 carried the corpse through the mud, but Dr. Levi Blum, surgeon of Berlin, husband to Ruth, walked beside him, invisible to the guards but growing stronger with each step.

16

The Healer - The Compromise

Birkenau, April 1944

Spring came to Birkenau with green shoots pushing through soil fertilized with human ash. The air warmed, carrying both the sweet scent of distant flowering meadows and the acrid stench of the crematoria working at full capacity as trains arrived daily.

Levi had survived fourteen months in this place. His body had adapted to chronic starvation, finding equilibrium at a skeletal thinness that would have horrified his former self. His mind had developed necessary defenses, but something inside him had hardened. Each compromise etched another mark into this protective shell, a record of his survival and his shame.

Three days each week in Block 10, assisting Kramer with experiments whose scientific value was as questionable as their morality was clear. Four days in the main infirmary, using his privileged position to save those he could while condemning others through the weekly selections that had become routine.

"You look tired," Anna observed one April morning as they prepared the infirmary for Müller's daily inspection. She had become his most trusted ally, her quiet strength a reminder of why his compromises might be justified.

"I didn't sleep well," Levi admitted. Dreams of Ruth had haunted him, terrible fantasies of her final moments in a gas chamber not unlike the ones at Birkenau.

Anna nodded. She understood without explanation. No prisoner slept well here.

Over the past months, Levi had watched Müller carefully, noting small signs of... not humanity exactly, but perhaps unease. The way he paused sometimes during selections, the manner in which he questioned certain protocols from Berlin. These observations meant nothing in practical terms, but Levi filed them away nonetheless.

"Dr. Müller seemed distracted yesterday," Anna mentioned, echoing his thoughts. "Did you notice how he questioned the new medication rationing orders?"

"I noticed," Levi replied carefully. Even with Anna, such observations carried risk.

Anna's eyes caught his across the infirmary, that particular look that meant information worth risking punishment to share.

"The Hungarians," she whispered, leaning in as she pretended to check his clipboard.

Levi paused. "How many?"

"Trainloads. Beginning next month."

Levi had heard whispers of Hitler's recent occupation of Hungary, one of the last European countries with a substantial Jewish population. "Your source?"

"The Sonderkommando. One came for treatment yesterday."

The man had spoken freely, enjoying the strange privilege of the Sonderkommando. What did it matter what secrets they shared? They lived on borrowed time, walking corpses who hauled actual corpses from the gas chambers to the crematorium.

"If it's true," Levi said, "the infirmary will be overwhelmed."

"Not if they follow the usual pattern," Anna countered. "Most will go directly to the gas. Only the strongest will enter the camp."

The infirmary door slammed open and conversation died instantly.

Dr. Müller arrived for inspection, followed by a stocky SS officer Levi had never seen before.

"Attention," Müller announced. "This is *Hauptsturmführer* - Captain Neumann from Berlin. He will be observing our medical operations today."

Levi and Anna stood rigid as the officers moved through the ward. Neumann carried himself with the overbearing confidence of Berlin headquarters, a man who had designed death on paper and now came to admire his blueprints in action.

"Your record keeping is excellent," Neumann commented to Müller. "Berlin appreciates efficiency."

"We strive for German standards, even here," Müller replied.

"And these?" Neumann gestured toward Levi and Anna. "They appear relatively healthy for inmates."

"Medical personnel receive additional rations," Müller explained. "It's necessary for them to function effectively."

Neumann approached Levi, studying him with the detached interest of a man examining livestock. "You're the Berlin surgeon, yes? The one assisting Kramer?"

"Yes, Herr Hauptsturmführer." Levi kept his eyes downcast, focusing on the shine of Neumann's boots, polished to a mirror finish.

"Remarkable," Neumann said to Müller. "Using Jewish medical knowledge to advance Reich science. There's efficiency in that, don't you think?"

"Indeed," Müller agreed. "Dr. Blum has proven quite valuable."

Neumann continued his inspection, questioning Müller about mortality rates, medication usage, and selection protocols. Only when they reached the far end of the ward did Levi's lungs remember how to function.

"Berlin is watching," Anna whispered, barely audible.

Levi nodded once. Nothing good ever came from Berlin's attention.

Later that day, as Levi completed his rounds, he noticed a new patient had been admitted, a gaunt man in his sixties with a badly infected hand. The infection had traced angry red lines up his forearm, the skin hot and swollen. Something about him seemed vaguely familiar.

"Name?" Levi asked, picking up the chart.

"David Goldstein," the man replied in educated German with a distinct Austrian accent. "Professor of Philosophy, University of Vienna. Before."

The voice triggered a memory, a dinner party in Berlin, years earlier. Animated discussion about Kant's categorical imperative over wine and Ruth's excellent roast duck.

"Professor Goldstein," Levi said slowly. "We've met before. I'm Levi Blum. My wife Ruth hosted you for dinner in Berlin, 1936."

Recognition dawned in the professor's eyes. "Dr. Blum? The neurosurgeon?" He gave a soft, bitter laugh that dissolved into a cough. "What a place for a reunion."

Levi examined the professor's hand, a deep laceration, badly infected, likely sustained during labor detail. Without treatment, sepsis would develop within days.

"I'll clean this and start you on antibiotics," Levi said, keeping his voice professional. "How long have you been here?"

"Since January," Goldstein replied. "Vienna to Theresienstadt, then here. The usual journey."

Levi cleaned the wound with gentle efficiency. As he worked, he leaned closer, voice dropping to a whisper. "The next selection is tomorrow. This infection is serious but not immediately life threatening. Keep your fever down if you can. Cold compresses when the guards aren't looking."

Goldstein studied Levi's face. "You conduct the selections now," he said. The words hung between them, neither question nor accusation.

"Yes."

"Yet here you are, telling me how to survive one." Goldstein's cracked lips twitched, not quite a smile. "Fascinating."

"We're all contradictions here," Levi said finally.

"Ah." Goldstein's eyes brightened momentarily. "You've been reading philosophy in your abundant free time, I see."

For a moment, they might have been in a university seminar room rather than a concentration camp infirmary.

"Something amusing, Doctor?" The voice came from behind him. Müller, returning unexpectedly.

"Professor Goldstein was reminding me of a philosophical debate from my university days," Levi replied, composing his features.

"Philosophy," Müller repeated, his tone suggesting he found the concept quaint. "A luxury of peacetime, I suppose." He examined Goldstein's chart. "Infection of the right hand. Prognosis?"

"With antibiotics, good," Levi said. "Without, uncertain."

Müller's eyes met his, a silent challenge. Resources were limited; allocating antibiotics to an elderly professor rather than a younger, stronger prisoner was questionable triage.

"He's a teacher," Levi added. "His knowledge could be valuable for record keeping, perhaps in Block 10."

It was a calculated risk, suggesting Goldstein for the experimental block. Better the administrative side of Kramer's operation than the infirmary's next selection.

Müller considered this. "Very well. One course of antibiotics. If he responds well, I'll speak to Kramer about utilizing his... intellectual capabilities."

That evening, as Levi made his final rounds, he stopped by Goldstein's bed. The professor was awake, his eyes reflecting the dim light.

"You recommended me for Block 10," Goldstein said. "I've heard what happens there."

"Administrative work only," Levi assured him. "Record keeping, data analysis. Your hand won't heal well enough for manual labor."

"And in exchange for this reprieve, I presume you want something from me."

Levi sat on the edge of the bed. "Not what you think. I need perspective, Professor."

"Perspective? Here?"

"Especially here." Levi leaned forward slightly. "I compromise daily. I assist with procedures to gain resources to prevent other deaths. I select some for death to save others."

"You want absolution," Goldstein interrupted. "I can't give you that."

"Not absolution," Levi insisted. "Understanding. How does one remain human while participating in inhumanity?"

Goldstein was silent for a long moment. Finally, he spoke.

"There's a story in the Talmud about a man who saved a single life. The rabbis said it was as if he had saved the entire world." He paused. "Perhaps that's all we can do in such times: save what worlds we can, even as others burn."

"And the cost to one's soul?"

"That," Goldstein said with the ghost of a smile, "is between you and God, Doctor. Or between you and yourself, if you prefer."

The next day's selection proceeded with mechanized efficiency. Levi and his fellow prisoner doctor, Dubois, moved through the ward, making notations, consigning some to life and others to death with marks that carried the weight of divine judgment without its wisdom.

When they reached Goldstein's bed, Levi noted with relief that the antibiotics were working, the angry red streaks receding from the wound, the fever reduced. He marked the professor for continued treatment, adding a note about transfer to Block 10 for clerical duties.

"Eighteen for transfer to Block 7," Dubois summarized when they finished.

Block 7 meant the condemned. Eighteen more deaths on his conscience.

"The new treatment protocols are working," Levi replied. The "new protocols" were largely his creation: triage systems that prioritized patients with the best chance of recovery, prophylactic measures to prevent infection, nutrition plans that maximized the impact of meager rations.

Müller reviewed their list with his usual clinical detachment. "Acceptable," he pronounced. "Though Hauptsturmführer Neumann might question the declining numbers."

"Improved efficiency," Levi suggested. "Fewer deaths means more workers for the Reich."

Müller nodded, almost approvingly. "You've learned our language well, Doctor."

The compliment stung worse than any slap.

That afternoon, Levi reported to Block 10 for his regular duties. Kramer was in high spirits, practically beaming as he greeted Levi in the laboratory.

"Excellent timing," Kramer said. "We've received approval for the next phase of our bone regeneration study. Berlin is most interested in our results."

The "next phase," Kramer explained, would involve surgical breaks rather than blunt trauma, creating clean, controlled fractures that would better demonstrate the effects of their experimental treatments. Levi's surgical skills would be central to the procedure.

"I'll prepare a protocol," Levi said, his voice steady despite the nausea rising in his throat. "Proper anesthesia would be necessary for precise results."

Kramer waved this away. "Local only. General anesthesia interferes with the biochemical processes we're studying."

"The subjects will be in considerable pain," Levi pointed out. "That introduces variables: stress hormones, muscle tension, movement that could displace the fracture."

It was a clinical argument, framed in terms of research validity rather than human suffering.

Kramer considered this. "You make a valid point. I'll requisition additional local anesthetic. And perhaps sedatives for the postoperative period."

It was a small victory: pain reduction, not prevention. But in Birkenau, such victories were all that existed.

As Levi prepared to leave Block 10 that evening, Kramer called him into his office. On the desk lay a copy of Levi's pre-war research paper on orthopedic trauma treatment.

"Remarkable work," Kramer commented. "Your techniques for managing compound fractures were quite innovative."

"Thank you," Levi replied, uncertain where this was heading.

"You know, after the war, there will be tremendous opportunities for medical advancement," Kramer continued. "Our research here, combined with minds like yours..." He trailed off, looking at Levi with what appeared to be genuine collegiality. "The Reich will need skilled physicians to help rebuild."

Levi stared at him, momentarily speechless. Kramer truly believed in some future rehabilitation, some world in which his atrocities would be recast as necessary sacrifices for medical progress.

"Do you have a question, Doctor?" Kramer asked, noting Levi's expression.

"No," Levi managed. "I was just... considering the possibilities."

"Do so," Kramer encouraged. "Skill and dedication are always rewarded, regardless of... previous circumstances."

Over the following weeks, as rumors of Hungarian transports intensified, the infirmary prepared for an influx of new prisoners. Anna organized existing resources while Levi quietly expanded their hidden network of diverted medications.

The system they had developed was simple but effective. During medication distribution, small amounts were set aside, hidden beneath loose floorboards, inside emptied pill bottles, even sewn into uniform seams. Never enough to be noticed in official inventories, but sufficient to save additional lives when the opportunity arose.

"The new shipment arrived," Anna reported one evening as they completed their rounds. "I've hidden what I could."

"How much?"

"Enough for perhaps twenty additional treatments. Antibiotics mostly, some pain medication."

It was a substantial risk. Discovery would mean immediate execution for both of them. But the alternative was watching patients die who might have been saved.

Professor Goldstein, now recovered and installed as a clerk in Block 10's administrative office, became an unexpected source of information. His position gave him access to transport records, camp statistics, even snippets of news from the outside world.

"The Allies are advancing," he whispered to Levi during a routine check-up in early June. "Normandy. The Germans are retreating on multiple fronts."

Hope in Birkenau was dangerous, more lethal than typhus, more insidious than starvation. Yet Levi couldn't excise it completely.

"How long?" he asked.

"Unknown," Goldstein replied. "But the SS officers are nervous. Files are being destroyed. Contingency plans are being discussed."

This aligned with what Levi had observed: increased tension among the guards, hushed conversations, unusual activities after dark. Something was changing.

One evening in late June, as Levi worked late organizing medical records, Müller appeared unexpectedly in the infirmary office. The camp director looked haggard, his usual pristine appearance slightly disheveled.

"Dr. Blum," he said, closing the door behind him. "I need to speak with you."

Levi looked up from his paperwork, immediately alert. Müller had never visited the infirmary alone, never closed doors for private conversation.

"Yes, sir?"

Müller moved to the window, looking out at the darkened camp. "The war situation has... evolved. Contingency plans are being implemented."

Levi remained silent, uncertain where this was leading.

"There may come a time when this facility requires... evacuation." Müller's voice carried a weight Levi had never heard before. "Such operations present logistical challenges."

"I understand," Levi said carefully.

Müller turned from the window, studying Levi's face. "You've proven yourself valuable here. Your medical skills, your... administrative capabilities."

"Thank you, sir."

"What I'm about to say must remain between us." Müller reached into his coat, withdrawing a small package wrapped in brown paper. "Medical supplies. Antibiotics, morphine, basic surgical instruments. Not much, but better than nothing."

He placed the package on Levi's desk.

Levi stared at it, uncomprehending. "Sir?"

"Hide it. If evacuation becomes necessary, there will be no medical support during transport. Prisoners will be moved on foot, likely in winter conditions." Müller's voice dropped to barely above a whisper. "Many will not survive such a journey."

The implications were clear. Evacuation would mean forced marches, likely designed to eliminate witnesses rather than preserve prisoners.

"Why are you telling me this?" Levi asked.

Müller was silent for a long moment, his hands clasped behind his back in a gesture Levi recognized from countless inspections.

"Because I am a physician, Dr. Blum. Whatever else I have become, that training remains." He paused. "Perhaps I wish to believe that some small portion of my oath might still be honored."

"I don't understand."

"You don't need to understand," Müller replied. "Simply be prepared."

He moved toward the door, then paused. "The choices you've made here, Doctor. The lives ended as well as saved. I want you to know that I... recognize the impossibility of your position."

The words hung in the air, an acknowledgment that violated every protocol of their relationship.

"Sir, I..."

"No," Müller interrupted. "Nothing more needs to be said."

After he left, Levi sat alone with the package of medications. Outside, the night sounds of Birkenau continued: distant shouts from guards, the rumble of transport trains, the ever-present whisper of smoke from the crematoria.

That night, he hid the medical supplies beneath the same loose floorboard where Anna stored their diverted medications. The cache was growing, a small arsenal against the suffering that seemed inevitable.

The next morning, as he made his rounds, Levi shared Müller's warning with Anna. They spoke in whispers, their conversation disguised as routine medical discussion.

"How reliable do you think this information is?" Anna asked.

"Reliable enough," Levi replied. "Müller wouldn't risk such a conversation without cause."

"Then we need to prepare. Stockpile more supplies, identify the strongest patients, decide..."

She didn't finish the sentence, but Levi understood. Decide who might survive a winter march and who would require a different kind of mercy.

"How many could we help during evacuation?" he asked.

"With what we have now? Perhaps fifty. If we can gather more supplies..." Anna shrugged. "Every life saved is a world preserved."

She was quoting Goldstein's Talmudic wisdom, the philosophy that had become their shared justification for impossible choices.

As summer deepened, Hungarian transports began arriving as predicted. The camp expanded rapidly, new barracks hastily constructed, crematorium operations increased to handle the massive influx. The infirmary saw hundreds of new prisoners, those deemed strong enough for temporary usefulness.

Levi worked eighteen-hour days, sleeping only when exhaustion made continued function impossible. The selection process became more brutal as space limitations demanded faster turnover. His hidden medicine network saved what lives it could, but the numbers were overwhelming.

One sweltering July evening, after a particularly difficult day that had seen thirty-seven patients marked for Block 7, Levi found himself alone in the infirmary office. The weight of his choices pressed down like the oppressive heat.

Anna entered quietly, carrying a small cloth bundle.

"You need to eat," she said, placing it before him. Inside was half a potato and a crust of bread, precious items she must have traded her own rations for.

"You should keep this for yourself," Levi protested.

"I already ate," she lied, her sunken cheeks betraying the falsehood.

As they organized the day's remaining medications, Anna spoke in a voice barely above a whisper. "There's talk among the guards. About evacuation procedures."

"What kind of talk?"

"Preparation for prisoner transport. Winter clothing requests, route planning." She paused. "They're not planning to leave witnesses."

The confirmation of Müller's warning sent a chill through Levi despite the stifling heat.

"Timeline?"

"Unknown. But they're accelerating certain... operations. The crematoria are working around the clock."

Levi understood. The camp was destroying evidence, eliminating prisoners who might testify about what had occurred here.

"We should identify core supplies," he said finally. "Medications that could make the difference between survival and death during forced marching."

Anna nodded. "And we need to decide about... the others. Those who couldn't survive such an ordeal."

The unspoken words hung between them. They had discussed this possibility before, obliquely, carefully. If evacuation meant certain death for the weakest prisoners, perhaps a quicker end would be mercy.

"The morphine supply is sufficient," Levi said quietly. "If it comes to that."

Anna touched his arm briefly, a rare physical gesture in this place where humanity had been stripped away. "We should have a plan. For ourselves as well."

The thought had occurred to Levi before. If marching meant certain death, if capture meant torture and execution, perhaps they should consider their own escape from suffering.

"Let's hope it doesn't come to that," he said.

That night, as he lay on his bunk, Levi's thoughts turned to Ruth. If she had been sent to a camp like this, she too might have faced such choices. The uncertainty of her fate remained its own special torture, but in that not-knowing, he found strange comfort. As long as he couldn't know for certain, he could imagine her alive, could dedicate his survival to the possibility of reunion.

He thought of Goldstein's Talmudic wisdom about saving worlds. In the months since his assignment to the infirmary, he calculated that his actions had directly saved perhaps 150 lives. 150 people who might otherwise have died in selections, from untreated infections, from despair.

A hundred and fifty lives against millions lost. A drop in an ocean of suffering. Yet each life represented a world entire, as the Talmud taught. Each person saved might bear witness, might remember, might rebuild if they survived to see liberation.

His hands, once dedicated solely to healing, were now stained with the blood of collaboration. Yet they still saved, still soothed, still did what good they could within a system designed for evil. It wasn't enough. It could never be enough.

But it was something.

As sleep finally claimed him, Levi's last conscious thought was of balance, that precarious state between resistance and complicity, between saving others and saving himself, between maintaining his humanity and surrendering to the inhumanity that surrounded him.

17

The Healer - August 1944

Birkenau, August 1944

August arrived with news that Warsaw had fallen to the Soviets. The camp guards spoke in hushed tones, faces tighter than usual, their actions more unpredictable. Transports continued to arrive, but rumors spread of dismantled crematoria in other camps, of documents being burned, of plans for evacuation if the front came too close.

In the daylight hours, Levi moved through the infirmary triaging the salvageable. At night when the guards thinned, he slipped between pallets with a different purpose. The vial of morphine felt heavy in his pocket, a weight he had grown accustomed to carrying.

The first weeks of August brought a steady stream of new patients from the Hungarian transports. Most were beyond help, their bodies already surrendering to starvation and disease. But among them were those who might survive with proper care, and it was for these that Levi reserved his hidden medications.

One evening, as summer heat lingered in the still air of the infirmary, Anna found him taking inventory of their concealed supplies. She looked thinner than ever, her once-robust frame whittled to angles and hollows by years of starvation. Yet her eyes remained alert, intelligent, undefeated.

"There's a new patient," she said quietly. "Just arrived from the Hungarian transport. She's asking for you specifically."

Levi looked up from counting antibiotic tablets. "For me? By name?"

Anna nodded. "She says she knew you in Berlin."

Intrigued and wary, Levi followed Anna to a far corner of the women's section, where new arrivals too ill for labor assignments were temporarily housed. On a thin pallet lay an emaciated woman, perhaps fifty though privation made precise age impossible to determine. Her head was shaved like all new arrivals, but wisps of gray showed where hair had begun to regrow.

"Dr. Blum?" the woman whispered as Levi approached.

He knelt beside her, studying her face carefully. Her features shifted in his memory, the gaunt angles gradually aligning with the plump cheeks he remembered from his Berlin practice.

"Yes," he said cautiously. "You asked for me?"

"Frieda Klein." The name came with a faint smile. "You treated my husband's heart condition in Berlin. 1938."

Recognition flooded through him. Friedrich's wife, the woman who had canceled theater plans when the political winds shifted. "Frau Klein," Levi said, taking her thin hand in his. "I remember you. I remember Friedrich."

"I knew it was you," she said, her voice barely audible. "Someone mentioned a Dr. Blum in the infirmary. I thought it might be you." Her grip tightened slightly. "I had to see for myself."

Levi examined her quickly, noting advanced malnutrition, respiratory distress, and signs of severe dysentery. She had likely been ill before deportation, her condition worsening catastrophically during the transport. Even with unlimited resources, her chances would be minimal. Here, they were nonexistent.

"Friedrich?" Levi asked, though he already knew the answer from her presence here alone.

Frieda shook her head slightly. "Theresienstadt. Two years ago. His heart finally gave out." She paused, studying Levi's face. "He spoke of you often, especially near the end. How you had tried to help him when other doctors had given up."

The memory surfaced: Friedrich Klein, a jovial baker with severe cardiac problems, coming to Levi's office month after month for treatments that could slow but not stop his condition's progression. A kind man whose greatest joy had been his wife's laughter.

"He was a good man," Levi said.

"Yes." Frieda's voice grew weaker. "The nurse says you help people here. When there's no hope."

Levi froze, glancing around to ensure no one else was within earshot. Such conversations carried deadly risk for both of them.

"I treat all patients as best I can," he replied carefully.

"Please," Frieda said, her grip tightening with surprising strength. "I'm dying. We both know that. I've seen how people die here." Her voice dropped to barely a whisper. "I'd rather not suffer more than necessary. I'd rather go with dignity, thinking of Friedrich, thinking of better times."

The words hung in the stale air between them. Levi's mind moved toward his hidden supply of morphine, then pulled back as conscience wrestled with compassion. This was different from the anonymous mercy he had provided to strangers. This was Frieda Klein, who had served him coffee and cake in her Berlin kitchen, who had worried about her husband's failing heart.

"Let me see what I can do for your symptoms first," he said, avoiding a direct answer. "There might be medications that can help."

Frieda's eyes, sunken but still observant, registered his evasion. She had always been perceptive, he remembered. "We all wear different skins now, don't we, Doctor?"

"Rest now," Levi told her, adjusting her thin blanket. "I'll return later."

As he walked away, Levi felt the weight of her request settling on his shoulders like a physical burden. In the months since he had begun carrying the morphine, he had helped eight people find peaceful deaths. Each had been a stranger, someone whose suffering he could alleviate without the complication of personal history. Frieda was different. She carried memories of his former life, of who he had been before this place stripped away everything but the essential core of survival.

That evening, after completing his official duties, Levi sat alone in the small office he used for paperwork. The infirmary had grown quiet, the day's selection completed, the condemned already transported to Block 7. Twenty-three this time, including two children whose only crime was falling ill in a place where illness meant death.

A soft knock interrupted his thoughts. Anna stood in the doorway, her face grave.

"Frau Klein is worse," she said. "The fever has spiked dramatically."

Levi found Frieda delirious, her breathing labored, her skin burning with fever. The dysentery had accelerated, dehydration setting in with dangerous speed. Without aggressive intervention, she would die painfully over the next day or two. With intervention, she might linger for a week, suffering constantly.

"She won't last the night," Anna said quietly, echoing his assessment.

Levi nodded, feeling the vial in his pocket grow heavier. "I'll stay with her," he said. "You should rest. It's been a long day."

Anna studied his face, understanding in her eyes. "I'll make sure you're not disturbed."

After she left, Levi sat beside Frieda's pallet, bathing her forehead with a damp cloth. The fever had drawn her consciousness away, and she mumbled incoherently, occasional German phrases mixing with sounds of distress. Sometimes she called for Friedrich, her voice young and hopeful, as if calling him to dinner in their Berlin apartment.

From his pocket, Levi withdrew the small vial of morphine and a syringe. Five cubic centimeters would ensure a quiet death, one that would look natural among the daily tally of disease and starvation. He had done this before, but never for someone who remembered his other life.

As he prepared the syringe, a memory surfaced unbidden: Ruth in their Berlin apartment, arguing about medical ethics over dinner. Her eyes bright with conviction, her hands gesturing emphatically as she challenged his rigid stance on euthanasia.

"Life isn't simply about continued biological function, Levi," she had insisted. "It's about dignity, about meaning. When those are irretrievably lost, what exactly are we preserving?"

He had countered with principles, with the sacred trust between doctor and patient, with the Hippocratic Oath's injunction to first do no harm. She had listened, then smiled in that way she had when she believed he was missing the essential point.

"One day," she had said, "you may find that compassion requires more courage than principle."

At the time, he had dismissed her words as philosophical abstraction. Now, in this place where philosophy met the brutal reality of systematic murder, he understood what she had tried to tell him.

Ruth's voice faded. The syringe remained steady in his hand. Frieda's labored breathing filled the space between heartbeats.

Levi inserted the needle with the gentle precision of decades of medical practice. The *Shema* - the central prayer of Jewish faith passed his lips silently, words worn smooth by repetition, a thread stretching back to Berlin, to times when mercy hadn't required poison.

Frieda's breathing eased almost immediately, the tension leaving her body as the morphine took effect. Her eyes opened briefly, a moment of clarity cutting through the fever's chaos.

"Friedrich?" she whispered.

"He's waiting," Levi replied softly.

Her eyes closed again, her breathing slowed, and within minutes, she was gone.

Levi sat with her body for a time, as had become his practice. This ritual felt essential, a final acknowledgment of the person rather than the number. Frieda Klein of Berlin, wife of Friedrich, baker's wife who served excellent coffee and worried about her husband's heart. Not prisoner 97423, not another anonymous victim, but Frieda.

The next morning, as her body was removed to join the day's collection for the crematoria, Levi made his notation in the death register: heart failure secondary to dysentery and malnutrition. In Birkenau's meticulous records, she would be merely another statistic.

But in Levi's private accounting, the ledger he kept only in his mind, she was the ninth person he had helped to die. Nine merciful deaths amid countless merciless ones. Nine choices made not by the camp's machinery but by his own moral judgment.

As summer deepened into its final weeks, the pace of change accelerated. Rumors of Allied advances grew more persistent, confirmed now by Goldstein's access to administrative records. The SS officers moved with increased urgency, their usual brutal efficiency tinged with something that might have been desperation.

In late August, Dr. Müller summoned Levi to his office for their second private meeting. The room had been further cleared since their last conversation, more bookshelves emptied, filing cabinets standing open with most of their contents removed. Müller himself looked haggard, his uniform still impeccable but his face betraying sleepless nights.

"The situation has evolved more rapidly than anticipated," Müller said without preamble. "Evacuation orders may come within weeks."

Levi remained silent, watching the other man carefully.

"I wanted to inform you personally," Müller continued, "because your... unique position requires special consideration."

"Sir?"

"You have established relationships here. Patients who depend on you, colleagues who trust your judgment." Müller paused. "The evacuation will not be... orderly. Many prisoners will not survive the journey."

The euphemism hung between them, both men understanding its true meaning.

"I see," Levi said carefully.

"I thought you should know," Müller said, "so that you might... prepare appropriately."

Again, the careful language that said everything while committing to nothing.

"Thank you for the warning," Levi replied.

Müller nodded, then moved to his desk and withdrew another small package, similar to the one he had given Levi weeks earlier.

"Additional medical supplies," he said, placing it before Levi. "For... humanitarian purposes."

As Levi reached for the package, Müller spoke again, his voice barely above a whisper.

"The choices you've made here, Dr. Blum. The lives ended as well as saved." He paused, seeming to struggle with his words. "I want you to know that I understand the impossibility of your position."

"Do you?" Levi asked quietly.

Müller's eyes met his for a moment, then looked away. "Perhaps not entirely. But I understand enough to know that judgment belongs to God, not to men like us."

That evening, Levi shared Müller's warning with Anna as they conducted their final rounds. The infirmary held fewer patients now, as selections had become more frequent and more ruthless.

"How long do we have?" Anna asked.

"Weeks, perhaps less." Levi paused beside a patient whose infection they had successfully treated with their hidden antibiotics. "We need to make final preparations."

They had discussed this possibility many times in whispered conversations, planning for the day when evacuation would force impossible choices. Their stockpile of medications had grown substantial enough to help perhaps sixty people during a forced march. But they both knew that many patients would be too weak to survive such an ordeal under any circumstances.

"The morphine supply?" Anna asked.

"Sufficient," Levi replied, understanding her question. If evacuation meant certain death for the weakest prisoners, perhaps a peaceful end would be the final mercy they could provide.

"And for ourselves?"

The question hung between them. They had saved enough medication to ensure their own quick deaths if capture and torture seemed inevitable.

"Let's focus on helping others first," Levi said. "We can make that decision when the time comes."

Over the following days, they quietly identified patients who might survive an evacuation march and those who would not. It was a grim accounting, made more terrible by the necessity of secrecy. Too many people aware of their plans would mean exposure and execution for everyone involved.

One evening, as September approached and the nights grew cooler, Levi found himself alone in the infirmary office, reviewing the mental lists he had compiled. Sixty patients who might survive evacuation with medical support. Forty who would not. His hidden supply of morphine was sufficient to provide peaceful deaths for all forty, if that became necessary.

The mathematics of mercy, calculated in doses of poison.

Outside, the night sounds of Birkenau continued their familiar rhythm: distant shouts from guards, the rumble of late transport trains, the ever-present whisper of smoke from the crematoria. But even these sounds seemed muted now, as if the camp itself sensed the approaching end.

From his jacket, Levi withdrew Ruth's final letter, the paper now so thin from handling that it was nearly transparent. Her words, written in a Paris apartment years earlier, seemed to speak directly to his current situation.

I wait for you, always. Ruth.

Whether she still waited somewhere, in this world or beyond it, he could not know. But he carried her with him, just as he carried Sigmund's journal, just as he carried the accumulated weight of every choice he had made in this place.

Dr. Levi Blum of Berlin was gone, transformed by Birkenau into someone who administered mercy through morphine and salvation through selection. Yet something essential remained: the capacity to see humanity even in this place designed to obliterate it, the determination to preserve dignity where possible, the courage to make impossible choices when necessary.

It wasn't enough. It could never be enough against the immensity of what surrounded them. But as he felt the hidden vials in his pocket, his final medicines, Levi understood that it was all he had to offer.

The man he had been would have condemned these compromises without hesitation. The man he had become understood that moral purity was a luxury that Birkenau did not permit.

Nine peaceful deaths. Sixty lives that might be saved during evacuation. Forty more merciful endings if the worst came to pass. Each number represented a world, as Goldstein's Talmudic wisdom taught. Each choice was a prayer that someone, somewhere, would remember and bear witness.

Levi Blum, prisoner 73829, camp doctor, administrator of mercy, navigated by memory and necessity through the darkness, saving what worlds he could along the way.

18

The Wolf Meets Miriam

Birkenau, 1944

The door opened and he walked in.

Miriam Weiss looked up from her desk as the door to Administration Building 2 creaked open. A prisoner she hadn't seen before entered, carrying a wooden crate filled with documents. He moved with purpose, while most inmates shuffled through their tasks with vacant expressions. This man still had physical presence. His shoulders strained against the striped uniform, blond stubble catching the harsh light from the single window.

"These need to be filed," he said, setting the crate on her desk.

His voice caught her attention, controlled and deliberate. Most prisoners' voices faded like their bodies, but this man spoke with clear intention. Something in her chest tightened, a flutter she hadn't felt in months.

Miriam rarely spoke to other prisoners beyond necessary instructions. She had watched too many people fade away.

"You're new to this detail," she said quietly, glancing toward the door.

His blue eyes met hers, surprise visible for just a moment. "Yes. Lucky me."

Bitter humor colored his voice. It struck her memory, the sound of irony and minds playing with words, a language from before this place.

"I'm Miriam," she offered, knowing names were always valuable here.

He studied her, calculating risks with familiar precision. She recognized the assessment, the same one she made daily when deciding who might be trusted.

"Yakov," he finally said. "Some call me Wolf."

"Wolf," she repeated, testing the name. It felt right on her tongue. "It suits you."

His mouth twitched. Not quite a smile, but its ghost. "It used to."

Boots scraped in the hallway. Wolf straightened, face going blank, the perfect prisoner mask sliding into place. His entire body transformed, shoulders hunching inward, head dropping. Miriam did the same.

"I'll be back tomorrow with the rest," he said at normal volume.

Miriam nodded, turning back to her papers. "See that you do."

Once he left, she found herself glancing at the door. Wolf's presence had cracked through her numbness. Perhaps recognition. Not just another survivor, but someone playing a role, as she had done in Berlin.

Before Birkenau, false papers and dyed blonde hair had let her hide in plain sight as a translator at Reich Headquarters. She became too valuable, too skilled. Her superiors grew suspicious, investigated, discovered her true identity, and sent her here. Now she was using those same skills to survive.

The smell of sawdust from his crate lingered. So did the memory of his voice, of the flash of humor in his eyes. In months of isolation, Miriam felt awareness stir within her.

He returned the next day, as promised.

This time, the guard accompanied him but stayed outside. Wolf had already earned enough trust to be unsupervised briefly.

"More files," Wolf said as the door closed. He placed the crate on her desk, then paused. "How long have you been here?"

The question was personal. A risk. Yet Miriam answered.

"Eight months." Eight months that stretched longer than all her years before.

Wolf nodded slightly. "You work in Administration. You see things."

"Some. Not everything they think."

"More than most." His gaze held hers. "You notice patterns."

Miriam checked the door, then turned back. She shouldn't trust him, shouldn't talk, shouldn't risk the safety built through invisibility. But his presence made her want to speak. Her pulse quickened when his eyes stayed on hers.

"Why are you asking?"

Wolf leaned closer, pretending to arrange files. She caught his scent beneath the camp smell, something distinctly him. "I'm trying to understand this place. How it works. Where the weak spots are."

"Weak spots?"

"Every system has them." A flash crossed his eyes, the memory of someone who once found cracks to slip through. "Even here."

The door opened before she could reply. *Oberscharführer* - Senior Squad Leader Müller entered, scanning the room before settling on Wolf.

"Taking your time with those files, Jew?"

Wolf's transformation was remarkable. His shoulders collapsed, head bowed, entire presence shrinking. "Sorry, Herr Oberscharführer. I was asking about the filing system."

"He was," Miriam confirmed quickly. "I was explaining our procedures."

Müller looked between them, suspicious but uninterested. "Hurry up. There's more waiting."

"Yes, Herr Oberscharführer," Wolf mumbled, all confidence gone.

When Müller left, Wolf stayed hunched for several seconds before slowly straightening.

"You're good at that," Miriam observed.

"At what?"

"Becoming invisible."

Recognition crossed his face. "We're all acting to stay alive."

"Some better than others," she replied, studying the way his jaw tightened when he thought.

The guard's boots sounded in the hall. Wolf gathered the empty crate and moved toward the door.

"Same time tomorrow?" Miriam asked, then caught herself. Too eager.

Wolf nodded once. "I'll bring the files from Building 7."

After his departure, Miriam returned to her work, but her mind kept circling back to their conversation. Wolf was dangerous, not like the guards, but in the way hope was dangerous. He made her remember what it felt like to want beyond mere survival.

On the third day, Wolf arrived when Miriam was alone in the office. She had been waiting, checking the clock, this anticipation troubling her. Attachment meant weakness here.

"You're early," she said.

"Müller checks his watch twice before lunch. Means he's eager to leave," Wolf replied, placing the crate on her desk. "We have twelve minutes, maybe fifteen."

His calculation told her this wasn't a coincidence. He had been watching, learning patterns, finding gaps. Just like her.

"Fifteen minutes for what?" she asked.

Instead of answering, Wolf reached beneath the documents and pulled out a small package wrapped in cloth. He placed it on her desk, hidden by the crate.

"Bread," he said softly. "And some cheese. From Müller's personal stash."

The smell reached her then, familiar, impossible. Her stomach responded painfully, a physical memory of food that tasted like nourishment.

Miriam stared at the package, then at Wolf. "How did you get this?"

"Better not to ask," he answered.

The risk he'd taken was astronomical. This wasn't trading or scavenging. This was theft from an SS officer's quarters.

"Why?" she asked, hand hovering over the cloth without touching it.

Wolf's face remained neutral, but something shifted in his expression. "You have access to information. I have resources. Maybe we can help each other."

A transaction, not kindness. That made sense, felt safer. Miriam understood transactions. But the way his voice softened on the word "help" suggested something more.

"What do you want to know?"

"Guard schedules. Administrative procedures." He paused. "Transport information."

Transport information. The lists that determined who lived and who disappeared.

"That's dangerous," she said.

"So is this," Wolf replied, nodding toward the package.

Miriam decided. She took the package and quickly slid it into her desk drawer. "I can tell you about the guards now. The rest will take time."

While Wolf arranged files for show, Miriam leaned close and quietly spoke. "Braun does his final sweep at 3:47, not 4:00. Always. He counts steps. Mueller gets distracted by paperwork between 2:15 and 2:30. Never looks up. Hartmann falls asleep at his post every Thursday after lunch. Exactly twenty minutes."

Wolf listened intently, eyes on the files but attention fixed on her words. She noticed how still he became when concentrating, like a predator waiting.

When she finished, Wolf asked, "Wednesday would be best for deliveries? During Müller's extended lunch?"

"Fifteen minutes guaranteed. No one checks this room then. But come early, before the clock tower chimes."

"Good," Wolf said, closing the empty crate. "Next Wednesday."

As he prepared to leave, Miriam found herself reluctant to end their conversation. These brief exchanges had become the only time she felt truly present.

"Why Wolf?" she asked suddenly. "Why do they call you that?"

He paused, hand on the crate. For a moment, she thought he wouldn't answer.

"Before," he said finally, "I was a thief. Used this face to get close to rich Germans. Take what I wanted."

"And now?"

A shadow crossed his features. "Now I'm just trying not to disappear."

Their eyes met, and in that moment, Miriam felt something beyond their transaction. Recognition of shared experience, of countless calculations that had kept them alive. Her breath caught.

"Be careful, Wolf," she said softly.

He nodded. "You too, Miriam."

After his departure, Miriam placed her hand on the drawer with his gift. In another life, what she felt might have been gratitude, or connection. Here, she had no name for it.

By the fourth week, they had established their routine.

Every Wednesday during Müller's lunch, Wolf arrived with his crate. They exchanged what they had: food from Wolf, intelligence from Miriam. Then spent precious minutes in conversation that reminded them both of the world before.

Today, Wolf looked thinner. The camp was taking its toll despite his warehouse position. His cheekbones stood sharper now, and the uniform that had once strained against his shoulders hung loose.

"You're losing weight," Miriam said while she sorted his files.

Wolf shrugged. "They've increased the work detail. Less food, more labor."

It was the pattern. Work prisoners to death through exhaustion and starvation.

"I might be able to get you assigned to the records warehouse permanently," she said. "I've made myself useful to them. They listen sometimes."

Wolf looked at her more intently. He had suspected Miriam navigated the system somehow, but this was the first time she'd offered to use her influence for him.

"Why would you do that?" he asked.

"Maybe I'm tired of watching people be consumed," she said. Then, with a flicker of something warmer: "Maybe I miss real conversation."

Wolf understood then that she had done this before, used her position to shield others. He didn't ask how many or what it had cost her.

"I would appreciate that," he said simply. The words felt inadequate for what she was offering.

As Wolf prepared to leave, he reached into his pocket and pulled out something small. A wildflower, somehow still fresh, its petals pale yellow against his palm.

"Found this by the fence," he said, almost awkwardly. "Thought you might..." He trailed off, as if unsure why he'd taken it.

Miriam stared at the flower. It served no purpose, had no survival value. It was beautiful, and beautiful things didn't exist here.

"Thank you," she whispered, taking it carefully.

Wolf looked surprised by his own gesture. As if his hands had acted without consulting his mind.

"Be careful, Wolf," she said, their parting ritual.

"You too, Miriam," he replied.

Once Wolf left, Miriam sat motionless at her desk. She thought about his face when she'd offered to secure his position, the surprise that flickered across it. It had cost her to build her small store of influence with the camp authorities: moments of perfect German, flawless translations, careful investments in their trust.

Using it for Wolf gained her nothing tangible beyond the food he brought. Food she could likely obtain elsewhere if needed.

In the drawer, hidden beneath papers, lay half the bread he'd brought today. She'd insisted he take the rest back with him. His body was shrinking while hers remained merely thin. Self-preservation dictated she take everything offered, but she couldn't watch him fade.

She looked at the flower in her hand. Such a small thing. Such a dangerous thing.

As Wolf pushed his cart back to the records warehouse, wind biting through his thin uniform, he realized something important had

160

shifted. He was building instead of taking: connections, trust, perhaps something he had no name for yet.

The old Wolf, the Wolf of Berlin, would have scorned such things as weaknesses.

But here, with death omnipresent and dignity stripped away, these fragile human connections had become the only wealth that mattered.

In the darkest corner of his mind, a thought formed and was immediately pushed away: The things you care about are the things they'll take first.

He wasn't ready to face that truth. Not yet.

19

Josef's Story - Der Fälscher

Block 19, Birkenau, January 1944

A single finger tremble led to death. Josef's hands stayed steady when *SS-Sturmbannführer* - SS Major Krüger breathed down his neck, the air thick with morning schnapps and yesterday's cigarettes. The guard waited, Luger in hand, thumb drumming against the weapon. Josef put the finishing touches on the American hundred-dollar bill. His third perfect lie since dawn.

"Faster, Kleinman," Krüger barked, his riding crop beating rhythm against polished boots. "The Reichsführer demands results, not excuses."

Josef bit back his response. "Three minutes, Herr Sturmbannführer," he said, eyes down, voice flat. You couldn't rush perfection, and perfection was the only thing keeping him breathing.

At Birkenau, precision meant survival. They were the same thing.

Through the window he could see the maze of wooden huts. Skeletal figures shuffled between them. Smoke poured from the chimneys day and night, that sweet-sick smell clinging to everything. Above it all, the January sky burned bright enough to hurt.

He stared at Franklin's face on the counterfeit bill. These same hands used to forge papers that got families across borders to safety. Now the Reich owned them. The irony tasted like acid in his throat.

"Excellent work, Kleinman." Krüger held the hundred-dollar bill to the light, examining the watermarks Josef had spent hours perfecting. "Your consistency remains remarkable."

162

Josef nodded slightly, showing no emotion. "Thank you, Herr Sturmbannführer."

At the next table, Dr. Levi Blum leaned forward. The former Berlin surgeon now served the Reich through different medical work, treating guards' minor ailments to keep himself useful.

"The woman from Administration mentioned they used to call you *'Der Fälscher* - The Forger,'" Blum whispered under the machine noise.

Josef kept working on his next bill, hands moving with practiced precision. "Maybe."

"We should talk. Later."

Josef's nod was barely visible. He'd been watching Blum just like the doctor had been watching him. Skilled men keeping each other alive by serving the forces that would normally kill them.

Time was running short. Josef heard the rumors, saw the growing tension in the guard ranks. Russians advancing. Reich retreating. When Operation Bernhard became useless, so would he. And the Reich didn't leave witnesses.

Franklin's face stared up at him from the counterfeit bill, seeming to ask what kind of freedom he was fighting for.

His hands worked automatically, finishing the details while his mind explored escape routes and tiny opportunities beyond the wire.

Berlin, 1929

"You've got a gift, Josef. But gifts can turn dangerous."

The Ypres gas had chewed up Ludwig Kleinman's lungs, leaving his voice nothing but a whisper. January's bite was hard that year. No coal meant the print shop stayed cold as the street. His father's fingertips had turned blue-black with frostbite.

Fourteen-year-old Josef perched on the edge of his bed, print samples scattered across his lap. His father was dying, and they both knew it. Nobody had to say it out loud.

Ludwig's grip on Josef's wrist came sudden and fierce. "Listen well, boy." A coughing fit doubled him over, blood speckling his handkerchief. When he straightened, his voice scraped like sandpaper. "Paper makes truth. Certificates, licenses, banknotes. Control the paper, control who lives, who marries, who gets to exist at all."

Josef's stomach tightened. His father's eyes burned with something desperate.

"Use those hands to create. Not to deceive."

"I promise, Papa." The lie slipped out smoothly. Just last week he'd forged his first document, a school excuse note. Watching his teacher buy it completely had awakened something inside him. Something hungry.

Ludwig Kleinman died in his sleep that night. Officials came for the corpse. Josef's mother Rebekka sat silent, tears cutting tracks down her cheeks. They handed over the death certificate that erased his father from the world.

Josef watched his mother sign it, her hand shaking. He studied every detail. The watermark. The typeface angle. The official's signature with its backward curve.

That's when Josef learned the truth his father had been trying to tell him. Documents don't just record reality. They create it.

Berlin, 1935

The job at Müller's shop kept them from starving, but barely. The old craftsman cared more about perfect impressions than bloodlines, and his government printing business was booming under the new regime's paper obsession.

"Perfection is the only standard they accept now," Gustav Müller hammered into Josef's head daily. "Especially now."

Now. Three years since the Kleinman family print shop had lost every government contract overnight. Regular customers stopped coming. Nobody said the word "Jewish" out loud, but the empty ledger books spoke clearly enough.

Müller watched Josef reset type with quick, sure movements. "You're lucky to be here. Good jobs are getting scarce for your kind."

Josef caught the warning underneath. The old man was protecting him the only way he knew how.

Evenings, Josef stayed late after Müller left. He'd slip into the cabinet where they kept government seals and stamps. Not stealing. Learning. His memory absorbed every detail. Official stamp designs. Tax form paper texture. Ministry typefaces.

Show him a document twice and he could copy it perfectly.

When his sister Esther's lungs seized up that winter, Josef created a prescription form. Added the pharmacy discount stamp for government workers. The pharmacist never blinked. Esther breathed easy that night.

Later, alone in his bedroom, Josef held his hands up to the weak light. Printer's hands. Ink-stained, strong from gripping metal type. But they'd become something else now. Hands that could print permission. Print possibility.

His father's voice echoed back: "Paper makes truth." Josef was starting to understand just how much power that meant. And how much danger.

Berlin, 1939

By twenty-four, Josef lived two lives. Days at Müller's, nights as the paper man. Word spread through whispers about someone who could solve "document problems." Josef was careful about his clients. He weighed need against risk, fairness against convenience.

Viktor Altmann's bookshop became his headquarters. The old man had a back room with perfect northern light and a discreet alley entrance. Josef turned it into a workshop. Printing equipment, darkroom, everything arranged precisely.

In certain circles, they called him "Der Fälscher." The Forger. Rich industrialists paid through the nose. Desperate families got the friend rate. Sometimes he worked for free when a case got to him.

Like the night Miriam Weiss appeared at his door.

She'd been different from his usual clients. Poised, intelligent, with a translator's precise way of speaking. But her request was the most dangerous he'd ever heard: complete identity transformation to infiltrate the Reich Ministry.

"You want to work for the people who want to destroy you," he'd told her that night in the tobacco shop's backroom.

Her response had impressed him: "Because that's where the information is. Where I might actually do some good."

Creating Layla Brandt had been some of his finest work. Birth certificate registered in Dresden's city records. University diploma that would pass the closest inspection. An entire ancestry traced back four generations.

He'd warned her about the ongoing arrangement. She would owe him translations, document analysis, and her skills in exchange for her new life. What he hadn't expected was how often he'd think about her courage.

The work was steady until everything collapsed with Viktor Altmann's arrest.

The Trap, January 1940

Karl Winkler showed up in December 1939, calling himself a fellow forger looking to partner up. Josef turned him down flat. The man's work was sloppy and his security nonexistent. But Winkler kept coming around, making himself useful with rare supplies when wartime rationing bit hard.

Josef never knew Winkler had been arrested months earlier and cut a deal. Deliver "Der Fälscher" or die.

The Swedish passports were finished when Josef heard the bookshop door chime after hours. Altmann was visiting his sister and wasn't due back until evening.

Josef hid his work and crept toward the front. Through the curtain he saw four men asking about American architecture books, using the code words his clients sometimes did.

Relief lasted about two seconds. Then he caught the man's accent. Wrong rhythm. Trap.

"Sorry," Josef said, a professional smile in place. "Schlosser's on Unter den Linden has the best architecture collection. We specialize in German classics."

The man's smile never touched his eyes. "Herr Kleinman misunderstands our needs. Karl Winkler suggested we have this conversation."

Winkler. The name hit Josef like a blow.

"Don't know any Winkler. I just mind the shop for Herr Altmann."

"Disappointing." Hand signal to his men. They started tearing the place apart. "The Gestapo has evidence of document manufacturing on these premises. Winkler gave us very detailed information about your operations."

Josef didn't fight when they found the workshop. Didn't resist the handcuffs. He was still calculating angles when they dragged him outside and Viktor Altmann came shuffling home.

The old bookseller's face went from confusion to understanding in a heartbeat. He tried to reach Josef. The Gestapo shoved him aside hard enough to send him tumbling into a bookshelf. Altmann grabbed his chest and went down.

"He needs a doctor!" Josef fought against his captors.

"The Jew lover needs nothing from us."

Viktor Altmann died there among his books while Josef watched, helpless in handcuffs. The weight of that moment would follow him through everything that came after.

Auschwitz-Birkenau, 1943-1944

Transfer orders came with heavy escort. Twenty specialists loaded onto a modified passenger car with seats, windows, and water. Not cattle cars. They were too valuable for that.

Through the window Josef watched Germany become occupied Poland. Ruined cities. Burning villages. Empty countryside stretching to the horizon.

Morning fog lifted to reveal Auschwitz-Birkenau. Watchtowers and wire surrounding a factory designed for processing humans.

No selection line for the specialists. No tattoos, no head shaving. They got Block 19, a converted workshop in the wooden barracks. SS-Sturmbannführer Bernhard Krüger ran the show. Operation Bernhard alongside other document work the Reich needed.

They handed Josef materials and instructions. Told him to prove himself with an American banknote. He delivered perfection because anything less meant death.

That first night in Block 19, Josef took inventory. His skills. His knowledge. His intact body. Most important, the mental discipline that had carried him through four years of this hell.

From his bunk he watched the crematoria burn against the night sky. The acrid smell never left your nostrils once you knew what it was.

Staring at that hellish glow, Josef made his choice: survive this place, use his skills to escape if the chance came, bear witness to horrors the world might not believe.

The next day he started studying the other prisoners in the workshop. A translator who worked with camp officials and had somehow earned unusual privileges. A former surgeon treating minor injuries. A tailor doing uniform repairs. A man with the look of black market dealings.

Josef didn't approach them yet. Like any good forger examining paper, he watched first. Studied their patterns, survival methods, small kindnesses in this place of death.

He'd need allies for what came next.

A week later, the translator appeared in his workshop. Not just any translator. The woman he'd known as Miriam Weiss, who had become Layla Brandt, now back to being Miriam Weiss in this place where false identities meant nothing.

"I need files processed," she said formally, setting a crate on his desk.

Their eyes met for just a moment. Recognition flickered, quickly hidden. She'd made it inside the system, just as she'd planned. Josef felt something he hadn't experienced in months: hope.

"Of course," he replied, voice steady. "I'll handle them personally."

As she prepared to leave, she paused. "They say you're the best at what you do."

"I try to meet expectations."

"Good," she said softly. "Because I think we might have mutual interests."

After she left, Josef stared at the files she'd brought. Administrative documents. Guard schedules. Transport information. Not random paperwork. Intelligence.

He smiled for the first time since arriving at Birkenau. His father's words echoed back: "Paper makes truth."

The most important forgery Josef would ever create wouldn't be on paper at all. It would be six prisoners vanishing from a place designed to make people disappear forever.

He had a name for the plan already: Operation Exit. Every perfect counterfeit he created for the Reich was really building a path to his own goals.

In Birkenau, Josef would forge his most ambitious identity yet. Not a prisoner or a forger.

A survivor.

20

Whispers in the Dark

The barracks door slammed shut. I counted twenty-three sets of footsteps before silence returned, broken only by muffled weeping from the far end of the building. Beside me on the wooden shelf we called a bed, Miriam's breath came quick and shallow.

Another selection. The third this month. Autumn was deepening toward winter, and the SS were choosing who would see spring. Those chosen walked out the main gate. The rest of us knew better than to ask where.

"Tell me about before," Miriam whispered. Her voice barely carried over the symphony of coughs and moans that filled our nights. "About Krakow."

I hesitated. Talking about before invited pain, let it crawl into spaces where I kept it buried. But she'd shared her story last week, about working as an interpreter in Berlin, about diplomatic conferences where men in expensive suits hung on her every word. Fair was fair.

"I grew up in Kazimierz," I said, keeping my voice low. "The Jewish quarter."

"Your accent sounds different. Not fully Polish."

Sharp ears. Nothing escaped Miriam's notice, a dangerous trait in a place where knowledge could kill. "My father was German. Lieberman. A professor at Jagiellonian University."

A woman cried out in her sleep nearby, then went quiet. We both listened, waiting for the sound that didn't come. It didn't.

"You don't say 'was' because he died," Miriam observed. "You say 'was' because you don't know if he's still alive."

I almost smiled. "Yes."

170

"So you spoke German at home?"

"With my father. Polish with my mother. She insisted I know both perfectly."

Footsteps outside. Leather on dirt, the familiar drag of the left heel. Müller, night shift, who preferred his rifle butt to his hands. The sound passed, faded into distance.

"I became a police sergeant," I continued. "Only female detective in Krakow Central."

"A Jewish woman? In the police?" Her voice caught on the impossibility.

"Eight years fighting for scraps. Men spitting in my coffee. Reports disappearing before they reached the captain." I remembered the small victories, the slow grinding progress. "I specialized in observation. Details others missed."

"That's how you've survived here."

"Partly."

The searchlight swept past our window, ten seconds of harsh brightness, then darkness again. Someone sobbed quietly in the corner, the sound quickly muffled.

I found myself talking about Kowalski. How we'd shared patrol cars for seven years, cigarettes, case files. How he'd carried me home drunk from the department celebration without ever mentioning it again. Partners in everything but name.

"What happened when the Germans came?"

The question I'd been avoiding. "His brother was an officer in my precinct. The one who turned me in."

"Officer Piotr Kowalski. That quick, efficient nod when the Germans asked about Jewish officers. Seven years of shared duty, erased with a single gesture. His eyes hadn't even met mine."

"My chief warned me to leave," I said. "But where? Palestine? America? Those doors were already closing."

"I had a chance to go to England," Miriam said. "The British Foreign Office offered to sponsor me when war broke out. I stayed for my parents. They were too old to travel."

"Where are they now?"

She didn't answer. The silence said enough.

A guard shouted somewhere outside, disciplining someone. We held our breath, waiting for the rattle of our door. It didn't come.

"I lasted longer than most," I said finally. "My uniform protected me at first. When they took it, I had nothing."

"Nothing but your wits."

"Sometimes even those fail here."

Miriam's hand found mine in the darkness, fingers cold as bone. "I saw you with the Commandant yesterday. Translating those supply reports."

My stomach knotted. "Yes."

"You understood more than you translated."

Words could kill here, but the nights were long, and Miriam had kept my secrets so far. "The guards think language is just words. That we're talking dictionaries with no thoughts of our own."

"But you understand."

"I was police. Reading people, reading situations. That kept me alive more than my badge ever did."

"And what do you read now?"

I pitched my voice lower. "The guards are nervous. Supply lines cut. Berlin screaming for more production while sending fewer trains. The Commandant's reports are lies."

"Lies about what?"

"Numbers. Output. Conditions. The efficiency he claims while everything falls apart around us."

Miriam's fingers tightened on mine. "So there's hope."

"Hope is dangerous here."

"Yesterday Kraus hanged herself with her headscarf," Miriam said quietly. "Tell me again about danger."

The words hit like a slap. I'd known Kraus from the translation pool. A professor's wife from Vienna who spoke five languages. She'd given up.

"My mother used to make *challah* - braided bread every Friday," I said, changing the subject. "The smell would fill our apartment. Flour dusting every surface. My father coming home from the university with ink on his fingers."

"You miss them."

"I don't think about what I miss. Thinking is how you break."

"What do you allow yourself?"

I considered the question. "Anger. It burns steady."

"Not tonight," Miriam said, pressing closer. "Tonight you have me."

Body against body. Human contact without violence. The shock of it made me realize how long it had been since anyone had touched me without cruelty.

"My apartment overlooked a small park," I heard myself saying. "In spring, the chestnut trees bloomed white. I'd drink coffee by the window before my shift, watching people. Old habit."

"Coffee," Miriam sighed. "Real coffee."

"With sugar. Sometimes a pastry from Starski's bakery, the kind that flaked all over your uniform."

"You're killing me."

"Sorry."

We lay quiet, listening to the night sounds. Distant trucks. A shout from the guard tower. The collective breathing of two hundred women packed into space meant for fifty.

The memories kept coming. "My neighbors used to ask me for help. Legal problems. Missing items. They trusted the woman police officer more than the men."

"Were you good at it? Being police?"

"Yes," I said without false modesty. "I saw what others missed. Connections. Patterns. It's why I was promoted despite..." I didn't need to finish.

"Same skills keep you alive here."

"Us alive," I corrected. "I saw Gruber eyeing your bread ration yesterday. She won't try again."

The threat in my voice wasn't subtle. Miriam squeezed my hand once in acknowledgment.

"Sleep," I said. "Morning comes early."

"Tell me one more thing," she murmured, voice heavy with approaching sleep. "Something beautiful from before."

I thought for a moment. "My father's library. Shelves from floor to ceiling. Books in German, Polish, English, French. I'd run my fingers along the spines while he worked, leather soft from years of handling. He let me read anything I wanted. Said minds shouldn't have borders even when countries do."

"Beautiful," she agreed.

Outside, the camp stirred in its restless sleep. Our shoulders touched. Hair that hadn't been washed in weeks brushed against skin. Neither of us pulled away. In this place, that was as close to trust as anyone got.

"We'll speak more tomorrow," I whispered, but Miriam's breathing had already deepened into sleep.

I closed my eyes, allowing myself to remember the smell of books in my father's library, the weight of them in my hands. For the first time in months, I dreamed not of death, but of words on pages. Of worlds beyond barbed wire.

But even in sleep, part of me stayed alert. Listening. Watching. Calculating odds and exits. Because somewhere in this machine of death, my children were still alive. Sarah and David, taken from me in that gymnasium in Krakow. I'd made them a promise in that cattle car, whispered it to myself in the darkness.

Find them. No matter what it cost. No matter who I had to become.

The promise that kept me breathing when breathing felt like betrayal. The promise that would carry me through whatever came next.

21

The Last Days in Birkenau

The boot prints in the frozen mud had stopped appearing three days ago.

I pressed my face against the crack in the barracks wall, watching the last columns of prisoners shuffle through the gates. Their breath rose like prayers in the January air. Machine guns prodded them forward into the gray morning. Some stumbled and fell. None stood again.

The death march. That's what Wolf called it, his voice flat as he calculated distances and odds with eyes that had learned to read angles in desperate places. The SS were driving everyone who could still walk westward, ahead of the Soviet guns growing louder each day.

We were six, hidden beneath the floorboards of Barracks 14. The space had been hollowed out by dead men's hands, and we pressed ourselves into the frozen earth while German boots thundered overhead. Wolf, Josef, Daniel, Levi, Rivka, and myself. Six survivors who'd found each other in the chaos of evacuation, bound together by nothing more than the shared understanding that alone meant death.

"They'll sweep before leaving," Levi muttered, his doctor's training making him catalog the sounds above us. "Execute anyone they find."

Rivka's words tumbled between German and Polish, her police instincts never quiet. "*Ja* - yes, they will check, *sprawdzą wszędzie* - they will check everywhere, everywhere." Her fingers tapped against her thigh in the rhythm I'd learned was prayer.

Hours crawled past. The sounds above faded to sporadic gunshots echoing from distant barracks, then silence broken only by explosions as the Germans destroyed evidence of what they'd done here.

"Now," Wolf whispered, pushing up on the floorboard.

We crawled out like pale shadows emerging from a grave. Winter light hit my eyes, making them water. Our bodies were bone draped in striped cloth. A shard of broken glass caught my reflection: skull with hollow eyes, skin stretched thin. Miriam Weiss, translator of seven languages, reduced to spite and determination. Not alive exactly. Just not quite dead.

Josef pulled Wolf aside, urgent words I couldn't catch. I watched his hands move with the same precision I'd seen him use on camp documents, those careful forgeries that had kept him breathing.

"Need to secure something before we leave," Wolf announced. "Josef says it's critical."

Daniel measured distances with his tailor's eye, always precise. "Guards could return."

"Worth the risk," Josef said. "I've been preparing for this."

The revelation that Josef had been planning beyond mere survival should have surprised me. Instead, I felt only a dull recognition. Of course someone had been thinking ahead. Someone always was, in places like this.

Josef led us through the deserted camp, past the empty roll call square where we'd stood countless mornings waiting to be counted like livestock. We moved silent as the ghosts we nearly were, my mind cataloging escape routes from habit.

Behind the administration building, Josef knelt and clawed at frozen ground. Wolf and Daniel helped without question while Rivka, Levi, and I watched for movement.

Josef uncovered a metal box containing printing plates, specialized tools, and inks. "Perfect forgeries," he said, his smile sharp as winter. "Could pass inspection anywhere. The SS had me making Allied currency for their own escapes."

More caches followed. Equipment, chemicals, papers. All buried by a man who'd understood what the rest of us were only now realizing: this day would come, and survival would require more than just staying alive.

"This is why you lived," Levi observed. "Not just for documents."

176

Josef's fingers brushed a printing plate with something like tenderness. "Their insurance. Their future." His eyes found mine. "Now ours."

A truck engine growled in the distance, freezing us in place.

"Barracks. Now," Wolf hissed.

We ran low, Josef's equipment clutched against our ribs. The final sweep had found us.

We barely made it under the floorboards before German voices approached, angry and hurried. Through the cracks, boots moved across our ceiling with methodical precision.

Rivka shook beside me, her frame hollow under my palm. The woman who'd commanded respect on Krakow's police force now reduced to silent terror. I caught her eyes, mouthed words: "Slow breath. Stay calm."

The Germans moved through the barracks like a machine, bayonets piercing mattresses. One stopped directly above us. Through the crack I could see worn leather, smell tobacco as he bent to examine something.

Please move on, my mind begged. We're already ghosts.

He straightened. Moved away. Voices receded. The engine started again, fainter now.

We waited. None of us moved for what felt like hours. Night stretched around us while my mind circled the same questions: What happens after survival? Who is Miriam when she's no longer prisoner 37529?

"They're gone," Wolf finally said, peering through the crack. "Last trucks left an hour ago."

We emerged into a world emptied of its purpose. The camp that had consumed so many lives now stood hollow, already becoming a memory.

"No food," Rivka said, her voice finding its old authority. "No water. Stay and we die slowly."

Levi looked at me with understanding. "*Kanada* - the warehouse complex. We need supplies from Kanada."

The warehouses of stolen belongings. Everything torn from the dead, sorted by efficient hands. Shoes, coats, valuables sewn into seams. Our last chance at the tools of survival.

We moved through the darkened camp like thieves, which I suppose we were. My grandmother would have wept to see me pawing through strangers' belongings, pocketing gold torn from dead mouths. But grandmother was ash now, and I was whatever I needed to be to see another dawn.

Kanada's door hung open. Inside: chaos. Overturned trunks, spilled jewels, tangled heaps of clothing. The guards had grabbed what they could in their haste, but riches remained.

"Take necessities," Wolf said, already sorting with practiced hands. "Nothing flashy. Nothing that screams Jewish. But remember, survival has a price."

I found a coat, fur-lined, that draped over my skeleton like a tent. Eighteen months earlier I'd had flesh, curves, substance. I'd taken up space without apology.

Josef worked methodically, pocketing small valuables. "Diamonds. Gold. Universal currency."

My translator's mind categorized and prioritized. Wedding bands hidden in shoes. A diamond brooch sewn into a coat lining. Only pieces that could pass unnoticed.

Daniel moved through the piles with purpose, his tailor's fingers testing fabric quality. "For you, Doctor," he said, offering Levi a wool coat. "German cut. Makes you look professional again."

Levi nodded, but I saw him calculating more than warmth. Survival odds, not just from cold or hunger, but from the camp that would always live inside us.

Rivka found a leather purse containing cosmetics. She held the lipstick in trembling hands like an artifact from another civilization.

"Take it," I told her in Polish. "All of it. *Będziemy znowu kobietami* - We'll be women again."

But would we? The question cut deep. Or were we forever marked by what we'd become?

We collected systematically. Clothes, valuables, even food: chocolates, tinned fish, hard bread. Josef secured identity papers and stamps. Wolf found documents that might serve us.

"Look for pearls," Levi suggested quietly. "Swallowable if necessary."

The observation from Berlin's most celebrated surgeon struck me as both horrible and essential. We'd become people who calculated which valuables could be hidden inside our bodies to avoid detection.

Hours passed. Dawn approached through dirty windows. Time to face whatever waited beyond the wire.

Josef gathered us with the authority of someone who'd been planning while the rest of us merely endured. "We need strategy. Not villages, they'll report strangers. Germans still control most of Poland."

"Forest," Wolf said. "Until we know which way the wind's blowing."

I thought of the massive pines surrounding the camp. Hiding places, but January would bite deep without proper shelter.

"War isn't over just because Birkenau's empty," I said. "We're escaping into a world still burning."

The realization crossed their faces. In our desperate hope, we'd forgotten the fighting continued. The distant artillery confirmed it.

"We stay together," Levi said, the doctor's authority returning to his voice. "None of us survives alone out there."

"We barely know each other," Daniel said, fingers worrying at loose threads on his stolen coat.

Wolf hefted a sack of valuables, testing its weight. "We're still breathing. That's enough introduction."

But I studied their faces and saw the truth we weren't speaking. We had no grand plan, no destination beyond away. We were simply six people taking advantage of changing circumstances, bound together by shared desperation and the understanding that survival meant adapting to whatever came next.

Perhaps that was enough. We'd learned to read the shifts in power, to bend without breaking, to find opportunity in chaos. The camp had taught us that survival was less about long-term strategy and more about recognizing the moment when circumstances changed.

This was that moment. The wire that had held us was gone, but so was the terrible certainty of our place in the world. Now we were truly free: free to live, free to die, free to choose what we became in the space between.

As we prepared to leave the only world we'd known for months or years, I felt something shifting inside me. Not hope exactly, but possibility. The woman who walked out of Birkenau would be different from the one who'd entered. Harder, certainly. More ruthless. But also more alive than I'd been in longer than I could remember.

We shouldered our stolen goods and walked toward the gate, six survivors carrying everything we owned in the world. Behind us, the watchtowers stood empty against the gray sky. Ahead lay the forest, branches heavy with snow.

And somewhere between the past that had tried to kill us and the future we were about to invent, we took our first steps as free people. Whatever that meant now.

22

Drexler

The camp had been empty for three days.

I stood at the broken window of the women's barracks, watching smoke rise from the administration buildings. The Germans had torched what they could before fleeing westward, ahead of the Russian guns that grew louder each hour. The stench of burning paper and metal cut through the ever-present smell of ash that would never quite leave this place.

Around the camp, bodies lay where they'd fallen. The dying had been left to die. The Germans no longer had time for bullets when the end was so close.

"Fire's almost out," Wolf said behind me. We'd built it small, just enough for warmth. Six survivors huddled around embers in a barracks meant for two hundred.

Josef sorted through his forged documents by the dim light. His hands moved with the precision that had kept him alive eighteen months, checking each paper, each stamp. "These should get us through checkpoints," he said. "If we're careful."

"How far to the Russian lines?" Daniel asked. His tailor's fingers worked constantly, mending tears in our stolen clothes, preparing us for whatever came next.

Rivka looked up from cleaning the Luger she'd taken from a dead guard. Her police training never stopped, even here. "Twenty kilometers east. Maybe less." She tested the gun's mechanism with professional competence. "But the Germans are still fighting. Retreating, but fighting."

Dr. Levi examined each of us in turn, his medical eye cataloging our condition. "We're stronger than we were three days ago," he said finally. "The food helped. But not strong enough for a long march."

We'd found the officers' kitchen that morning, looted what remained. Tinned meat, hard bread, even coffee grounds. A feast compared to what we'd eaten for months. My stomach still ached from eating too much too quickly.

"We leave before dawn," I said. The translator in me had somehow become the voice that spoke our collective thoughts. "While it's still dark."

"North or east?" Wolf asked.

"North first," Rivka said with certainty. "Away from the fighting. Then east when we're clear."

The fire died to embers. We settled into sleep as best we could, six bodies pressed together for warmth on wooden boards that had held so many others. I closed my eyes but stayed alert, listening to the sounds of an abandoned place slowly dying.

The motorbike engine woke me near dawn.

I sat up, instantly awake, heart hammering. Beside me, Wolf's eyes were already open. He'd heard it too.

The sound grew closer, then stopped somewhere near the administration building. A single rider. German, from the engine's sound.

Wolf touched Daniel's shoulder, gestured toward the window. They moved like shadows, years of survival training taking over. The rest of us stayed motionless, barely breathing.

Through the gray pre-dawn light, I watched them peer through the broken glass. Wolf held up one finger. One rider. Daniel pointed toward the administration building, mimed digging.

Someone had come back for something buried.

Wolf and Daniel crept back to us. "SS officer," Wolf whispered. "Alone. Digging behind the building."

Josef's face went hard. "They all buried things. Insurance for after the war."

"We should go," Daniel said. "Circle around him."

"No." The word came out before I'd thought it through. "We need to see who it is."

Something had changed in me during those three days of freedom. The woman who'd entered this place would have hidden, would have run. But that woman was gone.

Rivka checked her weapon. "If it's someone we know..."

She didn't finish the sentence. We all understood.

We moved through the barracks like ghosts, using shadows and broken walls for cover. The motorbike sat near the gate, engine ticking as it cooled. Expensive leather saddlebags hung from its sides.

Behind the administration building, a figure knelt in the snow, clawing at frozen ground with desperate hands. Even from a distance, I recognized the perfect posture, the precise movements.

Hauptsturmführer Karl Drexler.

My breath caught. Eighteen months of watching that man decide who lived and who died. Not the worst of them, but bad enough. I'd seen him sip coffee while pointing at names on lists, sending children to the gas with the same casual gesture he'd use to swat a fly.

"Drexler," Josef whispered. His hands clenched into fists.

The SS officer pulled a leather pouch from the hole he'd dug. Even from thirty meters, we could see it bulge with stolen treasures. Gold teeth, wedding rings, diamonds pulled from the mouths and fingers of the dead.

He never heard us coming.

Years of moving silently through barracks, of avoiding guards' attention, served us well. We surrounded him in seconds. Six shadows emerging from the gray dawn.

Drexler looked up to find us standing in a circle around him. His perfect uniform was stained with mud and grave dirt. His face, always so composed during selections, went white with recognition.

"Please," he said in German. The word came out like a prayer. "I have money. Gold. I can pay you."

None of us spoke. We studied this man who'd held our lives between his fingers for so long. The immaculate appearance now disheveled, the absolute authority reduced to begging.

"I kept you alive," he said, trying to stand. Rivka's gun stopped him halfway up. "I could have sent you to the chambers any day. I chose not to."

Daniel made a sound that might have been laughter if it hadn't been so broken. "And we should thank you? For deciding each morning not to murder us?"

"You don't understand," Drexler said, desperation creeping into his voice. "Orders came from Berlin. Quotas. I did what I could to minimize..."

"Minimize?" The word exploded from Josef. "You minimized? Tell that to Sarah Goldberg. Tell that to the Roth twins."

Drexler's hand moved toward his holster. Rivka's shot took off two of his fingers before he could reach it. The sound echoed across the empty camp like a judgment.

He screamed, clutching his ruined hand. Blood seeped between his fingers, staining the snow.

"The children you selected," I said in German, my voice steady despite the fire in my chest. "Do you remember their names?"

"I was following orders," he gasped. "You would have done the same in my position."

The silence that followed felt absolute. Even the wind stopped.

"No," Levi said quietly. "We are not the same."

I knelt and picked up a chunk of concrete from the ruined building. The others followed without words. Rivka set the gun aside and found a jagged stone. Wolf hefted a piece of rebar. Daniel hesitated longest, his gentle hands trembling.

"The boy who shared his bread with his sister," Wolf said. "You took him in October."

Daniel's fingers closed around a brick.

My arm rose before my mind decided. The concrete caught Drexler above the eye, opening a gash that sprayed blood across the snow. Then we were all there, eighteen months of helplessness finding voice in stone and steel.

Drexler tried to scream. The sound died under our fury.

I felt my arm rise and fall, rise and fall. Memory flashed with each impact: Drexler's polished boot on a starving man's face; his pointer finger selecting children for death; his casual sip of coffee while mothers wept.

When it was over, we stood in the growing dawn light, breathing hard. Vapor rose from our mouths. The only sound was wind through broken buildings.

Daniel stared at his hands like they belonged to someone else. Blood specked his stolen coat. Josef spat on what remained of our tormentor. Rivka holstered her weapon with mechanical precision.

"One debt paid," I said quietly. The words felt like stones in my mouth. "The first of many."

We worked in silence to scatter the stolen treasures, hiding evidence of why Drexler had returned. Gold and diamonds disappeared into our pockets, not for greed but for survival. A missing SS officer might not be investigated in the chaos of retreat, but scattered wealth would raise questions we couldn't answer.

Wolf found papers in Drexler's jacket. Travel documents, false identity cards, maps showing routes west. "He planned to disappear," Wolf said. "New name, new life."

"Not anymore," Rivka said.

We dragged the body behind the building. We dug out a clumsy hole and threw him in it, covering it up with rubble and dirt.. Just another casualty of war, another piece of debris in a place built for death.

The motorbike was too valuable to leave. Josef examined the engine with a forger's attention to detail. "Still has fuel," he said. "Could get us twenty kilometers."

"Too conspicuous," Rivka said. "A motorbike draws attention."

"Then we take what we can carry and go," I said.

We stripped the saddlebags of useful items: more false papers, German marks, even a bottle of schnapps. The bike itself we rolled into the ruins, another piece of war's wreckage.

As we prepared to leave, I felt something fundamental shift inside me. The woman who'd entered this place had believed in law, in justice, in civilization's rules. She would have been horrified by what we'd just done.

But that woman was dead, killed by the same machine that had tried to kill us all. What stood in her place was harder, more ruthless. Someone who understood that in a world without rules, survival required abandoning everything except the will to continue.

"Any regrets?" Wolf asked as we shouldered our packs.

I searched inside myself, probed the edges of guilt, tested its weight. "No," I said finally. "But I don't know what that makes us."

"It makes us alive," Josef said, "when he's not."

"Is that enough?"

Levi adjusted his stolen medical bag. "It means we remember. Their faces, their names. All of them."

The others nodded. I understood what they were suggesting. Not just survival, but purpose. Justice for those who would never see it themselves.

"How many will walk free when this war ends?" Wolf continued. "How many will burn their uniforms, change their names, go home to wives and children?"

The question hung in the cold air. We all knew the answer.

"We can't bring back the dead," Daniel said.

"No," I agreed. "But we can ensure the living don't sleep well."

We walked toward the forest as full daylight broke across the empty camp. Six survivors carrying everything we owned, plus something new: the weight of crossing from victim to something else entirely.

Behind us, watchtowers stood empty against the gray sky. Ahead, pine branches heavy with snow offered concealment and the promise of whatever came next.

The forest accepted us reluctantly. Every footstep in the snow sounded like an alarm. But we moved with a new purpose now, not just fleeing but carrying forward the memory of justice delivered, the knowledge that some debts could be paid even in a world gone mad.

We were no longer just survivors. We had become something new, something necessary. Six broken pieces walking out of a graveyard, not heroes, not victims anymore.

Whatever that made us, we would learn together.

23

The Journey Begins

The forest darkness moved and breathed, nothing like Birkenau's dead stillness.

Pine needles crunched under my stolen boots as we made our way through the trees. Behind us, the camp's watchtowers disappeared into gray dawn. Ahead lay only questions and the faint hope that survival might mean more than simply not dying.

We walked single file, Wolf leading with the instincts of someone who'd learned to read danger in faces and shadows. Josef stumbled behind him, exhaustion weighing his steps. Three days of real food had strengthened us, but eighteen months of starvation couldn't be erased so quickly.

"Need to rest," Josef gasped, leaning against a pine trunk.

I studied his face in the dim light. Not the flush of fever, just bone-deep weariness. "Five minutes," I decided. "Then we keep moving."

Rivka scanned the treeline with police-trained eyes. "Dogs could still track us."

"Guards ran west ahead of the Russians," Wolf said. "We're ghosts now."

Daniel picked at invisible threads on his sleeve, the tailor's nervous habit unchanged even in freedom. "Ghosts," he repeated. "Is that what we are?"

Dr. Levi stood apart, maintaining the surgeon's posture that seemed all he had left of his former self. "We're whatever we choose to become," he said quietly.

We moved deeper into the forest until mud sucked at our ankles and the smell of wet earth replaced the stench of ash that would always live in our lungs. When Josef's legs finally gave out, we stopped by a stream to rest and take stock.

"Can't feel my feet," he muttered, pulling off his boots.

I knelt to examine them. Blisters, some burst and weeping, but nothing that wouldn't heal. "You'll live," I told him. "We all will."

But surviving and living, I was learning, were different things entirely.

By afternoon, we could smell woodsmoke and hear the distant sound of an axe. Through the trees, a farmhouse emerged: stone walls, thatched roof, lamplight glowing in windows. The scent of bread and cooking meat made my stomach clench with longing.

"Too dangerous," Daniel said immediately.

"Too necessary," I countered. "We can't live in the forest forever."

Wolf studied the layout with calculating eyes. "One farmhouse. No close neighbors. Good sightlines." He looked at me. "You and I go first. Test the waters."

I nodded. As the group's translator, I'd become our voice by default. But Wolf's street instincts made him our scout when physical danger threatened.

We approached carefully, hands visible, posture non-threatening. A man emerged from the barn, medium height, work-weathered hands that held an axe with comfortable competence.

"Good day," I called in Polish, my university training serving me well. "We're travelers seeking shelter. We can pay."

The man's eyes took in our appearance, the striped fabric barely hidden under stolen coats, the way we moved like beaten animals expecting blows. Recognition dawned in his face.

"I'm Marek," he said finally, setting down the axe. "How many of you?"

"Six," Wolf answered in his accented Polish.

Marek glanced toward neighboring farms, then back at us. Something shifted in his expression. "After dark," he said quietly. "Come to the barn. It's safer."

Relief flooded through me. "Thank you."

188

He shrugged, uncomfortable with gratitude. "I'm still human," he said. "They tried to make us all into animals. I refuse."

That evening, we approached the farm as shadows lengthened. Marek met us at the barn door, a woman beside him.

"My wife, Sophia," he said. "She has food ready."

Inside the farmhouse, warmth and light surrounded us like a forgotten dream. Sophia looked up from her stove, wooden spoon frozen as she took in all six of us. She crossed herself quickly, not in fear but in sympathy.

Two boys peeked from behind her skirts, eyes wide.

"Jews," the younger whispered.

I tensed, but there was no alarm in his voice, just recognition of what we were.

Sophia spoke in Polish to Rivka, who stepped forward. "She says to wash first, then eat. No Germans will come. Russians are advancing."

A wooden tub sat near the fire, steam rising from hot water. Clean clothes appeared, patched but without stripes. The simple act of washing felt like resurrection.

At the wooden table, I held a spoon with trembling hands. Potato soup thick with vegetables, dark bread with rendered fat. My stomach, shrunken by months of starvation, rebelled against such richness.

Josef ate slowly between coughs of exhaustion. Daniel chewed with his eyes closed, as if the act of eating real food might disappear if he looked. Dr. Levi's medical training showed as he paced himself, knowing the dangers of eating too much too quickly.

None of us spoke. Words would have shattered the moment.

That night in the barn, clean straw and horse blankets felt like luxury. I lay awake listening to Josef's ragged breathing, Rivka's quiet prayers, the sound of Daniel weeping silently into his makeshift pillow.

Through cracks in the barn wall, I watched the farmhouse windows for signs of betrayal that never came.

Dawn brought porridge with milk and the beginning of our transformation from camp prisoners to something approaching human beings. But it was Marek's morning news that changed everything.

"War's not over," he told Wolf as they stood by the woodpile. "Germans still control the west, fighting as they retreat. Russians coming from the east, but slowly."

Wolf's face went pale. "We planned to go west. To the Americans."

Marek shook his head. "The west is still German territory. They see you, you're dead. Cornered animals bite hardest."

I felt something cold settle in my stomach. In our desperate hope for freedom, we'd imagined the nightmare was over. But the world beyond the wire was still burning.

When Wolf shared this news, our group fell silent. Daniel slumped against the barn wall. Josef closed his eyes, calculating new impossibilities.

"So where do we go?" Dr. Levi asked.

"Nowhere," I said finally. "Not yet. We wait."

And so we stayed, paying our way without money. Josef's forger's hands proved as skilled with broken machinery as with false documents. He fixed Marek's clock, repaired a harness buckle, even coaxed life back into Sophia's sewing machine.

Daniel's tailor skills transformed torn clothing into presentable garments. His fingers worked with precision that came from years of creating beauty from cloth, now applied to making us appear like ordinary refugees rather than escaped camp prisoners.

Dr. Levi pulled the younger boy's rotting tooth with gentle competence, his medical authority returning as he found purpose again. Watching him work, I saw glimpses of the celebrated surgeon he'd been before the world went mad.

Rivka kept watch with police instincts that never slept, scanning approaches to the farm, listening for unusual sounds. Though she was the only Polish native among us, my professional fluency proved equally valuable in conversations with neighbors who stopped by, deflecting curiosity with casual lies about displaced relatives.

I found myself in long conversations with Sophia, my fluent Polish allowing us to share recipes and folktales, stories of life before the war. She taught me to braid bread, I helped her understand the herbs her grandmother had used for healing.

Wolf remained vigilant, reading threats in every shadow, but gradually something in him began to uncoil. The con man's perpetual wariness softened into merely careful observation.

As days passed, we began to look less like walking skeletons and more like people. Hair grew back. Flesh slowly returned to our bones. The hollow-eyed stare of the starving gave way to something approaching normal human expression.

But normalcy was fragile. At night, I heard Marek and Sophia whispering through the walls.

"Let them stay until it's truly over," Sophia said.

"Someone talks, we all die," Marek replied. "The Kowalskis, shot last month. All of them."

"God doesn't see us anymore," Sophia whispered.

"Maybe not. But we see each other."

Their kindness came at mortal risk, and we all knew it.

Josef surprised me during our second week. As we sat by the stream where he soaked his healing feet, he spoke quietly about the future.

"Been thinking about what comes after," he said. "When this war finally ends."

"After survival, you mean?"

He nodded. "The men who built these camps, who ran them, who profited from them. Most will disappear into new lives. New names, new papers." His forger's hands clenched into fists. "I could track them. My skills, your languages, Wolf's street knowledge."

I studied his face. "You're talking about justice."

"I'm talking about payment. For all of it."

The idea settled into my mind like a seed finding soil. Not revenge exactly, but accounting. Making sure that what happened to us mattered, that it had consequences.

"We'd need resources," I said carefully. "Money. Connections."

Josef's smile was sharp as winter. "There are ways to acquire both. Banks, for instance. They foreclosed on Jewish homes, stored Jewish wealth. Some of that wealth could be... redistributed."

The audacity of it took my breath away. "You're talking about robbery."

"I'm talking about recovery. Taking back what was stolen."

Daniel, who'd been listening from a few feet away, looked up from mending a sock. "That would make us criminals."

"We're already killers," Josef said quietly. "Drexler proved that."

The truth of it hung between us. We'd crossed lines in the camp, crossed more when we killed Drexler. Each step had taken us further from who we'd been before.

"Think about it," Josef continued. "But don't think too long. Opportunities won't last forever."

As our third week at the farm began, the sound of artillery grew closer. Russian guns, Marek confirmed, advancing steadily westward.

"They'll be here within days," he told us over breakfast. "When they come..." He spread his hands helplessly.

I understood. Poles and Russians had never been friends. Soviet occupation might prove as dangerous as German, in different ways.

"You're worried about us being here when they arrive," I said.

Marek nodded reluctantly. "Six Jewish refugees might be... complicated. Questions about how you survived, where you've been."

That evening, our group gathered in the barn for what had become our nightly planning session. We'd grown comfortable in these discussions, six minds working together on the problem of continued survival.

"Time to move," Wolf said simply. "Russians or no Russians."

"Where?" Daniel asked. "West is still German. East brings us to the Soviet advance."

"South," Rivka suggested. "Toward Czechoslovakia. Or Hungary."

Dr. Levi shook his head. "Those borders will be chaos. Armies moving, refugees fleeing. We'd be lost in the confusion."

192

"Maybe that's good," I said. "Easier to disappear in chaos."

Josef looked up from the map Marek had given us. "First we need to survive the immediate future. Then we can plan for the larger one."

I studied the faces around me, these five people who'd become my family through shared suffering and mutual dependence. Whatever came next, we'd face it together.

"We leave tomorrow night," I decided. "One more day to rest, to prepare."

Agreement passed between us without words. We'd stayed as long as we dared, recovered as much as possible. Now uncertainty called again.

Our final day at the farm passed quietly. Sophia prepared extra food for our journey. Marek sketched routes on his map, marking safe houses he knew of, warning of areas to avoid.

"Where will you go?" he asked as we prepared to leave.

"Don't know yet," Wolf answered honestly. "Away from here. Toward whatever comes next."

Marek nodded, understanding the impossibility of planning in a world still at war.

At sunset, six bundles waited by the barn door: bread, cheese, meat, a knife for Wolf, extra bandages for Josef's feet, a silver cross for me.

Sophia embraced each of us, whispering prayers in Polish. Marek simply nodded, too moved for words.

At the edge of the clearing, I turned back. "Why help us?" I asked. "You could have been killed."

Marek studied me, then looked past at something I couldn't see. "You survived," he said finally. "Now live."

We walked into the morning mist, six shadows against the pale light. Behind us, smoke curled from the farmhouse chimney. Ahead lay nothing but questions and the knowledge that we were no longer just trying to survive.

We were learning to live. Whatever that meant in a world still burning.

24

The Farm

The sound of artillery had grown closer during our final night at Marek's farm.

I stood at the barn door in the gray dawn, watching Soviet patrols move through the distant treeline like shadows hunting shadows. The war was catching up to us again, and Marek's kindness could only protect us so far.

"Time to go," I told the others as they gathered their few possessions. Three weeks of safety had strengthened us, but our welcome was ending. Marek's worried glances toward his neighbors, his wife's nervous prayers, told us everything we needed to know.

Sophia pressed a bundle of food into my hands, her eyes bright with unshed tears. "*Bóg z wami* - God be with you," she whispered.

Marek simply nodded, understanding that goodbyes in wartime were dangerous luxuries. We slipped away before full daylight, six figures dissolving into the winter landscape.

The road twisted through barren fields, frozen mud cracking under our boots as Poland's winter closed around us. Snow dusted the naked trees, turning the world gray and white. Behind us, the sound of distant guns reminded us that the war's end was still measured in blood.

We walked for hours through the empty countryside. Our stolen coats, taken from Drexler's quarters when we killed him, kept out the worst of the cold. But cold was an old enemy now. We'd learned to make friends with worse things.

"A house," Josef said, his voice cutting through the falling snow.

Through the white curtain, a farmhouse materialized. Squat and wooden, with smoke rising from its chimney. A barn hulked nearby, its roof sagging under winter's weight. Yellow light leaked from a window, the kind of light that belonged to people who still believed in normal lives.

"Someone's home," Wolf observed, his con man's instincts reading the scene.

Dr. Levi shifted the rifle we'd taken from a dead German patrol. No ammunition, but people didn't need to know that. A rifle was authority enough.

We approached as darkness settled completely over the landscape. I knocked on the door and stepped back, letting the others position themselves in the shadows.

Footsteps from inside. A pause. The door creaked open.

A man filled the doorway, his face flushed with indoor warmth. Middle-aged, broad through the chest, wearing clothes too fine for a poor Polish farmer. His gaze moved from face to face, cataloging what he saw: strangers, desperate, dangerous.

"Who are you?" His Polish carried harsh German consonants that made my translator's ear twitch.

"We need food and shelter for the night," Rivka said, her police authority creeping into her voice.

The man's fingers whitened on the doorframe. "Go to the village. There's a church there."

"We've come from the camps," Josef said, the words stripped of everything but fact. "Birkenau."

Something flickered in the man's eyes. Not sympathy. Recognition of what we might be capable of.

"I can't help you." His voice hardened as he glanced past us toward the empty road.

Dr. Levi's grip on the rifle tightened.

The man started to close the door.

Josef wedged his foot in the gap. "You're German, aren't you?"

Blood rushed into the man's face, and I saw Wolf's assessment had been correct. This man was playing a role, just as poorly as most amateurs.

My gaze swept the interior of the house. The furniture was too solid, too fine. Heavy wool tapestries, china dishes, silver candlesticks.

None of it belonged to a Polish farmer struggling through occupation.

"Whose house was this?" Josef asked quietly.

The man's silence answered for him.

Josef pushed inside, his boots thudding against polished wood planks. "You were resettled here, weren't you? When the Germans came, they took Polish farms and gave them to good Aryan men like you."

The man swallowed, the sound wet and desperate.

"I know you," Dr. Levi said suddenly, his medical precision cutting through recognition. "Block 27. You beat Szymon to death for hiding bread."

The German's face went white. "I had orders. I had no choice."

Josef moved closer, his shadow falling across the man's terrified features. "We all have choices."

I turned away as Josef nodded to Dr. Levi. The rifle butt came down once. Twice. Then silence.

We buried him behind the barn that night, the frozen ground fighting us for every inch of depth. None of us spoke about it. Some conversations were luxuries we couldn't afford.

The farmhouse became ours.

For two weeks, we lived like people again. Real beds with actual mattresses. Hot food shoveled into our mouths until our shrunken stomachs rebelled. We scrubbed the blood from the floorboards and settled into rooms filled with stolen Polish treasures.

Josef found a radio hidden beneath the kitchen floorboards. Each night we gathered around it, straining to catch news through static about Soviet advances, German retreats, and a world being dismantled and rebuilt. The war gasped toward its end, but endings could be as dangerous as beginnings.

I repaired our clothes by firelight, needle flashing as I transformed stolen garments into something approaching respectability. Daniel discovered books on the shelves, German poetry and philosophy. He read passages aloud, translating words about beauty and truth that made Rivka laugh until tears streamed down her hollow cheeks.

Wolf sketched maps on the kitchen table, using salt for borders and matchsticks for roads. "We need to decide what we're doing," he said one evening. "Survival's not enough anymore."

Dr. Levi cleaned the rifle daily, though we'd found no bullets. The metallic scraping of the cleaning rod became a ritual, a promise of some kind.

But it was Josef who finally spoke what we'd all been thinking.

"The banks," he said one night as we sat around the radio, listening to reports of German retreats. "They hold everything stolen from Jewish families. Assets, valuables, property deeds. All of it sitting in vaults while the owners are ash."

The room grew quiet except for the radio's static.

"You're talking about robbery," Daniel said carefully.

"I'm talking about recovery," Josef replied. "Taking back what was stolen."

Wolf leaned forward, his con man's mind already working angles. "Banks have guards. Alarms. Police."

"Banks also have vulnerabilities," Josef said. "I know forgery. You know people. Miriam knows languages. Rivka knows police procedures. Dr. Levi knows anatomy." His smile was sharp as winter. "Daniel knows precision."

I studied the faces around me, these five people who'd become my family through shared suffering. "You're serious about this."

"Dead serious. The men who built the camps, who ran them, who profited from them? Most will disappear into new lives after the war. New names, new papers." Josef's hands clenched into fists. "But their money, their stolen wealth, is sitting in bank vaults. Waiting."

Rivka set down her coffee cup with deliberate care. "It would be dangerous."

"Everything's dangerous," Wolf said. "At least this has a purpose."

Dr. Levi stopped cleaning the rifle. "What kind of purpose?"

"Justice," I said quietly. "Evidence. Resources to track down the ones who escape."

The word hung in the air like smoke from the fireplace.

"I'll need supplies," Josef continued. "Tools, contacts, information. There's a network in Krakow, people who deal in documents and favors. If the Russians haven't taken the city yet."

"That's a big if," Wolf said.

"It's worth the risk. We need proper equipment for this kind of work."

Daniel looked up from his book. "You want to go to Krakow?"

"I want us to have options. Right now, we're hiding on a dead German's farm, eating his food and sleeping in his bed. That's survival, not living."

I felt something shift inside me, the same feeling I'd had when we killed Drexler. The woman who'd entered Birkenau would have been horrified by what Josef was proposing. But that woman was dead, killed by the same machine that had tried to kill us all.

"There's a truck in the barn," Wolf said thoughtfully. "German military. Needs work, but it runs."

We'd discovered it our first day, hidden under canvas and hay. The former owner had probably planned to use it for his own escape before we arrived.

"I'll go with you," Daniel said suddenly. "To Krakow."

Josef raised an eyebrow. "Why?"

"Because you'll need help. And because..." Daniel's fingers worried at a loose thread on his sleeve. "Because I want to do something that matters."

We spent the next three days getting the truck operational. Wolf's street knowledge included enough mechanical skill to coax the engine to life. Josef mapped routes through the Polish countryside, avoiding main roads where Soviet patrols might be operating.

I found detailed maps in the German's papers, carefully marked with military positions and supply routes. Useful for more than just finding our way to Krakow.

"What do you need?" I asked Josef as he prepared for the journey.

"Lock picks, cutting tools, chemicals for document work. Maybe weapons if I can find them." He paused. "And information about banks. Which ones hold the most assets, which are vulnerable."

Rivka studied the maps with police precision. "If the Russians have taken Krakow, you'll need different papers. Soviet identification."

"I can handle that," Josef said. "It's what I do."

The night before they left, we gathered around the kitchen table for what felt like a war council. The radio crackled with news of German retreats and Soviet advances, but our focus was on a different kind of battle.

"The Dresdner Bank has branches throughout this region," Josef said, pointing to marks on the map. "Small ones, minimal security. If we're going to start somewhere, it should be manageable."

"Start?" Dr. Levi asked.

"This won't be a one-time thing," Wolf said with certainty. "Not if we're serious about finding the ones who escaped."

I spread the detailed maps across the table. "These show transport routes, communication lines, administrative centers. We'll need to know the territory if we're going to move around safely."

As dawn approached, Josef and Daniel loaded their small packs into the truck. The rest of us would remain at the farm, planning and preparing for whatever they brought back.

"Be careful," I told them as they climbed into the cab. "The world's still burning out there."

Josef's smile was grim. "We've been burned before. We know how to heal."

I watched the truck disappear into the morning mist, carrying two of our family toward an uncertain future. Behind me, the farmhouse waited with its stolen warmth and hidden radio.

We'd survived the camps. We'd escaped the march. We'd found safety and lost it and found it again.

Now we were planning to become something else entirely.

The maps spread across the kitchen table showed us a country in chaos, armies moving like pieces on a board too large to comprehend. But somewhere in that chaos were the men who'd built our cages, and somewhere in those banks was the wealth they'd stolen from the dead.

For the first time since liberation, we had more than survival.

We had purpose.

25

The Dresdner Bank Job

The truck coughed to life in the gray dawn, and I watched Josef and Daniel disappear into the winter landscape with a mixture of hope and terror. Four days stretched ahead of us like an eternity.

Wolf, Rivka, Dr. Levi and I spent those days studying the maps Josef had left behind, marking potential escape routes and safe houses. But mostly we waited, starting at every sound, wondering if our family would return at all.

When the truck finally rumbled back into the barn on the fourth evening, Josef and Daniel looked like different men. Not just the exhaustion of the journey, but something harder in their eyes.

"Krakow's in chaos," Josef said as we gathered around the kitchen table. "Russians control the east side, Germans still hold the west. Fighting in the streets."

Daniel set down a canvas bag that clinked metallically. "But chaos has advantages."

Josef emptied his own satchel: lock picks, glass cutters, small hammers, chemical vials, and what looked like professional burglary tools. "Met some old contacts. Black market dealers who remember me from Berlin."

"And this," Daniel added, producing a German Luger pistol and two clips of ammunition. "From a dead SS officer."

Dr. Levi picked up the gun with clinical precision, checking the mechanism. "Just a couple of weapons between the six of us."

"Better than none," Wolf said. "What about the banks?"

Josef spread a hand-drawn map across the table. "Three Dresdner branches within fifty kilometers. This one in Breslau is our best target." He pointed to a small building sketched in careful detail. "Small staff, light security, processes local business accounts."

"How do you know all this?" I asked.

Josef's smile was grim. "Heinrich Mollenhoff. Used to fence stolen goods for me in Berlin. Now he's running black market currency exchange. He cased the bank last month for his own purposes."

"And you trust him?" Rivka's police instincts were sharp.

"I trust his greed. Paid him well for the information."

Daniel opened a notebook filled with his precise handwriting. "Five staff members. Manager with a limp, two tellers, one guard during the day, cleaning woman at night. No alarm system yet installed."

"Yet?" Wolf caught the word.

"They're planning to upgrade security next month. We have a window."

Dr. Levi studied the sketched floor plan. "This vault... how do we access it?"

Josef's hands trembled slightly as he held up the lock picks. "In Sachsenhausen, before they sent me to Birkenau, I worked in the administrative building. Learned to open filing cabinets when the guards weren't watching." He flexed his fingers. "Locks are locks."

The simplicity of it terrified me. "Josef, a bank vault isn't a filing cabinet."

"It's not Fort Knox either," he replied. "Small branch, older building. Mollenhoff says it's a Mosler safe from the twenties. I've opened them before."

Over the next three days, we planned with desperate intensity. Wolf sketched surveillance routes around the bank. Rivka worked out timing for guard rotations. Daniel measured cloth and thread, preparing disguises that would make us look like ordinary citizens instead of escaped prisoners.

I practiced German phrases for different scenarios, while Dr. Levi studied the building's layout for medical emergencies - both ours and potential victims'.

But planning and executing were different universes.

The morning of the robbery, my hands shook so badly I could barely button my coat. We'd stolen better clothes from the German's wardrobe, but they hung loose on our still-skeletal frames.

"Remember," I told the group as we prepared to leave the farm, "we're not killers unless we have no choice."

"We're already killers," Wolf said quietly. "Drexler and the farmer proved that."

The drive to Breslau took two hours through back roads clogged with refugees fleeing the Russian advance. Our truck looked like any other military vehicle pressed into civilian service.

By the time we reached the city outskirts, my stomach was churning with more than hunger.

Breslau wore the war like scar tissue. Bombed buildings, boarded windows, and the constant smell of smoke. German forces still controlled the city center, but barely. Soviet artillery rumbled in the distance.

Josef parked three blocks from the bank. "Last chance to change our minds," he said.

No one moved to leave.

The Dresdner Bank branch squatted between a bakery and a shuttered bookshop, its granite facade speaking of prewar confidence. Through the windows, I could see exactly what Daniel had described: two teller windows, one occupied. A guard by the door, reading a newspaper.

"God help us," Daniel whispered.

Wolf squeezed his shoulder. "God helps those who help themselves."

Josef and Daniel would enter through the front as planned customers. Wolf and I would circle to the service entrance. Dr. Levi would position himself across the street with a clear view of both exits. Rivka would create a distraction if needed.

My heart hammered against my ribs as Wolf and I walked casually toward the alley behind the bank. Every German uniform on the street made me want to run.

The service door was exactly where Josef's contact had said it would be. Wolf knelt with the lock picks, his con man's hands steadier than mine had ever been.

"Got it," he breathed.

We slipped into a narrow corridor that reeked of cigarette smoke and fear. Through thin walls, we could hear Josef's voice at the front counter.

"I need access to my safety deposit box," he was saying in perfect German.

Wolf and I crept toward the manager's office, following the floor plan burned into our memories. Behind Hitler's portrait hung a small safe, just as described.

Then everything went wrong.

"Wolfgang Adler," a voice said loudly in the main lobby. "I know that name."

Wolf and I froze. Through the office doorway, we could see a bank clerk staring at Josef with growing recognition.

"You sold my father a painting," the clerk continued, his voice rising. "In 1938. It was a fake."

Josef's face went white. Wrong identity, wrong city, wrong life coming back to destroy him.

"I think you have me confused with someone else," Josef said, but his voice cracked like thin ice.

The clerk's hand moved toward what had to be an alarm button.

In the office, Wolf grabbed my arm. "We abort. Now."

But before we could move, the front door opened. Three Wehrmacht officers entered, bringing cold wind and the authority of the dying Reich.

One of them glanced at Dr. Levi through the window and frowned.

"Shit," I whispered.

Wolf was already working on the safe, his hands moving with desperate speed. "We're committed now."

The safe opened with a soft click. Inside: documents, some Reichsmarks, and a small velvet bag that clinked with the sound of jewelry.

"Jewish assets," Wolf breathed, recognizing what we were looking at.

In the main lobby, Josef made his decision. He grabbed the clerk's wrist as the man reached for the alarm.

"Don't," Josef said quietly, but with the voice of someone who'd learned violence in darker places than this one.

Daniel stepped forward, blocking the guards' view of the struggle.

One of the Wehrmacht officers was studying Dr. Levi through the window with growing interest. He said something to his companions and started toward the door.

Rivka saw it happening. She burst into the bank, deliberately stumbling into the dozing guard.

"Help!" she cried in broken German. "Thieves! In the market!"

The guard jumped up, confused. The officers turned toward the commotion.

Josef used the distraction to force the terrified clerk toward the vault area. "Open it," he hissed. "Or people die."

My legs felt like water as Wolf and I crept through the chaos toward our escape route. The small safe's contents burned in my coat pocket.

The suspicious officer was no longer fooled by Rivka's distraction. He approached Dr. Levi with his hand on his holster.

"Your papers," he demanded.

Dr. Levi hesitated, then slowly reached into his coat. "I served in the Great War," he said with dignity. "Perhaps you remember Dr. Levi from the surgical corps?"

The officer's eyes widened slightly. Recognition and confusion warred in his face.

"I operated on Colonel Weber's son," Dr. Levi continued quietly. "In 1939. The boy lived because of these hands."

The officer wavered, caught between duty and memory.

Josef had the vault open now, the clerk trembling beside him with Daniel's hand on his shoulder. Safety deposit boxes lined one wall. Stacks of currency sat behind a metal cage.

"Take what we can carry," Josef whispered to Daniel. "Quickly."

But Josef's hands were shaking now, the reality of armed robbery hitting him like a physical blow. Documents scattered as he fumbled with the boxes.

Daniel, surprisingly, was steadier. His tailor's precision served him well as he systematically emptied boxes of jewelry and currency.

The Wehrmacht officer made his decision about Dr. Levi. "Stay where you are," he ordered, then turned back toward the bank entrance.

Wolf and I reached the service door. "Go," he urged. "I'll cover Josef and Daniel."

"We stay together," I said, though every instinct screamed to run.

Inside, the situation was deteriorating rapidly. The bank manager had emerged from his office, noticed his missing clerk, and was asking loud questions.

One of the officers finally understood that something was wrong. He drew his pistol.

"Everyone on the ground! Now!"

Josef and Daniel heard the commotion. "Time's up," Daniel said, stuffing the last handful of documents into his coat.

They ran for the service exit, leaving the bound clerk in the vault.

The officer fired, but his shot went wide as Rivka deliberately fell against him.

Wolf waited at the corridor entrance, waving Josef and Daniel through. "Move! Move!"

We burst through the service door into the alley, four people running for their lives through the narrow passages of a city at war.

Behind us, alarms began wailing.

Dr. Levi appeared at the mouth of the alley, walking quickly but not running. "This way," he called. "I know these streets."

We followed him through a maze of bombed buildings and rubble-filled lots, our stolen goods weighing us down like guilt.

Rivka caught up to us three blocks later, breathing hard but smiling grimly. "Got away clean," she panted. "Told them the thieves ran toward the river."

We reached our truck as the first police vehicles screamed past, heading in the wrong direction.

Josef's hands shook so badly he couldn't start the engine. Wolf took over, coaxing the truck to life with the same steady competence he'd shown with the locks.

We drove in silence through the back roads, each lost in our own thoughts about what we'd just done. What we'd become.

Night had fallen when we finally reached the farm. In the kitchen, by candlelight, we spread our take across the wooden table.

Reichsmarks, jewelry, documents, and Swiss bank account numbers. More wealth than any of us had seen since before the war.

"Not bad for amateurs," Wolf said, but his voice lacked its usual confidence.

Daniel sorted the jewelry with trembling fingers. "I thought I was going to be sick there."

Josef stared at his hands, which had finally stopped shaking. "When that clerk recognized me... I thought we were dead."

"We almost were," I said. "A dozen times."

Dr. Levi bandaged a cut on Wolf's hand where he'd scraped it on the safe. "We learned something today. We're not professionals. We're just desperate people doing desperate things."

Rivka studied the documents Josef had grabbed. "Transfer records. Account numbers. Names and addresses." She looked up at us. "This could be valuable after the war. Evidence."

"Evidence of what?" Daniel asked.

"Of who stole what from whom," I said quietly. "Who needs to pay it back."

Wolf loaded the Luger with practiced movements. "There are other banks. Other branches."

"And we'll be better prepared next time," Josef added, flexing his fingers. "We know what to expect now."

But I could see the toll in all their faces. The bank job had changed us, pushed us further from who we'd been before the camps, before the war, before we learned that survival sometimes required becoming something you never thought you could be.

"What are we doing this for?" Daniel asked into the silence.

The question hung in the air like smoke from the dying fire.

"Justice," I said finally.

"Evidence," Rivka added.

"Money to track down the ones who escaped," Josef said.

Dr. Levi's stare was distant. "Perhaps all of those. Perhaps none. Perhaps we're just trying to feel human again."

The candle flame burned low, shadows dancing across our hollow cheeks. Outside, snow continued falling, covering our tracks and the tracks of a world still at war with itself.

We'd survived the camps. We'd escaped the march. We'd found safety and lost it and found it again.

Now we'd committed our first real crime, stolen back a small piece of what had been taken from people like us.

And we were just getting started.

Wolf blew out the candle, plunging the kitchen into darkness. "Next time, we will do better."

In the darkness, Josef's voice was steadier than it had been all day. "Next time, we'll be ready."

They went to their sleeping areas, each carrying their share of the day's haul and the weight of what we'd become.

Tomorrow would bring new plans, new preparations, new questions about how far we were willing to go.

But tonight, we'd proven something to ourselves: we were more than survivors now.

We were hunters.

26
The Kraków Opportunity

The candles flickered in the drafty farmhouse as Wolf sorted Reichsmarks into neat stacks on the scarred wooden table. The paper felt crisp between his fingers, still carrying the metallic scent of the bank vault. Outside, a cold wind drove snow against the rattling windows like fingers tapping for entry.

"Just over twenty-six thousand Reichsmarks," Wolf announced. Three days since their Dresdner Bank job, and the roads were still impassable. Good for hiding fugitives.

Daniel smoothed his stolen SS coat, the black wool rough against his tailor's hands. He whistled low. "Not bad for three days' work."

Dr. Blum cleaned surgical instruments by the fire, his movements steady despite the tremor that hadn't left his hands since Birkenau. The beard he'd grown transformed him from a walking skeleton back to something resembling a doctor. Steam rose from the basin of hot water, carrying the smell of carbolic soap.

A sound outside made them all freeze, a crack that might have been wind or might have been footsteps.

Rivka's hand found the knife in her belt. At the window, she peered through frost-covered glass that turned the world into crystal fragments. "Just wind. Brenner's not going anywhere."

Miriam watched Dr. Blum work, noting how he still scraped beneath his fingernails with religious precision. Dirt from the shallow grave they'd dug for *SS-Rottenführer* Kurt Brenner. The earth had been thawing from solid, requiring picks and shovels that left blisters none of them mentioned.

Josef sat apart at the small desk, methodical as always. He scraped beneath his own nails with a metal tool, discarding invisible evidence fleck by fleck.

Wolf finished dividing the money into equal shares, the bills making soft rustling sounds. "Modest haul, all things considered."

"Modest compared to what's in Kraków."

Five pairs of eyes turned toward Josef. The room went still except for the pop and hiss of burning wood. Even the wind seemed to pause.

Wolf's jaw worked like he was chewing something bitter. "What the hell are you talking about?"

Josef reached for his leather satchel with deliberate slowness. "Dresdner was a test," he said, placing it on the table with a soft thud that seemed to echo. "To see if we could work together. I've always had a bigger target in mind."

Daniel's neck flushed red above his collar. "What else haven't you told us?"

Wolf slammed his fist on the table, sending Reichsmarks flying like startled birds. The sound made everyone jump except Josef. "After everything we've been through? After we trusted you with our lives?"

Josef's voice stayed level, but his knuckles whitened around the satchel's leather handle. "Not held back. Waited." He spread hand-drawn maps across the wooden surface with the precision of a man laying out surgical instruments. "If Breslau had failed, would Kraków even be possible?"

Rivka left the window, her boots creaking against the floorboards. "What's in Kraków that's worth risking what we've already gained?"

Josef met each of their stares in turn. In the candlelight, his face looked carved from shadow. "The future. Our future."

Dr. Blum studied the drawings, his finger tracing building outlines like he was examining a patient's chart. "Commerzbank Kraków. What makes this so special that you'd gamble our lives?"

Josef got that distant look, the same expression he'd worn in the barracks when planning their escape. "I worked Operation Bernhard in the camp. Counterfeiting for the SS. When you handle enough shipment manifests, you notice patterns." His voice took on the flat tone of someone reciting facts to avoid feeling them. "Kraków kept appearing. Always the Commerzbank."

Wolf pushed back from the table so hard his chair scraped against the floor. "You bastard. You knew all along, didn't you? You planned this from the beginning."

Josef pulled documents from his satchel, papers yellowed with age and handling. The candlelight made the ink look like dried blood. "These were on the manager's desk at Dresdner. Transfer orders. Shipment records." He arranged them with mathematical precision. "Breslau was just a collection point. Everything valuable went to Kraków."

Miriam moved closer, examining the papers with the careful attention she'd once given to manuscripts. The German was bureaucratic, cold, the language of systematic theft. "These are genuine." Her gaze locked with Josef's. "But you knew before we ever hit Dresdner, didn't you?"

Josef nodded once.

"You used us." Wolf's temple vein pulsed like a trapped animal. "We were your fucking test subjects."

"Did I?" Josef's eyes flicked toward the barn where Brenner lay buried under three feet of frozen earth. "Who suggested killing the officer instead of taking him prisoner? Who said we needed to send a message?"

Wolf's mouth opened, then closed. The accusation hung in the air like smoke.

"I asked you to be my partners," Josef said quietly. "Now I'm asking again. For a much bigger prize." He pulled out one last document, handling it like it might explode. "I processed this order in Birkenau eighteen months ago. Read it."

Miriam took the paper. The first line stole her breath and made her sit down hard on the wooden bench. "Currency printing plates. British pounds, Swiss francs, Swedish krona, American dollars."

"Jesus Christ," Daniel whispered.

"More than money," Josef said, his voice gaining intensity. "The power to create currency. Identity papers. Passports. Everything we need to become whoever we choose to be."

The fire split a log with a crack that made Daniel jump and spill wine down his shirt front.

"Why now?" Dr. Blum asked, setting down his instruments with deliberate care. "Why reveal this now when we're finally safe?"

Josef's finger traced a route on the map, following roads that led west toward uncertainty. "Soviet advance. The Germans are evacuating assets west. My sources say the plates and other vault contents will move to Germany in three days."

"Three days?" Daniel's voice cracked like a teenager's. "That's insane. Breslau took weeks to plan, and even then we nearly got ourselves killed."

"Sometimes panic creates the best opportunities," Josef said. "The evacuation means confusion. Bank personnel reassigned. Guards who don't know the procedures. Right now, they're vulnerable in ways they'll never be again."

Wolf stood and began pacing the small room like a caged wolf. "How long have you known? How long have you been planning this while we thought we were partners?"

"Since before we escaped the camp."

Rivka spat on the floor. The sound was sharp and final. "You didn't trust us. Even after we killed for you."

The room went quiet except for the wind and Wolf's pacing. Their shared killing of Drexler had bonded them beyond words, creating trust through blood. Now Josef threatened to shatter it.

"I trust you with my life," Josef said, and for the first time his voice carried emotion. "The timing wasn't right until now. You needed practice working together, we all did. We needed Dresdner's money to finance this operation. And we needed the chaos of German retreat for cover."

"What about security?" Rivka asked, her police instincts cutting through the emotion. "If this place is so valuable, it won't be guarded by farmers with hunting rifles."

"Regular German personnel transferred out yesterday. They're using local collaborators as replacements. Poles, Ukrainians. Desperate men with nothing left to lose when the Russians arrive."

"Which makes them more dangerous, not less," Rivka pointed out. "Men like that don't follow procedures. They shoot first and ask questions later."

"Exactly." Josef pointed to building blueprints that looked hand-copied from memory. "Service entrance to the vault level. Manager's private entrance in back. Four shifts, three men each. Two extras at key positions because of the evacuation, but no coordination between them."

"Can you crack it?" Daniel asked. "Really? Or is this another one of your educated guesses?"

Josef's face stayed neutral, but his eyes flashed with something that might have been pride or might have been desperation. "Yes."

Dr. Blum studied the documents, his medical training making him examine details others might miss. "The risk is enormous. Even compared to Dresdner. We're already hunted. If we're caught with counterfeiting plates..." He didn't finish the sentence.

"The reward matches the risk," Josef said, meeting each of their gazes in turn. "With that vault's contents, we don't just survive. We prosper."

He looked at Daniel. "That tailor shop in Tel Aviv you told me about when you thought I was sleeping. This makes it real."

To Dr. Blum: "Your medical practice. Your new identity. No more hiding what you were before the war."

A nod to Wolf: "The business empire you've already built in your head. I've heard you planning it at night."

To Rivka: "Complete disappearance. No one remembers the Warsaw police officer who knew too much."

Finally, to Miriam: "Your translations don't have to stay hidden anymore."

Miriam's breath caught. She'd kept her nighttime work secret, translating Polish poetry to Hebrew by candlelight when she thought everyone was asleep.

"How did you know?" she whispered.

Josef's mask slipped for just a moment, revealing exhaustion and something that might have been loneliness. "I stayed alive by watching everything. Noticing things others missed. It's not trust, it's survival."

Wolf stopped pacing and turned to face him. "The timeline's impossible. Three days isn't enough."

"Tonight for reconnaissance. Tomorrow to prepare. Execute the following night."

"What if they've already moved the plates?" Daniel asked. "What if your sources are wrong?"

"Then we walk away with Dresdner's money and find another opportunity. But the documents show a specific schedule, and my contact confirmed the timeline yesterday." Josef's voice carried absolute certainty. "I believe the plates are still there."

Dr. Blum cleaned his glasses with trembling fingers. "This isn't just theft anymore. It's escalation. Someone will hunt for these plates when they disappear."

"Who?" Josef challenged. "Nazis who are fleeing west ahead of the Russians? Soviets with their hands full establishing control? Western Allies who are still hundreds of kilometers away? We'll be gone before any real investigation starts."

Wolf stopped pacing and stared at the maps. "The speed bothers me. But Christ, I see the opportunity." He looked at the others. "We should discuss this. Without you, Josef."

Josef stood, gathering his documents except for the map. "I'll check the perimeter. Decide before I return."

He left them sitting around the candlelit table and walked into the freezing night, taking their certainties with him.

The door clicked shut. For three heartbeats, silence except for settling wood in the fire and the distant howl of wind through broken shutters.

Wolf hit the table with his open palm. "Son of a bitch played us from the very beginning."

"Does it matter if we all profit?" Daniel asked, but his voice lacked conviction. "Three days is madness, though. Pure madness."

"We succeeded at Dresdner," Dr. Blum pointed out. "Passed two checkpoints with Josef's forgeries. The man knows what he's doing."

Rivka faced them, her hand still resting on her knife handle. "Desperate men are more dangerous than time constraints. I've seen what frightened collaborators do when they're cornered."

"Can we trust him?" Wolf asked bluntly. "He's admitted withholding information. What else is he hiding?"

Miriam considered this, staring into the candle flame. "He tells us what he thinks we need when he thinks we need it."

"That's not trust," Wolf said. "That's manipulation."

"It's survival," Dr. Blum said quietly. "Josef outlasted two and a half years in Birkenau by keeping secrets. Liberation doesn't erase those instincts overnight."

Daniel ran fingers through his hair, leaving it standing at odd angles. "Why involve us at all? With his skills and connections, Josef could do this alone. Take all the profit."

"No." Rivka shook her head. "Even Josef can't be everywhere at once. Dresdner proved that. He needs us, even if he won't admit it."

"This isn't just about money," Miriam said slowly, pieces clicking together in her mind. "It's power. With those plates, we can create new identities, rewrite our histories completely." She studied each face in the candlelight. "Everyone here wants to start over, become someone the camps never touched."

Dr. Blum nodded, his expression thoughtful. "They took our identities, reduced us to numbers tattooed on our arms. Using their tools to rebuild ourselves, there's justice in that."

"I'm in," Miriam said suddenly. "Josef's right about the timing. This chance won't come again."

"Agreed," Dr. Blum said. "But I want detailed contingencies for everything that could go wrong."

Daniel exhaled slowly, the sound carrying all his doubts. "Yes. Though I hate the timeline with every fiber of my being."

Rivka gave a single nod. "The reward justifies the risk. And I trust my ability to handle whatever goes wrong."

All eyes turned to Wolf. He looked at each of them, then at the money stacked on the table, then at the maps Josef had left behind.

"You're all insane," he said finally. Then: "Fine. Yes. But we do this my way. Backup plans for everything."

The door opened, admitting Josef and winter air that made the candles gutter. He read the room with those neutral eyes that missed nothing.

214

"We start immediately," he said, returning to the table as if he'd never doubted their answer. "Wolf and I handle vault access. Rivka, your police experience is crucial for reading the collaborators."

He handed her an identity card. "Tomorrow you visit the bank as a customer. Helena Nowak, Warsaw banker's widow. Observe procedures, guard rotations, transportation schedules."

Wolf glared at him. "You really did plan this from the beginning. You even had her papers ready."

Josef handed Daniel a handwritten list. "Locksmith shop, three blocks from the bank. The owner was a criminal before the war, smuggling, black market trading. Tell him Josef from Berlin sent you."

Dr. Blum raised an eyebrow. "You have connections everywhere, don't you?"

"Not everywhere. Just where they matter." Josef turned to him. "Emergency medical plans. Escape routes if we get separated. And..." He hesitated. "Prepare for casualties. Ours or theirs."

The night passed in planning, transforming Josef's outline into operational reality. Maps marked with escape routes, timing sequences developed down to the minute, assignments distributed based on each person's skills. By dawn they had something that resembled a workable plan.

Miriam sat across from Josef as the others finally sought sleep, unable to quiet her racing thoughts.

"You never mentioned Kraków at the beginning," she said softly. "When we were planning Dresdner, you acted like that was everything."

Josef's hands kept moving, pen scratching across paper in the candlelight. "You would have refused. All of you. Too big, too dangerous after one small success."

"Trust works both ways, Josef."

He stopped writing and looked at her, really looked at her for the first time in days. "Trust is currency, Miriam. You spend it when it yields the highest return."

"We're not in Birkenau anymore."

"Aren't we?" he asked quietly, glancing toward the window where dawn was breaking gray and cold over the shallow grave beyond. "The world works by the same rules, just with different uniforms. Survival to the strong. Survival to the prepared."

He resumed his work, but his voice stayed soft. "They took everything from us. Families. Homes. Names. Our very selves." He met her eyes again. "Those plates are tools to reclaim what was stolen. They erased our past. With these plates, we write our future."

Dawn light crept across the Polish countryside, turning the snow the color of old bones. In three days, they would either have the power to reshape their destinies or be dead in a ditch outside Kraków. No middle ground existed in this new world they'd inherited.

Through the window, a crow settled on the disturbed earth behind the barn. Josef and Miriam watched it in silence, sharing the knowledge that their futures would be written in the papers they were about to steal, or in their blood on the bank floor.

27

The Kraków Heist

Gray fog spread across Kraków's streets like smoke from a dying fire as the truck stopped three blocks from the Commerzbank. Stefan, their locksmith ally, had been dropped off earlier, his weathered case in hand, shoulders hunched beneath a worn maintenance uniform that smelled of machine oil and old tobacco.

Wolf checked his watch, the glass fogged with condensation. 7:28. Stefan would enter in two minutes.

Josef's fingers traced Wolf's SS collar, the silver threads cold under his touch. "They'll notice the uniform first, then your confidence. Give them nothing to investigate."

Wolf nodded, his face hardening into the mask he'd learned to wear. Beside him, Daniel straightened his own subordinate officer's collar. The black fabric settled on Wolf's shoulders, and his body straightened automatically. Necessary. Revolting.

"Remember, you're Wilhelm Richter," Josef said quietly, his breath visible in the morning cold. "Daniel, you're Dietrich Müller."

"Wilhelm Richter, *Sturmbannführer*," Wolf said, his voice already taking on the clipped authority of the SS.

"Dietrich Müller, *Untersturmführer*," Daniel replied, though his hands trembled slightly as he adjusted his cap.

"Miriam and I follow at 8:50," Josef continued, checking his forged papers one last time. "Blum and Rivka stay with the truck unless signaled."

Rivka checked her pistol, the metal warming under her fingers. "If anything changes, I handle it." She slipped the weapon into her coat, feeling its weight against her ribs.

Dr. Blum checked his medical bag. Bandages and morphine instead of his usual instruments. His hands were steady now, the surgeon's calm returning when lives hung in the balance.

The church bell rang the half hour, its bronze voice cutting through the fog. Stefan shuffled through the service door, playing his part perfectly.

Stefan had been Warsaw's finest locksmith before the war, before they'd burned his shop and killed his apprentice son. Now his skills served darker purposes, but the money Josef paid would let him disappear into the chaos of postwar Europe. Sometimes survival meant becoming someone else entirely.

The service entrance worker squinted at Stefan's work order through sleep-crusted eyes. "Boiler inspection?"

Stefan kept his expression empty, just another tradesman grinding through another job. "Special order from Hauptmann Fischer. The transport team needs the heating system checked before the officers arrive."

The worker glanced past Stefan to the empty street, his breath steaming in the cold air. "Christ, just hurry. The Germans are breathing down my neck about the evacuation."

Stefan entered, his shuffle masking sharp eyes that catalogued security positions. The corridor ahead led straight to the vault, exactly as Josef's drawings showed. Twenty-three years of opening locks had taught him to read buildings like blueprints.

In the utility room beside the vault, Stefan opened his case. Locksmith's instruments of extraordinary quality, tools he'd crafted himself in better days. He began working on the access panel to the vault antechamber, his fingers remembering old skills.

The black Mercedes arrived at 8:45, its engine purring with Teutonic precision. SS insignia made pedestrians scatter into doorways like roaches fleeing light. Everyone knew the Soviets were coming. The Germans knew it too, which made them more dangerous than cornered animals.

Wolf emerged first. Tall, black uniform stark against the morning gray, silver death's head insignia gleaming wetly in the fog. Daniel followed two steps behind, a portfolio tucked under his arm containing impeccable forgeries.

218

The entrance guards stiffened like puppets jerked by strings. Wolf ignored them completely, his gaze fixed on something beyond their comprehension.

All movement stopped when they entered the lobby. Conversations died mid-sentence. Even the ticking of the wall clock seemed to pause.

The bank manager appeared, nervous sweat breaking through his professional smile despite the morning chill. "*Sturmbannführer* Richter, what an unexpected honor. We would have prepared if we'd known of your visit."

Wolf let the silence stretch until the manager's face flushed red above his starched collar. "Advance notice defeats the purpose." His tone could freeze blood in January. "I'm assessing security before today's transport. I need immediate vault access."

The manager blinked rapidly, his Adam's apple bobbing. "Of course, but protocols require..."

His voice trailed off as Wolf's stare intensified, pale eyes like winter ice.

Daniel produced the forged identification, every stamp and signature flawless. "Would you prefer explaining to *SS Oberführer* Müller why his direct orders were questioned? He's particularly concerned about security breaches."

The manager stepped backward, swaying slightly. "No, that won't be necessary. Please, proceed to the vault immediately."

Wolf maintained his bearing throughout the tour, noting guard positions and staff reactions. Every employee they passed pressed themselves against walls, fear radiating from them like heat from a furnace. Their terror fed his performance.

Josef and Miriam arrived at the staff entrance at 8:52 to find a locked door and armed guard whose eyes held the desperate alertness of a man expecting bad news.

"No personnel in or out except through main security." The guard's hand hovered near his holster. "Manager's orders since yesterday."

Josef nodded at his forged employee credentials. "Security protocols for the transport. We'll use the main entrance."

As they walked around the building, Miriam touched his arm. "This changes things. Wolf and Daniel are already inside."

"We adapt," Josef said quietly, but she could see the tension in his jaw.

Inside, Wolf was berating the bank manager in the lobby's center while Daniel watched with the impassive expression of a man accustomed to witnessing brutality.

"Incompetence," Wolf's voice carried through the marble space like the crack of a whip. "All nonessential personnel out immediately. This building will be empty in twenty minutes."

Staff members hurried away, some running for the exits. Papers scattered from desks. A secretary knocked over her inkwell in her haste.

Josef and Miriam approached the reception desk. Josef went cold when he saw Hermann Gruber, a bank examiner from Berlin, at the currency counter. Gruber had worked a forgery case connected to Josef before the war. The man's memory for faces was legendary.

Recognition would destroy everything.

Josef turned his face away and addressed the receptionist softly. "We're here for the special inventory. Vault section 4B."

The receptionist's hands shook as she fumbled through papers. "You're not on today's list."

"Check again," Miriam said firmly, her voice carrying quiet authority. "Herr Schreiber personally added us yesterday for transport preparation."

As the receptionist rechecked, Josef sensed movement. Gruber was walking toward him, his bureaucrat's instincts apparently triggered. Josef's pulse jumped like a trapped bird.

In the utility room, Stefan finished bypassing the alarm and began modifying the vault system. He could hear Wolf's voice, higher pitched now, trying to manage Wilhelm Richter's performance. The diversion was working, but the vault mechanism was more complex than expected.

Then he encountered a backup security system exceeding all intelligence predictions. Fifteen minutes minimum vault access even with all requirements met. The Germans had been more paranoid than Josef anticipated.

Only the bank manager could override it.

Stefan tapped the established pattern on the wall. Three quick, pause, two. The signal for complications.

Wolf heard the tapping during the manager's briefing about transportation schedules. His face showed nothing as he interrupted the man mid-sentence.

"Enough talk. I need to inspect the vault mechanism personally. Open it."

The manager's face drained of color until he looked like a walking corpse. "Sir, there are procedures. The timing mechanism requires..."

"Are you suggesting the SS security team should wait for your bureaucratic obstacles?" Wolf stepped closer, close enough that the manager could smell the soap he'd used that morning. The man whimpered. "Perhaps you're hiding something?"

"No! Of course not." The manager fumbled with his keys, dropping them twice before his shaking fingers could grip them properly. "Protocol demands dual authentication. The timing mechanism..."

"Override it. Now."

Daniel positioned himself between the manager and the desk telephone, his hand resting casually near his holster.

The manager inserted a brass key into a panel beside the vault door with trembling fingers. "The delay will be disabled, but I need head cashier authorization."

"Summon him. Immediately."

The head cashier hurried over, his breakfast still visible on his chin, and entered his code. Heavy mechanical thuds sounded as the vault locks disengaged, each one like a gunshot in the marble silence.

"You and the cashier stay here," Wolf instructed, his voice brooking no argument. "*Untersturmführer* Müller will document procedures while I inspect the interior."

Wolf entered the vault quickly, checking the utility room wall. Stefan's eye appeared through a small hole he'd drilled.

"Time delay triggered. But the plates aren't here."

Wolf's stomach dropped like a stone down a well. "What?"

Stefan pointed to a massive door at the vault's rear, steel reinforced with what looked like ship's armor. "Secondary security room. Special materials in high security storage. Additional keys required."

Wolf returned to the officials, his mind racing through options. "Security arrangements are inadequate. I need immediate access to the high security storage."

The manager went beyond pale into a sickly gray shade. "Sir, that area requires authorization from..."

"My authorization comes directly from Berlin." Wolf's voice dropped to a menacing whisper that seemed to leach warmth from the air. "Would you prefer I report this obstruction to SS Headquarters?"

The manager's knees buckled visibly. "No, please, I'll open it immediately."

Minutes later, the manager unlocked the secondary vault with keys that rattled against the metal. A small room with superior security, walls lined with metal containers that gleamed under electric lights.

Wolf held the manager's gaze until the man retreated like a whipped dog. "Wait outside the main vault. *Untersturmführer* Müller will record inventory."

Alone in the secure area, Wolf and Daniel worked fast, their movements urgent but controlled. The cases revealed printing plates by the dozens. British pounds, American dollars, Swiss francs, plates for identity documents and official stamps. The tools of financial resurrection.

"There," Daniel whispered, his tailor's eye cataloguing the treasure. "Now we need Josef and the others."

Outside in the lobby, Josef's situation was deteriorating rapidly. Hermann Gruber now stood directly behind him, close enough that Josef could smell the man's breakfast sausage on his breath.

"Excuse me," Gruber said, his voice carrying the persistence of a man who made his living noticing details. "Haven't we met? You look remarkably familiar."

Josef turned with forced surprise, arranging his features into polite confusion. "I don't believe so, sir. I recently transferred from the Łódź branch."

Gruber frowned, his bureaucrat's memory working like a filing system. "No, I'm certain. Berlin, perhaps? 1938 or '39? You were involved in some currency irregularities..."

Before Josef could answer, Wolf's voice cut through the bank like a blade. "Security protocol! Everyone out! Now!"

The confusion allowed Josef and Miriam to slip toward the vault area as Gruber lost track of them in the sudden exodus of frightened employees.

Across the street, Rivka watched through her newspaper, the print blurring as she focused on movement patterns. A man exiting the bank caught her attention. He moved with purpose rather than the panicked confusion of the other employees, his eyes scanning the street with professional alertness.

The man hurried to the staff door, key already in hand before he reached it.

Rivka folded the paper as Dr. Blum tensed beside her in the truck's cab. "Something's wrong. I'm going in."

She crossed the street, hand reaching for the Walther P38 in her coat, its grip worn smooth by her fingers during sleepless nights.

In the vault's secure room, Wolf and Daniel faced complex locking systems on the protective containers, mechanisms that would have challenged a master safecracker.

"We need Josef," Wolf said, sweat beading on his forehead despite the cold. "And more time."

Josef and Miriam reached the vault entrance, joining them in the steel-walled chamber.

"We have a problem," Josef said without preamble. "Hermann Gruber, bank examiner from Berlin. I knew him before the war. He was investigating some of my earlier work."

Wolf cursed under his breath. "Where is he now?"

"I don't know, but he won't give up easily. Men like that never do."

"Then we accelerate." Wolf's decision was instant, born from years of making life-or-death choices. "Daniel secures the entry. Miriam helps Josef with the plates. I keep the manager occupied."

They worked urgently to identify the highest value plates, Josef's hands moving with the reverence of a man handling religious artifacts. "These passport plates could create new identities for dozens of survivors."

A disturbance outside the vault stopped their work. Shouting, the sound of running feet. A Nazi loyalist had snuck back inside, triggered by the suspicious inspection procedures and his own paranoid instincts.

The man broke free from Daniel's restraining hand and sprinted toward the alarm station. "Imposters!" he shouted, his voice cracking with hysteria. "They're imposters! Call security!"

Daniel's strike sent him down, but he broke free and raced toward the manager's office telephone, driven by fanatic determination.

Rivka moved through service corridors, hearing the struggle ahead, her police training mapping the building's layout. Turning the corner, she saw a man sprinting toward administrative offices while Daniel pursued, his SS uniform incongruous with his desperate chase.

If he reached that telephone, the operation failed. Six people would be captured, tortured, executed.

She stepped into the corridor, blocking his path. He stopped abruptly, breathing hard.

"Move," he commanded in German, his voice shrill with authority he didn't possess.

The Walther P38 emerged with its suppressor, the weapon an extension of her will. Before he could speak again, she fired twice. The suppressed shots sounded like books dropping. The man crumpled without another sound, his fanaticism extinguished.

Daniel appeared around the corner, his face pale. "Rivka," he whispered.

"What was necessary." Her voice remained steady as stone. "Hide the body. We have maybe seven minutes."

Wolf maintained his position with the bank manager, knowing departure would destroy his carefully constructed cover. "The transport vehicles will arrive shortly. We should..."

"You take no action without my explicit permission." The manager flinched as if struck. "The security inspection continues."

The lobby security guard approached, his boots echoing on marble. "Herr Manager, there's a problem in the administrative area. Kluge is missing."

Wolf stepped forward, and the guard took a step backward instinctively. "My personnel are conducting complete security sweeps. Standard procedure for sensitive operations."

The guard hesitated, caught between duty and self-preservation. "Should I investigate?"

"Return to your post. Interference with SS security operations would require extensive explanation in Berlin."

Josef and Miriam had finished loading valuable plates into transport cases, the metal containers heavier than they'd expected. Daniel appeared at the vault entrance. "We leave now. Rivka's inside. There's been a situation."

A sharp gunshot echoed inside the bank, the sound carrying clearly through the marble halls.

The security guard had found Rivka in the administrative corridor, her posture among the scattered papers triggering his suspicion and survival instincts.

"Halt. Identification," he demanded, drawing his pistol with the practiced motion of a man who'd done this before.

Rivka evaluated instantly. She began raising her hands in apparent compliance, then dropped to one knee as he approached. He fired through the space she'd occupied seconds before, the bullet chipping marble from the wall.

Rivka closed the distance before he could redirect his weapon. Police training proved superior to military drill. A wrist strike disabled his gun hand, grappling techniques learned in Warsaw's streets took him down hard.

The guard's eyes widened during their struggle, recognition mixing with hatred in his gaze. "Jew," he said, the word carrying all the venom of the dying Reich.

She pressed her suppressed Walther against his chest and fired twice, feeling his life leave him through the vibration in the steel.

Standing over the body, she looked up to see Josef in the corridor, his face unreadable.

"He's dead," Josef said simply.

"Yes." She met his gaze directly. "We have minutes. Get the others. We're leaving."

Wolf abandoned his inspection charade with the cold efficiency of a man shedding a disguise. "This building is under complete SS control. A security breach has been identified. All personnel remain inside until the threat is neutralized."

The manager's suspicions were increasingly visible despite his terror, his bureaucrat's mind finally beginning to function. "Sir, shouldn't I contact local SS headquarters for additional support?"

"Silence." Wolf's voice dropped to deadly quiet. "Your security incompetence has already caused this breach."

Daniel whispered beside him, "The cases are ready. Josef and Miriam are bringing them out."

Josef and Miriam emerged from the vault carrying metal transport cases, the weight making them move carefully. Rivka followed, blood on her sleeve like a badge of necessity.

The bank manager saw it too, his eyes widening. "Is that blood? What's happening in my bank?"

Wolf made his choice. "You," he snapped at the manager, who jumped like a startled animal. "With me. Now. Everyone else stays put."

He physically guided the trembling manager toward the exit, his hand firm on the man's shoulder. Passing Daniel, Wolf muttered, "Extraction protocol three. Rendezvous point."

Daniel nodded, then moved toward the side door where Stefan waited with the others, his locksmith's case packed and ready.

Outside, Dr. Blum watched from the truck, counting minutes. Twenty-seven minutes total. They'd exceeded that without anyone appearing, and his medical instincts were screaming warnings.

Then he saw movement. Daniel emerged through the main door at a measured pace, playing his role to the end. Josef, Miriam, and Rivka followed, heading toward the eastern extraction point with the deliberate calm of people walking away from an explosion.

"Move," Dr. Blum told the driver. "East one block. Now."

The rendezvous point was a loading dock at an abandoned textile factory, the building's broken windows like dead eyes. The team converged from different directions as the truck arrived, their breath steaming in the cold air.

"Go, go," Wolf ordered as they loaded cases and climbed aboard, the truck springs groaning under the sudden weight. "Head west out of the city."

The truck accelerated through Kraków's streets, its engine noise lost among the sounds of a city preparing for siege.

Nobody spoke until they cleared the city center, the silence heavy with unspoken questions.

"What happened?" Wolf demanded, meeting Rivka's gaze in the truck's dim interior.

"A Nazi loyalist recognized something was wrong. He was heading for the telephone. I stopped him."

"You killed him," Josef said flatly, the words hanging in the air.

"Yes."

"And the guard," Miriam added quietly.

Dr. Blum had gone pale, his medical oath warring with reality. "Two people?"

Rivka showed no weakness, her voice carrying the finality of someone who'd made peace with necessary choices. "Two people who would have seen us all executed. Yes."

Extended silence filled the truck. They'd planned theft, not murder. The distinction seemed academic now.

"It was necessary," Rivka continued, her hands steady on her lap.

"Was it?" Dr. Blum challenged softly. "Did we know we'd become killers ourselves?"

"We already are killers, Levi," Wolf said quietly, his SS uniform a reminder of the roles they'd played. "Everyone in this truck has blood on their hands from the camps. From surviving."

"Not like this," the doctor insisted. "Not calculated execution."

Daniel spoke up, his voice thoughtful. "The guard recognized Rivka as Jewish. Called her 'Jew' with hatred. He would have killed her given the chance."

"Does that make it different?" Josef, who had clubbed Brenner to death, asked with genuine curiosity in his voice. "Where's the line between justice and murder?"

No one had answers. The truck rolled on through the Polish countryside.

Miriam finally broke the silence. "What's done is done. We have the plates. We escaped. Now we decide what comes next."

Wolf nodded, pulling off his SS cap and throwing it to the truck floor. "We stick to the plan. Back to the farmhouse to regroup, then head for the coast. The contact in Gdańsk expects us in five days."

"And from there?" Miriam asked.

"Palestine perhaps, or some better opportunity. We have the tools now to become whoever we choose to be."

The truck carried them away from Kraków, away from the bodies they'd left behind, toward an uncertain future written in stolen ink on forged paper. Behind them, the city disappeared into winter fog, taking their old selves with it.

28

The Promise Remembered

The snow had begun to melt around the farmhouse, though the ground still crunched underfoot. It was the kind of cold that settled into the joints like memory: dull, persistent, impossible to ignore.

Inside, the fire crackled. Not for comfort, just for warmth. They never lit it unless they needed it. The smoke traveled too far.

Miriam sat near the hearth, boots off, ankles crossed, staring at the flames like they held an answer. She hadn't spoken all day. That wasn't unusual. She wasn't the sort to fill a room with chatter, and the others had learned to let the silences breathe.

Wolf cleaned his pistol in the corner, methodical as always. The metal clicked against metal in a rhythm that might have been soothing if you didn't know what the sounds meant. Levi thumbed through a list of names on a torn envelope, his lips moving silently as he read. Daniel sat at the table with a pencil and a map, drawing arrows that had no clear destination. Josef smoked with one hand and sharpened a knife with the other, the blade singing against the whetstone. Rivka, sleeves rolled despite the cold, counted money from the Zurich job, her eyes flicking up at the others every so often, checking the air.

They had pulled it off without blood. That was always the goal now. Money moved. Locks broken. Gold rerouted to their hands instead of the hands that had broken theirs. They didn't speak about it like revenge. Not even like justice. They called it a correction.

The stack of Swiss francs grew under Rivka's fingers. Enough to last them months, maybe a year if they were careful. Enough to disappear completely if they wanted to. The thought hung in the room like smoke.

Miriam stood, finally. She didn't pace. Just moved to the window and looked out. The sky was low and gray, the kind that threatened snow but never delivered. Her reflection stared back from the glass, pale and sharp-angled. She touched the window with her fingertips, feeling the cold seep through.

"I have to go to Germany," she said.

No one moved. The knife stopped singing. The money stopped rustling. Even the fire seemed quiet.

After a moment, Wolf said, without looking up from his pistol, "For what?"

She faced them. Her hands were steady, but something in her eyes wasn't. "I made a promise. In Birkenau. To a woman. Her name was Elsa Rosenberg."

That name meant nothing to the others, but the camp did. The name Birkenau had its own weather. It settled on their shoulders like ash, heavy and gray and impossible to shake off.

"They had a boy," Miriam continued. "David. Three years old when they arrived. Blonde hair, pale skin. Pretty enough to make the guards look twice." She paused, her voice catching on something. "They took him away on the ramp. Said it was for medical care. We both knew what that meant, but she made me promise anyway. If I lived, I would look for him."

Daniel's pencil stopped moving. "You think he's alive?"

"I do."

Josef raised an eyebrow, ash falling from his cigarette. "And if he is, he'd be what, Germanized? Hidden? One of their good Aryan orphans they liked so much?"

"Exactly." Miriam's voice was flat now, matter-of-fact. "He would have fit their image. They would have used him."

Levi spoke quietly, the words dropping into the silence like stones. "*Lebensborn* - the breeding program."

That word stilled the room completely. They'd all heard of it, whispered about in the camps. Children taken, renamed, reconditioned. Taught to forget who they were, if they lived long enough to learn anything at all. A different kind of murder, slower and more thorough.

Wolf finally looked at her, his dark eyes unreadable. "You want to find him."

"I have to."

"And then?"

"Get him out. Whatever it takes."

The silence stretched between them, thick as the smoke from Josef's cigarette. Outside, the wind picked up, rattling the windows. The fire popped, sending sparks up the chimney.

Then Rivka spoke, her voice cutting through the quiet: "You're not doing it alone."

Miriam nodded once, but said nothing more. She didn't need to. The decision had been made the moment she'd spoken Elsa's name.

Wolf stood, stretched his arms above his head until his shoulders popped, then pointed to the table where Daniel's map lay scattered with pencil marks. "We've got contacts. We've got money." He glanced at Josef. "And we've got the best forger this side of hell."

Josef flicked his cigarette into the fire, where it hissed and died. "Of course you do."

"So we do what we always do," Wolf continued. "We plan it. We do it quietly. We do it clean." He looked at each of them in turn. "We find the boy. We bring him home."

"And what about the people who took him?" Daniel asked. His voice was soft, but there was steel underneath.

Miriam's reflection stared back from the window, her face hard as winter ground. "After David is safe," she said, "we settle accounts."

The fire crackled. The wind howled. And somewhere in the ruins of Germany, a little boy who had forgotten his name played with toys that weren't his, in a house that wasn't home, with people who had stolen more than just his childhood.

The promise would be kept. Whatever it cost them all.

29

The Hunt Begins

The train compartment smelled of unwashed bodies and stale cigarettes. Josef sat in the corner, his forged papers declaring him to be Heinrich Mueller, a clerk from the denazification office in Munich. The uniform fit well enough. The briefcase contained enough official stamps and letterheads to convince anyone who didn't look too closely.

He wasn't the only one playing a role.

Three hundred miles north, Wolf and Rivka worked the displaced persons camp outside Hamburg. She wore a Red Cross armband and carried a clipboard thick with forms. He posed as her translator, his accent carefully scrubbed clean of anything that might sound too familiar. They moved through the rows of tents and makeshift shelters, asking questions about children, about families torn apart, about names that might have been changed.

In Frankfurt, Daniel had found work as a clerk in the city records office. The supervisor was a nervous man who drank too much and asked too few questions. Daniel filed papers during the day and copied them at night, building a catalog of adoption records, orphanage transfers, and family relocations. His fingers were stained with ink, and his eyes burned from squinting at faded carbon copies, but he kept searching.

Dr. Levi Blum had the easiest cover and the hardest job. His medical credentials were real, his knowledge genuine. The Allied authorities welcomed him with open arms. He interviewed doctors, nurses, anyone who might have worked with the *Lebensborn* - breeding program. Most claimed ignorance. Some were lying. A few told the truth, their voices dropping to whispers when they spoke of what they'd seen.

And Miriam moved between them all, a ghost in gray traveling clothes, carrying messages and money and the weight of a promise made in hell.

They'd been at it for three weeks when Josef found the file.

The SS records office in Berlin was a tomb of paper and dust. Half the building had been bombed out, but the basement archives had survived. The new German clerks who worked there were eager to prove their cooperation with the occupying forces. They unlocked doors, provided translation, and pretended they'd never seen these files before in their lives.

Josef worked methodically, section by section. Birth certificates. Medical records. Transfer orders. The Nazis had documented everything, their obsession with paperwork ultimately becoming their betrayal.

He found it on a Thursday afternoon, filed under "Successful Placements, Frankfurt District, 1942-1943." A single sheet of paper, typed on official letterhead, signed with a flourish by someone who'd probably been dead for two years.

Subject: David Rosenberg, male, age 3, transferred from Birkenau processing center to Frankfurt *Lebensborn* facility for evaluation and placement. Physical characteristics: blonde hair, blue eyes, suitable for Aryan family integration. Psychological evaluation: minimal resistance to cultural adjustment. Assigned new identity: Dieter Reimann. Placed with Friedrich and Anneliese Schmidt, Frankfurt suburb, January 1945.

Josef stared at the paper for a long time. Then he folded it carefully and slipped it into his briefcase, next to the other documents that would never see the light of day.

The telegraph office was six blocks away. The message he sent was brief: "Product located. Meeting required."

They gathered in a safe house in Wiesbaden, a bombed-out apartment building where the landlord asked no questions as long as the rent was paid in American cigarettes. The room was cold and damp, with newspapers covering the broken windows and a single kerosene lamp for light.

Josef spread the file across the table. "Friedrich Schmidt, formerly *SS-Untersturmführer*, served with *Einsatzgruppe* C - mobile killing unit in Ukraine. Transferred to administrative duties in 1943 after suffering wounds in a partisan attack. Married to Anneliese

Hoffman, daughter of a Party official from Munich. No children of their own."

"Where are they now?" Miriam asked.

"Still in Frankfurt. Same address as the placement records. Suburban house, quiet neighborhood. He works as an insurance adjuster. She volunteers at the local church." Josef's voice was flat, clinical. "Model citizens."

Levi leaned forward. "What about the boy?"

"David." Miriam's voice was firm. "His name is David."

"David," Levi repeated. "Any recent records? School enrollment, medical visits?"

Josef shook his head. "Nothing official. But that doesn't mean anything. Half the records in Germany are missing or destroyed."

Wolf studied the address on the file. "We need to see him first. Confirm it's really him. Then we figure out how to approach this."

"Approach?" Daniel's voice was sharp. "We're not negotiating. We're taking him back."

"It's not that simple," Rivka said quietly. "He's been with them for over a year. He probably doesn't remember his real parents. Doesn't remember being Jewish. For all he knows, the Schmidts are his family."

The silence that followed was heavy as lead. Outside, a truck rumbled past, its engine coughing in the cold night air.

"So what do we do?" Daniel asked.

Miriam touched the file with her fingertips, tracing the edges of the paper that had recorded a stolen life. "We watch. We learn. We find a way to bring him home without destroying what's left of him."

"And the Schmidts?" Wolf asked.

Miriam's eyes reflected the lamp's flame, steady and unblinking. "One thing at a time."

They left Wiesbaden the next morning, traveling separately, taking different routes. By evening, they were all in Frankfurt, scattered across the city like pieces of a puzzle waiting to be assembled.

The house at 47 Beethoven Strasse looked ordinary enough. Two stories, red tile roof, small garden in front. Lace curtains in the windows. A child's bicycle on the porch.

From across the street, hidden behind a newspaper in a café window, Wolf saw the boy for the first time.

He was playing in the garden, building something with wooden blocks. Five years old now, still blonde, still pale. He wore short pants and a clean white shirt, like any other German child on a spring afternoon.

But there was something in the way he moved, careful and quiet, always glancing toward the house as if expecting to be called inside. Something in the way he flinched when a dog barked somewhere down the street.

Wolf lowered his newspaper and lit a cigarette, his hands steady despite the rage building in his chest.

They'd found David Rosenberg.

Now came the hard part.

30

The Child Who Forgot

They watched for a week before they understood what they were seeing.

The boy woke early, before dawn. Wolf could see the light go on in the small window under the eaves, third floor, back of the house. By the time the sun touched the rooftops, David was already in the garden, pulling weeds from between the vegetable rows with hands too small for the work.

He moved like an old man, careful and deliberate. When Friedrich Schmidt emerged an hour later, coffee cup in hand, the boy would straighten up and wait. Schmidt would inspect the work, sometimes nodding, sometimes pointing to spots that needed more attention. The boy never argued. Never complained. Just returned to his knees in the dirt.

"Christ," Daniel whispered from their position behind the cemetery wall. "Look at his arms."

Miriam focused the binoculars. The boy's forearms were mottled with bruises, old ones fading to yellow, fresh ones dark as storm clouds. When he reached for a particularly stubborn dandelion, she could see him favor his left side, the way people moved when their ribs hurt.

"He's five years old," Levi said, his voice tight. He was supposed to be watching for neighbors, but his eyes kept drifting back to the garden. "A five-year-old shouldn't know how to garden like that."

"A five-year-old shouldn't know fear like that," Rivka added. She'd been watching through the kitchen window with a different set of binoculars. "Look how he moves when Schmidt comes outside. That's not normal caution. That's terror."

The boy finished the weeding as the morning grew warm. He gathered the pulled weeds into a neat pile, carried them to the compost behind the garden shed, then stood waiting by the back door until Schmidt let him inside. Even from fifty yards away, they could see how he kept his head down, how he pressed himself against the doorframe to make room for the man to pass.

"This isn't a family," Wolf said. "This is slavery."

The kitchen window gave them the clearest view. Anneliese Schmidt moved through the morning routine like a woman underwater, slow and deliberate and slightly off-balance. She drank her coffee from a bottle that smelled like gin even from their hiding spot. When she spoke to the boy, it was in short, sharp German phrases that made him flinch.

Schneller. Vorsichtig. Halt den Mund.

Faster. Careful. Shut your mouth.

The boy set the table, served breakfast, and cleared the dishes. He ate standing at the counter, whatever scraps were left after the adults finished. When he dropped a fork, the sound of it hitting the floor made him freeze like a rabbit in headlights.

Schmidt backhanded him casually, the way someone might swat a fly.

"Enough," Miriam said, lowering the binoculars. "We've seen enough."

But they hadn't. Not yet.

The afternoon brought new horrors. The boy spent it cleaning the house from top to bottom, carrying a bucket and rags that were almost as big as he was. They watched him scrub floors on hands and knees, polish windows he could barely reach, dust furniture with the concentration of someone who knew there would be consequences for missing a spot.

When he finished, Schmidt inspected his work like a drill sergeant. Found dirt in a corner the boy had missed. Made him do the entire room again.

"He's training him," Josef observed. "Breaking him down, building him back up. Classic technique."

"For what?" Daniel asked.

"Perfect obedience. The boy's not their son. He's their project."

By evening, they had established a routine. Miriam would approach the next day, during the afternoon when the boy was alone in the garden. She would speak German of course, claiming to be from a church charity checking on children in the neighborhood. Nothing threatening. Nothing that would spook him into running.

But when afternoon came, the boy wasn't in the garden.

They waited. Watched. Finally, around three o'clock, they heard it: crying. Muffled and desperate, coming from somewhere inside the house.

"Cellar," Wolf said grimly. "Punishment."

The crying went on for an hour. When it stopped, they waited another hour before they saw movement in the kitchen window. The boy emerged, moving even more carefully than before, his face streaked with dirt and tears.

He returned to his chores as if nothing had happened.

"What did he do wrong?" Rivka whispered.

"Probably nothing," Levi answered. "Or something so small it wouldn't matter in a real family. Spilled something. Said the wrong word. Looked at them wrong." His hands were shaking. "This is systematic abuse. They're not just keeping him. They're destroying him piece by piece."

That evening, they regrouped in their safe house, a rented room above a bakery that still smelled of flour and yeast despite being closed for two years.

"We go in tomorrow," Daniel said. "We can't watch this anymore."

"And then what?" Rivka asked. "He doesn't know us. For all he knows, we're strangers trying to kidnap him. He'll fight us. He'll scream for the people who've been torturing him because they're the only family he remembers."

"So what's the alternative?" Wolf's voice was flat, dangerous. "Leave him there?"

"No." Miriam spoke quietly, but everyone turned to look at her. "We approach carefully. We remind him who he really is. Give him a choice."

"He's five," Josef pointed out.

"He's David Rosenberg," Miriam corrected. "Son of Elsa and Fritz Rosenberg. He had a life before this. Somewhere in his mind, he remembers."

"And if he doesn't?"

Miriam was quiet for a long moment, staring at her hands. When she looked up, her eyes were as hard as winter stone. "Then we save him anyway. And deal with the Schmidts after."

"Deal with them how?" Levi asked, though his tone suggested he already knew the answer.

"However we have to."

Outside, Frankfurt settled into evening. Somewhere in a house on Beethoven Strasse, a little boy who had forgotten his name lay on a thin mattress in a cold cellar, dreaming dreams he couldn't remember of people he'd lost and a mother who sang lullabies in a language he no longer understood.

The promise was becoming a rescue.

The rescue was becoming a war.

31

The Extraction

The telegram arrived at eight in the morning, delivered by a boy on a bicycle who didn't look twice at the address. Josef had crafted it carefully, official paper with proper stamps, the kind of urgent communication that made people drop everything and run.

URGENT - MOTHER GRAVELY ILL STOP COME IMMEDIATELY STOP TIME CRITICAL STOP

Friedrich Schmidt read it twice, his face going pale. He showed it to his wife, who was already three drinks into her morning. They argued in harsh whispers by the kitchen window while the boy scrubbed dishes at the sink, pretending not to listen.

From across the street, Wolf watched through borrowed binoculars as Schmidt packed a small bag. The man moved with military efficiency, checking train schedules, counting money, and making decisions. But he kept glancing at the boy, and Wolf could see the calculation in his eyes.

Evidence. Liability. Risk.

At ten-thirty, Schmidt made his choice. He grabbed the boy by the shoulder, dragged him to the elderly woman next door, and had a brief conversation that ended with him pressing money into her palm. Frau Weber nodded and took the boy's hand, leading him into her house as the Schmidts hurried to catch their train.

"Phase one complete," Wolf said into the radio. "Shepherds have left the flock."

Miriam's voice crackled back through the static. "Give them an hour to clear the city. Then we go."

The waiting was the hardest part. Josef chain-smoked by the window. Daniel cleaned his pistol twice. Rivka paced the small room like a caged animal. Only Levi sat still, his medical bag open beside him, checking and rechecking supplies they might need.

"What if he fights us?" Daniel asked for the third time.

"He's five," Wolf said. "If we can't handle a five-year-old without hurting him, we shouldn't be doing this."

"It's not about physical force," Levi said quietly. "It's about psychological trauma. We're going to terrify him no matter what we do. The question is how to minimize the damage."

At eleven-thirty, they moved.

Miriam wore a Red Cross uniform that Josef had modified the night before. The armband was regulation, the clipboard genuine, borrowed from Rivka's contacts in the displaced persons office. Levi dressed as a medical officer, his papers identifying him as Dr. Heinrich Muller from the Allied health authority.

They approached Frau Weber's house like officials on routine business: confident, unhurried, boring. The kind of people who dealt with paperwork and regulations and the endless bureaucracy of post-war Germany.

Frau Weber answered the door on the second knock. She was seventy if she was a day, with gray hair pinned back and suspicious eyes that had seen too much to trust easily.

"*Guten Tag*," Miriam said, showing her identification. "I am Nurse Hoffman from the International Red Cross. This is Dr. Muller from the Allied medical authority. We are conducting health and welfare inspections of displaced children in this district."

"Displaced children?" Frau Weber's voice was cautious. "There are no displaced children here."

"Our records indicate otherwise." Miriam consulted her clipboard. "We have documentation of a child placed with the Schmidt family next door. As they are temporarily absent, we understand the child is in your care."

"Dieter is not displaced. He is their adopted son."

"I'm sure that's what you've been told," Levi said gently. "But our records indicate otherwise. May we see the child, please? This is routine verification, nothing more."

Frau Weber hesitated, but the uniforms and official papers carried weight. She stepped aside, gesturing them into her small parlor.

"Dieter," she called. "Come here, child. Some people want to speak with you."

He appeared in the doorway like a ghost, small and pale and ready to run. He wore the same clothes as yesterday, wrinkled now and stained with whatever breakfast he'd been allowed. His eyes darted between the strangers and Frau Weber, looking for cues about how afraid he should be.

"Hello, Dieter," Miriam said in German, crouching down to his level. "We just want to ask you some questions. Is that all right?"

The boy nodded, but said nothing. His hands were clasped behind his back, and Miriam could see the telltale bruising on his wrists where someone had grabbed him too hard, too often.

"How old are you?" she asked.

"Five." His voice was barely a whisper.

"And you live with Herr and Frau Schmidt?"

Another nod.

"Have you always lived with them?"

This time he hesitated, his small face creasing with concentration. "I... I think so. Yes."

But there was uncertainty in his voice, a flutter of something that might have been memory trying to surface.

Miriam asked him if he still had his wooden train? He pulled it out of his pocket.

It was painted red and blue and worn smooth by small hands. The boy's eyes went wide. His mouth opened slightly, and for a moment he looked younger than five, like the three-year-old he'd been when his world ended.

"Where did you get that?" he whispered Mama.

"I remember," he said suddenly, his voice so quiet Frau Weber couldn't hear. "I remember the lady who sang to me. She had dark hair. She smelled like... like flowers."

"What was her name?" Miriam asked.

The boy's face scrunched with effort. "Mama. Her name was Mama."

"Do you remember her real name?"

A long pause. Then, like sunlight breaking through clouds: "Elsa. Her name was Elsa."

Frau Weber was watching now, her face growing confused and alarmed. "What is this about? What are you doing to him?"

"David," Miriam said, ignoring the old woman. "That's your real name, isn't it? David Rosenberg."

The boy looked up at her, tears starting to form in his eyes. "Am I in trouble? Did I do something wrong?"

"No, sweetheart. You did nothing wrong. Nothing that happened was your fault."

"But Herr Schmidt said... he said I was bad. That my real parents didn't want me. That they gave me away because I was... because I was..."

"Jewish?" Miriam finished gently.

The boy flinched as if she'd struck him. The word was forbidden, dangerous, something that brought punishment and pain.

"Being Jewish isn't bad, David. Your parents loved you very much. They didn't give you away. You were taken from them."

"That's enough," Frau Weber said sharply. "I don't know what game you're playing, but I won't have you filling the child's head with nonsense."

Levi stood, his presence suddenly commanding. "Frau Weber, this child has been the victim of war crimes. Identity theft, illegal adoption, systematic abuse. We have documentation, photographs, witness statements. The people you know as the Schmidts are criminals who stole this boy from his murdered parents."

The old woman's face went white. "That's impossible. Friedrich is a good man. He works for an insurance company. He goes to church."

"Friedrich Schmidt was *SS-Untersturmführer* in *Einsatzgruppe* C - mobile killing unit," Levi continued relentlessly. "He participated in mass murders in Ukraine before being assigned to the *Lebensborn* - breeding program. The boy was one of thousands of children stolen to be raised as Germans."

David was clutching the wooden train so tightly his knuckles had gone white. "Are you going to take me away?" he asked.

Miriam looked into his eyes, seeing fear and hope and confusion all tangled together. "Would you like to come with us? To a place where no one will hurt you? Where you can remember your real parents without being afraid?"

"Will Herr Schmidt find me?"

"Never. I promise you, David. He will never hurt you again."

The boy was quiet for a long moment, thinking with the careful consideration of someone who had learned that choices had consequences, that the wrong answer brought pain.

Finally, he nodded.

"I want to go," he whispered. "I want to remember my mama."

Frau Weber started to protest, but Levi was already moving, showing her more papers, official stamps, authorizations that looked real because they were real, just not for the reasons she thought.

"The child will be placed in proper care," he told her. "You will be contacted by the appropriate authorities regarding testimony about his treatment by the Schmidts."

They left through the front door, David walking between them with the wooden train clutched against his chest. He didn't look back at Frau Weber's house, didn't ask about his clothes or toys or anything he was leaving behind.

The car was waiting at the corner, engine running. Wolf at the wheel, Josef in the passenger seat. David climbed into the back between Miriam and Rivka, still holding his train.

As they drove away from Beethoven Strasse, he asked one question:

"Will you teach me how to be David again?"

"Yes," Miriam said, her throat tight with emotion. "We'll help you remember everything."

Behind them, Frau Weber stood in her doorway, watching the official car disappear around the corner, wondering what she should tell the Schmidts when they returned.

She wouldn't have to worry about that for very long.

32

The Ship to England

The safe house in Cologne reeked of carbolic soap and boiled potatoes. It was a Red Cross way station, one of dozens scattered across Germany to process displaced persons before they were shipped to new lives in other countries. Josef's contacts had arranged David's placement there under his current identity: Dieter Schmidt, a German war orphan bound for institutional care in England.

The boy had not spoken since leaving Frankfurt.

He sat on the narrow bed in the small room they'd given him, clutching the wooden train and staring at nothing. He ate when food was placed in front of him, used the toilet when told, followed simple instructions without argument. But he moved like a sleepwalker, present in body but absent in spirit.

"Trauma response," Levi explained to the others as they watched through the small window in the door. "Complete emotional shutdown. His mind is protecting itself the only way it knows how."

"How long will it last?" Miriam asked.

"Could be days. Could be months. There's no way to predict."

Josef appeared in the doorway, a telegram in his hand. "Transport's confirmed. Ship leaves Ostend tomorrow evening. We need to have him ready."

"Ready for what?" Miriam's voice was sharp. "To be handed over to strangers? To start over again with new names, new language, new everything?"

"Ready to have a chance," Wolf said quietly. "Which is more than he had with the Schmidts."

That afternoon, Miriam sat with David on the bed. She had changed out of her Red Cross uniform into civilian clothes, trying to look less official, less threatening. The boy watched her with those too-old eyes, waiting for instructions or punishment or whatever adults brought with them.

"Dieter," she said softly, then paused. "Actually, I think David is a better name for you. Do you like the name David?"

The boy considered this seriously, as he seemed to consider everything. "David," he repeated, testing the sound. Something flickered in his eyes, as if the name touched a memory buried deep. "Yes. I like David better too."

"Good. David it is then." She smiled at him gently. "Can you tell me about your train, David?"

He looked down at the wooden toy in his lap. For a moment she thought he wouldn't answer. Then, in a voice barely above a whisper: "Someone made it. The wheels are blue."

It was all he seemed to remember.

"That's nice," Miriam said gently. "It's a very special train."

She wanted to tell him more. Wanted to give him back the pieces of himself that had been stolen. But looking at his fragile state, she realized that might be another kind of cruelty. If his mind had buried those memories to protect him, perhaps it was better to let them stay buried.

At least for now.

"You're going on a journey," she said instead. "To England. It's far away from here, far from the Schmidts."

His small face brightened slightly at that. "They won't find me there?"

"Never. I promise you that."

"Will you come too?"

The question broke her heart. "Not right away. But someday, when you're older, we'll see each other again."

"Promise?"

"I promise. And David? In England, people will be kind to you. They'll give you food and a warm place to sleep. You'll learn new things, maybe even learn to speak more English."

The boy nodded, clutching his train a little tighter.

"Are you going to be my new mama?"

The words hit Miriam like a physical blow. She saw the hope in his eyes, fragile as spun glass, and knew she was about to break it.

"No, David. I can't be your mama. But there are people in England. Good people who want to take care of you. They're going to give you a home where you'll be safe and loved."

The hope died in his eyes, replaced by something that looked like resignation. "More strangers."

"Yes," Miriam said honestly. "But these are different. They know about you. They know you've been hurt, and they want to help you heal."

That evening, the team gathered in the common room while David slept. The other displaced persons gave them space, recognizing grief when they saw it even if they didn't understand its source.

"I don't like this," Daniel said. "Shipping him off to England. How do we know what kind of place he'll end up in?"

"We don't," Wolf admitted. "But we can't keep him. We're not set up for that kind of life."

"The institutions there are better than what he had here," Levi said quietly. "At least he'll be fed properly. Educated. Given a chance."

"A chance at what? Being processed through the system like cargo?"

"Better than being with the Schmidts," Wolf said flatly.

"What about them?" Daniel asked. "When do we go back?"

Miriam was quiet for a long moment, staring at her hands. When she looked up, her eyes were hard as winter stone. "After the ship leaves. After he's safe."

"And then?"

"Then we finish what we started."

The next evening, they stood on the dock at Ostend, watching the ship that would carry David to his new life. He wore his old coat over new clothes that the Red Cross had provided - Miriam had insisted he keep the coat, saying it would be familiar in a world of strangers. His hair had been cut and combed. He looked like any other refugee child, anonymous and lost.

The ship was crowded with displaced persons - adults and children, all clutching cardboard suitcases and official papers. David would be processed through the system like all the others, assigned to whatever institution had space for another war orphan.

"Remember," Miriam told David quietly, "you're going somewhere safe. England is far from here, far from people who might hurt you."

He nodded solemnly.

"Keep your train safe," she added. "And remember that you're a good boy, no matter what the Schmidts told you."

David looked up at her, and for a moment he looked like the little boy he should have been instead of the damaged child he'd become.

"Will I see you again?"

"Someday," Miriam said. "When you're older. But it might be a long time."

"Will you remember me?"

"Always," she said fiercely. "I will never, ever forget you."

The ship's whistle blew. Time to go.

David walked up the gangplank without looking back, the wooden train clutched in his coat pocket. At the top, a Red Cross worker checked his papers - still identifying him as Dieter Schmidt - assigned him a number, and led him toward the crowded lower deck where dozens of other displaced children waited for the journey to begin.

Miriam watched until the ship was a dot on the horizon, carrying David toward whatever future awaited him in England. Somewhere behind her, the others were already talking about travel arrangements, about getting back to Frankfurt, about settling accounts with the Schmidts.

But all she could think about was a promise made in hell and the little boy who carried the weight of two names: the one stolen from him and the one that might save him.

The promise was kept. The cost was still being calculated.

33

Settling Accounts

They waited three days after the ship disappeared over the horizon before returning to Frankfurt. Long enough for David to be processed through Dover, assigned his number, transported to whatever institution would house him. Long enough for the Schmidts to return from their fabricated emergency and discover their "son" missing.

The house on Beethoven Strasse looked different in the late afternoon light. Curtains drawn tight. No movement in the windows. A newspaper yellowing on the front step.

Wolf positioned himself across the street, watching the back garden through binoculars. "No sign of life. Could be they haven't come back yet."

"They're back," Josef said from his spot near the corner café. "Saw Friedrich this morning, talking to Frau Weber. Looked agitated."

"What did she tell him?" Miriam asked.

"Officials came. Medical inspection. Boy was taken for proper care." Josef's smile was thin and cold. "She believed every word."

They had discussed the approach during the drive from Cologne in the stolen Opel. No surveillance this time. No careful planning. The Schmidts had tortured a child for over a year. They had participated in genocide. They deserved no consideration, no chance to explain or bargain or run.

This was execution, pure and simple.

Daniel checked his watch. "Six-thirty. Dinner time. They'll be in the kitchen."

"Front and back?" Wolf asked.

Miriam shook her head. "Front door only. We go in together. Clean and quick."

They walked up the garden path like visitors paying a social call. Wolf carried a bottle of wine wrapped in brown paper. Rivka held a small bouquet of flowers from the market. To any neighbor glancing out their window, they looked like friends arriving for dinner.

Miriam knocked politely.

Footsteps inside. The sound of the lock turning.

Friedrich Schmidt opened the door, and his face went white.

He knew immediately. Not who they were specifically, but what they were. His hand moved instinctively toward his waistband, reaching for a weapon that wasn't there.

"Herr Schmidt," Miriam said pleasantly in German. "We'd like to speak with you about Dieter."

"I don't know what you're talking about." His voice was hoarse, strained. "There's no one here by that name."

"Of course not," Wolf said, stepping forward. "He's gone now. Far away from you. Forever."

They pushed past him into the hallway. Schmidt stumbled backward, his military training warring with the reality that he was outnumbered and unarmed.

"Anneliese!" he called. "Come here!"

She appeared in the kitchen doorway, swaying slightly, a glass in her hand that smelled of gin even from ten feet away. When she saw the strangers, her face crumpled with confusion and fear.

"Who are these people, Friedrich? What do they want?"

"They took the boy," Schmidt said, his voice gaining strength as anger replaced shock. "They're the ones who took our son."

"Your son?" Levi stepped forward, his medical bag in his hand but his voice carrying the authority of a man who had seen too much. "You mean the Jewish child you stole from his murdered parents? The boy you tortured and starved and beat?"

"That's a lie," Anneliese slurred. "Dieter is our boy. We saved him from those people. We gave him a good German home."

"You gave him nightmares," Rivka said quietly. "You gave him bruises. You gave him the kind of fear that follows children into their dreams."

Schmidt's face twisted with rage. "You think you understand? You think you know what we did? We civilized that little animal. We taught him discipline. We made him into something worthy."

"You made him into a victim," Daniel said.

"Better a victim than a Jew."

The words hung in the air like poison gas.

Miriam stepped closer to Schmidt, close enough to smell the sweat and fear on him. "Where were you stationed during the war, Friedrich?"

"That's none of your business."

"*Einsatzgruppe* C - mobile killing unit. Ukraine. We know all about your service record." Her voice was conversational, almost friendly. "How many children did you murder there, Friedrich? How many families?"

"I followed orders. I did my duty."

"Your duty." Wolf's voice was flat as hammered steel. "Tell me about your duty, Friedrich. Tell me about the children you lined up at the edge of mass graves. Tell me about the babies you threw into trucks like sacks of grain."

Schmidt's composure cracked. "You don't understand! It was war! We had to! They were going to destroy Germany, destroy everything we built!"

"So you destroyed them first," Levi said. "And when the war ended, when you couldn't murder Jewish children anymore, you decided to steal one instead. To complete the job in a different way."

"We saved him!" Anneliese screamed suddenly, her glass falling to shatter on the floor. "We took him from those filthy camps and made him clean! Made him proper! Made him German!"

"You broke him," Miriam said simply. "Just like you broke thousands of others."

Schmidt tried one last gambit, appealing to whatever mercy he imagined they might possess. "The boy is safe now, isn't he? You said so yourself. He's far away. So what's the point of this? What do you want?"

"Justice," Josef said from the kitchen doorway, where he'd positioned himself to cut off any escape route. "For David Rosenberg. For his parents. For all the others."

"David Rosenberg?" Schmidt's face showed genuine confusion. "Who the hell is David Rosenberg?"

"The boy's real name," Miriam said. "His real identity. The one you stole from him along with everything else."

"His name is Dieter Schmidt. Has been for over a year. That's who he is now."

"No," Miriam said quietly. "That's who you tried to make him. But you failed, Friedrich. Just like you failed at everything else. Just like your precious Reich failed."

Schmidt lunged for Miriam, his hands reaching for her throat. Wolf intercepted him, slamming the man against the wall with enough force to crack the plaster. Schmidt tried to fight, throwing wild punches that connected with nothing but air.

He was soft now, weak from his comfortable post-war life. The others were hardened by survival, sharpened by purpose.

The gunshot exploded through the small house like thunder.

Miriam spun around, her left shoulder erupting in fire. Anneliese stood in the kitchen doorway, swaying but steady enough to hold the small pistol she'd pulled from a drawer. Her eyes were wild with rage and gin.

"You communist filth!" she screamed. "You won't destroy my family!"

Daniel moved without thinking, his own pistol appearing in his hand. Two shots, center mass. Anneliese crumpled to the kitchen floor, the gun clattering away across the tiles.

Miriam collapsed against the wall, blood spreading across her coat. The shoulder was on fire, waves of pain radiating down her arm and up into her neck.

"Jesus," Wolf breathed, dropping beside her. "How bad?"

"Through and through," Levi said, already moving with his medical bag. "But we need to get her out of here. Now."

252

Friedrich Schmidt stared at his dead wife, all the fight draining out of him. Josef stepped behind him, hands moving with practiced efficiency.

It was over in seconds.

They carried Miriam to the car, Wolf and Daniel supporting her weight while Josef drove through the dark Frankfurt streets. She drifted in and out of consciousness, the pain making her vision blur and fade.

The safe house was a rented room above a bombed-out bakery. No electricity, no running water, just candles and a hand pump in the courtyard. Levi cleared the kitchen table, spreading out towels and instruments by lamplight.

"I need to get the bullet out," he said, examining the wound. "It's lodged against the bone."

"Do it," Miriam whispered.

"I don't have any anesthesia. This is going to hurt."

She nodded, biting down on the leather belt Wolf placed between her teeth.

Daniel held her legs while Rivka gripped her good arm. Josef positioned the lamp to give Levi the best light possible. The doctor's hands were steady despite the crude conditions, years of camp medicine having taught him to work with whatever tools were available.

The first incision made Miriam scream around the belt. Her back arched off the table, every muscle in her body trying to escape the white-hot agony in her shoulder.

"Hold her still," Levi commanded, his voice taking on the authority it had carried in the camps when life and death hung on his skill. "I can see the bullet. Almost there."

Thirty minutes later, it was over. The bullet sat in a small dish, deformed and bloody. Miriam's shoulder was bandaged with torn sheets, her arm immobilized in a makeshift sling.

She was pale as winter snow, but alive.

"You'll live," Levi said, washing blood from his hands in a basin of cold water. "But you'll carry that scar forever. And your left arm will never be quite the same."

Daniel stood by the window, staring out at nothing. His hands still shook from holding down Miriam while she screamed. The woman who'd been shot because he hadn't been watching Anneliese closely enough.

"This is my fault," he said quietly.

"No," Miriam said, her voice weak but firm. "This is war. People get hurt in war."

But Daniel couldn't shake the image of Anneliese falling, couldn't forget the sound of his own gunshots echoing through the kitchen. He had killed before, but always in the heat of survival. This felt different. Colder. More deliberate.

They burned the safe house records and moved Miriam to a different location before dawn. By the time the Frankfurt police investigated the fire on Beethoven Strasse, they were already crossing into Switzerland.

While Levi tended to Miriam, the others had searched the house. In a locked closet upstairs, they found Friedrich's collection: photographs, documents, jewelry, gold teeth. Trophies from his war service. Evidence of the families he had murdered, the children he had killed.

At the bottom of a wooden box, wrapped in oiled cloth, Josef found something that would have stopped Miriam's breath if she'd been conscious: a small prayer book, written in Hebrew, with "Elsa Rosenberg" inscribed on the inside cover.

David's mother's prayer book. Somehow, impossibly, it had ended up in Friedrich Schmidt's collection of stolen memories.

Josef wrapped it carefully and tucked it into his coat. Someday, if they ever found David again, it would be returned to him.

They scattered Friedrich's other trophies to the wind before setting the fire. Evidence of his crimes burned with his body, consumed by flames that lit the night sky.

The fire was visible for miles, a pillar of smoke against the dark German sky. By morning, there would be nothing left of 47 Beethoven Strasse but ashes and memories.

The neighbors would tell the police that the Schmidts had been acting strangely lately. That they'd seemed frightened of something. That they'd talked about leaving Germany, starting over somewhere new.

254

No one would mention the visitors with the wine and flowers. No one had gotten a good look at their faces.

By dawn, the team was already on the road to Switzerland in the stolen Opel, carrying the weight of another promise kept and another account settled.

In England, a small boy with a wooden train and a number instead of a name was learning that porridge tasted better when no one shouted at you while you ate it.

The circle was closing, but slowly. It would be years before all the pieces came together again.

Justice, they were learning, was a patient predator. It could wait.

34

The Weight of Promises

The farmhouse in the Swiss mountains looked exactly the same as when they'd left it three weeks ago. Snow still clung to the eaves. The wood pile still needed restacking. The silence still stretched between the peaks like a held breath.

But everything had changed.

Miriam sat by the window in the main room, her left arm immobilized in the sling Levi had fashioned from torn bed sheets. The bullet wound had healed cleanly, but her shoulder would never move quite right again. When the weather turned cold, it ached like an old memory.

She didn't mind. Scars were proof you'd survived something worth surviving.

Wolf cleaned his weapons at the kitchen table, the same methodical ritual he'd performed every evening since the camps. But now he glanced up at Miriam more often, checking her color, listening to her breathing. He'd carried her from the car to the house when they'd arrived, and something in the way he'd held her had been different. Careful. Protective. Almost tender.

Daniel sat in the corner, reading a letter that had arrived while they were gone. His hands still shook sometimes, a tremor that appeared without warning and disappeared just as suddenly. The sound of breaking glass made him flinch. Sudden movements caught his eye and set his jaw tightening.

"Who's it from?" Rivka asked, nodding toward the letter.

"My cousin in New York," Daniel said. "He wants to know if I'm planning to immigrate. Says there are opportunities for people with my... experience."

"What kind of opportunities?" Josef asked from his position by the fire.

"The kind where you don't ask too many questions about what someone did during the war."

Levi looked up from the medical journal he was reading. "Are you considering it?"

Daniel folded the letter carefully. "I don't know. Maybe. This work we're doing..." He trailed off, staring at his hands. "I killed a woman three weeks ago. Shot her twice in the chest. And the thing that bothers me isn't that I did it. It's that I didn't hesitate."

The room went quiet except for the crackling of the fire.

"She was trying to kill Miriam," Wolf said.

"I know. That's what I tell myself. Self-defense. Protection of a comrade. But it felt like something else at the moment. It felt like justice." Daniel's voice was barely above a whisper. "And that terrifies me."

Rivka set down her knitting. "What did you think justice would feel like?"

"I don't know. Satisfying, maybe? Like something had been balanced. But it just felt... empty. Like I'd crossed a line I can't uncross."

"You had," Miriam said from her chair by the window. "We all have. The question is whether we keep crossing lines or find a way to stop."

"Can we stop?" Josef asked. "After what we've seen? What we know? There are thousands of Schmidts out there, living comfortable lives, pretending they never murdered children."

"And there are thousands of Davids," Levi added quietly. "Children who survived but lost everything. They need someone to remember them, to fight for them."

Miriam touched her injured shoulder, testing the range of motion. The ache was constant now, a reminder of the price they paid for every mission.

"I've been thinking about what we are now," she said. "What we've become."

"What's that?" Wolf asked.

"Ghosts. We're the ghosts of the people we used to be, haunting a world that wants to forget we ever existed." She turned from the window to face them. "The war ended, but our war didn't. It just changed shape."

"So what do we do?" Daniel asked.

"We decide what kind of ghosts we want to be," Miriam said. "The kind that seeks revenge, or the kind that seeks justice. The kind that destroys, or the kind that saves."

Josef poked at the fire with an iron rod, sending sparks up the chimney. "What's the difference?"

"Revenge is about the past. Justice is about the future." Miriam's good hand moved to her injured shoulder, testing the range of motion. "We killed the Schmidts for what they did to David, to his parents, to thousands of others. That was revenge. But getting David out, getting him to safety, that was justice."

"And which one are we going to choose?" Rivka asked.

"Both," Wolf said simply. "We find the children who can still be saved, and we punish the people who hurt them. We make sure the dead are remembered and the living have a chance."

"That's a dangerous combination," Levi warned. "Rescue and assassination. Eventually, one will compromise the other."

"Then we'll adapt," Miriam said. "We'll learn. We'll get better at both."

Daniel stood up, walked to the window where the Swiss peaks caught the last light of day. "My cousin's letter mentioned something else. There's a network forming. Other survivors. Other people who refuse to let the world forget. Some of them are organizing, creating formal structures. Documentation projects. Legal proceedings."

"International courts," Josef said with a snort. "Trials that will take years and convict maybe a dozen of the worst offenders while thousands of others disappear into new identities."

"Maybe. But at least they're trying to do it officially. Legally."

"And we're not legal," Rivka observed.

"No," Miriam said. "We're not. We're something else. Something that works in the spaces between the laws, in the cracks where justice falls through."

Wolf finished cleaning his pistol and reassembled it with practiced efficiency. "So we continue."

"We continue," Miriam agreed. "But smarter. More careful. We learn from our mistakes."

"Like underestimating drunk Nazis with hidden guns?" Daniel asked, a ghost of humor in his voice.

"Like that." Miriam smiled, the first real smile any of them had seen from her since Frankfurt. "Among other things."

The fire burned lower. Outside, night settled over the mountains like a blanket. In England, a small boy with a number instead of a name was learning to sleep without nightmares. In Germany, the ashes of 47 Beethoven Strasse had been cleared away, leaving only empty ground where evil had once lived.

"There will be others," Wolf said. "Other Davids. Other Schmidts."

"I know," Miriam said.

"It won't be easy."

"Nothing worth doing ever is."

Josef stood, stretched, and headed toward his room. "Then we'd better get some rest. Tomorrow we start planning the next one."

As the others dispersed to their beds, Wolf lingered by the fire. Miriam remained in her chair by the window, watching the stars emerge between the peaks.

"Does it hurt?" he asked quietly.

"The shoulder? Sometimes."

"I meant the weight."

She looked at him, understanding immediately what he meant. The weight of promises kept and prices paid. The weight of becoming someone you never intended to be. The weight of choosing justice over peace, action over healing.

"Yes," she said. "It hurts. But it would hurt more to do nothing."

Wolf nodded and banked the fire for the night. As he passed her chair, he touched her good shoulder gently, a brief contact that said more than words could convey.

When he was gone, Miriam remained by the window, looking out at the starlit peaks. Somewhere in England, David was growing up without knowing his real name or his history. But he was alive, and he was free, and someday, maybe, they would find him again.

And give him back the truth he'd been too young to carry.

The promise had been kept, but the story wasn't over. It might never be over. Justice, Miriam was learning, wasn't a destination but a journey. A choice made new each day, with every sunrise bringing fresh opportunities to remember the dead and protect the living.

She finally went to bed, carrying the weight of promises made and promises yet to keep. Outside, the mountains stood high in the darkness, ancient and patient and strong.

They would be ready.

35

The Rosenbergs

Frankfurt, 1939-1944

The apartment on Fahrgasse wasn't large, but summer turned it into an oven. A third-floor walk-up overlooking a courtyard where puddles never quite dried and children no longer played. The smell of boiled cabbage hung in the air, a constant reminder of what they lacked. Fritz loved it for the morning light that slanted through eastern windows. Elsa loved it because it was theirs, perhaps the last thing in Germany that truly was.

Fritz Rosenberg watched his clock like a dying man watches heartbeats. Morning coffee at seven, never a minute before or after. Two cups, bitter and thick, the beans stretched with chicory when real coffee became impossible to find. After coffee, he turned to reading with the devotion of a monk attending morning prayers.

Real newspapers until 1940 when truth became contraband. Then smuggled foreign papers, creased and worn from too many hands, exchanged in fleeting moments at cafes where glances had become dangerous. Sometimes he retreated to books, classics and philosophy that the censors hadn't yet discovered or bothered to burn. He read them with desperate, fading hope.

He had once been someone in Frankfurt. A publisher of essays and art catalogues, books that outlived their makers. Until they didn't. Until his name disappeared from title pages and his office keys were confiscated on a Tuesday morning in March.

1940

Elsa clung to her music until they took that too. The upright piano, her grandmother's wedding gift, disappeared after the first "special tax assessment" on Jewish property. Forty years of polished wood and brass pedals, carried down three flights of stairs by men who wouldn't meet her eyes. She watched from the window as they loaded it onto a truck already half-full with other people's lives.

That evening, she sat at the kitchen table and wept for exactly five minutes. Fritz timed it on his watch, not from cruelty but because he needed to know how long grief was allowed before it became dangerous.

She kept a tuning fork in the nightstand drawer and a keyboard drawn on paper, the keys yellowed from her fingers tracing the notes. When she played this phantom piano, pressing down on nothing, David would freeze in place wherever he was. His small face grew serious, listening not just to the silence but to what made his mother's fingers tremble on certain soundless chords.

"Mama's playing," he would whisper to his wooden horse, the only audience left.

1942

David was born late spring during blackout hours when only bombers moved freely over Frankfurt. No doctor, since they had been forbidden to treat Jews months earlier. Just a midwife with worn hands who arrived at midnight and disappeared before first light, paid with Elsa's wedding ring.

He emerged into the world silent, eyes open, tiny fists clenched as if already prepared to fight. The following evening, Allied bombers returned, their distant drone growing to thunder as they passed overhead. The thin glass rattled until David's eyes widened, but he didn't cry. Even then, he seemed to understand that silence was survival.

They named him David because it was simple. Because it meant beloved. Because after three thousand years of history, the name still survived, and survival was the only prayer they had left.

During air raids, Elsa would wrap him in two wool blankets, one blue, one gray, and sing Yiddish lullabies in the cupboard under the stairs where the walls were thickest. They counted sirens together. One-two-three, danger coming. Four-five, all clear. By the time he formed complete sentences, he could identify planes by their engines and knew the precise sound of jackboots on the staircase below.

"Papa, the heavy one is coming," he would whisper, pressing his ear to the floor when the footsteps approached. His toy wooden

262

horse clutched against his chest, he would count each step. From the rhythm, he could tell which officer it was. The one with the limp who sometimes paused at their door. The young one who took the stairs two at a time. The heavy footfalls that caused his parents to stop breathing until they passed.

Fritz tried to maintain the illusion of productive life. Through coded letters and careful conversations, he made contact with a Dutch printer named Van Der Berg. Together they moved anti-fascist literature through channels that grew narrower each month. It wasn't resistance exactly, not the kind that made headlines or earned medals. It was defiance in low voices, matchlight cupped against a growing storm.

One November evening, a young student brought pamphlets hidden in a violin case. Fritz memorized the distribution points while Elsa fed the boy soup and bread. He couldn't have been older than nineteen, his hands shaking as he ate.

"They shot my professor yesterday," the boy said between spoonfuls. "For teaching the wrong kind of history."

Fritz wrote nothing down. He trusted no one fully. Yet impossibly, he hoped.

1943

In February, the ancient synagogue at Börneplatz collapsed during the night. The newspapers called it structural failure. Fritz knew better. The stones had stood for four centuries through wars and floods and the weight of countless prayers. They hadn't chosen this particular Tuesday to surrender to gravity.

That same month, his brother Jakob in Amsterdam stopped responding to their coded postcards. The silence from the west was absolute. Fritz continued writing anyway, sending letters to an address that might no longer exist, to a brother who might no longer breathe.

"Maybe the mail is just slow," Elsa said one evening, watching him seal another envelope.

"Maybe," Fritz replied, but they both knew better.

Spring 1944

Elsa stopped playing one gray afternoon without explanation. David had been humming along to her silent piano when she suddenly stood up, her face pale as winter sky.

"No more," she said, her voice barely a whisper.

She folded the paper keyboard into a cotton cloth and placed it atop the wardrobe, beyond reach. David, not yet two, pointed upward with confusion in his dark eyes.

"Why, Mama?"

She knelt beside him, smoothing his hair with trembling fingers. "Because some songs are too sad now."

The child, understanding everything and nothing, nodded once. He never asked again.

By summer, their street had emptied like a theater after the final curtain. The Kohns from the second floor vanished overnight, leaving their door standing open and breakfast still on the table. Neighbors whispered they'd gone to distant farms for agricultural work. Others spoke of labor camps in the east where strong hands were needed.

Everyone mentioned trains in low voices, but claimed they'd never actually seen one. Not personally. The fear clung to skin and clothes and dreams like smoke that wouldn't wash clean.

Mrs. Brandt from across the hall knocked one evening, her face hollow with hunger and something worse.

"They came for the Roths today," she whispered at their door. "Took them to the station. All three children too."

Elsa's hand found Fritz's shoulder. "Where?"

"East. That's all anyone knows. East."

October 1944

Then came the knock.

It arrived with the first hint of dawn, when the sky was the color of washed-out bruises and the streets still held traces of frost. The sound was precise, three sharp raps that traveled through the apartment like gunshots. Fritz sat up in bed, his mouth suddenly dry as sand. Elsa was already moving, wrapping her thin robe around herself with hands that barely shook anymore.

David slept on, one small sock sliding down his ankle, oblivious to the world turning on its axis.

Three men waited in the hallway. Two uniforms, one civilian with a clipboard and empty eyes that had seen this scene too many times to count. Papers were produced, official stamps glinting in the weak light filtering through the stairwell window.

"Ten minutes," the civilian said, consulting his watch. "One bag each. No exceptions."

Fritz packed papers first. Identification cards, their marriage certificate, David's birth record. Things to prove they had existed, had loved, had mattered. Elsa gathered clothing, the blue blanket, and the wooden horse carved by Fritz's father from a single piece of oak. David woke to find strange men in his home and didn't cry. He held his mother's hand and watched with eyes that missed nothing, filed everything away.

"Mama, are we going on a trip?" he asked.

"Yes, darling. A long one."

As they stepped into the hallway, Elsa paused at the threshold like a woman leaving church. She looked back once, her gaze sweeping over the cracked mirror that had reflected their faces for five years, the worn floorboards that creaked in the same places every winter, the small green mark on the wall where David had scribbled with a pencil stub. Her fingers touched the doorframe where they had measured his height just three weeks before, the pencil marks still fresh and hopeful.

She memorized the way morning light fell across their kitchen table, the view of the courtyard where she had hung laundry and watched seasons change. The place where they had been a family.

"Ma'am," one of the guards said, not unkindly.

She said nothing because there was nothing left to say. She turned and followed the guards down the stairs, her son's hand warm in hers, their footsteps echoing in the stairwell like stones dropped into a deep well. Behind them, the door stood open, waiting for new occupants who would never know the love that had lived within those walls.

At the bottom of the stairs, David looked up at his mother. "Will Papa's books be lonely?"

Elsa squeezed his hand. "Books remember everything, darling. Even when we're gone."

The truck waited outside, its engine running, exhaust visible in the cold air. Other families huddled in the back, their own bags clutched tight, their own children asking questions that had no good answers.

Fritz helped his wife and son climb into the truck bed, then took one last look at the building that had sheltered their small happiness. In the third-floor window, their apartment stared back with empty eyes.

The truck pulled away, carrying them toward the station, toward the trains everyone whispered about, toward an uncertain horizon where the sun was just beginning to rise.

36

The Train

They shuffled through Frankfurt before dawn, a column of shadows. No commands needed above a whisper. The Nazis had refined this to an art. By breakfast, nothing would remain of Jewish lives but empty rooms and disturbed dust. Fritz heard only the scratch of boots on cobblestone and the occasional German word that cut like glass.

David's fingers dug into Elsa's palm with surprising strength for a child not yet four. His eyes had gone flat and watchful, the warm brown of autumn chestnuts now resembling those of a much older person. He made no sound. The little oak train, carved by Fritz, remained firmly in his hands.

The station wasn't the grand *Hauptbahnhof* (main train station) where they had once waited for holiday trains to Munich or Berlin. This was a freight terminal on the eastern edge of the city, separated from the world by concertina wire that gleamed in the gray morning light. The guards were barely men, seventeen or eighteen years old with rifle straps cutting across chests that hadn't fully broadened. But their eyes held nothing of youth. Fritz recognized that emptiness. He'd seen it in photographs of the Great War.

The cattle cars squatted on the tracks, wooden boxes stained dark. Chalk numbers marked each door. Fritz looked at the cars and tried to count. How many people could fit? The numbers made him sick, but his mind wouldn't stop calculating.

"Move faster!" A guard with a pockmarked face shoved an elderly man who stumbled forward, nearly falling.

They climbed in. First twenty. Then forty. Then more. Bodies pressed against bodies until breath became difficult. The air thickened immediately with collective fear. Fritz wedged himself at the corner where two walls met, creating a pocket of protection. He braced one arm against the rough planks overhead, his other hand gripping David's narrow shoulder through his coat. Elsa stood between them and the press of strangers, her back against Fritz's chest.

Razor-thin cracks between the boards let in slivers of light but little air. Near the ceiling they'd cut a square, just high enough that prisoners couldn't reach it, just low enough that guards could check their cargo without risk.

The door slammed shut. No one breathed. No one moved. When the iron bolt slid home, the sound settled into Fritz's bones. He knew he would hear it in dreams if he lived to have dreams again.

David broke first. A single sob tore from somewhere deep inside his small chest. Elsa sank to the filthy floor, gathering him between her knees, her lips pressed against his ear. She whispered fragments that had lost their meaning: nursery rhymes about lambs and stars, the *Shema* (Hear, O Israel) prayer, broken pieces of lullabies her own mother had sung.

Fritz remained standing with one hand on Elsa's shoulder while the other counted the rough boards of the wall. Twenty seven planks from floor to ceiling. He counted again: twenty seven. His publisher's mind still sought order. Cataloged. Archived. Even as the world burned around him.

For an instant, Fritz closed eyes and saw their apartment on Fahrgasse. The eastern windows caught morning sun on the breakfast table. He smelled fresh bread from the bakery below. David's wooden blocks scattered across the floor, the oak train always within his reach. The memory felt thin, overexposed, already fading.

The train lurched forward. The wheels found their rhythm against the rails, a steady percussion that would mark the hours ahead. Through the ventilation square, Fritz caught glimpses of the familiar Frankfurt skyline disappearing behind them. The cathedral spire. The old bridge. Places where they had walked as a family on Sunday afternoons when the world still made sense.

Hour stretched into hour without form. Time became abstract, measured only by the changing quality of light through the slits and the rhythmic clanking of wheels against tracks. The heat built during day hours until sweat soaked through their winter clothes. David's fever began that first afternoon, his forehead burning against Elsa's palm.

"Fritz." Her voice cracked from thirst, the first word she'd spoken in hours.

He knelt beside them, feeling his son's cheek. The heat radiating from the child's skin terrified him more than the guards, more than the uncertainty of their destination. David's eyes fluttered open, unfocused, searching for something to anchor on in the dim light.

A Polish woman's prayers leaked from one corner, words running together like water. Across from her, an old man with wire spectacles retched into a monogrammed handkerchief. He folded it with hands that remembered dignity while his eyes forgot how to hope. Near the door, a younger man with a watchmaker's delicate fingers slid down the wall and didn't rise again. No one spoke of it.

The second day brought desperate thirst. David's lips cracked. His breathing grew shallow. Elsa tore a strip from her woolen scarf and pressed it against a crack where condensation had gathered. She laid the damp cloth across David's forehead and began to sing. No longer in whispers but in a thin, reedy voice that carried above the rattle of the train. Fritz remembered this lullaby from their first apartment, how she'd played it on the piano in the evenings, those long-ago evenings when music didn't feel dangerous.

A metal bucket in the center served as their only toilet. Soon it overflowed. The contents seeped across the floor, forcing everyone against the walls. The smell became overwhelming. Children whimpered. Adults closed their eyes and tried to breathe through their mouths.

Fritz became a human compass. The wheels changed rhythm through villages. They gained voice on hills, fell quiet on straightaways. His mind sketched maps from sounds, from subtle shifts in the carriage's sway. Southeast now, he thought. Through Bavaria, perhaps into Austria. The knowledge was useless, yet he clung to it.

The third day stretched endlessly. David's fever peaked, then broke into a different kind of stillness that frightened Fritz more than the burning heat had. The child lay limp in Elsa's arms, his breathing so shallow it barely moved his chest. His eyes remained open but distant, as if he were seeing something beyond the confines of their wooden prison.

"David," Elsa whispered, her voice barely audible. "Stay with me."

The child's gaze found her face. For a moment, the familiar spark returned to his eyes. He lifted one small hand to touch her cheek, his fingers cool now, no longer burning with fever.

"Mama," he said, the word clear despite his weakness. "The train is taking us somewhere far."

"Yes, darling. But we're together."

He nodded once, solemnly, then closed his eyes. His breathing deepened slightly. Not the labored gasps of illness, but something closer to natural sleep. Elsa held him closer, her own breathing matching his rhythm.

When night fell, the cold pounced. It seeped through every crack, turning breath to vapor and fingers to ice. Snow began to fall. Through the upper ventilation square, flakes drifted past like tiny ghosts. Inside, the crush of bodies created its own weather. Hot, then cold, then hot again.

Fritz watched his son's face in the dim light. Even in illness, David observed everything with unnatural focus for a child so young. Those eyes tracked the movement of light across the ceiling boards as if reading a story written there. The story of their journey, perhaps. Or something else entirely.

On what might have been the fourth night, Fritz bent close to Elsa's ear. "If they separate us."

The words lodged in his throat. She turned to look at him, her face ghostly in the dimness, all planes and hollows where roundness had been only days before. Her eyes met him with terrible knowledge. They'd both read accounts smuggled out of Poland. The underground papers Fritz had helped distribute now haunted him with their precise details.

"I know," she whispered back.

On the fifth day, the train's rhythm changed. It slowed, lurched forward, slowed again. The brakes screamed against the wheels, a sound that went through them like broken glass.

Then silence.

Voices outside. Dogs barking with trained fury. The sharp report of orders in German.

The door slid open with a shriek of rusted metal.

Cold air flooded in, shocking lungs accustomed to stagnant heat. The sudden light, though only the weak illumination of a winter afternoon, stabbed at eyes that had adjusted to perpetual twilight. With the light came the smell. Sweet and putrid, like flowers left too long in water. And beneath it all, the unmistakable scent of death.

"Out! Quickly!" The commands punctuated by the sharp crack of batons against the train.

Fritz jumped down first, his legs nearly buckling after days of standing. He reached up for Elsa, who passed David to him before descending. The child hung limp in his arms, his fever having broken into a different, more unsettling stillness.

A guard with wire-rimmed glasses approached them. His uniform was clean, pressed. His boots polished. He might have been a clerk in a bank, reviewing loan applications.

"Names?"

"Fritz Rosenberg. My wife, Elsa. Our son, David." His voice felt rusty, unused.

The guard made a mark on his clipboard. His eyes flicked to David, noting the child's condition. With a gesture suggesting routine rather than malice, he motioned to another guard, barely more than sixteen, with a face still spotted with acne.

"The child goes to the medical facility," he said, reaching for David.

Elsa's reaction was primal. She lunged forward. "No! He's just a child with fever. I can care for him!"

The young guard thrust the butt of his rifle forward, catching her in the stomach. She doubled over, gasping.

A woman in a white coat appeared beside them. She was perhaps forty, with graying hair pinned back efficiently. Her hands were clean, her manner professional. She looked like any doctor Fritz might have consulted in Frankfurt.

"The little ones receive proper medical attention," she said, her voice matter-of-fact. "We have a children's ward. Trained nurses. He needs treatment for the fever, yes?"

Her hand closed around David's arm with gentle firmness. Fritz felt the boy's weight leaving him. A terrible lightness replaced the solid form of his son. The child's eyes fluttered open for one brief moment, finding his mother's face with perfect clarity. His gaze moved with deliberate precision, as if memorizing every detail of her features, before the woman in the white coat turned away with him.

Elsa screamed. The sound contained every nightmare of every parent since time began. She lurched forward, hands grasping empty air. Fritz caught her around the waist, holding her upright as her knees gave way. Not out of cruelty. Out of certainty that following meant immediate death.

"David!" she called after them, but the woman was already walking away, the child's small form disappearing into the crowd of officials and guards.

The line continued moving forward. The snow beneath their feet had been trampled into a mixture of mud and darker substances Fritz refused to identify. Above them, floodlights illuminated a sign in wrought iron, its Gothic letters sharp against the gray sky.

ARBEIT MACHT FREI. Work sets you free.

Fritz tightened his grip on Elsa as they shuffled forward, two people where there had been three, moving deeper into the camp that had been constructed with German efficiency and precision. The precision he had once admired in their architecture, their literature, their music. The precision now turned to destruction.

Behind them, another trainload waited on the tracks, and another beyond that, stretching back toward a world that no longer existed for any of them.

As they walked through the gates, Fritz looked back once. In the distance, he could see the woman in the white coat entering a building marked with a red cross. David was no longer visible in her arms, but Fritz knew his son's eyes had remained open until the very end. Alert, watchful, missing nothing.

Those eyes that had learned to read danger in footsteps, that had tracked light across ceiling boards like words on a page, that had found his mother's face in that final moment with such perfect recognition.

The gates closed behind them with a sound like thunder.

37

Birkenau

This was Auschwitz! There were many camps that belonged to Auschwitz. Auschwitz 1 was the main camp, then Auschwitz 3 or Monowitz. Then there was this place called Auschwitz 2, Birkenau, the worst of all the death camps.

The gate loomed from the darkness, its iron words promising liberation through labor. Elsa knew lies when she saw them, even when forged in metal. Snow covered the ground while smoke rose from distant chimneys. The train had delivered them not just to another place but to a different world entirely.

Elsa's limbs obeyed basic commands but felt disconnected. Her legs moved: forward, stop, turn. Fritz had been separated from her, herded into the column of men being channeled toward a distant building. She had watched as his familiar shape became indistinguishable from the others, then disappeared entirely behind a corner. His hands had reached toward her once before the guards blocked her view.

The child was gone.

David and his walnut curls. The way his right lip lifted higher when he smiled. How he'd announce "tick-tock" whenever he heard a clock, his small voice solemn with authority. David, too exhausted by fever to resist when they took him, too small to fight, too precious to be allowed to remain.

Guilt pressed around her skull like a vise. Her eyes burned with pressure that wouldn't release into tears. If she had lunged at the nurse, if she had screamed earlier, if she had hidden David's fever, perhaps then he would still be with her. The rational fragment of her mind knew this was false, but rationality had become irrelevant in this place where children vanished into buildings marked with red crosses.

A woman in a striped uniform pulled her upright when she stumbled, another prisoner, but one who had survived long enough to be trusted with minor authority. Her expression was set in a rigid line, her cheekbones sharp with hunger.

"Keep walking. Don't fall. Falling attracts attention." The woman's voice contained neither compassion nor cruelty, merely critical information delivered in accented German.

They were directed to what the guards called the sauna, a name that promised warmth and cleanliness, a word stolen from civilization and gutted. Inside, the process of eradication began. Not of life, not yet, but of identity. The concrete floor was wet and cold beneath their feet. Industrial lights hung from the ceiling, casting harsh shadows that made everyone look corpse-like.

"Remove everything. Quickly." The instructions came in multiple languages, repeated by prisoners who had been there longer. Their voices were flat, mechanical, drained of emotion.

The smell hit her first: industrial disinfectant failing to mask human misery, sweat, fear, and something else. Something that reminded her of the butcher shop in Frankfurt, metallic and final. Clothes were stripped away and piled into enormous heaps. Elsa's fingers fumbled with buttons until a prisoner helper yanked her blouse open with practiced efficiency.

The shearing came next. Elsa watched clumps of her dark hair fall to the concrete floor, each snip of the dull scissors sending jolts down her spine. A girl no more than fourteen sobbed openly as her long blonde braids were severed. An older woman closed her eyes and recited something under her breath, prayer or poetry, her lips moving silently.

"Next," said a calm voice. The woman wielding the scissors had an economical grace to her movements. Unlike the others, she did not rush, though she worked with equal speed. Her eyes met Elsa's for a fraction of a second. Something passed between them, a current of recognition though they had never met. The woman looked away quickly, but not before Elsa noticed a small streak of premature gray at her temple and leather shoes instead of wooden clogs.

The tattoo followed, the final transformation from person to inventory. A prisoner with dead eyes operated the needle, puncturing the soft skin of Elsa's inner forearm with mechanical repetition. The pain registered as distant information, less immediate than the burning shame of standing naked among

274

strangers. She watched the numbers appear, blue-black against her pale skin. Numbers that would replace her name.

Then came the uniforms, coarse striped fabric sized for men, smelling of industrial soap and previous occupants. The material scraped against her skin like sandpaper. Wooden clogs replaced her shoes, immediately blistering her heels with each step. A slice of dark bread was thrust into her hand, along with a dented tin bowl. These, she learned, were possessions to be guarded with her life.

"Block 14, top bunk." The instruction came with a shove toward the door.

The barracks stretched in perfect rows, identical structures designed for animals now repurposed for humans designated as something less. Each building looked exactly like the next, numbered but otherwise indistinguishable. Inside Block 14, the smell struck her immediately: unwashed bodies, sickness, despair, and the sharp odor of the disinfectant they used to fight lice. Wooden bunks stacked three high contained multiple women on each platform. Elsa was directed to climb to an upper level already occupied by four others who shifted reluctantly to make space.

The boards were rough against her back. The straw mattress, thin and lumpy, provided no real cushioning. Above her, wooden rafters disappeared into shadows where she could hear the scratching of rats.

As she settled onto the hard surface, a woman with a shaved head and prominent cheekbones leaned close. Her breath smelled of hunger. "Don't cry. Not here. Not now. They look for weakness." Her accent was Polish, her advice delivered with the gravity of life-saving information.

"Where do they take the men?" Elsa asked, her voice strange and hollow in her throat.

The woman gave a small, tight shrug. "Other blocks. Different section entirely. You may see them at work details sometimes, but never speak. Never acknowledge them. The men's camp is separate, and contact means death for both."

A younger woman, perhaps twenty, turned toward them from the adjacent bunk. "I saw my husband once," she whispered. "Carrying stones near the fence. He looked right through me. Had to. But I knew he saw me." Her voice carried the weight of that single glimpse.

Elsa didn't cry. Her body remained in shock's protective embrace, emotions suspended like ice in winter air. That first night, she pressed herself against the barrack's rough wooden wall, splinters catching on her striped uniform. The woman beside her muttered in her sleep, Polish words that sounded like prayers or curses. Someone coughed repeatedly, a wet sound that spoke of illness. The thin blanket they shared provided no warmth against the February cold that seeped through every crack in the walls.

Where was Fritz now? She tried to picture him going through the same processing, his head shaved, his meticulous habits stripped away along with his clothes. Was he thinking of her? Of David? Did he know what had happened to their son, or was he tormented by the same terrible uncertainty?

And beneath that thought, the deeper wound: David. His small hands cold now, or worse. She couldn't allow herself to imagine what might have happened after the woman in the white coat carried him away into that building with its red cross that promised medical care.

The next morning began before dawn. A whistle shrieked through the barracks like a physical blow. "*Raus! Appell!*" (Out! Roll call!) The commands came with the crash of wooden clubs against bunks, against walls, against anyone who moved too slowly.

Roll call. They stood in frozen formation for hours while guards counted and recounted with deliberate slowness. Five rows deep, perfectly straight lines, no movement permitted. Elsa's wooden clogs rubbed raw spots on her heels. The cold bit through her thin uniform. Around her, women swayed on their feet but didn't fall. Falling meant attention, and attention meant death.

She learned the rhythm. Count off in German. Stand perfectly still. Wait. Count again when someone made an error. Wait longer. Her feet went numb. Her fingers turned blue inside the thin gloves they'd been given. But she stood.

After roll call came work assignments, distributed by the block elder, a German political prisoner who had been there since 1942. Her voice was hoarse from shouting, her manner brisk and impatient. Elsa was assigned to the laundry detail. Hauling massive baskets of soiled uniforms to the washing facility, scrubbing with caustic soap that ate through skin, hanging wet clothes in the freezing air.

The work was backbreaking, but it kept her warm during the day. Her hands cracked and bled from the chemicals. Her back ached from bending over the washing tubs. But she was alive. Each evening she returned to Block 14 exhausted but breathing.

Only later, after weeks of this routine, after the third time she collapsed from hunger during roll call and was kicked back to her feet, did it begin. The tears came silently during the darkest hours before dawn, a release of pressure rather than expression of emotion.

The girl on the adjacent section of the bunk turned toward her. Her face was young but her eyes belonged to someone much older. Dark circles shadowed her cheeks. "Your child?" she asked.

Elsa nodded, unable to speak David's name aloud.

"My sister. She was only twelve. They took her the first day." The girl's voice was flat, factual. No name offered, no details shared, no false comfort extended. She simply acknowledged their shared category of loss before turning away.

From the front of the barracks, the block elder shouted for silence. A sharp slapping sound followed by a muffled whimper indicated the consequence of disobedience. The single bare bulb hanging from the ceiling went dark, plunging them into complete darkness.

In the pitch dark, surrounded by the breathing and shifting of strangers, Elsa calculated how long it had been since she'd held David. Weeks now. The last moment replayed with perfect clarity: his small weight leaving her arms, the momentary flutter of his eyelids, the way his gaze had found her face with perfect recognition before the woman in the white coat turned away with him. The memory was a physical pain beneath her ribs, a hollow space exactly the size and shape of her child.

In the days that followed, time lost conventional meaning. Days began in darkness and ended in darkness, punctuated by roll calls, watery soup, and labor assignments that changed without pattern. Elsa worked wherever they directed her: hauling bricks when construction details needed extra hands, scrubbing latrines with caustic chemicals that burned through her cracked skin, sorting through mountains of clothing taken from new arrivals. Her body performed these tasks while her mind retreated to a protected inner chamber where David still existed.

She moved through the camp hollow but present. Words became unnecessary luxuries. Her vocabulary shrank to the essential: yes, no, thank you, please. Questions invited danger, observations risked punishment, complaints ensured swift reprisal.

She listened, and she watched.

She saw Fritz once, at a distance, his striped uniform hanging from shoulders already growing bony. He stood in a work detail sorting building materials near the fence that separated the men's and women's sections. She nearly called out before remembering the Polish woman's warning. Instead, she watched him for the brief seconds allowed. His hair had gone entirely gray in the month since their arrival. Or perhaps it was the dust from the rubble he moved endlessly from one pile to another.

His movements were careful, deliberate, the same methodical approach he'd brought to his publishing work. Even here, he maintained the precise habits that had defined him. When he lifted a board, he examined it first. When he placed it on the pile, he ensured it lay straight. This small insistence on order, meaningless though it was, filled her with fierce love and desperate worry. Was this precision keeping him alive, or would it mark him as too slow?

Even in this designed hell, patterns emerged. Hierarchies formed. Information circulated through whispered exchanges during work details, fragments of news traded like currency. Some prisoners had been there for years and knew which guards could be reasoned with, which *kapos* (prisoner supervisors) showed occasional mercy, and how to avoid the selections that came without warning.

There was a woman prisoner the others called Miriam. Unlike the others, her hair had grown back several centimeters, dark with a streak of premature gray at the temple. She was the one who had cut Elsa's hair that first day, the woman whose eyes had briefly met hers with recognition. Miriam wore real leather shoes rather than wooden clogs, and her uniform, while still striped, appeared almost fitted.

Her German was flawless, her Polish and Russian nearly as good. She worked as a translator for the camp administration when they needed someone to communicate with new arrivals or process paperwork for the various nationalities that arrived daily. When there wasn't enough translation work, she was assigned to other details: sometimes the laundry, sometimes sorting confiscated belongings, sometimes assisting in the camp hospital.

"She knows things," the girl with the dead sister whispered one night. "They say she can find out if someone is still alive in the men's camp. She has access to records."

Elsa stored this information away without reacting, filing it like the extra crust of bread she kept hidden in her mattress. She observed Miriam during work assignments, noting how she spoke to guards not with the obligatory servility of other prisoners but with the measured tones of someone engaged in professional discussion. The guards listened, nodded, and departed without the casual cruelty that characterized most interactions.

"She worked as a language teacher in Germany before the war," an older woman offered during the soup line one evening. "That's why they need her. Too many different languages coming through the gates."

That night, curled on her section of the crowded bunk with hunger gnawing at her stomach like a living thing, Elsa made a decision. It arose not from hope. Hope had become incomprehensible in this place where smoke rose from chimneys day and night. Rather, it emerged from the most primal instinct that remained functioning within her: the drive to verify her child's existence, to confirm that some trace of David remained in the world.

She would find a way to speak with this Miriam.

She needed to know if the hospital kept records of the children. If David's fever had been treated or if he had been sent immediately elsewhere. If he had suffered, or if his passage had been swift. If his name existed on any page anywhere, confirming he had been more than just her memory.

Not because Elsa believed her son could have survived. The camp had already taught her the foolishness of such fantasies. But because she needed to know the truth. It was the last maternal act available to her, to ensure her child had not vanished without witness, to establish that David Rosenberg had existed beyond the memories she carried.

In a place designed to erase individuals entirely, this small insistence on specific truth became her private rebellion. She would find Miriam. She would learn what had happened. And in doing so, preserve some fragment of the world as it should have been, a world where children were not smoke, where mothers knew where their sons lay, where names still mattered.

Tomorrow, she decided. During the morning work assignment when the laundry crews passed near the administration building. She would find a way to catch Miriam's eye. She would risk the single question that consumed her days and haunted her nights.

Elsa turned her face to the rough wood of the barracks wall. In the darkness, she allowed herself to silently form the words she would say to Miriam. Each syllable precise, rehearsed, necessary.

"My son's name was David Rosenberg. Three years old. Dark curls. Observant eyes. Separated on arrival. Fever. Can you find what happened to him?"

Elsa repeated the words in her mind until they became a prayer, a mantra, the only truth that mattered in a world that had forgotten the meaning of truth.

Around her, the barracks settled into the sounds of exhausted sleep. Breathing, shifting, the occasional sob quickly stifled. Tomorrow would bring another roll call, another work assignment, another day of survival. But tomorrow would also bring the possibility of answers.

She closed her eyes and saw David's face as clearly as if he lay beside her. His serious dark eyes that missed nothing. The way he held his wooden train like a talisman. The trust in his voice when he asked if they were going on a trip.

"Yes, darling," she whispered into the darkness. "We went on a trip. And I'm going to find out where it took you."

38

Fritz Rosenberg

The men's line moved forward through the camp's central pathway. Each step brought Fritz closer to the processing station. When someone ahead collapsed, the line compressed briefly before flowing around the fallen man. A gunshot cracked the air. Fritz didn't flinch. They came every few minutes now, as regular as his heartbeat.

Fritz kept his eyes forward after they separated him from Elsa. Not from lack of desire to find her among the women's ranks. That impulse pulled at him constantly, made his neck ache from the effort of not turning. But survival here demanded absolute focus. One backward glance, one moment spent searching for his wife, and he might stumble. Stumbling meant falling. Falling meant death.

The guards never shouted, never threatened. They watched, silent and patient, waiting for mistakes. Fritz felt their attention on his neck like cold breath, waiting for him to give them a reason.

Makeshift barracks lined the path, resembling livestock pens more than human shelters. Mud sucked at their shoes with each step. A cart creaked past, loaded with shapes Fritz refused to identify. A week ago that cart would have horrified him. Today, he only wondered if one day he'd be loaded onto it. The thought came without emotion, just practical consideration.

No one in line reacted, no heads turned. They had entered a state where horror became simply background noise.

Focusing on the man ahead, Fritz counted the vertebrae visible beneath his thin shirt. One, two, three. Facts instead of fear. Details instead of despair.

The men's processing exhibited brutal efficiency. Guards communicated through physical contact. Rifle butts to kidneys for those who moved too slowly. Open-handed slaps for those who made eye contact. Closed fists for anyone who spoke without being addressed.

A prisoner with a green triangle sheared Fritz's hair with clippers that pulled before cutting, leaving his scalp raw and spotted with blood. The metal teeth caught and tore. Each pass sent jolts of pain down his neck. They stripped him next, guards evaluating his naked body with the dispassionate gaze of livestock inspectors. His clothes disappeared into a mountain-high pile where hundreds of lives had been reduced to fabric.

The striped uniform they gave him carried rusty brown stains on the right sleeve and smelled of its previous owner's final sweat. The fabric felt coarse against his skin, like wearing sandpaper. The wooden clogs were two sizes too small, forcing him to shuffle instead of walk. Each step sent pain shooting through his compressed toes.

Fritz had once published books about humanity, about art, about the finest expressions of human culture. Now he was learning what it meant to have his own humanity stripped away, layer by layer, until only the most basic functions remained.

A guard with pockmarked skin tattooed a number on Fritz's arm, the needle puncturing deeper than necessary. The ink burned as it entered his flesh. Fritz watched the digits appear on his forearm but didn't immediately memorize them. That instinct would come later, after he understood that names had become luxuries from another life.

"Block 17," barked the processor, shoving him toward the door.

Block 17 housed sixty men in a space designed for twenty. Fritz's lungs rebelled at the first breath. The air was thick with urine, mold, and the metallic undertone of blood gone brown with age. Men occupied three-tiered bunks, coughing in their sleep with wet, rattling sounds that spoke of lungs filling with fluid. Some moaned. Others lay perfectly still, and Fritz couldn't tell if they were sleeping or something worse.

Rules existed here, unwritten protocols that determined survival, but they operated according to patterns he hadn't yet decoded. You learned by watching, by noting which behaviors earned beatings and which allowed you to become temporarily invisible to the guards. Invisibility was the closest thing to safety.

A man on the top bunk near the iron stove regarded Fritz with eyes that still held a flicker of something human. His cheekbones jutted sharply from his face, but his gaze was alert, measuring.

"Frankfurt?" The whisper barely traveled the space between them.

Fritz nodded once. No energy to spare for full sentences.

The man's face stayed granite-hard, but his eyes flickered with recognition. "Offenbach," he whispered back. The word hung between them like a bridge. Twenty kilometers apart in another life. A lifetime away now.

The exchange ended there. This wasn't friendship, just acknowledgment that they had once been human in the same place, that they shared some fragment of a world that no longer existed.

During evening distribution, Fritz received a dented metal bowl with gray liquid called soup. Unidentifiable particles floated in the broth like debris in stagnant water. He drank half, the thin warmth barely reaching his stomach, then set the remainder aside. Later, when the block supervisor turned to shout at someone else, Fritz offered the saved portion to an elderly man with wire-rimmed glasses who had collapsed during roll call.

The man ate it carefully, each swallow measured and deliberate, but offered no thanks. Gratitude was unnecessary here. Survival was its own acknowledgment.

That night, Fritz lay on his back on the hard wooden platform, feeling every knot and splinter through the thin straw mattress. His throat itched with a cough he refused to release. He had noticed how others shifted away from those who coughed, how men with respiratory problems were eventually removed during the night and never returned.

In the darkness, images of Elsa appeared behind his closed eyes. Not her face as he had last seen it, hollow-cheeked and shaven-headed, stripped of everything familiar. Instead, he saw Elsa from before. Elsa on their wedding day in 1938, dark hair arranged with white flowers, laughing at something he'd whispered during the ceremony. Elsa at the piano, fingers moving across ivory keys with the precision he'd fallen in love with. Elsa holding David for the first time, her face transformed by wonder and fierce protection.

David.

The memory struck him like a physical blow. Fritz curled his fingers into his palms until his nails drew blood. The boy was gone. Not just taken. Gone. His son had become smoke rising from chimneys, and Fritz hadn't even said goodbye.

He hadn't marked the moment when his son left his arms for the last time. Hadn't whispered anything meaningful into that small ear. No final blessing, no words of love, no promise to find him. The failure pressed against his chest like a stone. How could he have let that moment pass without understanding its finality?

Fritz bit down on his knuckle to keep from crying out. The sound would bring attention, and attention meant death. But the pain inside him demanded some physical expression, some way to acknowledge what had been lost.

He forced himself to focus on immediate sensations. The rough wood beneath his right hand. The ache in his compressed toes. The throb of the new tattoo. Physical pain became salvation, a tether to the present when the past threatened to consume him entirely.

"I'll find you," he whispered into the darkness, his voice barely breathing. "Elsa. Somehow." The promise held no plan, no strategy, just the assertion that some connection remained between him and the woman he loved.

The man from Offenbach shifted on his bunk, coughing quietly. Wind found its way through a crack in the wall, carrying the smell of smoke and something else. Something sweet and terrible.

Morning arrived gray and harsh, bringing no renewal, only continuation. The guards' shouts triggered immediate response regardless of physical readiness. Men rose and fell into formation with the speed of those who understood that hesitation meant death.

Work details were assigned arbitrarily, names called from lists that seemed to change without logic. Some men received shovels and marched toward massive pits beyond the inner fence. Others went to sorting sheds where they processed belongings stripped from new arrivals. Fritz found himself assigned to an ash detail, collecting residue from crematorium chimneys and spreading it on icy pathways for traction.

The work began immediately. No instruction, no explanation. Just buckets and shovels and the expectation that he would understand what needed doing. The ashes were gray and white, fine as flour in some places, chunky with unidentifiable fragments in others. As Fritz scooped the material, his mind tried to classify what he was handling. Residue from coal, he told himself. Industrial waste. Nothing more.

But sometimes his shovel struck something harder. Something that looked like a piece of bone. Or a tooth. And Fritz understood why the men in Block 17 never asked questions about their work details. Some answers would crack you open from the inside.

He shoveled methodically, moving neither too fast nor too slow, attracting no attention from the guards who supervised the detail. He had been a publisher before, a man who dealt in ideas and beautiful objects. Now he was a mechanism for transferring ash. Yet something still functioned inside him that wasn't mechanical: a capacity for memory, for the possibility that meaning existed beyond the electric fences.

The irony wasn't lost on him. He had spent his career preserving human thoughts on paper, ensuring that words and ideas survived their creators. Now he was handling the literal remains of people whose thoughts, words, and dreams had been reduced to ash. The symmetry was obscene.

He worked for hours, his back aching, his hands growing raw from the wooden shovel handle. When the guards called for a break, Fritz leaned against a concrete wall and watched the smoke rising from the distant chimneys. Always smoke. Day and night, the chimneys worked.

The camp had been designed to suffocate hope. What kept Fritz moving was something rougher: a stubborn refusal to disappear while his heart still beat. Not optimism, which would have been madness here. Just the animal determination to continue existing until existence became impossible.

Late in the afternoon, Fritz looked up briefly from his work when a new group of women prisoners marched past, fifty meters away on the path that led to the laundry facility. His heart seized, then began beating too fast.

Third from the end, her head down but her posture unmistakable: Elsa.

She walked with the same careful precision she'd always had, even in the striped uniform, even with her head shaved. The way she held her shoulders, the particular rhythm of her steps. His wife. Alive.

Their eyes didn't meet. He knew better than to call out or wave. The sighting lasted three seconds, long enough to confirm she still existed but not long enough to attract attention from the guards.

He returned to his shoveling with mechanical precision, but something fundamental had changed. She was alive. She was here. The knowledge didn't bring comfort exactly, but it hardened into resolve. If she was surviving, he would survive. If she was enduring, he would endure.

That evening, as prisoners returned to their blocks, the man from Offenbach leaned close during the brief moment when they collected their bread ration. His voice was barely audible above the shuffling of feet.

"Kitchen detail," he muttered. "Better food. Need someone who can count inventory, read supply lists. Someone with education." He paused, measuring Fritz with his eyes. "Tomorrow. Morning assembly."

Fritz understood. The man had connections, information, perhaps a way to survive beyond the next week. More importantly, he had recognized something in Fritz that might be useful. His years of managing publishing inventories, tracking book orders, maintaining precise records.

"I can count," Fritz replied, each word a calculated risk. "I can read German, some Polish."

The man nodded once, then moved away without another word.

Back in Block 17, Fritz recalculated his priorities. Simple survival wasn't enough anymore. He needed strength, information, a position slightly more valuable than anonymous labor. The kitchen might provide all three.

If he could establish himself there, perhaps he could learn more about the women's camp, about Elsa's location. Kitchen workers sometimes moved between sections. They had access to better food, which meant strength to think clearly. Most importantly, they had access to information about camp operations.

He would endure. He would find ways to help Elsa survive. He would honor David by living to speak his name when this nightmare ended. These weren't abstract hopes. They were concrete objectives, tasks to be accomplished through careful planning and patient execution.

As lights-out was called and the block plunged into darkness, Fritz committed the essential details to memory: Kitchen detail. Morning assembly. Offenbach. The man's real name, if he had given it. The location of the kitchen facility. He memorized each piece of information like weapons against the machinery of destruction surrounding him.

He slept lightly, waking at the smallest sounds. His mind already focused on what would come next. The night passed in increments of breath and heartbeat, each one a small victory against the camp that had been designed to erase him.

Somewhere in the women's section, Elsa was doing the same thing. Breathing. Counting heartbeats. Refusing to disappear.

Tomorrow he will try to position himself closer to survival. Not just for himself, but for the possibility that they might both live to remember their son together.

39

Elsa and Miriam

It took Elsa three days to find the right moment. During those days, she watched guard rotations and learned when whispers might go unpunished. Her academic's hands split open from the labor, blood seeping from lifelines that once promised futures. The black bread tasted of sawdust and cellulose, but she forced herself to eat every crumb.

She studied the camp's patterns like Fritz had taught her to observe the world. Bodies trudging through mud at dawn, huddled masses at roll call, then scattering to work sites where the SS expected them to produce but never to survive. Observation was the foundation of all worthwhile writing, Fritz had said. Now it kept her alive.

Where was David? The question gnawed at her constantly. Somewhere in this maze of barracks and electric wire, in the medical facility where they'd taken him, or already gone. She caught that thought, strangled it. Not now. Not while uncertainty still allowed for possibility.

During those three days of watching, Elsa learned to read the guards like weather patterns. Some roared constantly, their commands filling the air like thunder. Others struck without warning, their violence random as lightning. Worst were the silent ones with calculating patience who remembered faces and selected victims according to logic only they understood.

Through it all, she watched Miriam, the translator who moved between worlds.

Miriam navigated the camp with precision, never hurried, never hesitant. Her steps plotted the narrow space between invisibility and usefulness. When SS officers barked questions, she answered in perfect German, eyes downcast but spine straight. She never flinched at raised voices, never showed the fear that could make a person interesting to the wrong kind of attention.

Between translation duties, they sent her to *Kanada*, where prisoners sorted belongings stripped from new arrivals. Coats, shoes, wedding rings, dolls, photo albums. The last possessions of the erased, organized with German efficiency for redistribution or disposal.

Miriam returned from these shifts with particular stillness. Not the hollow shock that emptied other prisoners' eyes but something harder, more deliberate. A shell grown from strength, not weakness. She carried herself like someone who had seen everything and chosen to survive it.

The winter of 1944 had settled over the camp like a permanent condition. Three months had passed since Elsa's transport from Frankfurt. Three months since they'd ripped David from her arms on the platform. Those months had warped time itself, stretching minutes into years, compressing days into heartbeats.

Each day that passed made her plan feel more urgent and more impossible. What could she possibly say to convince this woman to risk everything? What did she have to offer except desperation? But the alternative was accepting that David had vanished without witness, that no record of his existence would survive beyond her failing memory.

The photograph had somehow endured. Hidden in the seam of her coat during processing, sewn deeper into the lining during her first week when she'd found a needle in the laundry detail. A miracle of oversight, or perhaps the guards simply couldn't imagine anyone preserving something so dangerous. The image had become her most precious possession and her greatest liability.

Elsa chose her moment like a thief planning a heist. Dusk, when the sorting shifts ended but night work hadn't begun. When tired guards huddled over cigarettes near the kitchen block. When shadows between barracks deepened enough to hide brief encounters from casual observation.

She cut across Miriam's path as the woman left the sorting shed, stepping too close, too suddenly. Before doubt could paralyze her, Elsa spoke.

"You speak German," she said, voice low but clear. "I need a word. Please."

Miriam's face gave away nothing. Only her eyes moved, flicking toward the guards by the kitchen, scanning the muddy path, then drilling into Elsa's face with an assessment that felt like a physical probe. For a moment that stretched endlessly, Elsa thought the woman would simply walk away.

"Not here," Miriam muttered, barely moving her lips.

She adjusted her course without breaking stride, heading toward her barracks with natural purpose. Elsa followed at the precise distance of coincidence rather than conspiracy. They rounded Block 23 toward the refuse pit where kitchen waste fermented in half-frozen layers. No guard lingered near that stench. The smell was overwhelming, a mixture of rotting vegetables, spoiled soup, and human waste that made breathing an act of will.

In the narrow gap between the building and pit, they faced each other. Their breath steamed in the bitter air. The ground beneath their wooden clogs had been trampled to gray mush that squelched with each small movement.

"My name is Elsa Rosenberg," she started, voice tight with control. "My son David. They took him on the platform when we arrived. Said he needed medical care for his fever." The words scraped her throat raw. "He's three years old. Dark curls, not blond. Had a wooden train in his pocket, carved oak. If you hear anything about the children who were taken to the medical facility."

Miriam's mask didn't crack, but something shifted behind her eyes. Not recognition of the boy, but recognition of desperation. She studied Elsa's face, weighing risks with the calculation of someone who had made such assessments many times before.

"What can I possibly do?" she asked, the question bare of hope but not of understanding.

"I don't know," Elsa said, honesty cutting through her prepared words. "I'm not asking you to risk yourself. Just listen. Watch. His name, if you see it somewhere. David Rosenberg. If there are records, lists, anything."

With movements that would be invisible beyond arm's length, Elsa pulled something from the hidden seam of her coat. A scrap of fabric wrapped around a smaller object. The fabric fell away to reveal a photograph, its edges soft with handling, surface webbed with fold lines from being hidden and reopened countless times.

The image showed David in their apartment, sitting by the window with morning light on his face. His wooden train rested in his lap. His smile was real, starting in his eyes before reaching his mouth. His small hands held the toy with the careful attention he brought to everything, as if the train contained secrets only he could understand.

Miriam didn't reach for the photograph immediately. She just looked, absorbing details with the efficiency of someone used to processing information that might vanish without warning. Her eyes moved across the image methodically: the child's face, his hands, the toy, the quality of light that spoke of mornings when the world still made sense.

"They don't keep proper records of children," she said finally, the words flat as a slammed door. "Taken from the platform for medical care usually means."

She didn't finish the sentence. They both knew what it meant.

"I know," Elsa said. "But if somehow. If there's any chance. If I die here and you live, at least someone will know he existed. David Rosenberg. Frankfurt. Born April 1942."

The silence stretched between them, filled with the distant sounds of the camp: guards shouting, dogs barking, the ever-present hum of the electric fence. Steam rose from the refuse pit, carrying its sickening smell over them like a blessing in reverse.

"If I live," Miriam said finally.

The promise held no comfort, no reassurance, no false hope. It offered something more valuable: truth tempered in shared knowledge. An acknowledgment that survival was never guaranteed, that the future existed only as a possibility.

Miriam's hand moved then, taking the photograph with quick efficiency. Her fingers were surprisingly warm as they brushed Elsa's palm. She slipped the image between her coat's lining and shell, into a hidden pocket that spoke of long practice at concealment.

"David Rosenberg," she repeated quietly, as if committing the name to the same secure place where she stored other dangerous information.

Without another word or backward glance, she turned and walked toward the main path. Within seconds, she had vanished into the haze that hung over Birkenau: part fog, part smoke, part the collective breath of twenty thousand souls caught between life and extinction.

Miriam

She walked the main path with the same measured stride as always. The photograph pressed against her ribs like a stone, warm from their brief contact but already cooling in the February air. No one stopped her. No one questioned her movements. No one noticed anything different about the translator who existed in the space between prisoner and collaborator, between the dying and the dead.

They rarely noticed her at all. She'd perfected the art of existing without being seen: useful enough to keep alive, invisible when guards scanned for targets, alert but never appearing to hear what wasn't meant for her ears. It was a delicate balance that required constant adjustment.

But Miriam was always listening.

Three years old. David Rosenberg. Born Frankfurt, April 1942. Dark curls. Wooden train. Medical facility.

She'd heard things about the children, fragments of information gathered over months of translation work. The trucks that left the medical facility full but returned empty within the hour. The tiny shoes and clothes sorted by size in *Kanada*. The "examinations" performed by men whose eyes were colder than their instruments.

She hadn't lied to Elsa Rosenberg. The children weren't documented properly. Their names, when recorded at all, existed on lists routinely burned, their identities erased from both life and the record of having lived. The Germans kept meticulous records of adults: numbers tattooed on arms corresponded to cards, to transport lists, to work assignments. But children were processed differently. More efficiently.

She could have told Elsa this. Could have explained exactly what happened to children under five delivered to the camp medical facility. The knowledge sat in her mind like broken glass, cutting whenever she moved it.

But she hadn't. Not because she didn't care, but because she couldn't afford to care completely. The SS couldn't shoot your

292

compassion, but they'd make you watch as they shot what you loved. Caring scraped you raw from the inside. Like smuggled bread or hidden valuables, it made you vulnerable.

Still, she'd taken the photograph. Made the promise. Why?

Perhaps because she recognized something in Elsa's desperation that reminded her of her own early days here, when she'd still believed information could change outcomes. Perhaps because the woman had offered truth instead of false hope, asked for witnessing instead of rescue.

Or perhaps because in a place designed to erase all traces of human love, preserving the memory of one child felt like the smallest possible act of rebellion.

That night, alone in the small room allotted to translators and record-keepers, Miriam sat on her narrow bunk. The others maintained their distance, each lost in private rituals of survival. Some prayed soundlessly, lips moving around words they dared not voice. Others traced invisible alphabets in the air, preserving languages they feared losing.

Miriam moved to the iron stove that barely warmed the room. With movements that seemed casual to anyone watching, she extracted the photograph and unfolded it with careful fingers. The paper was worn soft as cloth from being folded and refolded, but the image remained clear.

The boy smiled up at her. Not a posed smile but a real one, caught in a moment of genuine pleasure. Morning light touched his face like a benediction. His small hands held the wooden train with the careful attention children brought to their treasured possessions. His eyes held the bright curiosity of someone too young to understand that the world could be cruel.

David Rosenberg from Frankfurt. A child who had existed, who had been loved, who had played with toys and smiled in the morning light. Whatever had happened to him in the medical facility, this moment had been real. This joy had existed.

Miriam studied his face as if memorizing a map, fixing features that might never again be seen by eyes that recognized their significance. Then, with methodical care, she refolded the picture and slipped it back into her coat's hidden seam, next to the other small treasures that kept her human: a button from her mother's dress, a page torn from a book of poetry, a pencil stub no longer than her thumb.

And for the first time since her arrival at this manufactured hell, she spoke aloud to the empty air, her voice so soft it barely disturbed the silence:

"David Rosenberg. Frankfurt. April 1942."

The words contained neither hope nor despair. Just a marker placed between what was and what might be, a reminder that individual lives still mattered beyond the fences, that actions now might connect to consequences in some unimaginable future.

She would search the transfer records she sometimes translated, watch for mentions of children's transports, and listen when officers discussed "special treatment" procedures. She would look for any trace of a boy with dark curls and a wooden train. All while remaining Miriam the translator, Miriam the invisible, Miriam the survivor.

She would do this not because hope lived in this place, but because a woman with scholar's hands and desperate eyes had asked her to remember. To imagine a world beyond the electrified wire, a future neither might live to witness, where someone would need to know that David Rosenberg had been loved.

40

The Death March

Sirens shattered the January night. Guards who'd maintained methodical cruelty for months now ran between barracks, their boots crunching on ice, voices urgent with panic they'd never shown before. Dogs howled while orders became fragments as the camp's machinery of death jammed and seized.

The Russians were coming. The Red Army had broken through the eastern front. The camp was being emptied, its evidence scattered, its witnesses forced westward into the Polish winter.

Elsa had felt it building for days like tremors before collapse: fewer guards at roll call, officers snapping at each other in rapid German, and the chimneys standing cold since yesterday morning. Something fundamental had shifted in the rhythm of the place. The systematic murder had stopped, replaced by systematic panic.

They stumbled from barracks into the January night, thousands of prisoners blinking in the searchlights. Nearly sixty thousand from the Auschwitz camps. Elsa watched a woman ahead wrap a scrap of wool around bleeding feet. A man to her right had twisted paper into his wooden clogs. She'd stuffed her own shoes with straw that now froze against her skin like needles. The frozen ground drew heat from bare flesh with each step. Some screamed at first contact with the ice. Elsa had stopped feeling her toes an hour ago.

No one spoke as they assembled into columns. Words cost too much energy now.

The temperature had dropped to perhaps twenty below. Each breath stabbed her lungs with crystalline air. Her fingers, already damaged by months of labor, turned white at the tips. Around her, prisoners wrapped thin blankets around their heads like hoods, but the wind cut through everything.

Hope was something Elsa couldn't remember feeling anymore. Four months since they'd separated her from Fritz immediately upon arrival at the camp gates. Four months of accumulated suffering, each day stripping away another piece of herself until she wasn't sure what remained beneath the prison uniform and tattooed number.

But she'd endured. She'd survived the selections, the work details, the slow starvation. She'd even found someone willing to remember David's name if she died here. That fragile thread connected her to something larger than mere survival.

The chaos at the gate provided the impossible. In the darkness and confusion, as guards shouted contradictory orders and officers consulted maps by flashlight, the columns of men and women merged near the main gate. Guards focused on preventing escape rather than maintaining the rigid separation that had defined camp life. Bodies jostled together in the narrow space between the fences.

She knew his shoulders first. The slope of them, the particular forward tilt of his head when walking, etched in her memory from a thousand morning walks through Frankfurt. Fritz was a skeleton wearing her husband's posture. His face had hollowed to bone and skin stretched tight, his hair gone completely gray. Yet something remained unmistakably him, something the camp hadn't managed to kill.

He turned as if sensing her gaze. Her eyes found his across the narrow gap between columns.

The months since their separation vanished into this single moment of recognition. Not hope, as hope required energy they didn't have, but awareness that they both still existed despite everything designed to erase them.

Elsa broke from her line. Fritz jerked toward her. Around them, shouts erupted as guards tried to maintain order in the growing chaos. A rifle raised somewhere behind them, but another guard became distracted by movement at the perimeter where someone had stumbled into the electric fence. In the confusion and darkness, in the press of bodies and panic of evacuation, they slipped through the cracks of order like water finding its level.

No shots fired at them. No batons swung in their direction.

And then, impossibly, they walked side by side.

There was no embrace, no dramatic reunion. Their bodies, trained by months of camp discipline to avoid notice, kept careful distance. The miracle was proximity itself. Both alive, both moving, both here in this moment that yesterday would have been unimaginable.

Fritz's gaze dropped to her feet where thin wrappings had disintegrated, skin exposed to the ice. Dark spots marked her path behind them, blood frozen almost immediately in the brutal cold. He stared at her bleeding feet, helpless to do anything but witness her pain.

"David?" Elsa whispered, the word barely audible above the shuffling of thousands of feet.

His slight head shake told her everything. She'd known, but the confirmation still struck her like a physical blow.

"Found someone who might remember his name," she whispered back. She needed him to know about this small rebellion, this refusal to let David disappear completely from the world.

Fritz nodded once, understanding. His eyes held hers for a moment longer. The knowledge lived in their bones now, the terrible certainty they'd both carried but never spoken aloud.

They passed through the main gate at midnight. Behind them, floodlights stretched long shadows across the killing ground. Ahead, a road vanished into darkness and falling snow. The cold bit deeper outside the camp buildings as wind cut through their threadbare uniforms without mercy.

The column stretched ahead and behind them for perhaps a kilometer. Stronger prisoners moved toward the front, instinctively understanding that falling behind meant death. The weakest already struggled at the rear where rifle shots punctuated the night at irregular intervals. Fritz and Elsa found their place in the middle, avoiding both extremes.

They didn't speak again for hours. One foot before the other on the endless road. The sun rose pale and distant, offering light but no warmth. It crossed a colorless sky, then abandoned them again to darkness pierced only by the guards' flashlights sweeping back and forth across the column.

Snow fell in thick flakes, gathering on shoulders and covering the dark spots where prisoners had fallen. Bodies lined the roadside like mile markers. Guards sometimes bothered with a bullet for those who collapsed, sometimes let the cold finish the work. No stopping for the fallen, no looking back. The column flowed around the dead like water around stones.

Near midday on the second day, they passed through a small Polish town. Smoke rose from chimneys, carrying the smell of burning wood and cooking food. A woman stepped from a doorway, stared at the procession of skeletal figures, then hurried inside. Her door slammed shut, the sound sharp and final. Normal people living normal lives in heated houses with real food, a world that still existed parallel to their nightmare.

Fritz's throat worked as he swallowed repeatedly, his body betraying hunger it couldn't afford to acknowledge.

"*Bratkartoffeln*," he mouthed silently. Fried potatoes.

The word triggered a cascade of memory. Sunday mornings in their Frankfurt kitchen. Sizzling onions and crispy potato edges. Bach playing on the phonograph while David toddled in to watch his father flip potatoes with dramatic flourishes of the spatula. The smell of coffee brewing. Elsa at the table reading the newspaper aloud.

The memory struck her with unexpected force. Elsa stumbled, her balance gone as past and present collided. Without hesitation, Fritz's hand appeared at her elbow, not touching but hovering an inch away. She felt its presence, its readiness to catch her.

His fingers trembled near her skin, tendons tight with restraint. Touch meant attention from the guards, attention meant death, yet in that moment between falling and finding her feet, his hand waited to support her regardless of the risk.

She steadied herself. His hand withdrew to his side. Neither acknowledged the gesture because neither could afford gratitude. But as they shuffled forward, Elsa moved closer to him, near enough to feel the current of his movement, proof that he existed.

When the wind picked up and cut through her inadequate clothing, he shifted to block the worst of it. His skeleton body provided barely any shelter, but every degree of warmth mattered. When other prisoners around them ate snow to slake their thirst, he caught her eye and shook his head once. Snow would lower their body temperature further, steal precious energy from their failing systems. When they passed roadside corpses, he angled his body to shield her from the sight. Microscopic protections, each one a calculated risk.

298

The third day brought a blizzard. Wind howled across the open fields, driving snow horizontally into their faces. Visibility dropped to mere meters. The column bunched together as people instinctively sought shared warmth. Those who fell behind disappeared into the white curtain behind them. The guards themselves struggled now, their heavy coats and boots inadequate against the storm.

Evening brought no rest, just continued walking through darkness illuminated by swirling snow. Fritz began to stumble more frequently. Elsa could hear his breathing becoming labored, see the slight tremor in his legs that spoke of muscles failing. She moved closer still, ready to steady him as he'd done for her.

When guards finally called a halt near midnight, the column crowded into an abandoned barn that provided shelter from the wind but not the cold. The structure smelled of animals, creatures that had been better housed and fed than the humans now replacing them. Prisoners pressed together on the frozen dirt floor between livestock stalls, sharing body heat in a wordless agreement to survive the night.

In the barn's darkness, under cover of pressed bodies and whispered breathing, Fritz extracted something from his shirt lining. A bread crust no bigger than a matchbox, hoarded through impossible discipline. His fingers, frost-damaged and barely functional, broke it precisely in half.

"How?" Elsa whispered, unable to comprehend preserved food in their world of absolute starvation.

"Kitchen detail," Fritz murmured, his voice barely breathing. "Last week. Under the storage counter."

He'd worked in the camp kitchen for two months, she realized. The methodical habits that had once organized book publishing now applied to survival. He'd found this crust, hidden it, preserved it through the chaos of evacuation. The discipline required was almost incomprehensible.

He passed her portion with movements so subtle they registered as mere shifting in sleep. Her fingers closed around it, feeling its hardness, its impossible value. Perhaps thirty calories. A few crumbs of flour and water that represented everything words like "love" had once tried to capture before language, like all human constructs, had been stripped to its essential core.

She placed it on her tongue and let it dissolve slowly, savoring each particle. The taste was everything: sustenance, memory, hope distilled to its purest form. Her eyes closed as her mind escaped the barn briefly, traveling back to the bakery near their Frankfurt apartment where morning bread arrived still steaming from the ovens.

"Remember *Bäckerei Schmidt*?" The words escaped before she could measure their cost. Schmidt's Bakery.

Fritz didn't answer immediately. When he spoke, his voice carried years of Sunday mornings: "Christmas stollen. Orange peel and almonds."

They spoke in fragments after that, memories rationed like the bread. The apartment's morning light. David's first steps across the living room floor. The piano lessons that had filled their evenings with music. Each memory carefully selected, briefly shared, then packed away again.

They didn't speak of their son's fate directly. Grief, like joy, required strength they no longer possessed. They didn't speculate about their destination or their chances of survival. The future had shrunk to the next step, the next breath, the next moment of continued existence.

Before dawn, guards kicked them awake with boots and rifle butts. Bodies rose stiffly from the frozen ground, joints protesting after hours on the dirt floor. Those who couldn't rise received bullets. The shots echoed in the barn's confines, unnaturally loud after the whispered intimacy of the night.

The column reformed outside as dim light revealed white fields stretching toward distant forest. The sky promised more snow, heavy clouds pressing down like a gray ceiling. The wind had died, but the temperature had dropped even further during the night.

A man collapsed ten meters ahead of them, his legs simply giving way. He'd been walking beside them for three days, a teacher from Lodz who'd whispered mathematical formulas to himself like prayers. Now he lay in the snow, too exhausted to rise. A rifle cracked the morning silence.

Fritz's fingers brushed against Elsa's hand, contact so brief it might not have happened. Yet in that microscopic touch lived acknowledgment of what might come, what almost certainly would come if the march continued much longer. Neither had resources to sustain this indefinitely. Neither mentioned this probability.

But they had this moment. This step forward together. This shared breath in the brutal air.

Snow began falling again as they walked, thick flakes that covered their shoulders and the dark shapes scattered along the roadside. The column stretched ahead of them into the white distance, a river of human suffering flowing west toward an unknown destination.

Those who observed the marchers would have noticed nothing special about the two gaunt figures moving together. Their proximity seemed accidental, the careful distance between them revealing nothing of their connection. Just two more prisoners in striped uniforms, walking because walking was all that remained.

But they walked it together.

And in a world designed to erase every trace of human love, that small act of shared endurance became its own form of resistance. Not hope, which was a luxury they couldn't afford. Just the stubborn insistence on continuing to exist in the same space, breathing the same air, placing one foot in front of the other on the road that stretched endlessly ahead.

The march continued. The snow fell. The column moved west.

And somehow, impossibly, they were still together.

41

The Swiss Job - Miriam's Account

Basel, 1945: The streetlamps burn all night in Switzerland, wasteful and bright. I stand at my hotel window, counting them until my eyes water. Two blocks away, a baker slides morning loaves into an oven that hasn't gone cold since the war began. Three women laugh outside a café, their voices carrying through clean air. The sound makes me want to grab them by their shoulders, force them to understand what laughter cost elsewhere.

I press my hand against the cold glass and think of Sarah Goldstein. We shared a bunk at Birkenau until the fever took her. She used to whisper about a gold locket her mother gave her, hidden with family valuables in a Swiss bank. "After the war," she'd say, fingers tracing her collarbone where the chain used to rest. "It will all be waiting for us."

Sarah never made it to see the liberation. But her locket is down there somewhere, three blocks away in Alpenbank's vault, along with everything else they stole from us.

The bank squats on the corner like a well-fed animal, its sandstone facade scrubbed clean each morning. I've watched the same ritual for three days: guards changing positions with clockwork precision, wealthy clients stepping from automobiles that cost more than my father's entire library.

"More coffee, *Fräulein*?" Miss.

The waiter's Swiss German carries mountain inflections, nothing like the Berlin bark that still jerks me awake. I manage a smile and keep my own German clinical.

"Just the bill, please."

My forged papers rest against my ribs, tucked inside a pocket I sewed myself. Josef's work is flawless, but wearing someone else's name still feels like a costume that doesn't quite fit. Sometimes I catch myself responding to my real name before remembering it belongs to a dead girl.

A woman enters the bank, her fur coat heavy with money and indifference. The guard checks his watch. Fifteen seconds from curb to threshold. I make notes in my book, filling pages with timings, measurements, patterns. The mathematics of revenge.

"Ninety minutes," Wolf says, sliding into the chair opposite me.

He moves like smoke, this one. In the camps, he could appear beside your bunk without a sound, slip extra bread into your pocket while the guards weren't looking. Now he uses those same skills to cross a Swiss café unnoticed.

I sip my coffee before responding. "Four guards. Rotation every twenty minutes."

"The waiter's been watching you."

"Let him. Tomorrow he'll swear I was here alone." I close my notebook. "You look terrible."

Wolf's grin is sharp enough to cut glass. "Charming as always." But I see the exhaustion in his eyes, the way his hand trembles slightly before he controls it. None of us sleep well.

"Dresden was different," I say, keeping my voice low. "Half the records burned, guards looking over their shoulders at the Americans. This..." I nod toward the bank. "This is Swiss precision."

"Which is why we need to be better than precise. We need to be invisible." Wolf leans forward. "Rivka's found something. The blueprints Josef bought are wrong."

My stomach drops. "How wrong?"

"Wrong enough that Blum's having second thoughts. Not wrong enough to stop."

I think of Dr. Blum, how he stood over that dying SS guard in Krakow, watching him bleed out on the warehouse floor. Blum hadn't flinched then. If he's worried now, we should all be terrified.

"What else?" I ask.

Wolf's expression hardens. "Bauer takes lunch at Café Mozart. Same table, Tuesdays and Fridays. Predictable habits."

"You want me to approach him."

"You're the only one who can. Your German is perfect, you know banking, and..." He stops himself.

"And I'm a woman. Men like Bauer see a pretty face and stop thinking." I've played this role before, during our escape from the displaced persons camp. Amazing how quickly powerful men become stupid when they think they're being charmed.

Wolf doesn't like it. I can tell by the way his jaw tightens, how his fingers curl into fists on the table. In Birkenau, he'd position himself between me and the guards during inspections, taking beatings meant for others. Old habits.

"There's something else," I say. "I found her on the manifest."

"Who?"

"Sarah. Her locket is in safety deposit box 247. Along with her mother's wedding ring and her father's pocket watch." I pull the stolen document from my coat. "Look at this."

Wolf studies the list, his face growing pale. "These aren't just numbers. These are families."

"Every tooth pulled from every mouth. Every ring torn from every finger. All documented with German efficiency." My voice catches despite my efforts to stay clinical. "We're not just stealing money, Wolf. We're taking back pieces of murdered lives."

He reaches across the table and covers my hand with his. His palm is rough, scarred from the work details, but warm. "Then we make sure every piece finds its way home."

The touch lasts only seconds before he pulls away, but something passes between us. An understanding that goes deeper than shared survival. We're bound by more than trauma now.

Back at our rented rooms, the others wait. Josef hunches over his workbench, crafting new identities with an artist's precision. Rivka sits by the window, her detective's eyes cataloging every movement on the street below. Daniel spreads the building blueprints across the table while Dr. Blum checks his medical supplies.

The space feels crowded with more than people. We carry our ghosts with us: the friends who didn't make it, the families torn apart, the lives that ended in smoke. Sometimes I think the dead outnumber the living in this room.

"Found him," Josef announces, looking up from his papers. "Heinrich Bauer, Assistant Director. Thirty-eight years old, married, two children. Lives in Riehen, takes the tram to work."

"Habits?" Wolf asks.

"Café Mozart for lunch, Tuesdays and Fridays. Always orders the same thing: *schnitzel* and beer. Reads the financial papers. Sits alone." Josef's smile is cold. "Lonely man with expensive tastes." Breaded cutlet.

Dr. Blum looks up from his medical bag. "The compound is ready. Fast-acting for the guards, slower for the staff. No one dies."

"Unless they force our hand," Wolf says quietly.

We've had this argument before. After Krakow, after watching Rivka put two bullets in that warehouse guard, we swore no more killing. But we all know promises made in safety don't always survive contact with danger.

"Two weeks," Rivka says, speaking for the first time. Her voice is barely above a whisper now, damaged by screaming that no one heard. "They transfer major holdings on the fifteenth. Our window."

"Not enough time," Daniel objects. His tailor's precision extends to everything: measurements, timing, risk assessment. "We need at least three weeks to be sure."

"We don't have three weeks," I say. "The longer we stay, the more chance someone notices six refugees with expensive habits and no visible income."

Wolf nods. "Miriam's right. We move on the fifteenth or we don't move at all."

The room falls silent. Outside, Swiss church bells chime the hour. Normal people going about normal lives, unaware that six survivors are planning to rob their most secure bank.

"Roles," Wolf says finally. "Miriam approaches Bauer, gets him comfortable, maybe learns about internal security. I'll handle the guards. Rivka tracks police response times. Josef continues working on the vault combination. Daniel maps our escape routes. Blum prepares for medical emergencies."

"And if something goes wrong?" I ask.

"Then we improvise. It's what we're good at."

That night, I stand at my hotel window again, watching Switzerland sleep in its bubble of neutrality. The streetlamps burn steady and bright, wasteful with electricity while half of Europe still sits in darkness.

Wolf appears in my doorway without knocking. Another camp habit: privacy was a luxury none of us could afford.

"Can't sleep either?" he asks.

"Too quiet. In the camps, there was always noise. Crying, praying, guards shouting. Here..." I gesture at the peaceful street below. "It's like the world forgot what happened."

He joins me at the window. His reflection overlaps with mine in the glass, two ghosts haunting a hotel room in neutral Switzerland.

"Maybe that's why we're here," he says. "Someone needs to remember."

"Is that what this is? Remembrance?"

"Justice. Revenge. Does it matter what we call it?" His voice is soft but there's steel underneath. "They took everything from us. Our families, our homes, our futures. But they made one mistake."

"What's that?"

"They left us alive."

I turn to face him. In the dim light, his scars are barely visible, but I know they're there. We all carry marks, inside and out.

"After this," I say. "After we empty their vault and disappear. What then?"

Wolf considers the question. "There are others. Other banks, other Nazis who escaped with stolen wealth. Argentina's full of them."

"A lifetime of hunting?"

"If that's what it takes."

I think of Sarah's locket, waiting in that vault. Of all the other lockets, watches, rings, and photographs locked away like dirty secrets. Of the children who will never know their grandparents' faces because the pictures are trapped in Swiss steel.

"Then we better get this right," I say.

306

Wolf nods and turns to leave, but pauses at the door. "Miriam? Be careful with Bauer. Men like him..." He struggles for words. "They see what they want to see. But they can be dangerous when they realize they've been fooled."

"I can handle one Swiss banker."

"I know you can. That's not what worries me."

After he's gone, I return to the window. Down in the street, a man lights a cigarette and checks his watch. Just a late worker heading home, but my nerves are too sharp for casual assumptions.

Six survivors against Swiss precision. The odds have never been in our favor, but we've beaten worse. We survived the ghettos, the transports, the selections, the daily choice between humanity and survival.

Now we choose both.

I press my palm against the cold glass one more time, leaving a print that will fade by morning. Somewhere in this sleeping city, Heinrich Bauer lies in his comfortable bed, dreaming of profitable investments and Swiss efficiency. He has no idea that tomorrow, his orderly world will meet six people who learned mathematics in hell and graduated with degrees in impossible survival.

The streetlamps burn on, wasteful and bright, illuminating a country that sold its neutrality for Nazi gold. But not for much longer. We're about to collect what's owed, with interest.

I close my eyes and think of Sarah one more time. "Soon," I whisper to her memory. "Very soon."

42

The Swiss Job - The Plan

From our chalet, the Italian border wavers like a mirage on clear days. Josef's web of holding companies bought this place, with me playing my part: the Dutch widow, all pearls and grief. The locals leave me alone. Swiss discretion costs extra, just like the view.

Our basement has been transformed into something between a war room and a bank vault. Josef insisted on the same polish they use on teller counters, the same wax for the floors. Maps cover every wall. The eastern corner holds our recreation of Alpenbank's interior, built to exact specifications from stolen blueprints. Every pipe, every panel accounted for.

"This is madness," Daniel mutters, running his fingers along a replica wall panel.

"No," Josef says, adjusting a measurement with his ruler. "Madness was believing the Germans would keep their promises. This is just very expensive preparation."

Wolf studies the main blueprint spread across our table. He's rolled his sleeves back despite the mountain chill, and there's something different about him here. More focused. The random violence that kept us alive in the camps has crystallized into surgical precision.

"Tell me again why the service entrance?" he asks, though we've discussed this a dozen times.

"Because you're testing us," Rivka says without looking up from her street maps. Her pencil moves with detective precision, marking patrol routes and response times. "Making sure we can think on our feet when the plan goes wrong."

Wolf's grin appears, sharp and approving. "Maybe."

I watch them work and feel something I haven't experienced since before the war: the satisfaction of being part of something larger than survival. We've become a machine, each piece essential.

"Guards rotate at eight and noon," Wolf continues. "But there's a fifteen-minute window between eight-fifteen and eight-thirty when they're most vulnerable. Coffee break, shift change, attention wandering."

"Festival parade starts at eight-thirty," Rivka adds, making red marks on her map. "Pulls two patrol cars here and here. Response time to the bank stretches from four minutes to at least twelve."

Josef looks up from his forgery work, squinting through wire-rimmed glasses. "The internal alarm worries me more than the police. Direct line to the station, independent of the phone system."

"Won't be triggered," Daniel says. His tailor's fingers trace the vault mechanisms like he's measuring a customer for a suit. "Alarm requires a key turn from the manager's office. The manager will be occupied."

All eyes turn to me. I've spent three weeks crafting the perfect identity: wealthy, naive, vulnerable to masculine charm. The kind of woman men like Bauer think they can manipulate.

"Heinrich Bauer has agreed to a private consultation," I say, keeping my voice steady. "Eight-fifteen appointment. He's comfortable with me now, thinks I might transfer significant assets to his bank."

Wolf's expression darkens when I mention Bauer's name. His hands clench slightly before he forces them to relax.

"How comfortable?" Rivka asks.

"Comfortable enough to suggest lunch last week. Comfortable enough to close his office door and speak privately about my 'substantial Dutch holdings.'" I've practiced these lies until they feel like memories. "He'll give me thirty minutes minimum. Probably longer if I seem hesitant about committing funds."

"And if he tries something?" Wolf asks quietly.

The question hangs in the air. We all know what he's really asking.

"Then I handle it," I say. "I've handled worse."

Levi looks up from his medical supplies, precise movements unchanged since his surgery days in Vienna. "The compound requires exact timing," he says, closing a small vial with careful fingers. "Too little, they wake before we're clear. Too much..."

He doesn't finish. We all know about too much. After the farmhouse incident with Josef and Wolf and that SS officer, we made our pact: no unnecessary deaths. But 'unnecessary' can be a flexible word.

"Vault combination?" Wolf asks.

Josef sets down his pen. "Christoph thinks he has someone inside the manufacturer. Says he'll have it by week's end."

"Can we trust him?"

Wolf's smile contains no warmth whatsoever. "Christoph remembers what happened to Müller in Dresden when he tried to play both sides."

The casual menace in Wolf's voice should disturb me. It doesn't. Not after watching him share his bread rations with dying men. Not after he took a beating meant for me because I was too weak to stand for roll call. Not after finding hot tea outside my door on nights when the nightmares won't stop.

"Let's test the timing," Wolf says, moving toward our mock-up vault.

Daniel kneels beside the replica mechanism. Josef raises his stopwatch. The drill whine fills our basement war room.

"Twelve minutes," Josef calls.

Daniel swears under his breath, adjusts his angle. The bit slips.

"Fifteen minutes."

"Too slow," Rivka observes. "We'll be caught."

"Not finished," Daniel says through gritted teeth. He switches tools, working a thin metal probe into the mechanism. Sweat beads on his forehead.

"Eighteen... twenty... twenty-two minutes."

Daniel sits back, wiping his hands on a rag. "Without the combination, we're dead. Simple as that."

"Then we get the combination," Wolf says. "I'll meet Christoph tomorrow in Zurich."

The basement door creaks open. Rivka enters with a newspaper, her face grim.

"Problem," she announces, spreading it across our planning table.

The headline screams in German: "ALPENBANK ANNOUNCES SECURITY MODERNIZATION."

"In simple terms?" Wolf asks.

"New alarms, additional guards, completely new vault system next month." Rivka taps the article. "We wait, we face technology none of us understand."

Daniel stands, cleaning grease from his fingers. "So we attempt this without the vault combination? That's suicide."

"We proceed as planned," Wolf says. His voice carries the quiet authority that kept men alive in the barracks. "I'll have the combination by Friday."

"How can you be certain?" Levi asks.

Wolf's eyes are cold and fixed on the vault diagram. "Because the alternative is unacceptable."

Later, as the planning session winds down, I gather them back around the table. "There's something else we need to discuss. What exactly are we recovering."

The mood shifts, becomes heavier. We've focused so intently on the mechanics of entry that we've avoided thinking about what waits inside.

I spread Josef's stolen manifest across the blueprints. "I've decoded most of the inventory numbers. Location codes, origin markers, personal identification numbers."

"Meaning?" Rivka asks, though her detective instincts probably already know.

My finger traces down the columns. "Sarah Goldstein's locket. My mother's violin. Our family's silver *kiddush* cups." The Hebrew word catches in my throat. Ceremonial blessing cups.

Wolf leans forward. "My father's pocket watch. Gold case, inscription in Polish."

"Medical instruments from my Vienna practice," Levi adds quietly.

"Mother's diamond necklace," Daniel says. "Three carats in an emerald setting."

"My brother's Torah scrolls," Josef whispers. "Written in our grandfather's hand."

Rivka says nothing. I know she dreams about her police badge, the life she had before everything collapsed.

The silence stretches. These aren't just valuables. They're the physical remnants of murdered worlds.

"How much of it can we actually carry?" I ask.

Josef runs calculations in his head. "Priority items first. Personal effects that can be documented, then gold, then currency. Diamonds if we have space."

"And the rest?"

"Evidence," Wolf says simply. "Proof of what they did. Where it came from. Who it belonged to."

That night, I stand on the chalet's balcony, breathing mountain air that burns my lungs clean. The cold brings clarity at this altitude.

Wolf joins me without invitation, settling his jacket around my shoulders before I realize I'm shivering. His scent clings to the wool: soap, coffee, gun oil, and something uniquely him.

"You don't have to go through with the Bauer situation," he says, staring out at darkness. "We could find another approach."

I shake my head. "Each of us uses whatever weapons we have. You've killed to protect us. Rivka's killed to protect us. I can endure one banker's wandering hands."

His grip tightens on the railing. "It's not the same thing."

"Isn't it?" I turn to face him. "We're all doing what's necessary."

He's close enough that I can feel his warmth cutting through the mountain cold. In Birkenau, he used to position himself between me and the guards during inspections. Now he stands between me and the bitter wind.

"Three days," he says finally. "Rivka and Daniel finalize surveillance. Levi prepares the compounds. You confirm Bauer's routine. Josef and I retrieve the combination from Christoph."

I look out at the snow-covered peaks. "And when everything goes wrong?"

"Three escape routes. Six fallback positions. Emergency supplies cached between here and Milan. If we're separated, rendezvous in seventy-two hours."

His certainty should comfort me. Instead, it highlights how much can go wrong.

"Everything can fail, Wolf. We know that better than most people."

"And we know how to survive failure," he says, his voice softening the way it does when we're alone. His hand covers mine on the railing, rough palm against my knuckles. Just for a moment, then he pulls away. "We're not the same people they captured. We're not victims anymore."

The night air stings my lungs. Six damaged people preparing to rob Switzerland's most secure bank. The mathematics should terrify us. Instead, I feel something like peace.

"After this," I say. "After we empty their vault and disappear with Nazi gold. What then?"

Wolf considers the question carefully. "There are others. Banks in Argentina holding fortunes stolen from murdered families. SS officers living comfortable lives on money that isn't theirs."

"A lifetime of hunting?"

"However long it takes."

I think of Sarah's locket, waiting in that vault three days from now. Of all the other lockets, photographs, and heirlooms locked away like dirty secrets.

"Then we'd better not get caught," I say.

Wolf nods and turns toward the door, but pauses. "Miriam? Be very careful with Bauer. Men like him see what they want to see, but they can be dangerous when they realize they've been deceived."

"I can handle one Swiss banker."

"I know. That's not what worries me."

After he leaves, I remain on the balcony. The Italian border shimmers in the distance, promising escape routes and new identities. But first, we have promises to keep.

Six survivors against Swiss precision and Nazi gold. The odds have never favored us. But we've learned to make our own luck, and tomorrow we begin collecting what the world owes us.

I pull Wolf's jacket tighter and think of Sarah one more time. Three days, and her locket comes home.

43

The Swiss Job - The Execution

Dawn broke over the Swiss valley, turning snow-capped peaks to cold gold. In the chalet basement, the six of us crowded into too small a space. The concrete walls stank of floor polish and my own sweat.

Josef stood before us, pocket watch in hand. The back was engraved with a family name from Krakow. No living owners left to claim it. He tapped it against his thumbnail with nervous precision.

"Synchronize now. Six forty-seven and fifteen seconds."

We adjusted our timepieces in silence. For the next few hours, every minute could kill us or save us. I thought of Sarah's locket waiting in that vault, and my hands stopped trembling.

Wolf laid out the gear on the table. Field radios. Aerosol canisters disguised as breath fresheners. Forged papers that could fool Swiss bureaucrats. Levi's medical bag with its precise doses of chemical sleep.

"Final check," Wolf said. The charm he used on Swiss shopkeepers had vanished completely. This was the Wolf from the camp: hard edges and cold calculation. "Daniel?"

"Truck's behind the bakery." Daniel's fingers smoothed his pants leg, a tailor's habit even now. "Three minutes to the bank. Wire cutters ready. Uniforms pressed."

"Rivka?"

"First marchers at eight-thirty sharp." Rivka had the entire parade route memorized. "Two cops in the square, one patrol at the west end. Response time stretches to twelve minutes minimum once the music starts."

"Levi?"

The doctor's hands moved over his black bag like he was preparing for surgery. "Guards get the fast compound. Bank staff get the delayed version. Dosages calculated for body weight and stress levels."

"Josef?"

"Papers are perfect. Window opens at eight-fifteen, closes at nine-oh-one. Forty-six minutes to get in, get what we came for, and disappear."

"Miriam?"

I stood apart, already transformed into the wealthy Dutch widow. Good pearls, expensive enough to convince a greedy banker. Black suit that whispered money and respectability.

"Meeting with Bauer at eight-fifteen. His secretary has instructions to hold all calls. He's already suggested we discuss my holdings over lunch." The words tasted bitter, but my voice stayed steady.

Wolf's expression hardened like winter settling over the mountains. He said nothing, just nodded curtly, then looked at each of us in turn. No speeches, no dramatic farewells.

"We meet back here by two o'clock," Wolf said. "All of us."

It wasn't hope. It was an order from someone who'd kept men alive through hell.

At precisely eight-fifteen, my heels clicked across Alpenbank's marble floor. The sound echoed in the vaulted space like gunshots. The senior teller nodded, recognizing the wealthy widow who'd been courting their services. The bank reeked of lemon oil and old money.

Director Bauer materialized from his office with that predatory smile I'd learned to expect. His eyes remained fixed on what I represented: substantial assets waiting to be harvested.

"*Frau Van der Meer*, punctual as always." He gestured toward his private office. "Please, shall we continue our discussion about your substantial Dutch holdings?" Mrs. Van der Meer.

I gave him the smile I'd practiced for weeks, empty and inviting. "Of course, Director. I've brought the documentation we discussed."

My mind split in two as his office door closed behind us. One half recited memorized details about nonexistent Dutch securities. The other half wondered if Wolf was already in position, if Josef had talked their way past the service entrance guards.

Meanwhile, two blocks south, Daniel and Rivka approached the electrical junction box. Both wore gray coveralls stolen from a legitimate repair crew, caps pulled low over their faces. Daniel's toolbox weighed forty pounds and contained everything except legitimate electrical equipment.

The festival band was tuning up in the square, brass instruments catching morning sunlight. Children in traditional costumes ran between the vendors while their parents counted change for festival treats.

"Right on schedule," Daniel murmured, opening the junction box with Wolf's stolen master key.

"Band's warming up," Rivka confirmed, her detective's eyes scanning the crowd. "Two cops by the fountain, already bored. Old men drinking beer. Perfect cover."

Daniel traced the wiring inside the box with surgeon precision. Each wire had been memorized from stolen utility maps. "Ready when you give the word."

"Not yet," Rivka said, checking her watch. "Wolf goes first."

They stood in plain sight, just another utility crew fixing morning problems. In Switzerland, men in proper uniforms were invisible. Reliable. Background noise.

At eight thirty-eight, Wolf guided the delivery truck down the narrow street behind Alpenbank. Josef sat beside him, clipboard balanced on his knees, playing the role of nervous assistant.

"Guard change in two minutes," Josef said, consulting his meticulously timed notes. "Twenty seconds when neither guard watches the service door."

Wolf pulled into the loading area. "Christoph's combination better work."

Josef patted his breast pocket where three sequences waited on paper. "He says the middle one's most likely. For what we paid him, it has to be."

They sat in charged silence as the engine ticked, cooling. Josef checked his watch obsessively. "Eight-forty-two. Time to go."

They climbed out with practiced casualness. Wolf carried a clipboard and official scowl. Josef shouldered a crate marked "Accounting Supplies." Just two delivery men on a routine morning run.

Wolf pressed the service buzzer. A guard opened the door, alert but not suspicious.

"Identification," he said in Swiss German.

Wolf flashed the forged papers with bureaucratic efficiency. "Monthly supplies for the accounting department. Need a signature here." His German was flawless, carrying no regional accent that could be traced.

The guard scanned the papers while a second guard watched from behind. Neither looked particularly concerned. This was Switzerland, where routines were sacred and punctuality was holy.

Josef shifted the crate, letting it slip just slightly. The first guard's eyes flicked toward the movement. Wolf's hand found the aerosol canister in his pocket.

"Careful with that," the guard warned.

"Sorry," Josef replied, then deliberately dropped his clipboard. Papers scattered across the loading dock. Among them, clearly visible, lay a document with the Reich eagle letterhead, damning and unmistakable.

Both guards froze, eyes locked on that symbol. It still carried power, that eagle. Even in defeat, it commanded attention. In that split second of distraction, Wolf raised the aerosol and sprayed both men.

The compound worked exactly as Levi had promised. Within seconds, both guards swayed, confusion blooming in their eyes like opening flowers. Wolf caught the first as he collapsed. Josef grabbed the second. They lowered both men to the floor without sound.

"Clear," Wolf breathed into his radio.

Two blocks away, Rivka nudged Daniel. "Now."

Daniel's wire cutters closed on the telephone lines that connected Alpenbank to the police station. No alarm would reach help now.

"Lines cut," Rivka confirmed into her transmitter. "Moving to position."

Inside Bauer's office, I was explaining Dutch tax law when my compact vibrated against my leg. The signal I'd been waiting for. Something in my chest loosened fractionally.

"Director," I said, pressing one hand to my throat with practiced fragility. "I feel suddenly..."

I let my voice trail off, then executed what I hoped was a convincing faint, collapsing forward onto his mahogany desk. Papers scattered. A crystal water pitcher toppled, soaking my sleeve with genuinely cold water.

"*Frau Van der Meer*!" Bauer stood quickly, rounded his desk to help. The gentleman act, just as I'd predicted. He opened his office door to call for assistance.

But instead of finding his normal, orderly bank, Bauer saw Josef hanging a "Closed for Emergency" sign on the front door while unknown men in utility uniforms escorted his tellers toward the break room.

"What is happening?" he began, but Josef appeared beside him with an aerosol canister.

I caught Bauer as the compound took effect, his body heavier than expected, dense with good living and Swiss prosperity. Together, Josef and I dragged him back into his office.

"How long?" I whispered.

"Thirty minutes minimum," Josef replied. "Levi's dosages are precise."

"Clear here," I said into my radio.

In the main banking hall, Wolf moved like smoke between the marble columns. The "Closed for Emergency" sign hung on the front door, blinds drawn against curious eyes. In the break room, Levi had gathered the staff.

"Just a precaution," Levi was explaining in his educated Berlin German. "Possible gas leak from construction next door. Please drink this solution. It will counteract any effects."

The tellers sipped Levi's mild sedative without question. His medical authority and calm bedside manner made resistance unthinkable.

With the bank secured, Josef led Wolf and me toward the vault. We moved through the silent building like ghosts, our footsteps swallowed by thick carpet.

"Eleven minutes elapsed," I said, checking my watch.

"Festival music starting," came Rivka's voice through the radio. "Cops are moving toward the parade. Window is open."

Josef knelt before the vault, unfolding Christoph's paper with trembling fingers. He began the first combination sequence, movements precise despite the pressure.

Left 27. Right 46. Left 12. Nothing.

"First one's wrong," he muttered.

"Try the second," Wolf said, eyes on his watch.

Josef took a breath, wiped sweat from his palms, and started again. Left 16. Right 73. Left 34. Right 9.

I held my breath. Sarah's locket was behind that steel door, along with thousands of other stolen lives.

"Time check?" Wolf asked.

"Eighteen minutes since start," I replied. "Twenty-eight minutes until we need to move."

Josef's fingers completed the sequence. A subtle click echoed from within the mechanism. Tumblers falling into place. The vault had accepted the combination.

But the door didn't open.

"Secondary lock," Josef said, running his hands along the door frame. "Mechanical override. This wasn't in our blueprints."

My heart sank. We'd come so far, risked everything, and now...

"Let me," Wolf said, pressing his ear to the metal.

"You're not a safecracker," I protested.

"No, but I've opened locks before. Different kind, same principle." Wolf's fingers traced the door seam with delicate precision. "Everyone stay quiet."

He worked in absolute silence, face pressed against the cold steel, listening for vibrations only he could detect. Sweat beaded on his forehead despite the bank's chill.

One minute passed. Then another. I could hear my heartbeat in my ears.

"Window's closing," came Rivka's voice. "Need to hurry."

Wolf held up a hand for silence. His fingers found a nearly invisible depression near the hinge mechanism. He pressed, twisted, and pulled in one fluid motion.

A solid thunk from inside the door.

"Got it," Wolf said simply.

Josef and I grabbed the massive handle. The vault door swung open silently, revealing everything we'd dreamed of and feared to hope for.

The vault was smaller than expected but densely packed with stolen wealth. Gold bars lined one wall, each stamped with the Reich eagle. Foreign currency filled drawers in precise stacks. Loose gemstones sparkled in labeled trays.

But it was the safety deposit boxes that drew my attention. Brass numbers gleamed, and among them, the specific boxes listed in our Birkenau manifest.

"Twenty-two minutes," Josef said. "Load priority items first."

We worked with the efficiency of people who knew freedom measured in minutes. Gold bars disappeared into specially sewn pockets. Currency vanished into our clothing. I focused on the deposit boxes, using keys from Bauer's office to open those we'd identified.

The contents confirmed everything and broke my heart simultaneously. Wedding rings inscribed in Hebrew. Pocket watches engraved with family names. Pearl necklaces still in boxes from Warsaw jewelers.

In box 247, I found what I'd come for. Sarah's locket, exactly as she'd described it during those whispered conversations in our shared bunk. I opened it with trembling fingers. Inside, a photograph of a young woman with serious eyes and round cheeks.

"You knew her," Josef observed, watching me.

I closed the locket and slipped it into my pocket instead of our collection bag. Some things were beyond price. "Birkenau. Same barracks. She died believing her family's treasures were safe."

"Fifteen minutes," Wolf warned.

We finished loading in grim silence. Before leaving the vault, Josef placed a manila envelope on the center shelf. Inside were photocopied documents proving the bank's collaboration with Nazi theft. Evidence that would trigger investigations but not scandal. Swiss discretion would protect reputations while justice slowly ground forward.

As we prepared to leave, a sound from the front entrance froze us all. Someone knocking on glass.

Wolf motioned for us to continue toward the service exit while he investigated. From the shadows, he watched a middle-aged woman trying the front door, peering through the drawn blinds. She knocked again, harder, then consulted a small appointment book.

The woman checked her watch, frowned at the "Closed" sign, and finally walked away, muttering about Swiss efficiency.

Wolf rejoined us at the service entrance where Daniel was backing the truck into position.

"Close call?" I asked.

"Very close. But she's gone."

Before leaving, Levi made a final check of the sedated staff, ensuring all were positioned safely. He adjusted a young teller's head to keep her airway clear, the doctor in him unable to abandon his oath even here.

"Fifty-four minutes total," Josef noted as we loaded our transformed cargo. "Four minutes under schedule."

Daniel took the wheel with Wolf riding beside him. The rest of us hid in the modified truck compartment, surrounded by Nazi gold now liberated and transformed into justice.

"Drive normally," Wolf instructed. "Every traffic law, every speed limit."

Daniel nodded, pulling away from Alpenbank with painful normalcy. We passed the festival parade where children marched in traditional costumes and a brass band played cheerful songs. Local families cheered and applauded, completely unaware that one of history's most audacious thefts had just occurred three blocks away.

Only when we'd cleared the town and started climbing into the mountains did Wolf speak again.

"We did it," he said, wonder creeping through his careful control.

Daniel kept his eyes on the winding road. "We're not safe yet."

"No," Wolf agreed, watching Switzerland's perfect landscape slide past our windows. "But for the first time since Birkenau, I think we might actually make it home."

Hidden in our cramped compartment, I sat in charged silence with the others. My fingers traced the outline of Sarah's locket through my coat pocket. I thought of justice and revenge that looked too much alike sometimes. Gold for ashes. Money for lives. But also: stolen treasures returned to their purpose, wealth redirected toward rebuilding what had been destroyed.

The truck wound higher into the mountains, carrying its cargo of liberated riches and damaged souls toward whatever came next.

That evening, we sat around the chalet's dining table. Wine was poured but nobody drank much. Old habits from the camps, where alertness meant survival.

"To success," Wolf said, lifting his glass.

We drank, each lost in private thoughts. Daniel kept folding his napkin with mechanical precision. Josef stared at nothing, probably calculating distribution percentages. Rivka's fingers never strayed far from the knife beside her plate.

Later, when the others had retreated to their rooms, I found myself alone with Wolf on the balcony. The night air smelled of pine and distant snow, clean and sharp in my lungs.

"What now?" I asked.

Wolf turned the question over carefully. "We keep going. The money goes where it needs to: survivors, communities rebuilding, people hunting the ones who escaped. This was never about personal wealth."

"And the rest of it? The memories? The guilt?"

He turned toward me, his face softening in the mountain darkness. "We carry them forward. Like everything else we've survived."

I pulled Sarah's locket from my pocket, gold catching the faint starlight. "I keep thinking about what they stole. Not just lives or objects. They took our futures. Our possibilities."

"Not all of them," Wolf said quietly. He covered my hand with his, warm and solid and present. "We're still breathing. That's a victory they couldn't prevent."

I looked at our joined hands, then out at the Swiss valley spread below, peaceful and oblivious. Somewhere in that darkness stood Alpenbank, where tomorrow morning confused employees would discover their vault emptied and their complicity exposed.

"Yes," I said finally. "We're still here." I leaned into Wolf's warmth, allowing myself this small comfort after so much coldness. "I suppose that's enough for now."

Above us, stars pierced the black sky with ancient light. The mountains stood as they had for millennia, indifferent to human triumph or tragedy. And in a chalet balanced between earth and heaven, six survivors began to imagine what came after revenge, what could be built on the foundation of justice finally served.

44

The Swiss Job - The Aftermath

We kept the curtains drawn for three days. No one raised their voice above a whisper. Josef filled notebook pages with radio broadcasts while we took shifts at the windows, watching for Swiss police cars that never came.

On the third morning, the local newspaper finally mentioned Alpenbank. Page three, buried beneath advertisements for winter coats. Just an "incident" involving a medical emergency. Nothing about missing gold. Nothing about empty vaults.

"They're keeping it quiet," Wolf said, slapping the paper down on our kitchen table.

Rivka pushed her cold coffee away. "Won't last. Banking authorities know by now. Questions are being asked in Zurich."

"By which time we'll be gone," Josef said, though his voice lacked conviction.

I felt the weight of Sarah's locket in my pocket, warm against my fingers. Three days, and it still felt like stolen time. Every minute we stayed here increased our danger, but leaving meant accepting that the heist was really over.

"Bauer's been replaced," I announced, scanning intelligence from Wolf's contacts. "Officially it's 'health concerns following exposure to industrial chemicals.' Unofficially, he's been transferred to some village branch where he can't cause embarrassment."

I remembered his cologne, how he'd leaned close while examining my forged documents. His downfall should have felt like victory. Instead, I felt only cold satisfaction.

"They're closing ranks," Daniel observed.

"Which works for us," Josef replied, but uncertainty crept into his voice.

Levi had been silent all morning, sorting gemstones with mechanical precision. When he finally spoke, his words carried unexpected weight.

"Have you really looked at this?" He spread photographs across the table. "These aren't just valuable objects. They're fragments of murdered lives."

The kitchen went quiet. We'd inventoried every item, catalogued every piece, but suddenly I saw more than gold and currency. Levi held up a child's bracelet, so small it could only have belonged to someone under ten.

I pulled out Sarah's locket and opened it. The photograph inside showed serious eyes, round cheeks, a woman who believed her treasures would outlast the war.

"We need to decide what we're really doing here," I said. "Are we thieves or are we undertakers?"

Wolf leaned back in his chair. "Does it matter? The gold doesn't care what we call ourselves."

"It matters to me," Levi said quietly. "Every night I dream about the people who owned these things. They trusted Swiss banks to protect what mattered most."

The silence stretched until Josef cleared his throat. "The reinvestment plan is ready. Five banks, flawless documentation. Family heirlooms recovered from Nazi theft, Dutch investments hidden during occupation."

"How long?" Wolf asked.

"Three weeks if we're careful. Two if we take risks."

I stood and walked to the window. Below us, Swiss villages carried on their orderly lives, unaware that six refugees had just pulled off one of the country's most audacious thefts.

"I'll handle the banking," I said. "Different identity at each institution. Wealthy widow looking to invest recovered assets."

Wolf's expression darkened. "More performances. More Bauers."

"Each bank visit is a small victory," I replied. "Every deposit transforms stolen Nazi gold into something useful. Money for survivor relief, funds for hunting war criminals, resources for rebuilding communities."

"And reserves," Josef added. "For operations like Argentina."

The word hung in the air like smoke. We all knew what waited in Argentina: SS officers living comfortable lives on wealth that wasn't theirs.

"*Sturmbannführer* Helmut Seidel," Josef said, unfolding a map of South America. "Living in Buenos Aires under the name Ricardo Brenner. Government connections, legitimate business interests, all built on gold stolen from murdered families." SS major.

The room temperature seemed to drop. Helmut Seidel. Even his name carried the memory of polished boots and casual cruelty.

"Argentina's a long way from Switzerland," Daniel said.

"So was freedom, once," Wolf replied.

Two weeks later, I'd become our public face across Swiss banking. Zurich: navy dress, conservative pearls, old money discretion. Geneva: silk scarf, Italian leather, cosmopolitan sophistication. Lugano: understated elegance suggesting Mediterranean connections.

Each performance required becoming someone new while smuggling our liberated assets into legitimate financial channels. The irony wasn't lost on me: using Swiss banking discretion to launder gold stolen by the Nazis from murdered families.

At each institution, I smiled at men who reminded me of Bauer, signed papers with steady hands, became the kind of client Swiss bankers cultivated: wealthy, discreet, and unquestioning.

But each signature felt like justice served cold.

Each evening when I returned to the chalet, Wolf waited. He never asked if I was managing the strain, never mentioned the dark circles under my eyes. But he'd sit with me in comfortable silence, sometimes bringing tea I hadn't requested but always needed.

"Two more banks next week," I told him after returning from Geneva. We sat on the balcony while mountains rose around us like fortress walls.

"They believe every word you tell them," Wolf said. "You make them see exactly what you want them to see."

I looked at peaks touched with evening light. "Survival has always been performance."

"But this is different. You're not just surviving anymore. You're hunting."

After six weeks, most of our recovered assets had been redistributed throughout the Swiss banking system. Clean money for dirty purposes, as Josef called it. We prepared to leave.

The basement was sterile now, empty of planning maps and gold bars. We'd scrubbed the floors with bleach and removed every trace of our presence.

"The Italian border offers three crossing points," Rivka said during our final planning session. "I'll take the main road. My language skills and contacts will handle any problems."

"Wolf and Josef, mountain crossing," I said, consulting our escape plans. "Levi, Daniel, and I take the train. Wealthy travelers heading south for the climate."

"And after Milan?" Daniel asked.

Josef spread his South American map across the table. His finger pressed on Buenos Aires. "Helmut Seidel owns a shipping company. Imports from Europe, exports to North America. Perfect front for moving stolen assets."

"Are we deciding now?" Wolf asked. "Argentina?"

"Italy first," Josef said, folding the map precisely. "Then we choose."

But we all understood what hung unspoken in the air. Each operation had been larger than the last, carrying greater risks. Argentina would test everything we'd learned about survival and justice.

The border crossing went smoothly. Rivka secured our Milan safe house without incident. Wolf and Josef navigated mountain passes despite early snow. My group encountered only one problem: Italian guards showed too much interest in my expensive luggage.

I played the haughty widow, speaking rapid French with a convincing Dutch accent. When linguistics failed, I reached into my purse and counted out Swiss francs. The senior guard hesitated, then pocketed the money with practiced ease.

Only when we gathered in Milan did the reality settle in. We'd actually succeeded. The relief was physical, like setting down a weight I'd carried for months.

That night, we shared a genuine meal: Italian wine, fresh bread, and even laughter. The apartment forced us into close quarters, but I found I didn't mind. These five people had become something like a family.

"A toast," Wolf said, raising his glass. "To the most civilized bank robbery in history. No violence, no alarms, no running from the police."

"I'll take civilized," Daniel replied. He'd gained confidence since the heist, moved with new certainty.

"The real achievement was putting it back into Swiss banks," I said. "Full circle."

"Not quite," Levi corrected. "This time the money serves justice instead of genocide."

Josef raised his water glass. "To purposes worthy of what was lost."

We drank to that, each lost in private thoughts. We'd turned Swiss banking discretion against itself, becoming practitioners of economic justice through irony.

Later that night, as the others slept, I stood at the window watching Milan rebuild itself. The city sparkled with electric lights, people moving freely through streets that had known occupation and liberation.

I opened Sarah's locket again, studied her photograph in the window's reflection.

"It's finished," I whispered to her memory. "Not enough. Never enough. But something."

Josef appeared beside me, quiet as always.

"Are we criminals now?" I asked. "Or something else?"

Josef considered the question carefully. "I don't know if those categories matter anymore. But were we necessary? Yes."

"Argentina, then?"

"If we all agree."

"And after that?"

Josef had no answer. We both knew there would always be more Nazis escaping justice, more stolen wealth to recover, more communities needing resources to rebuild.

I looked at the locket one final time before pocketing it. "I want to find where her family lived. See if anyone survived."

"We'll help," Josef said simply.

From the next room came Wolf's steady breathing. Rivka murmured something in her sleep about police procedures. Life continued, even for people who'd just committed the perfect crime.

"We survived, Josef. Against everything they did to us."

"More than survived," he added quietly. "We remembered who we are."

Outside, Milan continued its night rhythm, oblivious to six people who'd transformed Nazi gold from a tool of oppression into a weapon for justice. The money would fund survivor relief, support war crimes investigations, and finance operations against escaped SS officers living comfortable lives on stolen wealth.

I finally turned from the window. My body ached for sleep, but my mind raced with account numbers, distribution plans, and the faces of men like Helmut Seidel who thought they'd escaped consequences.

I touched the locket through my coat one more time. "Sleep well, Sarah," I whispered. "We're just getting started."

Three days later, we stood at Milan's central train station. Rivka would continue south to establish networks in Rome. Levi and Daniel planned to return to displaced persons camps, using our funds to improve conditions and locate surviving family members.

Josef had already departed for Genoa, carrying documents and gold toward ship passages to Argentina.

Wolf and I watched the others disappear into crowds of travelers, refugees, and rebuilding Europeans. Six people who'd shared hell were scattering across the continent like seeds carried by wind.

"Regrets?" Wolf asked as our train approached.

I thought of Switzerland's mountains, of Alpenbank's violated vault, of Nazi gold transformed into justice. "None. You?"

"Only that it took us this long."

330

We boarded the southbound express, carrying new identities and old purposes. Through the window, the Italian countryside rolled past in golden afternoon light. Ahead lay Argentina, Helmut Seidel, and the next phase of our war against escaped evil.

I settled into my seat and opened Sarah's locket one more time. Her photograph smiled up at me, frozen in a moment before the world ended. But now her treasures served living purposes, and her death had meaning beyond mere loss.

"Almost home," I told her silently, then closed the locket and turned my attention to planning our next impossible thing.

Outside, Europe healed and rebuilt. Inside our compartment, two survivors planned justice for the dead.

45

The Haifa Operation

Haifa sparkled in the Mediterranean evening light, but Miriam saw only darkness in the testimony she was translating. Her pen moved across the Hebrew text with mechanical precision, converting one survivor's nightmare into clinical German that their target would understand.

"Subject B-7: Male twin, age six years, four months. Initial injection administered 0800 hours. Subject exhibited tremors within twelve minutes. Vomiting commenced at fourteen minutes. Convulsions began..."

She set down her pen and rubbed her eyes. Twenty-six years since Birkenau, and the words still had power to break her.

"Another medical research file?" Wolf asked from across their rented apartment's main room. At fifty-one, he carried himself with the careful economy of a man who'd learned violence as a survival tool and refined it into an art.

"Dr. Anton Meier's notes," Miriam replied. "Twin studies. He documented everything with German thoroughness."

Josef looked up from his printing press, where he was producing perfect Israeli identity documents. His counterfeiting operation had evolved far beyond wartime forgeries. These days, he funded their entire network through carefully crafted currencies and documents sold to refugees and intelligence services.

"How many children did Meier kill?" Josef asked, adjusting his glasses.

"Forty-seven documented cases," Miriam said. "Probably twice that number undocumented."

Rivka entered from the balcony where she'd been monitoring police radio frequencies. At fifty-three, her detective instincts had expanded into international intelligence coordination. She maintained contacts in a dozen countries now, all feeding information about Nazi war criminals living comfortable lives.

"We have a problem," she announced, her face grim. "The watcher isn't just watching Meier anymore. He's watching us."

Wolf was immediately alert. "How close?"

"Close enough to photograph our faces. Professional telephoto lens from the building across the street."

Daniel emerged from the bedroom where he'd been altering their appearance for tonight's operation. He'd become their master of disguise and infiltration, but unlike the others, he still questioned their transformation from survivors to hunters.

"Maybe we should abort," Daniel said. "If Israeli intelligence is onto us..."

"We can't," Miriam said firmly. "Meier received notification yesterday. He's planning to leave Israel next week. Damascus, according to our source."

Levi looked up from his medical bag where he was preparing specialized compounds. At fifty-nine, he retained the steady hands that had made him Berlin's most promising young neurosurgeon at twenty-seven, before the war destroyed his world. Now those same hands delivered justice with clinical precision.

"Syrian protection," Levi observed. "If he reaches Damascus, we'll never get another chance."

Wolf moved to the window and peered through the curtains. A man in a gray jacket sat on a bench across the street, newspaper open but eyes on their building.

"Professional surveillance," Wolf confirmed. "Military bearing. He's not trying very hard to hide anymore."

"Maybe that's the point," Josef said. "Maybe he wants us to see him."

The room fell silent as they processed this possibility. Through the window, Haifa's evening life continued: families walking to dinner, children playing in courtyards, normal people living normal lives because people like them hunted monsters in the shadows.

"This is our twelfth operation," Wolf said. "We've never had intelligence interference before."

"Meier's different," Rivka said. "He's been living openly, treating Israeli patients. Someone in government might feel protective."

Daniel wasn't satisfied. "All the more reason to reconsider. The others were different. Low-level SS guards, minor officials hiding in remote places. Meier's integrated into Israeli society."

"He's integrated by design," Miriam said, holding up the translated testimony. "Perfect cover for a child murderer. Rebecca Goldstein, age seven. He injected her with typhus to test treatment methods. She lived for six days. He documented her fever progression by the hour."

They'd had this conversation before, in different cities with different targets. It never got easier, but it always ended the same way.

Wolf spread photographs across the table. Surveillance shots from the past week showed a distinguished older man with silver hair and careful posture. He looked like someone's grandfather.

"Meier maintains strict routines," Wolf said. "Clinic in the morning, private consultations in the afternoon. Home by six. Synagogue on Fridays."

"Perfect cover," Rivka observed. "But his routine's been disrupted. Yesterday he visited his bank, then drove to the airport. He's preparing to run."

"The watcher spooked him?" Daniel asked.

"Or something else did. We're not his only enemies."

Levi closed his medical bag with a soft click. "Tomorrow evening, then. Medical consultation about research collaboration. I approach him as Dr. David Rosen from Hadassah Hospital."

"Too dangerous with surveillance," Daniel protested.

"More dangerous to wait," Wolf replied. "If he disappears to Damascus, those forty-seven children die a second time."

"Backup positions?" Rivka asked.

"Modified plan," Wolf said, his tactical mind adapting to new circumstances. "Rivka monitors the watcher. If he moves to intercept, you create a distraction. Daniel covers the clinic's back exit. Josef handles emergency extraction. Miriam translates if negotiations go wrong."

"And if the watcher calls for backup?"

"Then we improvise. It's what we're good at."

The next morning brought crisp Mediterranean air and unexpected complications. The watcher was gone from his usual position, replaced by a different man who didn't bother hiding his interest in their building.

"They're rotating surveillance," Rivka observed from behind the newspaper. "Professional operation."

"Or they're moving to arrest us," Daniel muttered.

"Only one way to find out," Wolf said. "We proceed as planned."

Levi, transformed by Daniel's skills into Dr. David Rosen, approached Meier's private clinic carrying genuine medical credentials Josef had obtained through their network. But as he rounded the corner, he spotted the original watcher stationed near the clinic entrance.

"Problem," Levi said into his concealed radio. "Surveillance at target location."

"Abort?" Wolf's voice crackled back.

Levi studied the clinic. Through the windows, he could see Meier moving around his office, packing files into boxes. Time was running out.

"Negative. Proceeding with modifications."

Instead of the front entrance, Levi circled to the building's service alley. A delivery truck was unloading medical supplies. He approached the driver with practiced authority.

"Dr. Rosen, Hadassah Hospital," he said, flashing credentials. "Emergency consultation with Dr. Meier. Which way to the service entrance?"

The driver pointed helpfully. Minutes later, Levi was inside the building, moving through service corridors toward Meier's office.

The receptionist looked up in surprise as he emerged from the back hallway. "Dr. Rosen? I thought you were coming through the front."

"Parking complications," Levi said smoothly. "Is Dr. Meier available?"

"He's in his office, but he's been quite agitated today. Something about travel arrangements."

Anton Meier looked up from his packing as Levi entered: silver-haired, distinguished, but with nervous energy that suggested imminent departure.

"Dr. Rosen, welcome," Meier said in accented Hebrew. "Though I'm afraid our consultation will need to be brief. Unexpected travel has arisen."

They settled in Meier's office, which was half-packed, medical texts in boxes and family photographs already removed from the walls.

"I'm particularly interested in your work with twins," Levi said carefully. "I understand you did extensive research during the war years."

Something shifted in Meier's expression. A brief flicker of recognition, quickly suppressed.

"My wartime work was... limited," Meier said, his hands stilling on a file box. "Difficult conditions. Few resources. Not something I discuss professionally."

"Of course. But the documentation I've seen suggests remarkably detailed observations. Particularly regarding physiological responses to stress and pharmaceutical intervention."

Meier's posture straightened. Through the window, Levi could see the watcher moving closer to the building.

"May I ask where you've seen such documentation?" Meier asked, his voice carrying a different accent now.

"Survivor testimonies. Medical records that survived the camps."

The pretense fell away like a shed skin. Meier stood abruptly, moving toward his desk where Levi glimpsed the outline of something metallic in the drawer.

"I see," Meier said, his voice now fully German, no longer hiding behind Hebrew inflections. "And what exactly do you want, Dr. Rosen? Or should I say, Herr...?"

"Levi Goldstein. Birkenau, Block 31."

Meier's hand froze halfway to the drawer. "Impossible. Block 31 was liquidated in '44."

"Some of us survived. Some of us remember."

"Memory is unreliable," Meier said, but his hand moved again toward the drawer. "Wartime trauma creates false narratives."

Levi shifted position, blocking Meier's access to the desk. "Rebecca Goldstein. Age seven. You injected her with typhus."

"I don't recall individual subjects."

The office door burst open. Not Wolf or Miriam, but the watcher: a lean man in his forties with the unmistakable bearing of military intelligence.

"Step away from the desk, Doctor," the man commanded in Hebrew, weapon drawn.

Meier's hand darted for the drawer, but Levi was faster, grabbing his wrist and forcing it away from whatever weapon waited there.

"Who are you?" Levi demanded of the newcomer.

"Mossad. Agent David Stern." His weapon remained trained on both of them. "Dr. Meier, you're under arrest for war crimes."

"Finally," Meier said, almost with relief. "I wondered when official channels would catch up."

"And you," Stern said to Levi, "are under arrest for planning assassination of an Israeli resident."

"Israeli resident?" Levi's voice carried disbelief. "This man murdered Jewish children."

"That's for courts to determine."

"Courts had twenty-six years," Levi replied. "They failed."

Stern's expression hardened. "Step away from Dr. Meier and put your hands where I can see them."

Instead, Levi moved closer to Meier, who was now pressed against his desk, trapped between the two men.

"Tell him," Levi said to Meier. "Tell him what you did to those children."

"I was following orders," Meier said, his composure finally cracking. "Medical research was assigned to me. I didn't choose the subjects."

"You chose to document their deaths in detail. You chose to note their final words."

Stern's weapon wavered slightly. "What are you talking about?"

"Hannah Rosenthal, age six," Levi continued. "He tested pain tolerance through systematic injury. She lasted three days. He wrote down everything she said, including when she asked why the doctor was hurting her."

"That's enough," Stern commanded, but uncertainty crept into his voice.

"David and Sarah Klein. Twins, age eight. He separated them to test psychological trauma responses. David died calling for his sister. Meier documented that too."

The room was quiet except for street sounds from below. Meier stood frozen between them, while Stern struggled with competing duties.

"My grandparents died at Treblinka," Stern said quietly. "The Kleins were their neighbors."

"Then you understand," Levi said.

"I understand the law," Stern replied, but his weapon lowered slightly. "There are proper procedures."

"Procedures that let him live freely for twenty-six years while his victims stayed dead."

The office door opened again. Wolf entered, followed by Miriam, both with hands visible but ready for action.

"Agent Stern," Wolf said calmly. "We need to talk."

"No talking," Stern replied, raising his weapon again. "All of you, hands on the wall."

"David Klein was eight years old," Miriam said instead, pulling out translated testimonies. "These are his words, recorded by Dr. Meier on the day he died: 'Please bring Sarah back. I'll be good. I promise I'll be good.'"

Stern's hand trembled slightly. "Stop."

"Sarah Klein lasted three more days. She kept asking for her brother. Meier noted that she stopped eating after David died. He was curious about grief responses in children."

"I said stop!"

"We have forty-seven documented cases," Wolf said quietly. "Children who trusted a man in a white coat. Children who died slowly while he took notes."

Meier finally spoke. "They were going to die anyway. At least my research served scientific advancement."

The words hung in the air like poison. Stern's expression changed, hardening into something cold and final.

"Scientific advancement," he repeated.

"Medical knowledge requires sacrifice. Wartime provided unique opportunities for research that peacetime ethics would never allow."

Stern lowered his weapon completely. "My grandmother's name was Sarah Klein."

The silence stretched. Through the window, Haifa carried on its afternoon business, unaware that justice was being negotiated in a doctor's office.

"Courts require evidence, appeals, international cooperation," Stern said finally. "Some war criminals will never face trial because of diplomatic complications."

"So what do you suggest?" Wolf asked.

Stern looked at the testimonies spread across Meier's desk, then at the man who had documented the murder of children with scientific precision.

"I suggest that some forms of justice require different approaches than others," he said. "I suggest that a Mossad agent might need five minutes to check the building perimeter."

He holstered his weapon and moved toward the door. "Five minutes. Then I return with backup."

After he left, they turned back to Meier, who had slumped into his chair.

"You understand what happens now," Wolf said.

Meier nodded slowly. "I've been expecting this for years. Every knock on the door, every unexpected visitor."

"Any last words?" Levi asked, preparing his medical kit.

"Those children... they weren't supposed to suffer. The research required clinical observation, but suffering wasn't the goal."

"Suffering was the result," Miriam said. "And you documented every moment."

Levi worked with the precision that had made him a surgeon. A small injection, barely visible. Meier's eyes widened, then began to glaze.

"Potassium chloride," Levi explained. "Heart attack. Quick and clean, which is more mercy than you showed them."

As the life faded from Meier's eyes, Levi felt the familiar weight settle on his shoulders. Twelve Nazi war criminals dead by his hand. Each one necessary. Each one carried forward into whatever came next.

They placed the translated testimonies on Meier's desk, spread around his body. Evidence of what he'd done, why justice had found him at last.

Exactly five minutes later, Agent Stern returned with backup officers. He surveyed the scene with professional detachment.

"Heart attack," he announced to his team. "Stress of the interrogation, probably. These older war criminals often have weak hearts."

The backup officers began their investigation while Stern walked Wolf's team outside.

"Dr. Meier won't be traveling to Damascus," he observed.

"No," Wolf agreed. "He won't."

They stood in the Mediterranean afternoon, two types of justice meeting on a Haifa street.

"There are others," Stern said. "War criminals living throughout the region. Some beyond our legal reach due to international treaties and diplomatic immunity."

"Are you making a suggestion?" Rivka asked.

"I'm observing that official channels have limitations. Unofficial channels sometimes achieve what official ones cannot."

They parted without handshakes, without formal agreements, without documentation. But understanding passed between them. The state of Israel would pursue justice through legal channels when possible. Six survivors would pursue it through other means when necessary. Both approaches served the same cause.

That night, they sat on their apartment balcony watching Mediterranean stars. Josef was already researching their next target: a former SS officer living in Damascus under Syrian protection. Rivka was coordinating with contacts in Lebanon. Daniel, despite his earlier reservations, was planning new identities for their expanded operations.

"Do you think Stern will really cooperate?" Daniel asked.

"He will," Wolf said with certainty. "Because he understands that time is running out. Another generation, and all the witnesses will be dead. All the criminals will die peacefully in their beds."

"And the children still alive? What do we leave them?"

"A world where monsters can't hide forever," Levi said. "Where there are consequences for evil, even if they come late."

Below them, Haifa settled into night. Somewhere in the city, investigators were cataloguing Anton Meier's death and the testimonies of his victims. Tomorrow there would be questions, investigations, eventually a quiet conclusion that a war criminal had met an appropriate end.

And somewhere else, other Nazi war criminals were sleeping peacefully in comfortable beds, secure in their belief that justice would never find them. They were wrong. Six survivors had made justice their profession, and now they had unofficial support from the very state built on the ashes of their murdered families.

"Damascus next?" Josef asked.

"Damascus next," Wolf confirmed.

The hunt continued, but now they hunted with purpose beyond personal justice. They hunted for a nation that understood the value of memory, the necessity of consequences, and the truth that some forms of justice could not wait for courts and appeals.

In the darkness, Agent Stern watched their building from a new position. Not surveillance now, but protection. Tomorrow he would begin providing intelligence about targets beyond Israeli law's reach. Tomorrow the partnership would begin in earnest.

But tonight, forty-seven murdered children rested a little easier, knowing their killer had finally answered for his crimes.

46

Harold and Margaret

Sussex England

I didn't mean to run at first.

I only meant to go out the side door of Blackwood Home for Displaced Children, past the yard with its splintered swing set, through the gate where the boy with the red shoes had gone once and not come back. The Home wasn't terrible like in stories. Nobody beat us or locked us in cupboards. But it wasn't a place where anyone touched you unless they were checking for fever or lice. It wasn't a place where anyone remembered if you liked strawberry jam or orange.

I waited till the cook was shouting about burned potatoes and the bell was ringing for supper. Miss Winters was counting heads in the dining hall, and Mr. Pierce was fixing the toilet that always backed up when it rained. No one saw me slip past the metal bins that stank of Victory Soup and cabbage. No one called my number. That's what they used instead of names, numbers sewn into our collars. I was 41.

I thought someone would call me back, but no one did.

The sky outside was bigger than anything at Blackwood. It went on forever, like someone had forgotten to build walls and a ceiling. I didn't know which way to go, so I just walked away from the gray building and the wire fence and the sign that said "Temporary Care Facility."

I walked and walked. My shoes hurt because they were someone else's. Everything I wore was someone else's: brown shorts that scratched, a shirt with a collar that rubbed my neck raw, socks that slouched around my ankles.

The cold came slowly, soaking in. I saw shops with windows half empty from rationing, a dog that looked at me then ducked its head, a man on a bicycle who stared right through me. His eyes were tired in that way all grown-ups' eyes were tired since the war ended.

I didn't cry. I slept that first night behind a fence near a big church. It smelled like stone and wet wood and old dust. I had the small wooden train in my coat pocket but didn't take it out. If I took it out, someone might see and want it, and it was mine.

The morning came with rain. My stomach had forgotten what full meant. I hadn't eaten since lunch the day before.

I was hiding behind the bins at the back of a baker's shop when I saw him: a man with white hair and a brown coat that hung straight and proper. He walked slowly, not rushing like everyone else. His shoes were polished but old, with little cracks in the leather.

He saw me and didn't shout or look angry like most adults did when they saw children where children shouldn't be.

"Are you playing soldiers or just hiding?" he asked quietly.

I didn't answer.

He crouched down slowly, like his knees hurt. "Got an empty stomach there, boy?"

I nodded before I could remember not to talk to strangers.

He held out a small sandwich wrapped in brown paper. I waited, watching his hands, watching his eyes. Then I took it and ate half in two bites. The taste of butter and cheese hit my tongue like a shock.

He sat down on the church steps, not looking at me but at the empty street, giving me space.

"Don't like it in there, do you?" he said.

I didn't say anything. My English was at best basic.

He looked at me again, not hard but like he wanted to see me, which was different from how anyone had looked at me for a long time.

"What's your name?" he asked.

I opened my mouth. David, I thought. The name arrived from somewhere certain inside me. But nothing came out.

"That's all right," the man said. "I'm Harold. Harold Rose." He studied my face, then added, "I think perhaps you need a proper breakfast and a warm place to sit. Would you like to come with me? Just for breakfast. Then we can sort out where you belong."

Something about his pale blue eyes reminded me of someone. I couldn't remember who.

I nodded.

He stood slowly and held out his hand. After a moment, I took it. His palm was warm and dry.

"It's not far," he said. "My wife Margaret makes a fine plate of eggs. She's been rather hollow since our James went to Oxford. I think she'd be glad of the company."

We walked six blocks to a narrow house with a blue door and window boxes with nothing growing in them yet. Inside smelled like toast and coffee and furniture polish.

A woman with gray-streaked brown hair looked up from the stove, surprise flickering across her face. Her apron had tiny flowers embroidered along the edge.

"Harold?" she asked.

"This young man was sheltering near the churchyard," Harold said. "Hasn't had a proper breakfast. I thought perhaps..."

Margaret Rose looked at me, really looked, and something in her face softened. I recognized the look. It's how adults look at children who remind them of children they've lost.

"Well," she said briskly, "we can't have that. Sit down, young man. The eggs are nearly ready."

I sat at their table with its checked cloth and blue ceramic salt and pepper shakers shaped like birds. I ate eggs and toast and drank milk from a real glass. I watched how Harold spread his jam in a perfect circle and how Margaret tucked a strand of hair behind her ear when she was thinking.

When I'd finished eating, Harold cleared his throat. "We should telephone the authorities, I suppose."

Margaret was washing dishes, her back to us. Her shoulders stiffened slightly. "I suppose we should," she said. "But perhaps it could wait until after lunch. The poor child looks exhausted."

"What do you think?" Harold asked me. "Would you like to rest here for a bit before we sort things out?"

I nodded.

"Can you tell us your name?" Margaret asked gently.

Again, I opened my mouth. Again, no sound came.

"That's all right," she said. "Names aren't the most important thing, are they?"

I slept on their sofa beneath a knitted blanket that smelled like cedar. Their kitchen voices woke me.

"Clearly from one of those camps," Margaret was saying quietly. "The way he flinches when doors close."

"If we call, they'll just put him back in that place," Harold replied. "Children falling through the cracks everywhere."

A pause. Then Margaret: "We have the room."

"It wouldn't be proper. We'd need to apply, go through channels."

"By which time he could be anywhere," Margaret said firmly. "Harold, perhaps this is our chance to set something right."

Another pause.

"We'll need to give him a name," Harold said finally.

Margaret leaned against him. "We could call him David," she said softly. "After your father."

Something inside my chest clicked into place.

That afternoon, Harold brought paper and colored pencils. "Would you like to draw?"

I drew a train with smoke coming from the top. I drew people standing beside it, their faces just circles with dots for eyes.

Harold looked at the picture for a long time. "Is this a memory?" he asked quietly.

I shrugged. I couldn't always tell the difference between what felt real and what felt like dreams.

He didn't telephone anyone that day or the next. Winter melted into spring before the government remembered I existed. Then came the women in wool suits, their pens scratching across official papers. Margaret and Harold answered questions, signed papers, and promised things. I started at the local school, where no one knew I hadn't always been David Rose.

At night, I kept the wooden train under my pillow.

But when I woke, Margaret or Harold would always be there, ready to tell me that I was safe now, that I was home, that I was their David Rose.

And little by little, I started to believe it.

One lovely spring morning we went for a walk to buy bread and cakes. Margaret liked the taste from the bakery sometimes, having made them herself for too many years.

As we walked along the moderately crowded street, two people walked slowly in front of us. The lady was pushing a stroller with a baby. I couldn't understand them even though they were loud enough. Their clothes looked different from ours.

I was skipping ahead and behind Harold and Margaret. At some point I found myself in front of the strangers. The lady was bending over and singing something to the baby.

I stopped and stared at her. The song flowed into my body. I began to sing with her, but it was not my language: "*Shlof, shlof, mayn tayer kind.*" Sleep, sleep, my dear child. Margaret and Harold formed a circle with the man and lady around me. The lady and I stopped singing at exactly the same time.

The man began talking to me and I didn't know the words but I felt them and nodded. Tears were running down my cheeks and I looked at Margaret whose face was changing and she hugged me.

"I'm sorry Mum! I don't know what is happening to me." I was scared and as she held me the man spoke to her and I understood everything except the word he kept repeating: Yiddish.

We left them and walked more quickly toward the bakery.

That evening, after I was tucked into bed, I heard their voices through the floorboards. Margaret was crying, something I had never heard before.

"We can't pretend we didn't see that," Harold said, his voice tight. "The boy knew every word of that song."

"What are we supposed to do with it?" Margaret asked through her tears. "Drag him through more trauma? Make him remember things that nearly killed him?"

"Perhaps we should ask someone. A doctor. Someone who understands these things."

"No." Margaret's voice was firm. "No doctors, no questions, no poking at wounds that have finally started to heal. Look at him, Harold. He's happy. He's safe. He's ours."

A long silence. Then Harold: "And if someday he asks? If he wants to know?"

"Then we'll tell him we tried to protect him. That we thought... that we hoped love would be enough."

I pressed my ear harder to the floor, but they had grown quiet. I clutched the wooden train tighter and wondered what Yiddish meant, why that song had made my chest hurt in a way that wasn't quite sad.

Years passed. They never once talked about that day, just as they never talked about before. But sometimes I would catch Margaret looking at me with something like fear in her eyes, and sometimes Harold would clear his throat and suggest cricket just as questions formed on my lips.

They meant well. In the years since Harold found me behind the baker's shop, they'd given me everything they thought a boy needed: a home with blue-painted walls in my bedroom, a school uniform with my name stitched in the collar (David Rose, not just a number), a shelf of books I could read anytime.

But they could never give me back the song that woman had sung, or explain why my tears had come without permission when I heard it. That remained mine alone, buried beneath their careful English love like a secret I wasn't allowed to tell myself.

47

Becoming Dr. David Rose

David – Age Sixteen Sussex, England

I'd been studying German for eighteen months when Dr. Patterson called me to her office after class. The corridors of Blackwood Grammar smelled like chalk dust and wet wool coats, the same institutional smell that sometimes made my chest tight for reasons I couldn't name.

"Sit down, David," she said, closing the door with a soft click. Her desk was covered with examination papers, mine somewhere in the stack with its perfect marks. "I wanted to discuss your language progression."

I settled into the hard wooden chair, wondering if I'd done something wrong. Dr. Patterson was severe but fair, with steel-gray hair pinned in a bun that never showed a strand out of place.

"Your German is quite remarkable," she said, studying me over her reading glasses. "Particularly your pronunciation. It's almost... native."

Something cold moved through my stomach. "Thank you."

"Where did you learn it?" she asked. "Before my class, I mean. Your parents mentioned you'd never formally studied it."

I opened my mouth, then closed it. The truth was, I didn't know. The words simply arrived in my mind when I needed them, the grammar patterns felt familiar rather than learned. Sometimes I dream in German, waking with the taste of foreign syllables on my tongue.

"I'm not sure," I said finally. "It just seems... natural."

Dr. Patterson leaned back in her chair, her expression thoughtful. "Yesterday you corrected my pronunciation of '*Vernichtungslager*.' Do you remember that?" Extermination camp.

I nodded. The word had made something twist inside me when she'd said it wrong.

"That's not a word we've covered in class, David. It's quite specific terminology. Where did you encounter it?"

"I don't know," I said, my voice smaller than I intended. "It just sounded wrong the way you said it."

She was quiet for a long moment, her fingers drumming against the desk. "Have you considered continuing with languages at university? You have a gift."

Walking home that afternoon, I couldn't shake Dr. Patterson's questions. The wooden train sat heavy in my blazer pocket, as it had every day for nine years. I pulled it out as I walked, running my thumb over its familiar scratches and dents.

When I arrived at the cottage, Margaret was in the kitchen preparing tea. She looked up as I entered, that careful smile she always wore when discussing school.

"How were your lessons today?" she asked, arranging biscuits on a plate with geometric precision.

"Dr. Patterson wants to discuss my German studies with you and Father," I said, setting my satchel by the door. "She says I have some kind of natural ability."

Margaret's hands stilled. The biscuit she'd been holding crumbled slightly between her fingers.

"Oh," she said. "Well, that's... that's wonderful, darling."

But her voice carried something else. Fear, maybe. Or guilt.

Harold emerged from his study as we sat down to tea, the newspaper folded under his arm. He'd been spending more time in there lately, claiming work but I suspected he was simply avoiding conversations that might lead to uncomfortable questions.

"David's German teacher wants to speak with us," Margaret said without preamble.

Harold's cup stopped halfway to his lips. "Oh? What about?"

"She says he has an unusual aptitude. Almost native pronunciation, apparently." Margaret wasn't looking at either of us, focusing intently on stirring her tea.

"I corrected her pronunciation of a word I've never studied," I said, watching both their faces. "She seemed surprised I knew it."

The silence stretched between us like a held breath. Harold set down his cup with deliberate care.

"Languages can be... inherited, in a sense," he said finally. "Perhaps you have a natural ear."

"But where would I have inherited it from?" I asked. The question hung in the air like smoke.

Margaret and Harold exchanged a look, quick, loaded with meaning I couldn't decipher. In that glance, I saw nine years of carefully managed conversations, nine years of deflected questions.

"Perhaps," Harold said, clearing his throat, "we should speak with Dr. Patterson. Understand what she's recommending."

Later that evening, I was supposed to be completing my mathematics assignment, but instead I found myself in Father's study, surrounded by his war histories and political biographies. I'd pulled down a volume about displaced persons after the war, telling myself it was for a history essay.

But as I read about children separated from their families, about the massive effort to reunite survivors, about the thousands who were never claimed, never identified, I felt that familiar tightness in my chest. The academic language couldn't quite mask the human tragedy beneath: Children who forgot their names. Children who stopped speaking altogether. Children who were given new identities and new families and told to be grateful.

"David?" Margaret's voice from the doorway made me jump. "It's quite late."

I looked up to find her watching me with an expression I'd seen before but never understood, something approaching worry, mixed with what might have been guilt.

"Just reading," I said, closing the book quickly.

She noticed the title anyway. Her face went pale.

"Why are you reading about that?" she asked, her voice carefully controlled.

"History project," I lied. "About post-war reconstruction."

She nodded, but I could see her hands trembling slightly. "Well. Perhaps it's time for bed."

As I passed her in the doorway, she reached out and touched my arm.

"David," she said softly. "You know we love you, don't you? That you're exactly where you belong?"

"Of course, Mum," I said, though something in her tone made the words feel more like a question than a statement.

That night, I lay awake holding the wooden train, studying its details in the moonlight filtering through my bedroom window. One wheel was slightly loose, wobbling when I rolled it across my palm. There was a mark along one side that looked like it might have been made by teeth, small teeth, a child's teeth.

Had I made that mark? I couldn't remember, but something about it felt familiar, like a half-recalled dream.

I thought about Dr. Patterson's questions, about the way certain German words felt right in my mouth while others felt foreign. I thought about my parents' reaction, the way they'd looked at each other like conspirators sharing a secret.

And I thought about the book I'd been reading, about children who were given new lives and told to forget their old ones. Children who sometimes remembered anyway, in dreams or in the way certain words felt on their tongues.

Something was hidden beneath the surface of my life. I could feel it there, like walking on ice that might crack at any moment. My parents loved me. I never doubted that. But there were doors in our house that were never opened, conversations that were never finished.

As I finally drifted toward sleep, I found myself wondering not just who I was, but who I had been before I became David Rose. And whether the answers to those questions were something my parents feared as much as I was beginning to need them.

The wooden train grew warm in my palm, as if it were trying to tell me something I wasn't quite ready to hear.

48

The Coat

I was supposed to be in Vienna that summer. Not just Vienna, but a residency at the university that would have my name on office doors, my signature on archival request forms for documents untouched since 1945. Twelve weeks in high-ceilinged halls where I'd lecture alongside scholars I'd once reverently footnoted. Career-making stuff.

Cambridge didn't just hint: they dangled lab space and research assistants. Oxford arranged one of those "informal conversations" about a Holocaust Studies chair, the kind where they serve Earl Grey in bone china while measuring your ambition against their endowment. There were books waiting to be written, conferences eager for my participation. The future sat there like a train with its doors open. All I had to do was board.

But I couldn't.

Instead, I drafted emails declining each opportunity, my fingers hovering over the keyboard before each send, questioning my sanity even as I knew the decision was final. I told them I'd be leaving for Poland indefinitely. Not as a researcher working from university libraries, but as a guide at Birkenau. Just for the season, I claimed, though I had no idea how long this would take. A calling I couldn't articulate in academic jargon they'd respect.

My department chair invited me to lunch, ostensibly to discuss my sabbatical plans. Across a white tablecloth in an overpriced Oxford restaurant, he studied me with the clinical gaze historians reserve for puzzling primary sources.

"This is unusual," he said, the words hanging between us.

I stabbed an asparagus spear, watched it bleed water onto the plate.

"Vienna requested you specifically." His tone suggested I was declining a royal summons. "People work decades for such invitations."

"I'm aware."

"And this guide position, it's not even affiliated with an academic institution? No research component?" He was offering me a lifeline, a way to reframe my inexplicable choice into something the university could stomach.

"Just a regular tour guide position," I confirmed. "With the memorial foundation."

He sipped his wine, the glass catching light like an artifact under museum glass. "I see. Well, perhaps you need a different perspective for a while. Though I must say, many would consider it a step down."

After that, they all mastered the same look: colleagues, friends, everyone. That careful tilt of the head, that manufactured neutrality. Academic faces trained to hide judgment but somehow broadcasting it louder. No one directly argued with my decision. I was already too far gone.

The dreams started three weeks before my scheduled departure.

Not the usual anxiety dreams about forgotten lectures or misplaced research notes. These were different. Vivid. Tactile. I would wake with the sensation of small fingers clutching wool, of weight settling around thin shoulders, of safety found in too-large sleeves.

A coat. Always a coat.

In the dreams, hands, adult hands, careful hands, would lift me, wrap me in grey wool that smelled of lavender and fear. The buttons never matched: one black, one brown, one grey. The hands would speak in whispers, urgent words in a language I understood but couldn't place upon waking. Stay brave. Remember. This will always be yours.

I would wake gasping, my flat suddenly too warm, my pajamas clinging to sweat-dampened skin. But the sensation of the coat remained, phantom fabric against my arms, phantom safety around my shoulders.

The dreams intensified. Each night, the same scene played with slight variations. Sometimes the hands moved quickly, urgently. Sometimes they lingered, stroking my hair, whispering
354

reassurances. But always, always, there was something being tucked into the coat's lining. Something small and precious and hidden.

So you'll remember who you are, the voice would whisper. So you'll never forget.

I began avoiding sleep. Coffee became my closest companion, academic papers my late-night refuge. But exhaustion eventually won, and with it came the dreams, more vivid than before.

On a rainy Thursday evening, while sorting through research materials I'd never use, the exhaustion finally overtook me. I dozed off in my chair, surrounded by boxes of books destined for storage.

This time, the dream was different. Clearer. The hands belonged to a woman with dark hair and eyes that held too much knowledge for her age. She was crying as she worked, tears falling onto the grey wool as she made her careful adjustments to the coat's interior.

They won't find this here, she whispered, her voice breaking. When you're older, when you understand who you are, you'll have this part of home with you.

Her fingers pressed something small and hard into a carefully created pocket in the lining, then sewed it closed with tiny, precise stitches. The needle caught the light as it moved, silver against the grey fabric.

Promise me you'll remember, she said, lifting my face to meet her eyes. Promise me you'll never forget who you are.

I woke up with a start, my heart hammering against my ribs. But this time, I didn't dismiss it. This time, I knew with absolute certainty that it wasn't just a dream.

The next morning, I drove to Sussex.

I didn't call ahead. I didn't second-guess what I had experienced. My hands were steady on the wheel, but my mind raced as early summer green smeared past my windows. The Roses' cottage appeared like it always did: ivy-strangled walls, hedges Harold trimmed with obsessive precision, the blue door he repainted every other year.

Margaret was already in the garden when my tires crunched the gravel drive, kneeling beside her roses with pruning shears in her gloved hands. The normality of it, her there among her flowers like any Friday morning, was both jarring and reassuring.

She smiled when she saw me, though something flickered behind her eyes. Recognition, perhaps. Or resignation.

"What a lovely surprise," she said, leading me inside. "Your father's in the village, but he'll be back for lunch."

We had tea in the kitchen, the same sturdy ceramic mugs she'd used since my childhood, the same McVitie's digestives arranged in concentric circles on the blue plate reserved for visitors. But I could barely focus on the familiar ritual. The dream pressed against my consciousness like a weight I couldn't shake.

When the pot was nearly empty, I set down my mug with a deliberate sound against the wooden table.

"Mum," I said, my voice steadier than I felt, "I need to see the coat."

The color drained from her face. Her hands, reaching for the teapot, froze mid-motion.

"What coat, darling?" she asked, but her voice was already defeated.

"The one I was wearing when you found me. The grey one with the mismatched buttons."

She stared at me for a long moment, her mouth opening and closing without sound. Then she placed her hands flat on the table, as if bracing herself.

"How did you..." she began, then stopped. "We never told you about the coat."

"I've been dreaming about it," I said. "For weeks. Every night. A woman's hands, sewing something into the lining. She said it would help identify me when the time came."

Margaret's eyes filled with tears. She pressed a trembling hand to her mouth.

"Oh, David," she whispered. "We wondered if this day would come."

The attic stairs creaked with each step. Cedar and old paper and dust motes dancing in the window's light. Margaret moved with purpose now, her earlier shock replaced by something that looked almost like relief.

She led me to a box wrapped in linen, secured with twine that had yellowed with age. Her fingers shook as she untied the knot.

356

"We could never bring ourselves to throw it away," she said, her voice thick. "Not even when you outgrew everything else. Harold said we should, said it would be better, but I..." She trailed off, lifting the small coat from its careful wrapping.

It was exactly as I'd dreamed it. Grey wool, soft and worn at the cuffs. The buttons that didn't match: one black, one brown, one grey. The careful hand-stitching around the collar, tiny and precise.

"She hid something in it, didn't she?" I said, though it wasn't really a question.

Margaret nodded, fresh tears spilling over. "We found it when we had it cleaned. In the lining. We didn't know what to do with it, so we..." She gestured helplessly. "We put it back. We thought someday you might..."

I took the coat from her hands, turned it over to expose the lining. There, in the front left corner near the bottom, I could see where the original stitching had been carefully opened and then resealed.

My fingers found the small pair of scissors Margaret offered, and I cut through the careful threads. Inside the small pocket, exactly where my dreams had shown me, was a silver Star of David, no larger than a coin. Its edges were worn smooth, as if it had been held many times by anxious fingers.

When I lifted it, the metal was warm against my palm.

Margaret and I sat in silence for what felt like hours, the coat spread between us, the pendant catching the light from the attic window. The weight of thirty-two years of unasked questions settled around us like dust.

"She loved you," Margaret said finally. "Whoever she was. We could see it in how carefully she'd prepared this coat, how she'd made sure you'd be warm, how she'd hidden this as something just for you to keep."

I closed my fingers around the pendant, feeling its edges press into my palm.

"Did you ever wonder who I was before?" I asked.

"Every day," she admitted. "But we were so grateful to have you, so afraid that if we looked too hard, someone might come and take you away. It was selfish, perhaps, but you were ours. You are ours."

That night, in my old bedroom beneath the sloped ceiling, I lay awake with the pendant warm against my chest, suspended on a simple chain Harold had found in his workshop. The coat lay folded on the chair by the window, no longer a mystery but not yet fully understood.

For the first time since the dreams began, I slept deeply. And for the first time in weeks, I didn't dream of the coat.

Instead, I dreamed of a train platform and a woman with dark hair who pressed a wooden toy into my small hands and whispered, "Remember who you are."

When I woke, I knew I was closer to finding out.

49

The Breakdown in Auschwitz-Birkenau

The bus fell silent as we rolled onto the gravel parking lot. The brick entrance of Birkenau stretched beyond tinted windows, its inscription visible even from this distance. Each person in our group grew still, their breathing shallow. I watched my students arrange their faces into expressions they thought history required. None of us knew yet how inadequate those masks would prove.

For weeks I had prepared these students for what they would encounter. We'd reviewed survivor accounts, studied maps, and analyzed documents. They believed they were ready. I had believed I was ready too. But this place cannot be prepared for.

The April wind cut through my coat as I stepped off the bus. Heavy clouds pressed down, swollen with unreleased rain. The students clustered together, their faces taking on the uncertain look they'd worn that morning at breakfast in Krakow. Twenty-two graduate students, Holocaust scholars all, became hesitant children facing history made real.

I caught my reflection in a window: a young Oxford academic who had built his research around analyzing genocide from the safety of university libraries. Brick and wire transformed theoretical knowledge into stark fact. But as I straightened my shoulders to begin my professional duties, something else stirred beneath my scholarly composure. A memory that wasn't quite a memory, pressing against my consciousness like a half-remembered dream.

I had been here before. Not as Dr. David Rose. As someone else.

At Auschwitz I, we moved through the exhibits in orderly fashion. The main camp presented itself through structured displays: confiscated belongings, official photographs, the preserved barracks. Students took pictures they understood would never leave their academic files. Not from disrespect, but self-preservation. Some held hands as we moved between blocks.

I led them with practiced calm, describing the barracks and bureaucracy in a voice that sounded foreign to me. The words were correct. The facts are accurate. But my scholarly training could not quiet what was stirring inside me. My coat felt unusually heavy. The air seemed thick. Each breath required effort.

Something was awakening. The same inexplicable knowing that had seized me just months before in this place, when the mist had carried a voice I'd tried to convince myself was hallucination. When Jacob, my grandfather, had spoken through the fog and told me to find Miriam Weiss. I'd searched for her then, scoured records, contacted survivors' organizations, but the trail had gone cold. I'd buried that failure, convinced myself it had been a breakdown, stress from leading too many academic tours to this cursed place.

But now the knowledge was flooding back, undeniable.

Birkenau proved worse. Where Auschwitz I offered the false comfort of exhibits, Birkenau revealed only vast emptiness that spoke louder than any display. The enormous scale of wooden structures and broken chimneys stretched to a horizon without escape. Open space and sky and absolute silence, disturbed only by spring wind moving through the ruins.

Our Polish guide spoke about the arrival platform, the selection process, "*links*" versus "*rechts*." Left versus right. I understood these German words too easily. I had taught them myself. But I was no longer listening to her professional explanation. I found myself walking away from the group, drawn toward the railway ramp where cattle cars once unloaded their human cargo.

My legs moved without conscious direction toward a patch of broken concrete and weeds near an old tree showing signs of spring growth. I had no reason to go there, no logical explanation for why it called to me. Yet I knew I had been in that exact spot before. Not as Dr. David Rose, Oxford academic on an academic tour. As someone much smaller.

The recognition was immediate and certain. The words emerged in German before I could stop them: "I believe I have been to this place before." The students formed a semicircle behind me, confusion replacing their scholarly composure. One nervous laugh vanished into silence.

With my hand I indicated empty ground to my left. The knowledge came from somewhere deep, unstoppable: "A barrier used to be here. The wire sagged in the middle because someone tried to climb it. They shot him. The blood on the snow turned black."

Our guide stopped speaking, staring at me. My statement exceeded any information she had prepared. Sarah, one of my doctoral students, moved closer with concern etched on her face.

"Dr. Rose?" she said quietly. "Are you all right?"

But I was beyond answering. I pointed to another empty section, my voice growing stronger as suppressed memories broke through: "A shed stood there. Blue door. Chipped paint. The wind made a sound when it hit it. Like tapping. Like someone trying to get in."

The group had moved from academic respect to genuine alarm. I could see them exchanging glances, recognizing trauma response from their training. Thomas, always the most practical of my students, was already reaching for his mobile phone.

I was no longer speaking to them but to something within myself. My voice dropped to a whisper as I spoke about a woman who had been there. Tall. Not a guard. One of us. She gave me a coat that was too big. She told me to be brave, that she would find a way to save me. She said...

A wave of dizziness hit me. I stumbled, catching myself against a concrete post. Blood appeared on my scraped palms as the present dissolved around me.

The person I had been for thirty-two years began to fall away. The historian who had recorded statistics was being replaced by a different truth. My breath came in short bursts. A whisper escaped: "I'm not supposed to be here." Then, worse: "I was here."

Images crashed through my mind in violent succession: mud that pulled at wooden shoes, the screech of train doors, a hand gripping mine with desperate strength, a voice urging me to stay brave, stay quiet, remember who I was.

A woman. Dark hair streaked with early gray. Eyes that looked through the wire as if seeing beyond it. The name surfaced from somewhere deep in my consciousness, carried on a wave of longing and terror: Miriam.

She had been real. Jacob's words hadn't been hallucination. Miriam Weiss existed, and she had saved me once, in this place where children went to die.

"Dr. Rose, we need to get you some help." Sarah's voice seemed to come from very far away. Strong hands gripped my shoulders, steadying me.

But I pushed away from them, staggering toward the railway platform. "She's still alive," I said, though I had no idea how I knew this. "She's waiting for me to remember."

The guide and two students helped me to my feet and back to the visitor center. The medical staff spoke of dissociative episodes and acute stress responses. Have I ever had panic attacks before? Was I taking any medications? Had I eaten breakfast that morning?

I nodded and shook my head at appropriate intervals, letting them construct their understanding. But I knew the truth now. The terror was absolute, but so was the certainty. My carefully constructed identity was crumbling, but something real was emerging from beneath it.

The sedative began to work as I felt the familiar object pressing against my hip. I reached into my coat pocket for the wooden train I'd brought from England. Its shape remained clear as the room faded. The train she had given me. David Rose no longer fully existed. I was someone who had faced the ramp while Miriam gave me a coat and a new name and somehow helped me survive what others could not.

As consciousness slipped away, one thought remained crystal clear: I needed to find her again. After all these years of searching in the wrong places, asking the wrong questions, I finally understood what Jacob had been trying to tell me.

Someone was still waiting for me to remember. And this time, I wouldn't let the trail go cold.

50

Pieces of Truth

I couldn't leave. That was the simple truth of it.

After they helped me to my feet at Birkenau, after the medical staff checked my pupils and asked their careful questions, after my students gathered their scattered notebooks and looked at me with a mixture of concern and professional fascination, I should have returned to the bus. I should have flown back to England with them, filed my trip report, and resumed my tutorials at Oxford.

Instead, I found myself in a cramped flat above a bakery in Oświęcim, three kilometers from the camp gates.

The decision happened without conscious thought. While Emily and Thomas packed their bags at the hotel in Kraków, discussing my "episode" in hushed academic tones, I was already asking Mrs. Kowalski about monthly rates for her spare room. She spoke little English, I spoke no Polish, but trauma translates in any language. She looked at my face and simply nodded.

The flat was sparse: a narrow bed, a small table, two chairs, a hot plate for cooking. A single window overlooked the town square where ordinary life continued. Mothers pushing prams, old men feeding pigeons, children walking home from school. Life that had learned to exist beside the shadow of what had happened here.

I called Oxford from the post office. My voice sounded foreign to my own ears as I spoke to Professor Matthews.

"Extended research leave," I managed. "Personal... family matters that have come to light. I need to remain in Poland for the foreseeable future."

Matthews was concerned but accommodating. Academic breakdowns weren't unheard of, especially among those who studied trauma. He would arrange for my tutorials to be covered, my research responsibilities suspended.

The call to Anna was harder.

"David, what do you mean you're staying?" Her voice crackled through the international connection. "The trip was only supposed to be a week. Your students are already back. Sarah called me. She said you had some kind of collapse?"

I pressed my forehead against the cold glass of the phone booth. How could I explain what I couldn't understand myself? That I'd recognized places that shouldn't exist in my memory? That my grandfather's ghost had appeared to me in the mist, speaking of secrets and survival?

"I need time, Anna. Something's happened here... something I can't explain properly yet."

"Then come home and we'll sort it out together. Whatever it is, we can—"

"No." The word came out harder than I intended. "I can't leave. Not yet. I'm sorry, but I can't ask you to understand something I don't understand myself."

The silence stretched between us, filled with static and the weight of everything I couldn't say.

"Are you... are you ending our engagement?" Her voice was very small.

"I don't know," I whispered, and heard her sharp intake of breath. "I don't know anything anymore, Anna. I need to stay here until I do."

After that conversation, I stopped answering the phone at Mrs. Kowalski's. She would call up the stairs when it rang, but I'd shake my head, and she'd return to tell whoever it was that I was unavailable. Anna called daily for the first week, then every few days, then not at all.

Margaret and Harold tried to reach me through the university, through the British consulate, through every channel they could think of. I wrote them one letter, posted from the center of town:

I am safe. I am not having a nervous breakdown. Something has happened that I need to understand before I can return to England. Please don't worry, and please don't try to find me. I'll contact you when I can explain properly. All my love, David.

I knew it wasn't enough. I knew they'd be frantic with worry. But what could I tell them? That their adopted son had discovered he'd been to Auschwitz-Birkenau before, as a child? That he could remember details of a place he'd supposedly never seen? That his dead grandfather was sending him messages through the mist?

The truth would destroy them. Better they think me temporarily mad than permanently lost.

Jacob had appeared to me in that same place just months before, emerging from the mist to tell me I was drowning in secrets. He'd given me a name: Miriam Weiss. He'd told me to find her, that she held the key to my survival.

I had tried then, rushing back to England to scour survivor records, contact Jewish organizations, write letters that went unanswered. The trail had gone cold. No Miriam Weiss in the databases I could access. No responses from the agencies. I'd convinced myself Jacob's appearance had been stress-induced hallucination, the product of too many academic visits to places that should have remained buried.

But the breakdown at Birkenau had shattered that rational explanation. Jacob hadn't been an hallucination. The memories weren't academic projections. The connection was real. And somewhere, Miriam Weiss was still alive.

So I stayed. Every day I walked the three kilometers to the camp. Sometimes I joined the tourist groups, listening to guides recite facts I already knew. Sometimes I stood alone at the railway ramp, waiting for something I couldn't name. The guards grew accustomed to seeing me, the strange young Englishman who came daily and stood motionless for hours.

The headache that had started during my breakdown never fully left. It lived at the base of my skull, spreading outward whenever I tried to force the memories to make sense. My small flat felt both like sanctuary and prison. Mrs. Kowalski brought me soup I barely touched, bread that grew stale on my table.

The dreams started two weeks after I'd arrived in Oświęcim. Not ordinary stress dreams. These came sharp and clear, too real. Often in German, sometimes Yiddish. My academic German was fluent, but this was different. These words carried emotional weight I'd never learned in tutorials, pronunciation that felt natural rather than studied.

No dream logic to them, no symbolic confusion. They arrived as precise fragments. A woman's hands folding a child's coat, fingers worrying a small tear in the lining. Snow through wooden slats. A bowl with thin broth, one slice of carrot floating on top.

And always footsteps. Behind me. Never seen. The measured sound of boots on wood. The synchronized crunch of gravel. The sound followed me into waking.

During the long Polish nights, I'd sit at my small table and hold the wooden train.

It had outlasted everything I owned. Predated university degrees and academic papers. Survived childhood illnesses and adolescent uncertainties. Older than David Rose himself, the identity I'd worn as far back as memory stretched.

I'd take it from my bag and hold it in the lamplight. Minutes sometimes. Hours others. Fingers tracing every groove, the misaligned wheels, the scorch mark along one side. Searching for messages hidden in its surface.

In the silence of my exile, I'd speak to it.

"Jacob was real, wasn't he? You knew I'd need to remember."

"Someone gave you to me. You're the thread that leads back to her."

"Why couldn't I find Miriam when Jacob told me to? What did I do wrong?"

Questions that daylight wouldn't tolerate. In darkness, aimed at a toy, they felt almost reasonable.

Then, one night nearly a month after my breakdown, something changed.

I was sitting at my small table, the wooden train before me in the yellow circle of lamplight. The flat was silent except for the distant sounds of evening life in the square below. I hadn't eaten properly in days, subsisting on tea and Mrs. Kowalski's worried offerings and the growing certainty that something was approaching.

A presence filled the room. Not threatening, but powerful. Warm like sunlight through windows, familiar like a half-remembered lullaby.

I'm with you, David. Hold on. You're not alone.

The voice bypassed my ears entirely, arriving directly in my consciousness. Female. Accented. Speaking English with the careful precision of someone for whom it wasn't a first language.

What you experienced at Birkenau was real. The memories are returning because it's time. Because I'm ready to help you carry them.

I gripped the wooden train so tightly my knuckles went white.

"Miriam?" I whispered to the empty room.

Yes, child. I've been searching for a way to reach you ever since I felt your pain at the camp. Jacob sent you to find me, but some connections can't be forced. They have to grow naturally.

"I tried to find you. After Jacob appeared. I searched everywhere."

I know. But you weren't ready then. The truth would have destroyed you. Now you're strong enough to bear it.

The presence intensified, and suddenly I could almost see her. Dark hair streaked with silver, eyes that held decades of sorrow and fierce determination. She looked older than the woman from my fragmented memories, but unmistakably the same person.

Tomorrow, go to the place where we last spoke. The railway platform at Birkenau. Stand there at sunset, and I'll be able to show you everything. Your real name. Your parents. Why you survived when so many others didn't?

"How? How can you reach me like this?"

Some bonds aren't broken by distance or time. Your mother came to me at Birkenau and made me promise to find you if she didn't survive. I kept that promise, David. I found you after the war and helped save you. Part of me has stayed connected to you ever since. Now that connection is strong enough for truth.

The warmth began to fade, but not before one final message.

Bring the train, David. It's been waiting twenty-six years to come home.

Then silence.

I sat motionless at my small table until dawn, the wooden train warm in my palm. For the first time since my breakdown, I felt completely present in my own life. Not relieved. The headache still pulsed, the isolation still pressed down like a weight. But focused on something real.

Tomorrow, at sunset, I would stand on the railway platform at Birkenau. I would face whatever truth Miriam Weiss had been protecting all these years. I would finally understand why I'd been unable to leave this place, why Anna's love and Oxford's certainties had felt like prisons, why every day I'd walked toward the camp like a pilgrim seeking absolution.

For the first time in twenty-six years, I was going home.

51

A Flicker of Recognition

I spent that final day in Oświęcim walking through streets I'd come to know by heart. Mrs. Kowalski watched from her bakery window as I passed, her eyes holding the gentle worry of someone who had seen too much history to ask direct questions. She simply nodded when I told her I would be leaving soon.

The morning felt different. Sharper. The April air carried scents I noticed for the first time in weeks: fresh bread from the bakery below, coffee from the café across the square, the faint sweetness of early flowers pushing through winter soil. Colors seemed more vivid, sounds more distinct. As if Miriam's presence the night before had cleared something from my vision.

I returned to my small flat above the bakery to wait. The wooden train sat on my table where I'd left it after her message, no longer just a mysterious possession but a bridge between past and present. I picked it up, feeling its familiar weight, the smoothed edges that spoke of years of handling.

For the first time, I allowed myself to truly examine it. The wood was old, darker in some places where oils from countless fingers had soaked in. One wheel was slightly misaligned, giving it a gentle wobble when rolled. Along one side, a scorch mark formed a rough pattern I'd never noticed before. Or perhaps had never allowed myself to see.

The mark looked deliberate. Not damage but design. A small star, carved or burned into the wood. The kind of star that might have meant something specific to someone specific.

I closed my eyes and let the memory come without resistance.

A woman's hands placing this train back in my coat pocket. Not the rough coat I'd worn at Birkenau, but something warmer, cleaner.

Blue wool with wooden buttons. Her fingers were quick but gentle as she tucked the train deep into the inner pocket.

"This will help you remember," she had said. "When you're ready."

The accent was there in the memory now, clearer than it had been during her psychic contact. Eastern European but softened by years elsewhere. Her English careful but confident.

I opened my eyes. The scorch mark on the train's side suddenly made sense. Not random damage but a deliberate mark. A way to ensure this particular toy would be recognizable years later.

Someone had marked it for me. A breadcrumb trail leading back to truth.

The afternoon passed slowly. I tried to read but the words wouldn't hold still. I attempted to write in my journal but found myself drawing circles instead of forming sentences. Restless energy filled my small flat until I could no longer sit still.

I walked to the camp gates, as I had every day for the past month. But today felt different. The guards nodded at me with familiarity. The tourists seemed louder, more intrusive. I found myself protective of the place in a way I'd never experienced before. As if it belonged to me now. Or I to it.

At the railway platform, I stood where I'd collapsed weeks before. The gravel looked the same, but my relationship to it had changed entirely. This was no longer foreign ground but something approaching home. The most unlikely, terrible home imaginable, but home nonetheless.

The sun moved across the sky with agonizing slowness. I watched shadows shift across the ruins, marking time until the moment Miriam had promised to appear. Sunset. The golden hour when day surrenders to night.

Other visitors began to leave as evening approached. Tour groups gathered at buses, individual travelers made their way toward the exits. Soon I stood alone on the platform, the wooden train warm in my palm.

A wind picked up, carrying the scent of grass and distant cooking fires from the town. The same wind that had blown here twenty-six years ago when I'd been four years old and terrified and somehow protected by a woman whose name I was only now beginning to remember properly.

Not Mira. Miriam.

As the sun dropped toward the horizon, painting the sky in shades of gold and rose, I felt the same presence that had filled my flat the night before. Stronger now. More focused.

She was coming.

I didn't know how I knew this, only that I did. The connection between us, whatever impossible link had formed all those years ago, was pulling tight again. Drawing us back to this place where our paths had first crossed.

The wooden train grew warm in my hand. Not from my body heat but from something else. Some energy flowing between us across whatever distance still separated us.

I thought of Anna back in England, probably wondering if I would ever return to the life we'd been building. I thought of Margaret and Harold, worried sick about their adopted son who had vanished into his own past. I thought of my colleagues at Oxford, covering my tutorials and wondering if I'd lost my mind entirely.

All of that felt like someone else's life now. David Rose the academic, the fiancé, the carefully constructed English gentleman. He was dissolving like morning mist, making room for whoever I'd been before. Whoever Miriam remembered.

The sun touched the horizon. Golden light streamed across the railway platform, transforming the place of death into something almost beautiful. Almost peaceful.

I stood waiting, holding the wooden train, ready to learn who I really was.

Ready to remember why I'd survived when so many others had not.

Ready to understand what Miriam Weiss had done for a terrified four-year-old boy, and what she was about to do for the man he'd become.

52

The Seamstress of Bratislava

1970 New York

Rabbi Gottlieb's voice faded as Miriam focused on the newcomer's hands. The woman's fingers worked the edge of a handkerchief, restless and quick. Miriam recognized these markers.

"Esther, would you like to introduce yourself?" the rabbi asked gently.

The woman, small-boned, perhaps forty-five, with silver threads running through brown hair, raised her gaze from the synagogue floor. Her words came carefully.

"My name is Esther Dahms. I was in Majdanek."

Beside Miriam, Wolf's hand found hers. His wedding band pressed against her skin, still strange after twenty-two years.

"For two years," Esther continued. "And afterward, Bergen-Belsen. Then Sweden. Now here." She gestured at the synagogue basement. "I still have the dreams. The doctor says they should have stopped by now."

The rabbi nodded. "Dreams often persist. Would you like to tell us about them?"

"It's always the same one. Always her."

Miriam felt her attention sharpen. Not abstract terrors, but specific nightmares with names, with faces.

"She was a guard. Young. Pretty, even." Esther's voice flattened, became clinical. "Ilse Hartmann. She worked in the women's section where we sewed uniforms."

Rain struck the synagogue windows.

"Other guards screamed. But not her. She moved between our tables without raising her voice. Checked our stitches. Her uniform never showed a wrinkle, her hair pulled back in those tight braids, wound so tight they left marks on her scalp."

Miriam listened carefully. The specific details. The sensory memory. This wasn't borrowed trauma.

"She had this small mirror," Esther continued, her voice barely above a whisper. "Checked her braids constantly. Made sure every strand was perfect. When she found a mistake in our work, she would call the woman forward. Very politely. 'Come, let me show you.' And then she had this whip. Thin, like a riding crop. She would point to the stitches, explaining what was wrong. 'This shows carelessness,' she always said. 'Carelessness reflects a careless soul.' And then she would strike."

The synagogue became still.

"In my dream," Esther whispered, "she never stops checking those braids. Never stops finding imperfections."

After the meeting, Miriam intercepted Esther in the foyer. Wolf read her intent and stepped outside to wait.

"Esther," Miriam said quietly. "Would you join me for tea? There's a café on Columbus."

Skepticism flickered across Esther's face, but something in Miriam's expression convinced her. She nodded.

Ten minutes later they sat facing each other. Rain transformed the café window into streaks of light. Esther warmed her hands around untouched chamomile tea, studying Miriam.

"Your husband," she observed. "The way he watches you. Like he's protecting something precious."

Miriam allowed a slight smile. "Wolf sees threats others miss."

"And you? What do you see?"

"Survivors," Miriam answered simply. Then, "Birkenau."

Esther stared into her cup. "Different hell."

"Same devils," Miriam said quietly.

After a moment, Esther reached into her handbag and withdrew a small newspaper clipping, creased from handling. She smoothed it on the table between them.

"Found this three months ago. German newspaper, library archive."

Miriam examined the clipping. A few lines announcing a tailoring shop opening in Bratislava, accompanied by a photograph of a slender woman standing before a storefront, her face partially turned from the camera.

"Anna Kovac, it says she calls herself now." Esther tapped the image. "But I would know that posture anywhere. The way she stands. That's her, Ilse Hartmann."

Miriam studied the image carefully. The angle of the chin. The stance that suggested military training.

"I dream of killing her," Esther said flatly. "Every night. But I wake up, and she's still alive somewhere, measuring fabric with the same hands that once held the whip." Her voice caught. "Living. While I can't sleep."

"What would you have me do with this?" Miriam asked, keeping her tone neutral.

Esther looked confused, then embarrassed. "Nothing. I don't know why I showed you. Something in your face, perhaps." She reached for the clipping. "Forgive me."

Miriam placed her hand over Esther's, stopping her. "Leave it with me."

"Why?"

"I know people who verify these things."

Hope and suspicion warred in Esther's eyes. "The Israeli agents? I tried contacting them. They're only interested in high-ranking officers."

"Not them," Miriam said. "Other people. People who care about the smaller monsters too."

They parted outside the café, Esther headed downtown, Miriam crossing to where Wolf waited. He straightened when he saw her approaching.

"Well?" he asked, falling into step beside her.

Miriam handed him the newspaper clipping. "Bratislava," she said. "As soon as possible."

Wolf studied the photograph, absorbing every detail. Then he folded the clipping carefully and tucked it into his jacket pocket.

"I'll call the others tonight," he said.

Bratislava, Three Weeks Later

The cobblestones of Bratislava's old quarter gleamed wet under street lamps as Rivka approached the corner of Michalska and Venturska. Her pace was unhurried, a woman returning home from evening shopping, the wrapped package under her arm adding to the illusion.

But her eyes tracked the figure in the second-floor window of the building across the street. A woman with dark hair pulled back severely, moving between cutting tables with familiar efficiency.

"Target confirmed," Rivka murmured as she passed Wolf's position at the café. "Second floor, northwest corner. Matches the description."

Wolf didn't look up from his newspaper, but his fingers drummed once against his coffee cup. Message received.

Twenty minutes later, Josef approached the same corner from the opposite direction. The woman had moved to the front window now, adjusting fabric on a display mannequin. The lamplight caught her profile clearly.

Josef slowed his pace, studying the face from multiple angles. The widow's peak. The pronounced cheekbones. The scar at the right temple, barely visible but unmistakable to someone who knew to look for it.

But something felt wrong.

He continued past the building, circling the block before returning to the team's staging point in a small hotel three streets away.

"It's not her," he announced as he entered the cramped room where the others waited.

Daniel looked up from the street map spread across the narrow table. "You're certain?"

"The physical markers are close, but not exact. The scar is on the left temple, not the right. And she's too young. This woman is perhaps thirty-five. Hartmann would be fifty-one by now."

Dr. Blum frowned. "A relative?"

"Possibly. The name on the shop registration is Maria Kovac, not Anna."

Miriam felt a chill of unease. "Sister-in-law, perhaps. Using a similar name."

"We need to verify," Wolf said quietly. "Before we proceed any further."

The next morning brought clearer intelligence. Dr. Blum, posing as a customer seeking alterations, engaged Maria Kovac in conversation. She was indeed a war widow, her husband killed fighting with the Slovak resistance. She had learned tailoring from her late mother-in-law, Anna, who had recently moved to a smaller shop on the other side of the old quarter.

"Anna Kovac," she explained as she measured Dr. Blum's jacket sleeve, "taught me everything I know about precision. She always said careless stitching reflected a careless soul."

Dr. Blum's hand stilled on the fabric. "An interesting philosophy."

"She learned it during the war, working in a factory. Very strict about quality. Some people found her intimidating, but she was just particular about her craft."

That afternoon, they found the real Anna Kovac.

Her shop occupied a narrow building wedged between a bakery and a bookstore, the kind of space easily overlooked unless one knew to search for it. The sign was smaller, more discreet: "Fine Tailoring - A. Kovac, Proprietress."

Rivka spotted her first, watching from a café across the street as the woman emerged to sweep her front step. The movement was unmistakable: the rigid military bearing, the way she held her spine perfectly straight even while performing mundane tasks.

And when the woman paused to adjust her hair, checking her reflection in the shop window, Rivka saw the tight braids wound close to her scalp, exactly as Esther had described.

"That's her," Rivka said quietly into the small radio. "No question this time."

The hotel room in Bratislava's old quarter fell silent as Josef spread the final photographs across the narrow table. The woman in the images adjusted her hair with familiar precision, fingers working the tight braids exactly as Esther had described.

"It's her," Josef said simply. "No question this time."

Wolf leaned against the window, watching the street below. "She mentioned closing the shop next week. Moving to Vienna. If we're going to act, it has to be tonight."

"After our mistake with the sister-in-law," Dr. Blum said quietly, "we cannot afford another error."

Miriam studied the photographs in the lamplight. When she looked up, her voice was quiet but firm. "This should be women's work."

The room stilled. Rivka's eyes met Miriam's across the table.

"She tortured women," Miriam continued. "Made them bleed for imperfect stitches. Let women answer for that."

Daniel frowned. "We've always worked as a team."

"And we will," Rivka said, understanding immediately. "But some justice requires the right hands to deliver it."

Wolf turned from the window, studying his wife's face. "Security?"

"You handle the perimeter," Miriam said. "Keep the police clear. But inside, this belongs to us."

Josef nodded slowly. "There's sense in this. Appropriate symmetry."

"It would be our first time," Daniel observed.

"Yes," Miriam said. "It would be."

At precisely 6:28 that evening, Miriam approached Anna's Fine Tailoring alone. Through the window, she could see Ilse inside, adjusting the lock on the front door. The CLOSED sign was already turned. As arranged, Miriam knocked lightly on the glass.

Ilse looked up, recognition on her face from their earlier appointment. She unlocked the door, opening it just enough for Miriam to slip inside.

"Forgive me," Miriam said, removing her coat. "Am I too late?"

"Not at all," Ilse replied, relocking the door. "I've set aside time for you. Do you have the blouse?"

"Yes, right here." Miriam withdrew a carefully folded silk blouse from her handbag. "The collar needs attention, as I mentioned."

"Let me see." Ilse took the garment, carrying it to her work table where a lamp cast bright light. She examined the collar with professional focus, her fingers tracing the seam lines. "Yes, I see the issue. Delicate work, but simple to repair."

As Ilse bent over the blouse, the back room door opened silently and Rivka stepped through, positioning herself between Ilse and the front door.

"How long have you been a seamstress?" Miriam asked conversationally.

"All my life, really," Ilse replied, not looking up. "My mother taught me as a girl. I've always had a gift for detailed work." She paused, reaching up to check her braids with unconscious precision. "Precision is everything in this trade."

"And during the war?" Miriam asked, her voice unchanged. "Where did you apply this gift then?"

Ilse's hands stilled on the fabric. "I worked in a factory," she said after a pause. "Making uniforms."

"Which factory was that?"

Now Ilse looked up, wariness entering her eyes. "I don't see how that's relevant to your blouse."

Miriam switched to German. "*Die Uniform steht dir immer besser als die Lumpen deiner Gefangenen, Ilse Hartmann.*" The uniform always suited you better than your prisoners' rags, Ilse Hartmann.

The sewing scissors clattered to the floor. Ilse backed against the cutting table, her eyes darting between Miriam and the shadowy figure by the door.

"I don't know what you're talking about." But her voice cracked on the lie.

"Clara Rothstein," Miriam said, stepping closer. "Eighteen years old. You made her unpick the same seam seven times because the stitches weren't uniform enough. Then you had her stand in the snow for three hours. She died of pneumonia two days later."

Ilse's face went white. "That's impossible. No one could know that."

"Survivors remember everything," Rivka said quietly from behind her. "Every detail. Every face. Every cruelty."

Ilse spun toward Rivka's voice, then back to Miriam, calculation replacing shock. "*Überlebende*," she whispered. Survivors. "You're survivors." Her eyes narrowed. "But not from Majdanek. I would remember you."

"Not from Majdanek, no. But that hardly matters now."

"What do you want? Money? Information?" Ilse's voice took on a pleading tone. "I was nothing. A minor functionary. I can tell you about the real monsters. Commanders who made actual decisions."

"We know exactly who and what you were," Miriam said evenly.

With surprising speed, Ilse lunged toward the back room, but Rivka was ready. The older woman might have lost some speed over the years, but her detective instincts remained sharp. She caught Ilse's arm, redirecting her momentum toward the rear exit.

"*Nicht so schnell*," Rivka murmured. Not so fast.

But Ilse twisted free with desperate strength, shoving past Rivka and bursting through the back door into the narrow alley behind the shop.

The chase began immediately.

Ilse ran through Bratislava's medieval streets like a woman half her age, muscle memory from another life driving her through the labyrinth of narrow passages. Her braids had begun to loosen, dark hair spilling across her shoulders as she gasped for breath.

Miriam and Rivka followed twenty meters behind, their footsteps echoing off stone walls that had witnessed centuries of pursuits. Rivka spoke quietly into her radio: "Target is running. Moving east toward the cathedral."

Wolf's voice crackled back: "Police responding to disturbance on Michalska Street. Daniel's redirecting them toward the university."

Ilse glanced back once, her face pale in the lamplight, then darted left into an even narrower alley. The passage curved between ancient buildings, barely wide enough for two people to pass.

She emerged onto a small square dominated by a medieval church, its spire black against the evening sky. For a moment she hesitated, looking for escape routes.

"The old quarter is a maze," Rivka said quietly to Miriam. "But she doesn't know it as well as she thinks."

They approached from opposite sides of the square, forcing Ilse toward the one exit that led to a dead end. She realized the trap too late, finding herself in a narrow court surrounded by high walls.

Ilse pressed her back against the stone, her hands flat against the wall as if she could push through it. Her carefully maintained appearance had deteriorated during the chase. Hair loose, clothing disheveled, the control she prized so highly finally broken.

"There's nowhere else," Miriam said, approaching slowly.

Ilse turned, breathing hard. "You don't understand. I was nobody. The women I supervised, they were going to die anyway. I just tried to maintain order."

"Order," Rivka repeated. "Is that what you called it?"

"I can give you names," Ilse said desperately. "Real war criminals. Officers who escaped justice. I'm just a seamstress now."

"You were never just anything," Miriam replied. "You chose every action. Every cruelty."

Ilse's hands moved to her hair, an unconscious gesture of control even now. "That was nearly thirty years ago. I'm not that person anymore."

"Aren't you?" Rivka gestured at Ilse's compulsive smoothing of her loosened braids. "You still need everything perfect. Still can't tolerate imperfection."

"I run a legitimate business. I help people look their best."

"You profit from skills learned while watching women die," Miriam said quietly.

Ilse straightened, and for a moment the mask slipped completely. The military bearing returned, the cold authority that had once held power over life and death. "They were prisoners. I was following orders. Maintaining discipline was necessary for the war effort."

"There it is," Rivka said softly. "There's the woman who killed Clara Rothstein."

"And Sarah Schrank," Miriam added. "And Ruth Stein. And dozens of others whose names we know."

Ilse's face hardened. "You think this makes you righteous? You're murderers, same as anyone."

"No," Miriam said simply. "We're seamstresses too. And we've come to fix your final imperfection."

What followed was swift and quiet. No speeches, no elaborate revenge. Justice delivered with the same precision Ilse had once demanded from her victims.

When it was done, Rivka knelt beside the body and withdrew a small pair of scissors from her coat.

"For Esther," she said, cutting through one of Ilse's braids near the scalp.

Miriam held the severed hair in her hands, feeling its weight. "She wore it like armor."

"And now it's evidence," Rivka replied.

They worked together to stage the scene, making it appear that Anna Kovac had suffered a heart attack while walking home from her shop. Two women who had survived the worst humanity could offer, delivering justice with the same attention to detail their tormentor had once prized.

As they walked back through the quiet streets, Rivka spoke softly. "It felt different. More complete somehow."

Miriam nodded, the braid secure in her coat pocket. "Some things can only be settled between women."

In the distance, Wolf waited at their rendezvous point, the others already dispersed according to plan. Tomorrow they would leave Bratislava separately, carrying with them the knowledge that Ilse Hartmann's long escape from justice had finally ended.

But tonight, for the first time, two women had claimed the right to answer for crimes against their sisters. And that felt like its own kind of justice.

New York, Two Weeks Later

Miriam attended the survivors' group meeting as usual. Esther Dahms sat in the same chair as before, but something had changed. Her hands no longer trembled as she spoke about a memory from before the war. Her voice seemed stronger.

After the meeting, Miriam approached her. "Would you walk with me for a moment? The air would do us both good."

Esther agreed. They strolled half a block in silence before Miriam withdrew a small envelope from her coat pocket.

"I have something for you," she said, placing it in Esther's hands. "No need to open it now."

Esther's fingers closed around the envelope, a question in her eyes.

"No explanations," Miriam said gently. "Some things are better left unspoken between us."

Later that night, alone in her small apartment, Esther opened the envelope with trembling fingers. Inside was a photograph of a woman slumped at a workbench, her face peaceful in death. And wrapped in tissue paper, a braid of dark hair, cut close to the scalp.

Esther held the braid to the light, recognizing the texture, the way it had been wound tight enough to leave marks. For the first time in twenty-six years, she smiled without pain.

At the next meeting, Esther sought Miriam out, taking the seat beside her. Midway through the session, she leaned close and whispered, "I can sleep now. The nightmares have stopped."

Miriam nodded, unable to speak.

That evening, as she prepared dinner in their kitchen, Wolf handed her a folded note that had arrived through their channels. Another name. Another location.

"*Soll ich den anderen Bescheid geben?*" Wolf asked. Shall I tell the others?

Miriam studied the name on the paper. A camp guard from Ravensbrück this time, reportedly living in Marseille. She thought of Esther Dahms, sleeping peacefully for the first time in years.

"Yes," she said. "Tell them we begin again next week."

Outside their window, New York continued its restless movement. Tomorrow, Miriam would teach her German class. Wolf would attend business meetings. They would shop for groceries, pay bills, exchange pleasantries with neighbors.

And beneath these ordinary movements, their true purpose would continue. The pact they had made would hold until death released them from it, or until the last monster had been found.

Whichever came first.

53

Miriam - The Call

She knew this would be the day because the connection had grown too strong to ignore.

Miriam sat in the small stone house, watching the Mediterranean catch the early morning light. Her companions still slept around her: Rivka curled near the window, Daniel breathing deeply in his corner, Josef and Levi on their separate mats. Wolf was already outside somewhere, checking the perimeter as he did each dawn.

Twenty-eight years since she'd watched David board the ship to England. Twenty-eight years of carrying his truth, waiting for the moment when he would be strong enough to bear it himself.

That moment had arrived.

The psychic contact she'd made with him the night before had drained her more than she'd expected. Reaching across continents, piercing through decades of carefully constructed amnesia, required energy she wasn't sure she possessed anymore. But it had worked. She'd felt his response, felt his understanding that today would bring answers.

She rose quietly, gathering her few possessions. The leather notebook where she recorded everything that must not be forgotten. The photograph of Elsa and Fritz Rosenberg, David's parents, taken before the war when they still believed the world made sense. David would need to know what had become of them, the terrible truth she'd carried alone for so many years.

"You're leaving us." Daniel's voice came softly from across the room. Always the most perceptive of their group.

She turned to find him watching her, his eyes alert despite the early hour.

"For how long?" he asked.

"I don't know." She folded the photograph carefully between the notebook's pages. "David needs me. The connection is strong enough now for a full revelation. I can't do that from here."

Daniel sat up, his movement causing Rivka to stir slightly. "Meier?"

"Will have to wait." She shouldered her small pack, feeling the weight of promises kept and promises yet to fulfill. "This is more important. David is breaking apart without his truth. If I don't help him remember who he is, we'll lose him entirely."

"You think he's ready?" Daniel's skepticism was gentle but clear. "You said yourself the last time you tried to contact him, years ago, he wasn't strong enough."

Miriam paused at the door, remembering those earlier attempts. The tentative psychic touches that had sent David into panic attacks. The way his mind had recoiled from memories too painful to process. She'd learned to wait, to let him come to the truth gradually.

"He's older now. Stronger. And months ago, when he collapsed at Birkenau, his defenses finally cracked open. The breakdown wasn't destruction, Daniel. It was preparation. Since then, he's been waiting there, ready for the truth even if he doesn't understand why."

She kissed his forehead gently, the same gesture she'd used to comfort him during their darkest days in the camps. "Continue watching Meier. Document everything. When I return, we'll finish what we started."

The journey to Poland felt both endless and instantaneous. Hours on planes and in airports, her consciousness split between her physical movement through space and her awareness of David waiting at Birkenau. She could feel his growing certainty, his readiness to face whatever truth she carried.

By the time she reached Kraków, the sun was already beginning its descent toward evening. She hired a car without hesitation, her hands steady on the wheel despite the magnitude of what lay ahead. The driver she'd initially contacted had canceled, claiming mechanical problems, but she understood. Some journeys had to be made alone.

The countryside rolled past her windows: fields where spring was finally asserting itself over winter, small towns with their careful distance from history, the gradually familiar landmarks that told her she was approaching the place where everything had changed.

As she drove through Oświęcim, she felt David's presence like a powerful pull. He was already at the camp, already waiting. The wooden train she'd given him all those years ago was warm in his hand, its carved star connecting them across the distance that remained.

She parked outside the camp gates as the last tour groups were leaving. The place felt alien to her now, transformed into something for visitors and education. This was her first time returning since she'd been a prisoner here, and the changes were jarring. Memorial plaques and guided pathways where there had once been only mud and desperation.

But tonight was different. Tonight she wasn't coming as a mourner or a witness. Tonight she was coming as the keeper of a promise finally ready to be fulfilled.

The sun hung low in the sky as she walked toward the railway platform. With each step, the connection between them strengthened. She could feel David's heartbeat, quick with anticipation and fear. Could sense his determination to finally know the truth, no matter how painful.

She could see him now, walking alone on the platform where cattle cars had once unloaded their human cargo. A tall man in a dark coat, holding something small and precious in his hands. No longer the terrified four-year-old she'd rescued from Schmidt's house, but carrying that child within him still.

The wooden train pulsed with warmth as she approached. The psychic bridge between them blazed with recognition, with homecoming, with the completion of a circle that had taken nearly three decades to close.

54

The Meeting

David saw the car first, a small rental sedan parked at the edge of the visitor lot as the last tour buses pulled away. The woman sitting behind the wheel had her hands pressed flat against the dashboard, staring through the windshield at the camp entrance with an expression he recognized immediately. Terror.

He approached slowly, his footsteps crunching on the gravel. She didn't move, didn't acknowledge his presence, even when he stopped beside the passenger door. Through the glass, he could see her shoulders rising and falling with quick, shallow breaths.

This was Miriam Weiss. The woman who had reached across impossible distances to contact him. The keeper of his truth. And she was paralyzed with fear.

David tapped gently on the window. She startled, her head turning toward him with wide eyes that held decades of carefully controlled panic. For a moment, neither of them moved. Then recognition dawned on her face, and something deeper. The same inexplicable knowing that had drawn him here day after day.

She rolled down the window with trembling fingers.

"David," she said, her voice hoarse. Not a question. A statement of fact, of completion.

"Miriam." He crouched beside the car so they were at eye level. Up close, he could see she was younger than he'd expected, perhaps in her fifties, with a custom-made sling supporting her left arm. The kind designed for permanent wear.

"You came."

She nodded, then looked back toward the camp entrance. The brick gateway with its railway line stretching beyond. Her hands were white where they gripped the steering wheel.

"I can't," she whispered. "I thought I could, but I can't."

David understood immediately. This wasn't just about meeting him. This was about a woman who had survived Birkenau returning to the place where everything had been taken from her. Where she'd made an impossible promise to a desperate mother. Where she'd somehow endured long enough to keep that promise.

"You don't have to go in," he said gently. "We can talk here. Or somewhere else entirely."

She shook her head, still staring at the entrance. "No. I have to. There's a place inside where I met your mother. Where she made me promise to find you. I have to stand there again. I have to tell you everything while standing on that ground."

Her voice was steady, but her body betrayed her. The trembling had spread from her hands to her shoulders.

"Then I'll go with you," David said. "Every step."

She turned to look at him again, and he saw her properly for the first time. A woman in her fifties, hair prematurely gray, wearing a simple dark coat over the custom sling that supported her left arm. But her eyes held the same fierce intelligence he'd sensed during their psychic connection. The same strength that had kept her alive long enough to rescue him.

"You don't understand," she said. "I haven't been back here since I escaped in January 1945. Twenty-six years since I walked out of this place, but I could never bring myself to return."

"Then why now?"

"Because I promised your mother I would tell you who you are when you were ready to hear it. And you can't be ready anywhere else. The truth belongs here, where it began."

David stood and walked around to the driver's side of the car. "Move over," he said. "I'll drive us in."

She stared at him. "Would you do that please?"

"You've been carrying my truth for twenty-six years," he said. "The least I can do is help you carry it the last few hundred meters."

Miriam hesitated, then slid across to the passenger seat and David got behind the wheel. They drove to the visitor parking area in silence, both staring at the entrance gates ahead. When David turned off the engine, neither of them moved immediately.

"Everyone has to walk through those gates," David said quietly. "There's no other way in."

A uniformed guard approached their car as they sat gathering courage. David rolled down the window.

"Good afternoon, Dr. Rose," the guard said with a polite nod. "I recognize you from your tours. We're officially closing now, but please, take all the time you need. I'll wait."

"Thank you," David replied, touched by the man's understanding. Word had clearly spread among the staff about his frequent visits and the emotional weight they carried.

As they walked toward the entrance, Miriam's steps became slower and more hesitant.

The entrance road was short, perhaps two hundred meters from the public lot to the gates themselves. But David could feel Miriam's tension increasing with each meter. Her breathing became more rapid, her hands clenched into fists in her lap.

"I came through those gates in a cattle car," she said, her voice barely audible. "October 1943. From Berlin. I was twenty years old. There were eighty-seven people in our car when we left. Sixty-one were still alive when we arrived."

David waited, understanding that this wasn't conversation but necessary preparation. She was building the strength to continue.

"I was twenty years old," she continued. "I thought I knew what suffering was. I thought I understood what humans were capable of doing to each other." She laughed, a sound without humor. "I knew nothing."

"Miriam," David said softly. "We can leave. Whatever you need to tell me, you can tell me anywhere."

"No." Her voice was stronger now, determined. "Your mother found me in there. She made me promise to find you when I was in there. If I'm going to honor that promise completely, I have to stand where she stood when she begged me to save you."

She looked at him, and he saw something shift in her expression. The fear was still there, but something else had joined it. Resolution.

"Let's walk to the gates," she said. "But slowly. Let me see it all."

They passed through the entrance gates and into the vast expanse of Birkenau. The railway tracks stretched ahead of them, leading to the platform where countless lives had been decided with a gesture.

"I wasn't there when your mother arrived," Miriam said as they walked along the tracks. "I had been in the camp for over a year by then. It was late 1944, and I was assigned to a work detail that day, nowhere near the selection platform."

David felt something twist in his chest. "But you learned what happened to me?"

"Later. Much later. Your mother found me weeks after her arrival. She had been selected for work and assigned to the women's camp. But you..." Miriam's voice faltered.

Miriam stopped walking and pointed to the platform ahead of them.

"She told me what happened. You were clinging to her when the selection officer pointed her toward the work line. But when the guards tried to take you with the other children, the officer noticed something about you. Your blonde hair, your blue eyes."

"And then?"

"He gave an order, and guards came and ripped you from your mother's arms. When she tried to stop them, to hold onto you, one of them hit her in the stomach with a rifle butt. She collapsed, and you were taken away. She never saw you again."

David felt the weight of this brutal separation, imagining his three-year-old self being torn away from the only safety he knew.

"That must have been when they selected me for evaluation," he said quietly.

"What name did she call out?" David asked quietly.

"David," Miriam said, watching his face carefully. "She screamed 'David!' as they took you away. David Rosenberg."

David stopped walking. The name hit him like a physical blow, not because it was unfamiliar, but because something deep inside him recognized it.

"David Rosenberg," he repeated slowly. "That's my name. My real name."

"Yes. You've never heard it before?"

"No, never. But it..." He struggled to find words. "It feels right. Like coming home."

Miriam nodded, then continued walking toward the area where the barracks had stood. "Weeks later, she found me in the women's camp. We didn't know each other, but she had heard I was asking questions about children who had been taken for evaluation. She was desperate for any information."

"When was this?"

"Early 1945. It was only a few weeks before the camp was liberated. She had been working in the camp for months, but she spent every spare moment trying to find information about you. That's when she found me and made me promise." Miriam reached into her coat pocket with her good hand and pulled out something wrapped in old cloth. "She gave me this."

David stared at the wrapped object. "She had something with her? In the camp?"

"I know how impossible it sounds," Miriam said, her voice defensive. "They stripped us naked, shaved our heads, took everything. But somehow, your mother had managed to keep this hidden." She began unwrapping the cloth carefully. "She said she sewed it into the lining of her coat before they were taken. During the chaos of processing, she managed to retrieve it."

Inside the wrapping was a small photograph, creased and faded but still recognizable. A young couple with a small blonde boy between them, all three smiling at the camera.

"Your parents," Miriam said softly. "Elsa and Fritz Rosenberg. And you."

David took the photograph with trembling hands. The faces looked back at him, strangers, but strangers who shared his features, his eyes, his smile.

"My parents," he whispered.

"She made me promise to give you this if I found you. She said, 'Tell him who he is. Tell him where he comes from. Tell him we loved him.'"

"What happened to her after that? And my father?"

"I don't know," Miriam said, her voice heavy with old pain. "I escaped from the camp just days before the Russians arrived in January 1945. It was only weeks after your mother gave me this promise. I never learned what happened to either of your parents when the camp was liberated."

"And me? Were you able to find out what happened to me?"

"Nothing," Miriam said, frustration evident in her voice. "You had vanished completely. I asked everyone I could, took terrible risks trying to gather information, but there was no trace of you. Children selected for evaluation just disappeared into the Nazi system."

"So how did you find me?"

"After the war," Miriam said simply. "It took me years, but I never stopped searching. I kept the promise I made to your mother."

They had been walking as they talked, and now Miriam stopped in front of an area where one of the brick buildings stood, its chimneys marking where barracks had once housed thousands of prisoners.

"This is where she found me," she said, pointing to the space between the building and what had once been another barrack block. "We walked around behind there, near where the refuse was dumped, so we could talk without being overheard."

David stared at the area she indicated. Where his mother had entrusted his future to a stranger. Where she had given away her most precious possession, a photograph of her family, in the desperate hope that someone would remember her son.

"Will you show me exactly where?" he asked.

Miriam looked toward the space between the buildings, her face pale but determined.

"Yes," she said. "I need to walk there again. I need to show you exactly where your mother made me promise to find you and tell you who you are."

But as she looked toward the area behind the building, her breathing became rapid again. The trembling had returned to her hands.

"Twenty-six years," she whispered. "And I still can't face walking back there."

David reached out and gently took her good hand. "Then we'll walk there together. One step at a time. You kept your promise to my mother for twenty-six years. Let me help you complete it."

She looked at him, and he saw something in her eyes he hadn't expected. Not just fear, but recognition. The child she had promised to find had grown into a man who could now offer her strength.

"David Rosenberg," she said softly, testing the name. "Yes. Let's go tell you the rest of your story."

55

The Burden of Truth

The Hotel Srodmiescie sat on a quiet street in Oświęcim's old quarter, its narrow facade painted a faded yellow that had once been cheerful. David had booked two adjoining rooms that morning, though he hadn't been entirely sure why. Some instinct had told him that whatever happened today, neither he nor Miriam would be ready to part ways immediately.

Now, as they climbed the wooden stairs to the second floor, David felt grateful for that impulse. Miriam moved slowly beside him, her good hand gripping the banister. The afternoon at Birkenau had drained them both, but he could see the exhaustion in her face went deeper than the day's revelations. It was the weariness of someone who had carried a burden for twenty-six years and was finally setting it down.

"Your room is here," David said, stopping at door 203. He handed her the key. "Mine's next door. We share a bathroom."

She nodded, fumbling with the lock. Her fingers, so steady when she'd unwrapped his parents' photograph, now trembled slightly.

"Miriam," David said quietly. "Are you all right?"

She looked at him, and for a moment he saw not the fierce woman who had rescued him, but someone fragile, uncertain. "I'm not sure," she admitted. "For twenty-six years, I've known exactly what I had to do. Find David Rosenberg. Tell him who he is. Keep the promise." She pushed open her door. "Now that it's done, I don't know what comes next."

"Rest," David said. "We'll have dinner. And you can tell me the rest."

"The rest?"

"The parts you haven't told me yet. About what happened after you put me on that ship." David's voice was steady, but she could hear the questions underneath. "I need to know all of it, Miriam."

She studied his face. "It won't be easy to hear."

"Nothing about today has been easy."

A small smile crossed her lips. "No. I suppose it hasn't." She stepped into her room, then turned back. "There's a restaurant downstairs. Karczma Pod Orłem. Seven o'clock?"

"I'll be there."

The restaurant occupied the hotel's ground floor, its low-beamed ceiling and wooden tables giving it the feel of an old tavern. At seven o'clock, it was nearly empty. Just a few locals nursing beers and an elderly couple sharing *pierogi* in companionable silence. Polish dumplings. David had arrived first and chosen a corner table where they could speak without being overheard.

Miriam appeared in the doorway precisely at seven. She had changed from her dark traveling clothes into a simple gray dress, and had attempted to tame her graying hair. But it was her face that struck David. The careful mask of composure she'd worn all day had slipped slightly, revealing something more vulnerable underneath.

She slid into the chair across from him, wincing slightly as her damaged arm settled against the table.

"How long have you had the sling?" David asked.

"Twenty-six years." Her tone was matter-of-fact. "Since the night we rescued you."

The waitress approached. A young Polish woman with kind eyes who seemed to recognize that her customers needed privacy. They ordered simply: *żurek* soup and dark bread, tea for both. Polish sour rye soup. When she'd gone, silence settled between them like dust.

"You said there were complications," David said finally. "When you rescued me."

Miriam nodded, her fingers tracing the rim of her teacup. "We had planned to take you and leave immediately. Get you to safety, then deal with Friedrich and Anneliese later. But they came home early."

394

Her voice dropped. "Friedrich walked through the front door just as Wolf was carrying you down the stairs."

David felt something cold settle in his stomach. "What happened?"

"He recognized us immediately. Not individually, but what we were. Survivors. He reached for a pistol he kept on the hall table." Miriam's eyes had gone distant, seeing that night again. "Josef shot him before he could draw it."

"And his wife?"

"Anneliese was behind him. She saw Friedrich fall and started screaming. Not from grief, from rage. '*Vermin*,' she called us, said we had no right to take '*ihr Sohn*.'" Miriam's voice hardened. "She ran for the kitchen. We thought she was trying to escape, but she came back with a gun." Vermin. Their son.

The waitress returned with their soup, steam rising from the bowls. Neither of them touched it.

"She shot you," David said. It wasn't a question.

"In the shoulder. The bullet went through and lodged against the bone." Miriam's good hand moved unconsciously to her damaged arm. "Daniel shot her twice in the forehead. It was remarkable, really. He hated violence more than any of us, but his aim was perfect."

David stared into his soup, and suddenly the numbness cracked. Heat flooded his chest, a mixture of gratitude and horror and something that felt dangerously close to rage.

"You nearly died," he said, his voice tight. "You nearly died saving a child you didn't even know. Keeping a promise to a woman who was already dead."

"David..."

"No." He looked up at her, his eyes bright with unshed tears. "Do you understand what you've told me? Six people risked everything, lost everything, became killers, spent twenty-six years hunting Nazis, all because you made a promise to my mother. A woman I don't even remember."

The raw emotion in his voice made other diners glance their way. Miriam leaned forward, her own voice gentle but firm.

"Your mother loved you. In the few moments we had before she died, her only thought was protecting you. That promise wasn't just words, David. It was her last act of love."

"But the cost." David's hands were shaking slightly. "Look what it cost you. Look what it cost all of you. You could have had lives, families, peace. Instead you became..."

"We became what we needed to become," Miriam said quietly. "And we chose it. Every day for twenty-six years, we chose it."

"What happened then?"

"We had to get out quickly. Neighbors would have heard the shots. Levi operated on me that night in a safe house outside Frankfurt. Crude conditions, no anesthesia, just candlelight and whatever medical supplies he could carry." She picked up her spoon, then set it down without eating. "The others burned the house with the Schmidts inside. Made it look like an accident."

"And you've never regretted it?"

Miriam was quiet for a long moment. When she spoke, her voice carried no doubt. "Friedrich Schmidt participated in mass murder in Ukraine before being assigned to the Lebensborn program. They stole you from murdered parents and spent a year trying to break your spirit. Do I regret that they're dead? No. I regret that thousands of others like them lived comfortable lives and died peacefully in their beds."

The elderly couple at the other table paid their bill and left, their footsteps echoing on the wooden floor. The locals at the bar spoke in low Polish, their voices a comforting murmur.

"After you healed," David said. "You could have come to England. Found me."

"We could have." She looked toward the window, where darkness was settling over the town. "But we had made a decision. The six of us. We were going to hunt down the men who had destroyed our families. SS officers who had escaped justice. Einsatzgruppen leaders hiding under new names. Camp guards living comfortable lives while our parents' ashes were still settling."

"Nazi hunters."

"Yes." She met his eyes directly. "We made a pact that night in the safe house while Levi dug the bullet from my shoulder. The six of us who had survived would dedicate our lives to finding the ones who

396

had slipped through the cracks. The minor officials, the local collaborators, the ones the Nuremberg trials would never reach."

David felt the weight of what she was telling him. "And you couldn't take a child into that life."

"It wasn't just dangerous, though it was. We were hunted ourselves, moving constantly, sleeping with weapons." She struggled for words. "But more than that, what we planned to do, what we have done, it changes you. We've spent twenty-six years becoming something necessary but terrible. I couldn't let that darkness touch you."

David's voice cracked slightly. "But you let it touch you. All of you. Because of a promise to a dead woman."

"Because of love," Miriam corrected. "Because some promises are worth keeping, no matter the cost."

"How many?" David asked quietly.

"Over the years? Dozens. Friedrich and Anneliese were the first, but not the last." Miriam's voice was steady, clinical. "*SS-Oberführer* Klaus Brandt, who ran medical experiments on children at Dachau. Otto Hoffner, who commanded an Einsatzgruppen unit that murdered three thousand Jews in Ukraine. Werner Kellner, who helped organize deportations from Vienna." SS senior colonel.

She recited the names like a prayer, each one carrying the weight of judgment passed and executed.

"Some we caught early, in the chaos after the war. Others took years to find. SS-Oberführer Klaus Brandt, who ran medical experiments on children at Dachau. We found him in 1948, three years after liberation. David tried to process this. The woman sitting across from him, who had risked everything to save him, had spent twenty-six years methodically hunting down and executing Nazi war criminals. She and her five companions had become something between vigilantes and avenging angels.

"I need you to understand," Miriam said, leaning forward slightly. "We didn't do this from bloodlust or simple revenge. We did it because no one else would. Thousands of war criminals escaped after 1945. They burned their uniforms, changed their names, and started new lives. The official denazification process was a joke. Too many people wanted to move on, to forget."

"But you couldn't forget."

"How could we? They murdered our families, our communities, our entire world. And then they expected to live peaceful lives as if nothing had happened." Her voice carried twenty-six years of controlled fury. "We lost everything, David. Our parents, our siblings, our children. Some of us lost spouses, lovers. They took our past and tried to take our future. The only thing left was to ensure they paid."

David understood the logic, even felt a certain justice in it. But the scope of what she was describing, decades of systematic killing, was staggering.

"Tomorrow," Miriam said, "before you leave, there's something else I want to tell you about. But not tonight. Tonight, you need to rest and think about what you'll do with everything you've learned."

David felt a chill that had nothing to do with the autumn evening. "What else is there to tell?"

"About what we became after we left this place. About the choices we made and the prices we paid." Her voice carried the weight of twenty-six years. "But that can wait. You have enough to process for one day."

They sat in silence for several minutes, the weight of twenty-six years of hidden history settling between them. The restaurant had grown quieter, shadows lengthening as evening settled over the town.

"Where are the others now?" David asked.

"They're waiting for me in Haifa. All five of them." Her voice carried a note of urgency. "There's a doctor there who has managed to evade justice for twenty-six years. Our intelligence finally tracked him down. He was a camp physician who performed medical experiments on children."

"And you're still active?"

"The Haifa job is far from our last. This is our life mission, David. We see no end to it." Her voice carried a grim determination. "There are always more. Former guards living comfortably in Argentina. Bureaucrats who organized deportations, now drawing pensions in Canada. Collaborators who betrayed their neighbors, teaching in American universities. We're all in our fifties and sixties now, but we'll continue until we can't."

The waitress approached hesitantly, clearly wanting to close. David reached for his wallet.

"Miriam," he said as they climbed the stairs to their rooms. "I need to ask you something."

"Of course."

"Do you regret it? Any of it? Sending me away, becoming killers, spending your lives hunting the past instead of building a future?"

She paused at her door, considering the question carefully.

"I regret that we lived in a world where such choices were necessary. I regret that you grew up without knowing who you were. I regret that I never got to watch you become a man." She looked at him directly. "But do I regret ensuring that the men who murdered our families paid for their crimes? Do I regret that Friedrich and Anneliese Schmidt will never steal another child? No. I don't regret that."

David nodded slowly. He found, to his surprise, that he understood. More than understood. He respected it. These six survivors had turned their trauma into purpose, their loss into a mission.

"Tomorrow," she said, "after you give your tour, we'll talk more. There are still things you need to understand. But for now, you need to decide what to do with the truth."

They said goodnight, each retreating to their rooms. But David knew neither of them would sleep easily. Tomorrow would bring more revelations, more pieces of a puzzle that had taken twenty-six years to solve.

As he lay in the narrow hotel bed, staring at the ceiling, David thought about the tour he was scheduled to give in the morning. For years, he had guided visitors through the horrors of Birkenau, speaking about history with academic detachment. Tomorrow, he would return not as Dr. David Rose, Holocaust historian, but as David Rosenberg, survivor and witness.

And afterward, Miriam would tell him the rest. Whatever darkness still remained to be revealed.

Outside his window, the quiet streets of Oświęcim slept peacefully, unaware that two floors above, a promise made in hell was finally, fully being kept.

56

The Tour Guide

David woke before dawn, his body stiff from a night of fractured sleep. Every time he'd closed his eyes, fragments of the previous day returned: his mother's photograph, Miriam's damaged arm, the weight of twenty-six years of secrets finally shared. He lay in the narrow hotel bed, staring at the ceiling, trying to process what it meant to be David Rosenberg instead of David Rose.

At seven o'clock, he dressed in his usual tour guide uniform: dark trousers, white shirt, the official badge that identified him as Dr. David Rose, Senior Historical Interpreter. The irony wasn't lost on him. Today he would guide visitors through a place that had shaped his life before he could even remember it.

Miriam was waiting in the hotel lobby, dressed in the same dark coat she'd worn yesterday. She looked as if she hadn't slept either.

"How are you feeling?" she asked.

"Like everything I thought I knew about myself was wrong," David said. "Which I suppose it was."

They walked to Birkenau in silence, arriving an hour before the tour was scheduled to begin. The morning mist hung low over the memorial, giving the ruins an ethereal quality that David had never noticed before. Or perhaps he was seeing everything differently now.

"I have something I want to show you," Miriam said as they approached the entrance. "Before your tour begins."

She led him past the main gate, beyond the tourist paths, to a section behind the women's barracks where the ground was rough and overgrown. David recognized the area. He'd walked past it hundreds of times during tours, usually pointing out the remains of the administration buildings.

400

Miriam stopped beside a patch of earth that looked no different from any other. She raised her foot and stomped hard on the ground, her face twisted with sudden fury.

"SS-Hauptsturmführer Karl Drexler is buried here," she said, her voice carrying twenty-six years of satisfaction. "We killed him in January 1945. The six of us surrounded him in the snow behind the administration building while he was trying to dig up treasures he'd buried. We beat him to death with rocks, pieces of ice and chunks of concrete from the bombed buildings."

David stared at the unremarkable patch of earth. "Here?"

"He came back on a motorbike three days before the Russians liberated the camp. The Germans had fled, abandoning us, but Drexler returned alone to dig up treasures he'd buried behind the administration building. Gold teeth, wedding rings, jewelry stolen from the murdered." She stomped again, harder this time. "We six survivors were hiding in the women's barracks when we heard his engine. We surrounded him while he was on his knees, clawing at the frozen ground with his bare hands, desperate to retrieve his stolen wealth before the war ended."

The casual way she described it chilled David more than the morning air. This woman who had saved his life, who had spent decades hunting war criminals, had beaten a man to death with stones and felt no remorse.

"We dug his grave ourselves," Miriam continued. "Six feet deep in the frozen ground. As far as I know, he's still here, rotting beneath the earth where so many of his victims died."

David looked around the memorial grounds with new eyes. Thousands of visitors came here each year to pay their respects to the dead, never knowing they were walking over the grave of an SS officer executed by survivors.

"Why are you telling me this?"

"Because you need to understand what the killing of Drexler began. That morning in the snow, we crossed a line. We became hunters instead of victims. When we rescued you two years later, it solidified our purpose. We realized we could deliver justice when the world wouldn't." She looked toward the ruins of the gas chambers. "How many war criminals escaped after 1945? How many lived comfortable lives while their victims' bones bleached in mass graves? We decided that some of them, at least, would pay."

"The promise was just about me," David said quietly.

"Yes. But saving you showed us we could act instead of just survive. We could deliver justice when the world wouldn't." She looked toward the ruins of the gas chambers. "How many war criminals escaped after 1945? How many lived comfortable lives while their victims' bones bleached in mass graves? We decided that some of them, at least, would pay."

David felt the weight of that revelation. His rescue hadn't just saved one child. It had created six instruments of justice, six people who would spend their lives hunting down the men who had tried to erase an entire people.

"Does it ever end?" he asked.

"No. There are always more. Former guards in Argentina, bureaucrats in Canada, collaborators in American universities. We'll continue until we can't."

A bus pulled into the parking area, bringing the first tour group of the day. David checked his watch. In thirty minutes, he would stand before twenty strangers and guide them through the history of this place. But which David would do the guiding?

"Would you stand with me during my tour today?" David asked.

Miriam looked surprised. "Are you certain? This is your moment."

"It's our moment. You saved my life. You kept a promise to a woman I never knew. I want them to meet you."

After a moment, she nodded. "Yes. I'll stand with you."

They walked toward the visitor center together, his mind churning. For twenty-six years, he had been Dr. David Rose, academic and historian. He had guided thousands of people through Birkenau, explaining the mechanics of genocide with scholarly detachment. He had been good at his job precisely because he could maintain that distance.

But David Rose was a fiction. The real person walking these paths was David Rosenberg, son of Elsa and Fritz Rosenberg, survivor of the Holocaust, living proof that sometimes promises made in hell could be kept.

The tour group assembled near the entrance: twenty-three people from various countries, ages ranging from teenagers to elderly couples. David recognized the usual mix. History students, curious tourists, descendants of survivors seeking connection to their family's past. He had given this same tour hundreds of times, but never as himself.

Miriam stood quietly beside him as he faced the group.

"Good morning," he began in English, his voice carrying across the group. "My name is Dr. David Rose, and I'll be your guide this morning through the Auschwitz-Birkenau Memorial."

The lie came automatically, but it sat differently in his mouth now. Heavy. Wrong.

They walked through the ruins methodically. David pointed out the remains of the gas chambers, explained the logistics of mass murder, described the daily life of prisoners with the same clinical precision he had always used. But something was shifting inside him with each stop.

At the women's barracks, a teenage girl asked about the children.

"Many children were murdered immediately upon arrival," David explained. "They were considered useless for labor. But some were kept alive for medical experiments or other purposes."

"What happened to them?" the girl pressed.

David had answered this question countless times with statistics, historical context, and cold facts. But standing in the place where his own story had begun, the words that came out were different.

"Most died. But some survived. Some were rescued by people who risked everything to keep promises to the dead."

The group sensed something had changed in his tone. They listened more intently as they moved through the memorial.

At the monument between the ruins of the crematoria, David stopped his usual recitation. The words he had spoken hundreds of times felt suddenly inadequate.

"We often talk about the Holocaust in numbers," he said, his voice quieter than usual. "Six million Jews murdered. Hundreds of thousands of Roma, disabled individuals, political prisoners. But each number represents a person. A life. A family destroyed."

An elderly woman in the group nodded, tears starting in her eyes.

David's voice grew stronger, carrying across the memorial grounds with a power that surprised even him.

"I am a Holocaust survivor."

The words hung in the air like a bell that had finally been struck after twenty-six years of silence. He felt them resonate through his chest, through his bones, through every cell of his body that had carried this truth without knowing it.

"And today I am its witness."

The silence that followed was absolute. Even the wind seemed to pause. David felt the weight of his true identity settling onto his shoulders, not as a burden but as a mantle he was finally ready to wear. For twenty-six years he had been a ghost haunting his own life. Now, in this place where his story began, he was finally, fully alive.

The group went silent. This wasn't part of any standard tour.

"My name is David Rosenberg. I was born in 1942. When I was three years old, I was stolen from my murdered parents and given to an SS officer and his wife who tried to erase my identity. I lived as Dieter Schmidt until I was rescued by six survivors who had made a promise to my dying mother."

A young man raised his hand tentatively. "You mean you're..."

"I'm a survivor. I was here, in this place, as a small child. I don't remember it, but it shaped everything that came after." David looked around the circle of stunned faces. "For twenty-six years, I believed I was someone else. I built my life around studying the Holocaust without knowing I was part of it. Only yesterday, I met the woman who saved my life."

He reached for Miriam's hand, drawing her forward. "This is Miriam. She was a prisoner here for two years before she escaped. She was shot rescuing me, and she has carried that bullet wound for twenty-six years. She and five other survivors risked everything to keep a promise made to my dying mother."

Miriam stood silently beside him, her damaged arm visible in its perpetual sling, living proof of the price paid for David's freedom.

The silence stretched for nearly a minute. Several people were crying openly now.

"Why are you telling us this?" asked a middle-aged man.

David considered the question. Why was he revealing himself to strangers when he had only learned the truth himself twenty-four hours ago?

"Because this place isn't just history. It's not just something that happened to other people in another time. The survivors, the victims, the perpetrators, they're all still with us. Some of the killers lived long, comfortable lives. Some of the survivors spent decades hunting them down. Some of the stolen children grew up never knowing who they really were."

He gestured toward the ruins around them. "This isn't a museum. It's a cemetery. A crime scene. A place where the worst of humanity tried to destroy the best of it. And somehow, impossibly, love survived. Promises were kept. Children were saved."

The tour continued, but everything had changed. The questions were more personal, the silence more profound. David found himself speaking not as a historian but as a witness, not about statistics but about the weight of memory and the power of human connection.

As they reached the end of the tour, the elderly woman who had cried earlier approached him.

"Thank you," she said quietly. "My grandmother died here. I've visited three times, but I never felt close to her until today. You made it real."

Others approached with similar words. The young man asked if David's story would be documented, preserved. The teenage girl asked about the rescue mission and the other survivors.

"There were six who saved me," David said, his hand still holding Miriam's. "This woman who had made a promise to my mother and five others."

"As the group dispersed, David and Miriam stood together among the ruins. For the first time in his adult life, he felt complete. Not Dr. David Rose, the respected academic who studied tragedy from a safe distance. David Rosenberg, survivor and witness, son of Elsa and Fritz, proof that some promises transcend death itself.

"How did it feel?" Miriam asked as they walked toward the memorial monument.

"Terrifying. And right." David looked back at where the tour group had been. "I've been giving tours here for eight years, and I never understood what this place really was until today."

"And what is it?"

"It's not a museum. It's a graveyard where the dead still speak, if you know how to listen."

Miriam nodded. "Your mother would be proud. She always said you would grow up to be a teacher."

They sat on a bench near the memorial monument as the afternoon shadows lengthened across the memorial. Around them, the ruins of Birkenau stood as testament to humanity's capacity for evil and, somehow, its capacity for hope.

"I have to leave tonight," Miriam said quietly. "Fly back to Israel. The others are waiting."

David felt a sudden pang of loss. After twenty-six years apart, they would separate again in a matter of hours.

"Will I see you again?"

"Yes. One day we must meet in New York. There is more to tell you, David. Much more. Some of it you will not like, and you will need to try to understand." Her voice carried a weight he was beginning to recognize. "But not today. Today was about truth. The rest can wait."

"What happens now?" David asked.

"Now you decide who you want to be. David Rose the historian, or David Rosenberg the survivor. Or perhaps both." She stood, preparing to leave. "I must go now. My flight leaves in three hours."

David felt the finality settling between them. "When we meet in New York, what will you tell me?"

"About what we became after we left this place. About the choices we made and the prices we paid. About things that happened in the years between then and now." Her voice grew softer. "About why some truths are harder to bear than others."

"I'm ready to hear it."

"Are you? It gets much darker from here, David. Much darker."

He thought about the patch of earth where Karl Drexler lay buried, about six survivors who had spent twenty-six years hunting war criminals, about a promise made in hell and kept through decades of patient justice.

"I'll be ready when the time comes," he said.

As they walked toward the parking area, David took one last look at the memorial. Tomorrow he would return as David Rosenberg, not David Rose. He would tell visitors about this place not as an outside observer but as someone whose life had been shaped by the forces that created it.

At the parking area, they embraced awkwardly, carefully avoiding her damaged arm.

"Thank you," David said. "For everything. For keeping the promise."

"Thank you for standing with me today. For letting them see that promises can be kept, even in a place like this."

Miriam climbed into the taxi that would take her to the airport. As it drove away, David stood alone in the parking lot of Birkenau, no longer the same person who had arrived that morning.

The promise was kept. The circle was closing. But the story, he was beginning to understand, was far from over.

57

The Whisper of Hope

David Rose couldn't look away from the photographs on the walls of the Wiener Holocaust Library. Each black-and-white image drew his attention with the pull of recognition, not of faces, but of something deeper. At thirty-three, he carried himself with the careful posture of someone who had learned to bear witness professionally, yet tonight felt different. Personal.

Outside, London disappeared behind a curtain of autumn rain.

For the past year, David had lived with Miriam's revelations about his past, attending memorial events like this one across Europe. Tonight's gathering had drawn Holocaust scholars and survivors, the usual mix of academic discourse and solemn remembrance. But Anna hadn't come with him this time.

"You need space to process this," she'd said that morning, her Polish accent soft with understanding. "These events are yours to navigate. I'll be here when you get back."

Her absence felt both liberating and lonely. Anna had witnessed what happened at Birkenau last year when Miriam's voice broke through decades of silence, and had seen him collapse under the weight of recovered memory. Since then, she'd given him room to find his footing in this new identity, but tonight he missed her steady presence.

"Excuse me." The voice was thin but insistent. "Are you Dr. Rose? Dr. David Rose?"

David turned to face an elderly man whose skin stretched over prominent bones. The faded blue tattoo on his outstretched wrist spoke volumes before he uttered a single word, but David's trained eye noted inconsistencies. The numbers appeared too fresh, the positioning slightly off from standard Auschwitz markings.

"Yes, I am," David replied, taking the man's hand with professional courtesy. The skin felt cool and dry.

"Elias Bernstein," he said, his accent carrying what sounded like Poland beneath decades of British inflection, though David detected traces that didn't quite align. "I read your article in the Journal of Holocaust Studies. When I saw the name Dr. David Rose, formerly Rosenberg, and Frankfurt as your birthplace, I had to meet you."

David's attention sharpened, but not entirely in the way Elias intended. Something felt rehearsed about the approach. "Oh?"

Elias studied David's face with theatrical intensity. "You see, I knew a Rosenberg family from Frankfurt at Birkenau. Your features... Fritz Rosenberg had the same forehead, the same way of holding his head."

The claim was too neat, too perfectly aligned with what someone might guess from David's published biographical details. As a historian, David had encountered fabricated testimonies before, not always malicious, sometimes born from trauma's need to create connections where none existed.

"I appreciate you reaching out," David said carefully, "but I should mention that many families shared surnames in pre-war Frankfurt."

"But the scar," Elias pressed, his finger tracing a line along his jaw. "Fritz had a scar here. And Elsa, she spoke languages: German, Polish, Russian. Even in the camps, she would translate."

David felt his breath catch despite his skepticism. The scar detail matched what Miriam had told him, but it was also the kind of specific detail that could be fabricated by someone who'd done research. Still, the language reference struck deeper. His own facility with languages had always puzzled him.

"Mr. Bernstein," David said, his historian's training taking over, "I'd be interested in hearing more, but I wonder if we might arrange a proper interview? These kinds of connections require careful documentation."

Something flickered across Elias's features. Disappointment? Relief? "Of course, of course. Professional standards." He pressed a folded paper into David's palm. "My contact information. I have documents, you understand. Records from the death march to Gross-Rosen."

David pocketed the paper without looking at it. "I'll be in touch."

As Elias shuffled away, David remained unsettled but not convinced. The encounter felt simultaneously significant and suspicious, like a puzzle piece that might fit but could also be forced into place.

The train back to Oxford gave him time to think. Through rain-streaked windows, the English countryside blurred past while David's mind worked through what he'd heard. Elias's story wasn't impossible. Death march survivors did exist, records were incomplete, mix-ups about who died where weren't uncommon. But the timing, the convenience of the encounter, the almost too-perfect details all raised flags.

Anna was waiting up when he arrived home, curled in the armchair with a book, her reading glasses perched on her nose. She looked up as he entered, studying his face with the attention she usually reserved for particularly challenging student essays.

"How was it?" she asked, closing the book but keeping her finger marking the page.

David sat on the couch across from her, pulling Elias's paper from his pocket. "Someone approached me. Claims he knew my parents at Birkenau."

Anna's posture straightened. "Claims?"

"An elderly man named Elias Bernstein. Says my parents survived the initial selections, were on the death march to Gross-Rosen." David unfolded the paper, reading the neat handwriting. "He had specific details. My father's scar, my mother's languages."

"But you don't believe him."

It wasn't a question. Anna knew him well enough to read the doubt in his voice.

"I don't know what to believe," David admitted. "The details were accurate, but they were also the kind of details someone could research. His tattoo looked... wrong somehow. And the whole approach felt staged."

Anna set her book aside completely now, leaning forward. "What would someone gain from lying about this?"

"Attention. Connection to a known historian. Maybe he's writing a memoir and wants credibility." David rubbed his forehead. "Or maybe he genuinely believes he knew them but is conflating memories. Trauma does that."

"Or maybe he's telling the truth."

The possibility hung between them like a bridge David wasn't sure he wanted to cross.

"That's what terrifies me," David said quietly. "What if Miriam was wrong? What if everything I've accepted about my parents' death is false?"

Anna moved to the couch beside him, her hand finding his. "Then we figure out what's true. Together."

"But what if they survived? What if they lived and never found me?" The questions he'd been avoiding spilled out. "What if they started new families, had other children? What if I'm just a ghost from their past they'd rather forget?"

"David." Anna's voice was firm. "You're catastrophizing. You don't even know if this man is legitimate yet."

"But if he is..."

"If he is, then we deal with that when we know for certain." She squeezed his hand. "You're the historian, love. Investigate. But don't let hope or fear run ahead of facts."

David looked at their joined hands, Anna's wedding ring catching the lamplight. "I need to verify his story independently. Check his details against records."

"Good. That's what you'd do with any historical claim."

"And I should probably contact Miriam. Ask her directly what she knew about the death march."

Anna nodded. "She loved you enough to find you, to give you back your identity. I doubt she'd lie about something this fundamental."

"Unless she thought the truth would be worse than the lie."

They sat in silence for a moment, the weight of possibility settling around them. Outside, the rain had stopped, leaving only the sound of water dripping from the gutters.

"The girls asked why you've been going to so many memorial events," Anna said eventually.

"What did you tell them?"

"That you're learning about family history. Which is true." She paused. "But if this leads somewhere real, if we find out your parents might be alive..."

"We'll need to decide what to tell them," David finished. "How do you explain to children that their grandfather and grandmother might exist when they've grown up thinking they died before Daddy was even found?"

"Carefully," Anna said. "And together. Always together."

David lifted their joined hands and kissed her knuckles. "What did I do to deserve you?"

"You married a Polish literature professor who understands complicated family histories," she said with a small smile. "Now, are you going to call this Elias tomorrow?"

"I'll start with the archives. Cross-check his details with death march records, survivor testimonies. If his story holds up, then I'll arrange a proper interview."

"And if it doesn't?"

David considered this. "Then I thank him for his time and continue believing what Miriam told me."

"And if it does hold up?"

The question opened onto territory David wasn't ready to explore. "Then everything changes."

Anna leaned against his shoulder. "Not everything. We're still here. The girls are still ours. This house is still home."

"But my parents..."

"Would be a gift. A miracle, even. But David, you were orphaned as a baby and survived. You built a life, a career, a family. You're not incomplete without them."

He rested his cheek against her hair, breathing in the familiar scent of her shampoo. "I know. But the possibility..."

"Is worth investigating. Carefully. Methodically. Like the historian you are."

That night, David lay awake staring at the ceiling while Anna slept beside him. Elias's paper sat on his nightstand, a small rectangle of potential that could rewrite everything. But Anna was right. He needed facts, not speculation. Tomorrow he would begin the work of verification, treating this like any other historical inquiry.

Still, as sleep finally claimed him, David found himself wondering: what did you say to parents who'd lost you seventy years ago? How did you bridge that kind of time, that kind of loss?

And underneath it all, the question that scared him most: what if they were still out there, somewhere, wondering what had happened to their son?

58

Shadows in the Archives

The archives consumed David's days like a fever. By the third week he'd memorized every crack in the Shoah Foundation's ceiling tiles, and his reflection in the monitor looked tired and hollow. The preservation chemicals from the document room had seeped into his clothing, a smell that reminded him of formaldehyde and old paper that Anna noticed the moment he walked through their front door each evening.

Marina set down tea that would go cold like the last dozen cups. "Fourteen hours today, Dr. Rose."

David didn't look up from the testimony playing on his screen. "I'll leave when I'm finished."

The routine had become automatic. Coffee at seven, archives by eight, testimonies until his eyes burned. Sixty-seven survivor accounts so far, each one meticulously cataloged in his notes. Every Holocaust survivor from Birkenau who might have seen Fritz or Elsa Rosenberg during the evacuation. So far, fragments and shadows, but nothing solid.

He reached for the next file, squinting at the timestamp. Hermann Kohl, recorded in 1995, age eighty-one at the time. As the video began, David noticed the man's nervous habit of touching his left temple, a gesture repeated every few minutes throughout the interview.

"The death march began January 18th," Hermann said, his accent thick with residual German. "They selected the strongest prisoners. The rest they left for the Russians."

David leaned forward. Hermann described the march in detail, the snow, the executions of those who faltered. But then the interviewer asked about specific people he remembered.

"There was a couple from Frankfurt. Rosenberg, I think the name was. The woman spoke excellent German, helped translate for the Polish prisoners. The man, he was thin but determined."

David's pen stopped moving. He rewound the video, played it again. Hermann continued: "Yes, Fritz and Elsa Rosenberg. The woman had dark hair, very intelligent eyes. She helped others understand the guards' orders."

This was it. David paused the video and noted the timestamp, his hands trembling slightly. Hermann described the couple making it through the first day of the march, helping other prisoners navigate the guards' increasingly violent commands.

"After Gross-Rosen, I lost track of most people," Hermann finished. "The camps emptied so quickly as the Allies advanced. But I remember thinking the Rosenbergs might survive. They had a determination about them."

David stared at his reflection floating over Hermann's frozen face. Finally, real evidence. His parents had survived Birkenau, and had made it to Gross-Rosen. He gathered his notes with shaking hands and headed home.

Anna was grading papers at the kitchen table when he arrived, her red pen tucked behind her ear. She looked up and immediately recognized something different in his posture.

"You found something," she said, pushing the essays aside.

David nodded, pulling his notebook from his briefcase. "Hermann Kohl. He was on the death march with them. Described them perfectly." His voice carried an excitement he hadn't felt in weeks. "They made it to Gross-Rosen alive."

Anna reached across the table for his hand. "What now?"

"I need to trace what happened after Gross-Rosen was liberated. If they survived that long..." David stopped, afraid to complete the thought aloud.

That night, David lay awake planning his next research phase. American immigration records, Displaced Persons camp documentation, survivor organization files. If his parents had lived through the war, there would be traces. There had to be.

The next morning brought disappointment that hit like a physical blow. David had contacted the International Tracing Service about Fritz and Elsa Rosenberg from Frankfurt, providing dates and camp information from Hermann's testimony. The response came quickly: their records showed Fritz and Elsa Rosenberg, originally from Frankfurt, had both died at Bergen-Belsen in March 1944.

David stared at the official documentation, his excitement crumbling. Different couple entirely. Wrong camp, wrong date, wrong story. The Rosenbergs Hermann had described were strangers who happened to share his parents' names and professions.

He called Anna from the archive's lobby, his voice flat with defeat. "False lead. The Rosenbergs Hermann knew died at Bergen-Belsen in '44. Different people."

"I'm sorry, love." Anna's voice carried across the connection like a lifeline. "Come home early today. The girls miss you."

David returned to his research the next day, but the enthusiasm had dimmed. He approached each new testimony with professional distance, guarding against hope that might lead to another crushing disappointment.

Three weeks later, an archivist named Margaret approached his usual table. "Dr. Rose? I may have found something relevant to your research."

She handed him a folder containing documentation from a different Displaced Persons camp near Munich. "Fritz Rosenberg, listed as arriving June 1945. The biographical details match what you've been researching."

David's pulse quickened as he read the intake form. Fritz Rosenberg, age thirty-one, mathematician, originally from Frankfurt. Wife deceased, status of children unknown. The handwriting was careful, educated.

This time, David forced himself to verify every detail before allowing hope to build. He cross-referenced the documentation with other camp records, checking arrival dates, processing numbers, physical descriptions. Everything aligned perfectly.

He spent two days tracking the paper trail from this DP camp, following Fritz Rosenberg through the immigration process. The records showed an application for passage to America in late 1946, approved for travel in early 1947.

But when David tried to trace the immigration further, the trail went cold. No Fritz Rosenberg matching these details appeared in Ellis

Island records. No follow-up documentation in American immigration files.

David sat in the archive's reading room, staring at the incomplete puzzle. Fritz Rosenberg had been processed for immigration to America but had never arrived. Or had arrived under different documentation. Or had changed his mind and gone elsewhere.

Another dead end.

That evening, Anna found him sitting on their bedroom floor, surrounded by scattered photocopies and notes.

"Tell me what you're thinking," she said, settling beside him.

"What if I'm chasing ghosts?" David's voice was barely audible. "What if I want this so badly that I'm seeing connections that don't exist?"

Anna studied the papers spread around them. "You're a historian, David. You know how to evaluate evidence objectively."

"But this isn't objective anymore. This is personal." He gathered a handful of documents. "Every lead seems promising until it falls apart. Maybe Miriam was right. Maybe they died at Birkenau and I'm torturing myself for nothing."

"Or maybe the records are incomplete. Maybe they immigrated under different names. You know how often that happened."

David nodded, but the doubt had settled deep in his chest. He'd been at this for three months, and despite occasional promising leads, he had nothing definitive.

The next morning, he called Miriam in New York. Her voice carried clearly across the Atlantic, warm but somehow guarded.

"David, how is your research progressing?"

"Slowly," he admitted. "I've found testimonies placing them on the death march, even some evidence suggesting my father reached a DP camp. But the trail keeps going cold."

There was a pause before Miriam responded. "These investigations can be quite difficult. Records from that period are often incomplete or contradictory."

"I know. I just... I suppose I hoped for clearer answers."

"David," Miriam's voice grew more serious, "when we meet in New York, there will be things we need to discuss. Things that may be difficult for you to hear."

"What kind of things?"

"It's better discussed in person. But I want you to be prepared. Sometimes the truth is more complicated than we initially understand."

After the call ended, David sat staring at his phone. Miriam's words carried an undertone he couldn't identify. Warning? Regret? Something about her tone suggested she knew more than she was sharing.

He returned to the archives with renewed determination, but also growing unease. What could Miriam need to tell him that required such careful preparation?

The breakthrough came in late August, buried in a batch of recently digitized records from the International Tracing Service. David had requested broader searches, expanding beyond his usual parameters. The document was faded, barely legible, but the name was clear: Fritz Rosenberg, Frankfurt.

This time, the details were unmistakable. Age, physical description, camp history, all matching perfectly. But what made David's breath catch was the destination listed on the immigration form: New York City, 1947.

His father had made it to America.

David's hands shook as he photographed the document from every angle. He cross-referenced the ship manifest, tracking the SS Marine Flasher's passenger list from July 1947. There it was: F. Rosenberg, age 33, destination: Bronx, NY.

For the first time in months, David felt hope that wasn't immediately tempered by doubt. This wasn't a false lead or mistaken identity. This was his father, alive, arriving in America just two years after the war ended.

But where was his mother? The ship's manifest listed Fritz as traveling alone, status: widowed.

David spent the rest of the day searching for any trace of Elsa Rosenberg in the same records. Nothing. If she had survived Gross-Rosen, she hadn't made it to America with Fritz. The implications settled over him like a weight.

From his London hotel room that evening, David called Anna with trembling hands.

"I found him," he said without preamble. "My father. He survived. He arrived in America in 1947."

"David." Anna's voice was breathless. "Are you certain?"

"Completely. Ship manifest, immigration records, everything matches. He made it to New York."

"And your mother?"

"No record of her. He's listed as widowed on the ship manifest."

Anna was quiet for a long moment. "What will you do now?"

"I have to go to New York. If he survived until 1947, he might still be alive. And I need to talk to Miriam." David paused, remembering her cryptic warnings. "She's been preparing me for some kind of difficult truth. I'm starting to wonder what she knows that she hasn't told me."

"When will you go?"

"As soon as I can arrange it. Anna, if he's still alive..." David couldn't finish the sentence. The possibility felt too large, too fragile to speak aloud.

"Then we'll deal with that together," Anna said. "All of us. But David, be prepared. Even if you find him, thirty years is a long time. People change. Survivors often build walls too thick for even family to breach."

After hanging up, David sat in the hotel's silence, staring at photocopies of his father's immigration documents. Fritz Rosenberg had survived the camps, survived the death march, and made it to America. But why had Miriam told him his parents died at Birkenau? What had happened in the years between 1947 and when Miriam found him as a baby?

The questions multiplied, each one leading to darker possibilities. Had his father abandoned him? Had Miriam lied to protect him from rejection? Or was there something else, something that explained Miriam's careful warnings about difficult truths?

David booked a flight to New York for the following week, but sleep wouldn't come. His father's signature on the immigration form haunted his thoughts. Somewhere in New York, the answers waited. But for the first time since beginning this search, David wondered if he truly wanted to find them.

59

The Reunion

Part I: Confronting Miriam

The limestone building on Park Avenue surprised David with its obvious wealth. He confirmed the address twice against Miriam's careful directions, feeling the disconnect between this Manhattan elegance and the spiritual guide who had connected with him at Birkenau. The doorman assessed his appearance with professional scrutiny.

"Your name, sir?"

"Dr. David Rose. I'm expected."

The doorman nodded after consulting his phone. "Someone will escort you upstairs, Dr. Rose."

David's footsteps echoed across marble floors as he followed a young man toward gleaming elevator doors. Crystal chandeliers hung overhead, and antique furniture filled spaces that spoke of generations of wealth. This display of Manhattan privilege felt completely at odds with the humble survivor he had imagined Miriam to be.

The elevator doors opened on the penthouse level. The young man who had escorted him extended his hand with a warm smile.

"Dr. Rose? I'm David Feldman. My mother asked me to bring you up."

David felt his confusion deepen. "You're Miriam's son?"

"Yes, sir." Young David pressed the elevator button for the penthouse. "She's been expecting you, though she hasn't told us much about why you're here."

Each floor they ascended challenged David's mental image of Miriam. A penthouse? A family he'd never known existed? During their psychic connection at Birkenau, she had never hinted at this lifestyle, this world of obvious comfort and resources.

The penthouse entrance opened onto spaces larger than David's entire Oxford home. Through floor-to-ceiling windows, Central Park stretched green and inviting in the afternoon light.

"David."

Miriam stood in the doorway to the living area. She looked shorter at home than he'd expected, wearing a simple black dress with expensive jewelry. Her silver hair was perfectly arranged, and she carried herself with the confidence of someone accustomed to comfort. The woman before him bore little resemblance to the concentration camp survivor who had guided him through his breakdown at Birkenau.

She approached and grasped his hands. Her skin felt cool and dry, her fingernails meticulously manicured. These weren't the hands he'd imagined belonged to someone who had reached across time to find him.

"Finally, we meet again here in person." Her eyes maintained their familiar intensity despite the luxurious setting. "Come, there's someone you should meet."

A distinguished man with gray hair rose from a leather chair beside the windows.

"Wolf Feldman," he introduced himself with a firm handshake. "Miriam has told me about your remarkable journey, Dr. Rose."

David accepted the handshake mechanically, his mind struggling to process these revelations. Young David mentioned something about his sisters before disappearing deeper into the apartment, leaving the three adults alone.

Miriam watched David with the same penetrating gaze he remembered from Birkenau.

"This isn't what I expected," David said, gesturing around the opulent room. "This is very different from the woman who found me in that camp."

Miriam's lips curved slightly. "You expected a shabby apartment? An old woman alone with her ghosts and memories?"

David nodded. "You never mentioned a family. A life like this."

"Our connection wasn't about my circumstances," Miriam replied. "It was about returning your past to you." She paused, studying his face. "But you didn't come here to discuss my living arrangements, did you?"

David straightened, feeling his months of research crystallizing into this moment. "I found documentation. Immigration records. My father survived the war, came to America in 1947." His voice gained strength. "I need to understand why you told me my parents died at Birkenau."

Wolf and Miriam exchanged a look that David couldn't interpret.

"Yes," Miriam said simply. "I know he survived. I know they both survived."

The admission hit David like a physical blow. "What? Even my mother survived?" "You knew? All this time, you knew they were alive?"

"David, sit down. Please." Miriam gestured toward the sitting area. "This is more complicated than you understand."

"More complicated?" David's voice rose. "I spent months researching, following false leads, questioning everything you told me. And you knew?"

Wolf moved closer. "Perhaps some refreshment while we talk? This conversation will take time."

"I don't want refreshment," David snapped. "I want answers. Where are they? Are they still alive?"

Miriam nodded. "They're alive. They live here in New York."

David sank into a chair, the weight of this revelation settling over him. "Here? In New York? How long have you known where they were?"

"I've always known," Miriam admitted. "I've been... keeping track of their welfare."

"Keeping track?" David repeated. "What does that mean?"

Wolf settled into a chair across from them. "It means she's been ensuring they have what they need. Medical care, housing assistance, emotional support when necessary."

"Without telling me?" David's anger was building now. "Without telling them I was alive?"

"They believe you died," Miriam said quietly. "Just as you believed they died."

David stared at her. "You lied to them too?"

"I told them what I thought was best at the time." Miriam's composure remained steady. "You were all so damaged, David. The war, the camps, the separation. Sometimes mercy requires difficult choices."

"Mercy?" David stood abruptly. "You call thirty years of lies mercy?"

"David," Wolf interjected, "your parents' condition after the war... It was severe. More severe than you might imagine. The medical reports from that time..."

"I want to see them," David interrupted. "My parents."

Miriam nodded. "I've arranged for that. But you need to understand what you're walking into. They're not the people from your recovered memories. The war changed them in ways that never fully healed."

"Where are they?"

"The Bronx. They live very simply, very quietly. They don't receive visitors often." Miriam paused. "I've contacted someone who works with them, helps coordinate their care. She'll meet you there, help facilitate the introduction."

David looked for a phone. "I'm calling Anna. She needs to know what's happening."

"Already arranged," Wolf said gently. "We contacted her yesterday, explained the situation. She's flying in this evening with your daughters."

David stared at him. "You contacted my wife without telling me?"

"We thought it best that your family be here when you... when this reunion happens," Miriam explained. "Some experiences are too significant to face alone."

The presumption of it, the careful orchestration, made David feel manipulated despite his desperate desire to see his parents. "I don't understand who you are anymore," he said. "The woman who connected with me at Birkenau, who helped me remember... that woman would never have kept families apart for thirty years."

"That woman," Miriam replied, "is exactly who would make such choices when she believed they were necessary for survival."

Wolf stood. "The car is waiting downstairs when you're ready. Helena Rosen will meet you at your parents' building. She's been working with Holocaust survivors for decades, and knows your parents well."

"Working with them how?"

"Providing support services. Medical coordination. Social assistance." Wolf's explanation was careful, revealing little. "Many survivors need ongoing help navigating American systems."

David headed toward the elevator, then turned back. "After I see them, you and I are going to have a much longer conversation about these thirty years of mercy."

Miriam nodded. "Yes. There's much more you need to understand about how all our lives have been connected."

Part II: The Search

The South Bronx air carried exhaust and urban decay, a stark contrast to the rarefied atmosphere of the Upper East Side. The building loomed before David, its brick walls stained by time and weather, graffiti covering surfaces in colorful tags he couldn't read. He checked Miriam's address against the faded numbers above the entrance.

A thin woman with papery skin and cautious eyes approached from across the street.

"Dr. Rose?"

"Yes. Helena Rosen?"

She studied his face with uncomfortable intensity. "You have his eyes. Fritz's eyes." She paused. "This is going to be very difficult for all of you."

Helena led him toward the building's entrance. "These people don't speak to strangers easily. Thirty years in America, and they still jump when someone knocks unexpectedly. I'll need to act as an intermediary, or they won't even open the door."

They climbed four flights of creaking stairs, the narrow hallway reeking of cabbage and industrial disinfectant. Helena moved slowly, giving David time to absorb the environment.

"Most Holocaust survivors in this country never achieved what people call the American dream," she explained quietly. "Many live like this, in buildings like this. The trauma... it doesn't just go away because you reach safety."

The faded apartment numbers were barely visible. Helena knocked gently on a door marked 4B. Long seconds passed before David heard movement inside, then a chain being unlatched.

The door cracked open, revealing a single watchful eye.

"Helena?" The voice carried a heavy German accent despite decades in America.

"I brought the historian I mentioned. Dr. Rose, from England."

Rapid German followed, whispering through the narrow opening. Helena responded in the same language, her tone reassuring.

Then the door opened reluctantly.

Helena pressed David's arm before stepping aside. "I'll return in an hour. That should give you time for initial introductions."

David entered a cramped but spotlessly clean room. A frail man sat by the single window while a thin woman positioned herself protectively between David and her husband. Both looked older than their years, their faces etched with lines that spoke of more than normal aging.

"I am Elsa," the woman said with formal politeness, evaluating David with sharp eyes. "My husband is Fritz. He is not well. We don't usually receive visitors."

David's heart pounded as he studied their faces, searching desperately for resemblance to his own features or to the handsome couple in Miriam's pre-war photograph. The decades had not been kind. This couple bore little physical similarity to the vibrant people he had imagined.

"Thank you for agreeing to see me," David began. "I'm researching Frankfurt families who survived the camps. I wonder if you might share some of your experiences."

The couple exchanged a look weighted with decades of caution.

Fritz gestured weakly toward a chair. Elsa fetched a glass of water, her movements economical and careful. After Fritz finished drinking, she began speaking.

"There is little to tell. We survived Birkenau, then Gross-Rosen. We came to America in 1947." The information came mechanically, as if she'd repeated it many times. "That is our story."

David nodded, his historian's training helping him maintain composure despite his racing pulse. "And before the war? In Frankfurt?"

"Fritzwas a publisher of books. I worked mainly as a translator. Technical documents mostly, some literary work." Elsa's responses remained guarded but precise.

The room seemed to sway slightly. A publisher and a translator. Exactly the professions Miriam had told him his parents held. David gripped his chair arms, preparing to venture into more dangerous territory.

"Did you have a family? Children before the war?"

The water glass slipped from Fritz's trembling hand, liquid spreading across his wrist and onto the floor. Elsa's entire demeanor shifted, her face hardening into protective suspicion.

"Why do you ask this?" Her words came sharp and defensive. "Who are you really? What do you want from us?"

David realised just how volatile the situation was becoming so he carefully opened his briefcase and withdrew a small bundle wrapped in soft cloth. His hands shook slightly as he set it on the table between them.

"I'd like you to look at something. Please tell me if you recognize it."

He unwrapped the tiny wooden train. The paint had worn away over the decades, but the craftsmanship remained evident. Delicate cuts, elegant curves, the work of someone who understood both wood and love.

Elsa's face went pale. She reached toward the toy but stopped just short of touching it, her hand hovering in the air.

"Where did you get this?" she whispered.

"Someone gave it to me. She said it was carved by a father for his son's birthday before the war."

Fritz made a sound deep in his throat, somewhere between recognition and pain. He pushed himself upright, gripping the chair arms with white knuckles.

"That toy..." His voice was rough from disuse. "I carved it. From oak. For David's third birthday."

Elsa shook her head frantically. "No, no. Many fathers made toys for their children. This proves nothing." Her hands fluttered like trapped birds. "It could be anyone's train."

David took the train and stuck his thumb into the crack underneath. He did it in a way that it was very clear to both of them what he was doing. Slowly he prised apart the wood and the tiny piece of paper stuck out. The train now in two parts was in the palms of his hand. He handed the wood and the paper to Fritz. Fritz's eyes were too weak to read the paper but he remembered the secret part in the train and he sat there dumbfounded.

David moved closer, and Elsa noticed the thin leather cord around his neck, the Star of David pendant barely visible beneath his collar. Her eyes fixed on it with sudden intensity.

"May I?" she asked, reaching toward the necklace.

David lifted the pendant free of his shirt. Elsa's fingers touched the worn leather cord with reverence.

"This star..." her voice broke. "I sewed this into his coat lining. The day they came for us. I hid it so deep..." She looked up at David's face with desperate searching. "The woman who found him said it was buried with his body."

"I never died," David said, each word careful and distinct. "Someone found me with a German family. She saved me and gave me this star, telling me my mother had sewn it into my clothing to protect me."

Fritz shook his head violently. "It's not possible. Too many people had such stars. This doesn't mean..."

"Fritz." Elsa's voice was urgent. "Look at him. Really look at his face."

Fritz pulled out the tiny piece of paper and handed it to Elsa. She stared at it and slowly read the word written so long ago: "Elsa, it says Elsa!"

Fritz raised his eyes reluctantly, as if looking might make hope too dangerous to bear. "I can't. If this is some mistake, some cruel joke..."

David made a decision then. Instead of more words or evidence, he moved to stand behind Elsa's chair. His adult body felt awkward, but some cellular memory guided him as he wrapped his arms around her shoulders from behind, resting his chin near her head. The position felt natural despite the years, as if his bones remembered this exact embrace.

Then he began to sing, the old Yiddish lullaby surfacing from memories buried so deep he hadn't known they existed:

"*Schlof, mayn kind, schlof keseyder, schlof, mayn tayer kind...*" Sleep, my child, sleep peacefully, sleep, my dear child...

Fritz froze completely. When he finally looked up, his eyes moved over every detail of David's face with the intensity of a man studying a miracle.

David continued the lullaby, the words flowing as if they'd never stopped. "Before the war, I used to stand behind Mother exactly like this while you both sang to me before sleep."

Fritz's water glass hit the floor, liquid spreading across the worn carpet. "Only our David stood that way," he whispered, each word torn from decades of grief. "Behind his mother, just so. And that song..." His voice broke completely. "No one else knew that song was his alone."

Part III: Recognition

Elsa covered her mouth with both hands, a sound escaping that was part sob, part laugh, part prayer. Her shoulders began to shake under David's embrace.

"Thirty years," she whispered through her fingers. "Thirty years I've heard that voice in dreams."

428

Fritz moved slowly across the small room, his legs unsteady. His hands trembled as he reached toward them, touching David's face with fingertips that traced familiar features.

"Your father's forehead," he murmured. "Your mother's eyes. But grown, so grown..."

The reunion was awkward and desperate. Elsa turned in David's arms, holding him with fierce intensity while Fritz embraced them both, his frame shaking with emotion too large for his frail body to contain.

"*Mein Sohn*," Elsa repeated in German. "Mein Sohn, mein Sohn." My son.

When David finally pulled back, his vision was blurred. He wiped his eyes, looking between these two people who were somehow his parents, yet strangers shaped by decades of trauma he could barely imagine.

"Why here?" he asked, gesturing around the small apartment. "Why like this?"

Fritz studied his twisted fingers, evidence of malnutrition and hard labor that had never fully healed. "After the camps, after believing you were dead... nothing else seemed to matter. We wanted only to disappear, to exist quietly."

"We thought you died at Birkenau," Elsa said, still gripping his hand as if he might vanish. "The woman who found us, she told us you didn't survive the war."

The scope of Miriam's deception began to crystallize for David. "She told you I was dead?"

"A fever, she said. In the first days after liberation." Fritz's voice carried thirty years of accepted grief. "She showed us papers, documents. We had no reason to doubt..."

"And she told me you both died in the gas chambers."

Elsa's grip on his hand tightened. "Why would she do this? Why keep us apart?"

"I don't know," David admitted. "But I intend to find out."

They talked for another hour, tentatively rebuilding connections across three decades. David learned about their struggles in America, their isolation, their continued battle with trauma that had never fully healed. He told them about England, about his education, his work as a historian, and his marriage.

"You have a wife?" Elsa asked, hope creeping into her voice.

"Anna. She's Polish, and teaches literature at Oxford." David smiled. "And we have two daughters."

Fritz repeated the word "daughters" as if it were foreign. "Granddaughters."

"They're here in New York. Miriam arranged for them to fly in today."

When Helena returned, she found them still sitting close together, hands linked, as if physical contact could bridge the lost years.

"Are you ready to leave this place?" David asked his parents. "Come with me to meet your granddaughters?"

Fritz and Elsa exchanged uncertain glances.

"We don't... we're not used to going out," Elsa explained. "People, crowds..."

"Just family," David assured them. "Your family."

With Helena's help, they gathered a few belongings and descended to the waiting car. In the taxi back to Manhattan, David's parents huddled together, watching the city transform from decay to prosperity as they traveled from the Bronx toward the Upper East Side.

Part IV: Family

Anna and the girls were already at Miriam's penthouse when the elevator doors opened. David's entrance with his parents brought all conversation to an abrupt halt.

Anna moved toward him immediately, her eyes taking in his emotional state and the two elderly people beside him.

"David," she said simply, understanding everything in that single word.

"Anna, these are my parents. Fritz and Elsa Rosenberg." The words felt strange on his tongue. "Mother, Father, this is my wife Anna."

Anna approached Fritz and Elsa with careful warmth. "I'm so glad to finally meet you. David has been searching for you for so long."

Miriam stepped forward, her composed expression showing the first cracks David had seen.

"Fritz. Elsa. After all these years."

Elsa met her gaze directly, thirty years of grief and confusion in her eyes. "You told us our son was dead."

"I thought I was protecting all of you," Miriam replied. "The decisions seemed right at the time."

"You had no right," Fritz said, his voice containing decades of suppressed pain. "Our son. Our choice to make."

Before the confrontation could escalate, David's younger daughter appeared at Anna's side, looking up at these new strangers with solemn curiosity.

"Daddy, are these my grandparents?"

David knelt beside her. "Yes, sweetheart. This is Grandfather Fritz and Grandmother Elsa."

His older daughter joined them, studying her newfound grandparents with the direct gaze children possess.

"I'm Elsa Rose," she said formally.

Elsa's breath caught. "Elsa? You named her...?"

"Even though I thought you were gone, I wanted your name to continue," David explained.

Elsa slowly lowered herself to the child's level. "I'm your Grandmother Elsa. We share the same name."

The younger girl pushed forward. "I'm Miriam Rose. Daddy says my name is special too."

Fritz settled carefully beside his wife, looking at these granddaughters with wonder. "You named them for your mother and your rescuer," he said to David. "You kept us with you, even when you thought we were lost."

Wolf positioned himself nearby. "Perhaps we should allow everyone time to rest before dinner. This has been an overwhelming day for all."

David looked around the opulent apartment, at Miriam whose wealth still puzzled him, at his parents who seemed diminished by the grandeur, at his wife and daughters who were processing their own wonder at this sudden expansion of family.

"There's still much we need to discuss," he said, looking directly at Miriam.

"Yes," she agreed. "Tonight, after dinner, there are things you all need to understand about these thirty years. Connections you're not aware of. Choices that were made for reasons more complex than simple deception."

Anna moved to David's side, taking his hand. "Whatever those reasons are, we're here now. All of us. That's what matters."

David squeezed her fingers, watching his daughter Elsa show her grandmother a book she'd brought, watching Fritz attempt conversation with young Miriam despite his obvious discomfort with strangers.

The family that war had separated and deception had kept apart was beginning to find its way back together. Not whole, perhaps never that. Too much time had passed, too much damage had been done. But alive, connected, and for now, that felt like enough.

As evening approached and Wolf began preparations for dinner, David realized this was only the beginning. Tonight or Tomorrow would bring more questions, more revelations, more difficult truths about the choices that had shaped all their lives.

But later tonight, for the first time in thirty years, Fritz and Elsa Rosenberg would go to sleep knowing their son was alive. And David would sleep knowing he was no longer an orphan with a manufactured past.

But there were far too many questions and not enough answers for Elsa. She pressed on deeper. It had to all come out. Some bits made sense but not much.

60

The Weight of Mercy

The silence in Miriam's elegant living room felt heavy. David stood between his newfound parents and the woman who had simultaneously saved and deceived him.

Elsa broke first. "Thirty years," she whispered, each word cutting. "Thirty years believing our son was ash."

"I never meant to..." Miriam began.

"Stop." Elsa's hand rose, trembling but certain. "You had no right to decide we were too broken to be parents."

Fritz's fingers found his wife's shoulder. "You found our boy." His voice caught, torn between gratitude and decades of loss. "We can never repay you for that. But the lies, Miriam, the years you stole from us."

The Feldmans' son and Anna had taken the children to another room, leaving the central figures to confront their shared past.

Miriam's composed exterior cracked. "You were both dying when I found you," she said. "The doctors gave you weeks. Fritz with tuberculosis. Elsa with typhus and starvation."

"And when we didn't die?" Fritz asked. "When we survived despite everything?"

Wolf Feldman stepped forward. "By then the adoption was final. The British authorities wouldn't have returned a child to displaced survivors with nothing." He gestured toward the terrace. "Perhaps we should continue outside. Fresh air might help."

They moved through French doors onto a terrace overlooking Central Park. Spring sunshine spilled over them, bright against the shadow of their shared past.

David pressed his palms against the cool stone balustrade. The woman he'd connected with at Birkenau now stood before him in cashmere and pearls, having rewritten his life through her choices.

"What I can't understand," he said, "is why maintain this fiction for decades? Why not tell me the truth when I was grown? Why not tell them once they were settled here?"

Miriam pulled a thick folder from her bag. "These are psychiatric reports from the DP camp." She held them out to David. "Your parents' trauma... The doctors believed it would take years before either of you could function, if ever."

She paused. "Remember, it was a time when thousands of children were being placed with new families. The experts insisted clean breaks heal best. They told us children should be spared their parents' nightmares. I followed their advice."

"If only you'd used your wealth to help survivors instead of playing God with families," Elsa said bitterly. "The Fallen Leaves Foundation saved Fritz when his heart failed. They help survivors who have nothing, while you live in luxury. Don't you feel ashamed?"

A strange expression crossed Wolf's face. He glanced at Miriam, who gave a barely perceptible nod.

"Elsa," Wolf said quietly, "there's something you should know about The Fallen Leaves Foundation."

Fritz's head snapped up. "What about it? It's kept us alive for years."

Wolf pulled a business card from his pocket and handed it to David. The logo showed a stylized tree with falling leaves. Beneath it: "The Fallen Leaves Foundation - Founder: Miriam Feldman."

"Miriam established it in 1951," Wolf explained. "Specifically to support Holocaust survivors struggling to rebuild lives in America."

Fritz stared at the card. "You... you're behind it?"

"Yes," Miriam said. "I've overseen your case files personally since the beginning."

Fritz's hand shook. "When my heart valve failed... the specialist from Boston..." He looked up. "That was you?"

"The least I could do," Miriam replied. "I couldn't undo my decision, but I could ensure you were cared for."

"And the experimental medications for my depression," Elsa added slowly. "The psychiatrist who finally stopped the nightmares. The rent subsidies when Fritz couldn't work...even now you pay all of the rent?" Her voice grew quiet. "All this time, you've been watching over us?"

"From a distance, yes."

David sank into a chair. "You've been caring for all of us, in your way."

Anna appeared at the terrace doors, her presence steadying him. Looking at her, David felt the impossible weight of it all: his education in England, his career, meeting Anna, their daughters. None of it would exist if Miriam had chosen differently.

"But why?" he asked. "Why separation rather than support? Why not help us be a family?"

Wolf moved to a side table and lifted a worn leather portfolio. "Miriam, it's time."

She nodded as Wolf placed the portfolio between them. Inside lay dozens of letters, yellowed with age, all in Miriam's handwriting.

"I wrote to both of you," she explained. "Letters explaining everything, asking forgiveness, suggesting ways to carefully rebuild connections. But I never sent them. The doctors convinced me reopening wounds would cause more harm than healing."

David picked up a letter addressed to him, dated 1960, his seventeenth birthday. His eyes caught phrases about truth and heritage.

Wolf settled beside Fritz and Elsa. "Those first months after the camps, children were shuffled between strangers like unwanted parcels. The lucky ones found relatives. The rest disappeared into orphanages, new families, new countries." His eyes darkened. "We were all drowning. Some of us made terrible decisions while struggling to survive."

As spring breezes swept across the terrace, Wolf took them back to 1945.

"When Miriam found David with the Schmidts, he was half-starved and mute. Allied authorities were overwhelmed with orphaned children. The British were accepting refugee children, offering them stable homes."

"Meanwhile," Wolf continued, "Miriam searched desperately for survivors from her own community. By the time she located you both, six months had passed. You were in a makeshift hospital in Munich, both critical."

Miriam picked up the thread. "The doctors said you wouldn't last the week, Fritz. Your tuberculosis was too advanced. And Elsa, you were lost in delirium. You didn't recognize anyone. You fought the nurses, called them guards. When anyone mentioned David, you'd scream until you collapsed."

David studied his mother, trying to reconcile this fragile woman with the description.

"I remember little from then," Elsa admitted. "It's like looking through dirty glass."

Fritz's hand covered hers. "There were months after liberation when you'd scream until your voice broke. Sometimes I'd find you huddled in corners, speaking to ghosts only you could see."

Silence settled between them, broken only by birds calling in the trees.

Wolf spoke again. "Miriam faced an impossible choice. David was safe in England, beginning to recover. You two were dying, with doctors insisting any disruption might kill you both."

"I made a choice," Miriam said, forcing herself to meet their eyes. "The Roses needed to believe David was truly theirs, so I told them you were dead. And when you both survived..." Her voice faltered. "I told you David was gone because everyone insisted it was the only way either of you would survive."

"And later?" David asked. "Years later, when they were stable? When I was grown?"

Miriam removed a particular letter from the portfolio, dated 1955. "I tried once. When you were both settled here and Fritz was working steadily, I approached you about the truth."

Fritz's brow furrowed, then cleared with recognition. "Rosh Hashanah, 1958. You came to our apartment. Started talking about 'new information' about David."

"Yes," Miriam confirmed. "I began explaining there was a possibility David had survived. But Elsa collapsed before I finished. You ordered me out, Fritz, and said never to mention his name again."

Fritz nodded. "Elsa didn't leave bed for weeks after. The doctor sedated her." His eyes softened on his wife. "We never spoke of it again."

Elsa's eyes brimmed. "I don't remember that day at all. But I remember the darkness that followed."

Miriam nodded. "After that, I decided silence was kindest. I had already established the foundation, and used my resources to ensure you had what you needed. I watched David from afar, made sure he thrived with the Roses."

She looked directly at David. "When you broke down at Birkenau, I had to reach out, to give you some understanding of your past. But I kept my promise never to disrupt the lives built on both sides of this divide."

David moved beside Anna, drawing strength from her presence. "So much lost time. Years we can never recover."

"Yes," Miriam acknowledged. "That burden is mine to bear."

Anna's fingers found his. "But think of what might never have been," she whispered. "That rainy Oxford morning. Our daughters."

David squeezed her hand, the realization striking him anew. His entire life had been shaped by Miriam's decision; the family he cherished might never have existed otherwise.

The French doors opened, and Miriam's son David stepped onto the terrace. "Hope I'm not intruding. Just wanted to let you know we've prepared the guest apartments downstairs for the Rosenbergs and the Roses. And tonight, we're hosting a small dinner. There are some people who've been waiting a long time to meet you all."

Miriam looked at her son with gratitude. "Thank you, David."

Young David smiled. "My father thought you might like to know that Rivka, Daniel, Dr. Blum, and Josef will be joining us. They all live in the building."

Fritz frowned. "I don't understand. Who are these people?"

Miriam's son glanced at his father before answering. "They helped rescue young David from the Schmidts. They've remained close to our family all these years."

Stunned silence followed this revelation. Fritz stared at Miriam. "The rescue wasn't just you? There was a team?"

Wolf nodded. "A carefully planned operation. Schmidt was Einsatzgruppe, death squad. Taking a child from them risked everyone involved."

"We thought perhaps tonight might be the time to share that story, if you're ready to hear it," Miriam's son added.

Fritz turned to Miriam, his weathered face softening. "There was real danger to save our boy?"

Wolf suddenly pulled Miriam's dress aside to expose a deep scar on her shoulder. "She wears this from the day that Nazi shot her. Yes, there was danger."

"We all took the risk," Miriam said simply, adjusting her dress. "We had lost so much already. We couldn't bear to lose one more child."

Elsa pushed herself up with effort and crossed to where Miriam stood. For a long moment, the two women faced each other, both survivors, both carried through decades by love for the same child.

"The foundation," Elsa said finally, "it saved Fritz's life. That night when his heart was failing... they sent doctors within hours. Without them, without you, he would have died."

"I'm glad I could help," Miriam replied softly.

"What you did," Elsa continued, voice unsteady, "keeping David from us... I may never fully understand it. But what you've done since, watching over us, ensuring we survived... that I begin to understand."

Not forgiveness, not yet, but acknowledgment. Recognition that within the tangled threads of their lives, Miriam's choices had been guided by something more complex than simple deception.

David stood between these women who had each, in their way, been mothers to him. "I think we've all been living in the shadow of impossible choices made in impossible times."

Anna approached with their daughters, sensing the storm had passed. The girls watched the adults with solemn eyes.

"Perhaps," David suggested, taking his younger daughter's small hand, "we should rest before dinner. It seems we have another chapter of this story waiting."

As they moved to leave, David's older daughter approached Fritz hesitantly. "Grandfather," she said, the word new on her tongue, "will you tell me about when my father was little? Before England?"

Fritz knelt with a wince and looked into the eyes of his namesake granddaughter. "Yes, Elsa," he said, voice thick. "I will tell you about a boy who loved wooden trains and songs under starlight."

David watched new connections forming across thirty years of separation. The anger and confusion he'd felt at Miriam's deception hadn't vanished, but now shared space with understanding of the impossible choices she'd faced.

David lingered on the terrace, Anna's hand finding his. "If she'd made different choices, I'd never have known Oxford." His voice dropped. "Never found you in that rainy lecture hall. Elsa and Miriam wouldn't exist."

Anna pressed her forehead against his shoulder. "Our daughters are flesh and blood, and they're waiting inside to know their grandparents."

They rejoined the others, prepared to hear the next chapter of a story that had begun in darkness but continued, improbably, in the spring light of a New York afternoon.

61

The Voice in the Garden

The morning at Miriam's had been beautiful and heartbreaking in equal measure. Levi had watched David embrace his birth parents for the first time since that terrified child had been rescued from his Nazi captors, three generations of a family made whole again. The reunion had been everything they'd all hoped for, but as Levi walked down Fifth Avenue toward the park, his happiness for David had settled into something heavier, a recognition of his own profound solitude.

At seventy, Dr. Levi Blum had everything a man could want. His Park Avenue apartment overlooked the city he'd conquered through intellect and determination. His practice had made him wealthy, his reputation had made him respected. He had dear friends like Miriam who worried about him and invited him to family celebrations, treating him like a beloved uncle to their children and grandchildren.

But he had never stopped being alone.

The October air was crisp as he walked down Fifth Avenue, the familiar sounds of Manhattan around him. Car horns echoed between the towering buildings, and the scent of roasted chestnuts from a street vendor mixed with the exhaust and energy of the city. He turned into Central Park, his usual refuge when the weight of his carefully constructed life became too much to bear. The autumn leaves crunched beneath his polished shoes as he walked past joggers and dog walkers, all of them part of the city's endless rhythm. He'd learned long ago that success could fill many voids, but not the particular emptiness that came from having no one to truly come home to. No one who knew the man behind the distinguished exterior, who remembered him when he was young and terrified and holding onto hope by threads as thin as spider silk.

He was thinking of Ruth, as he sometimes did on days like this. His wife, lost to the machinery of hatred before they'd even had a chance to build a real life together. But increasingly, when these moods took him, he found himself thinking of Anna. Anna with her gentle Bavarian accent and her steady hands in the infirmary. Anna who had understood without words that love could bloom even in hell, that two people could find solace in each other when the world had become unrecognizable.

The flower vendors near the Conservatory Garden were setting up their displays, the bright colors a sharp contrast to his gray thoughts. The smell of fresh blooms carried on the cool air, and he could hear the distant laughter of children playing on the lawns. He'd planned to walk past, but something made him slow his steps.

A voice. A woman speaking German to one of the vendors, her tone warm and concerned.

"Die Rosen sind so schön, aber werden sie lange halten?" The accent was unmistakable, Bavarian, with that particular lilt that softened the consonants. "I want them to last. They're important."

Levi's feet stopped moving entirely. His chest tightened as if all the air had been drawn from his lungs. It couldn't be. In a city of eight million people, after thirty years, it simply couldn't be.

But that voice. That exact caring tone she'd used when speaking to frightened patients, when whispering to him in the corners of the infirmary, when planning their impossible escapes and their final backup plan with the morphine they'd so carefully saved.

He turned slowly, afraid to look, afraid not to.

She was standing with her back to him, holding a small bouquet of white roses, speaking to a vendor who was clearly enjoying the conversation in their shared dialect. Her hair was longer now, silver and swept back in a style that was elegant and soft. Nothing like the brutal cropped hair they'd been forced to wear in the striped uniforms. The way she held her head, the graceful line of her neck, these things hadn't changed.

"Anna?"

The word escaped him as barely a whisper, but she heard it. She turned, and for a moment, time collapsed entirely. The lines around her eyes, the silver in her hair, the elegant coat and careful makeup, all of it fell away, and she was twenty-eight again, wearing the striped uniform in a place that should have killed them both.

Her eyes widened. The roses trembled in her hand.

"Mein Gott," she breathed. "Levi?"

And then he was crying, standing there on a path in Central Park with tears streaming down his face, reaching for her with hands that shook. The sounds of the city seemed to fade around them, the distant traffic and bird songs becoming nothing more than background to this impossible moment.

"Anna, I'm so sorry. I looked for you. I searched everywhere. I couldn't find you."

She stepped forward and touched his face, her fingers gentle against his cheek, catching his tears as she had once caught his blood when he'd been beaten by the guards.

"I waited," she whispered, switching to English. "I waited without knowing I was waiting."

Her own tears came then, and when he opened his arms, she stepped into them as if thirty years had been thirty seconds. He held her against his chest, feeling the solid warmth of her, the proof that she was real and alive and here. Other people walked past them, joggers with their headphones, tourists with their cameras, families with children pointing at the flowers, but they might as well have been alone in the universe. The cool October breeze stirred the leaves above them, and somewhere a street musician was playing violin, the melody floating across the park.

"I never married," she said into his shoulder, her voice muffled. "I couldn't. There was always... there was always you."

"Nor I," he managed. "How could I? You were... you are..."

They held each other without speaking, two people who had learned to live with an absence so fundamental they had built their entire lives around it. The flower vendor watched them with curious eyes, and finally, understanding that this was something sacred, turned away to give them privacy.

"Come home with me," Levi said finally, pulling back to look at her face. "Please. I have a beautiful apartment, and books, and music, and everything except what matters. Come home."

Anna looked up at him, this distinguished man with silver at his temples and expensive clothes, and saw the frightened young doctor who had held her hand in the dark. "Yes," she said simply. "Yes, I'll come home."

As they walked toward Fifth Avenue together, Anna still clutching her white roses, Levi felt something he hadn't experienced in thirty years. The sounds of the city returned gradually, the honking taxis and construction noise and endless conversations of eight million people, but now it all seemed different, vibrant rather than lonely. He felt complete. Not happy, happiness was too small a word for this, but whole. As if a piece of his soul that had been missing had suddenly, impossibly, been returned to him.

"You're really here," he said as they waited for a taxi.

"I'm really here," she confirmed, and when she smiled, he remembered exactly why he had never been able to love anyone else.

62

The Feast

Manhattan blazed gold at sunset. David watched amber light bounce off glass towers while the Feldmans fussed with place settings fifteen stories above Madison Avenue. Their rooftop garden shouldn't exist in this city of concrete and steel. Trees stood in massive concrete pots, while vines covered wrought iron trellises. The central table could seat fourteen but was set for twelve, white linen bright in the fading light.

Wolf surveyed the elegant scene with satisfaction. The penthouse, the garden, the expensive wines cooling in silver buckets. All of it paid for with money they had liberated from the banks of former Nazis, or printed in the sophisticated counterfeiting operation twelve floors below in specially built concrete bunkers. Justice had many forms. Sometimes it wore evening clothes and served champagne.

David couldn't stop staring at the city, couldn't look at the people behind him. His thoughts felt crowded after this afternoon's revelations.

Anna found him at the parapet. Her fingers found his forearm.

"You okay?"

"Christ, no." A laugh escaped, all wrong. "I woke up as David Rose. Oxford academic. Interesting refugee backstory. Now I'm what? David Rosenberg? Living survivor by proxy?" He gestured toward the dinner table. "And there's my personal rescue squad, eating canapés."

Anna's shoulder pressed against his bicep. No platitudes. Just there.

"You're still you," she said after a moment. "Just with more history than you had this morning."

His parents stood by the herb garden. Fritz and Elsa Rosenberg. Two survivors wearing clothes Miriam had bought them that afternoon. The fine wool and silk hung strangely on bodies shaped by poverty and trauma, but the colors brought life back to faces that had been gray for too long. But there was something in the way Fritz tilted his head toward the fading light. Something in how Elsa's fingers brushed against a rosemary plant and briefly closed her eyes. Like muscle memory from another lifetime.

Their granddaughters orbited them like satellites. Eight-year-old Elsa holding big Elsa's twisted fingers with careful gentleness. Six-year-old Miriam tried to make Fritz laugh by pretending the olive tree was eating her hair. The girls had accepted these strange new grandparents without hesitation. Children adapt. David never had that skill.

"Your father has a knack with them," Anna said. "Watch how he listens."

David watched Fritz kneel despite his bad knees to hear something Miriam whispered. The old man's face was as serious as state secrets.

"Never thought I'd envy my kids for having what I missed." The bitterness startled him.

The Feldmans played host naturally. Wolf stood tall among the guests, his blonde hair and blue eyes a stark contrast to the predominantly Jewish gathering. Miriam floated between guests in a black dress, switching effortlessly between languages. Their son shepherded his wife Sarah toward the Rosenbergs. David Feldman. Living embodiment of a boy they had once saved.

"It's still strange," David whispered. "They named their son after me. Kept my memory alive all these years."

Anna squeezed his arm. "A connection across time. They never forgot you."

Four new faces had joined the dinner party. Wolf Feldman approached, gesturing toward the newcomers.

Levi stood up at the table as if he was going to say something very important. "Today is one of the most important days of my life!" He looked at his watch as if it were going to say something. My wife Ruth was taken from me and there has been only one person for me ever since. I thought that she had been taken from me as well." There was an expected knock on the door and Levi walked over to it. He walked from the doorway holding the hand of a lovely old lady. " This is my Anna!" They sat down and Wolf thought that was an appropriate time to continue the introductions.

"David," he said warmly, "I'd like you to meet the people who helped save your life." He guided David toward the elderly man with that neatly trimmed white beard and wire rimmed glasses. "This is Dr. Levi Blum. In 1945, he was our medic and ensured you were healthy enough for the journey to England."

Dr. Blum looked like Santa with a medical degree, his white beard trimmed to mathematical precision. His handshake crushed David's fingers despite the man being at least seventy.

"You were a stubborn child," Blum said, a German accent thick as butter. "Four years old and skinny as a stick. Wouldn't eat unless we played airplane with the spoon. Bit me when I tried to check your throat." He displayed his right index finger. A tiny crescent scar. "Still have the mark."

David stared at the ancient scar. "Sorry."

"Bah." Blum waved away thirty years of apology. "Showed fighting spirit. Jews need that."

Rivka Lieberman had hands like a construction worker. Hair cropped so short her scalp showed through the silver. No makeup. No jewelry except a small Star of David that caught the light when she gestured.

"I drove," she said when Wolf introduced her. Just that. Nothing else.

"The truck," Wolf prompted. "Tell him about the border crossings."

Rivka's mouth twitched. "Three checkpoints between Frankfurt and the safe house. British, American, French zones. Had papers claiming we were delivering medical supplies." A harsh laugh erupted from her chest. "You were our medical supply. Hidden under bandages and plasma bottles in the back of the truck." Her eyes, sharp as flint, fixed on David. "You pissed yourself when the shots went off. Soaked through my only good shirt."

Wolf made a noise. Rivka shrugged, unrepentant.

"What? He was about four. All kids piss themselves." She squinted at David. "You want pretty stories or you want what happened?"

446

The woman's bluntness hit David like a slap. Then unexpected laughter bubbled up. "What happened," he heard himself say. "Always what happened."

Daniel Kraus stepped forward, stocky, with sharp eyes behind wire frames. "I coordinated the operation. Made sure everyone got where they needed to be." His mouth twitched. "Germans weren't the only ones who could plan efficiently."

Josef Kleinman stood slightly apart, a tall man with dramatic white hair. "Document forgery was my specialty," he explained. "I created new identities for hundreds during the war. But yours required something special because it had to fool the British authorities." His eyes twinkled. "I worked three days without sleep perfecting your papers."

The rich smell of cooking food wafted across the terrace. The group moved toward the long table, where staff had begun serving the first course. David found himself seated between his wife Anna and Miriam, with Fritz and Elsa directly across, flanked by their granddaughters.

During dessert, Fritz leaned toward Dr. Blum. "Tell me about finding my son," he said quietly. "I need to understand what happened."

Dr. Blum set down his fork, his expression turning serious. "Miriam and some of the others located him through their network of contacts. She discovered rumors of a Jewish child living with a German couple near Frankfurt. The man was a former SS."

David felt a chill. The words "former SS" hit him with physical force.

Daniel picked up the narrative. "The SS records showed everything. Friedrich Schmidt had been an Einsatzgruppe commander on the Eastern Front before being reassigned to the Lebensborn program. After the war, he was living openly under his own name in Frankfurt."

"How did they get David?" Elsa asked, her voice trembling.

Josef answered, "The Lebensborn program stole thousands of Jewish children from the camps and ghettos. Particularly Aryan looking children." He glanced apologetically at David. "With your blond hair and blue eyes, you matched their racial ideal. The records showed you were renamed Dieter Reimann."

David felt Anna's hand find his under the table. Across from him, Fritz was pale, his food untouched.

"I don't understand," Fritz said. "How did you get him out?"

The table fell silent, all eyes turning to Miriam. She set down her wine glass carefully.

"We observed the house for weeks," she said. "We saw them beat him and treat him like a slave. We had to make sure it was David and we had to be sure that we were not going to traumatize him any further or we would not take him. Then we planned to take him in three days' time, but Daniel was breaking under the pressure of watching David's terror and he insisted that we had to get him out today!" said Miriam touching a tear forming under her left eye. "Josef had created papers showing we were representatives of the Red Cross. Daniel arranged for a vehicle and secured the route. Dr. Blum came as our medical authority. Rivka drove."

As she spoke, David felt flashes of memory. Images he had never been able to place.

"We sent Schmidt a false telegram claiming his mother was gravely ill. He and Anneliese left you with their neighbor, Frau Weber, and rushed to catch a train." Miriam's voice continued steadily. "That's when we approached Frau Weber with our Red Cross credentials, claiming we needed to inspect displaced children in the district."

"She let him see you?" Fritz asked.

"She had no choice. We had official papers, uniforms, and proper authority." Miriam's voice softened. "You were so small, so frightened. But when I asked to see your wooden train, the one your mother had given you, you remembered. You remembered her name was Elsa."

"And the Schmidts?" Elsa whispered.

"They returned early from their journey. Found you gone, Frau Weber hysterical with explanations about Red Cross officials." Her voice hardened. "They came straight to their house, where we were gathering our things. Schmidt walked through the front door just as Wolf was carrying David's few belongings down the stairs. They had dressed you in a Hitler Youth uniform. A four-year-old in Nazi regalia."

Elsa made a small sound of distress.

"Schmidt recognized us immediately. Not individually, but what we were. Survivors. He went for his gun," Miriam continued. "Josef shot him before he could draw it. Anneliese was behind him. She saw

448

Friedrich fall and started screaming. Not from grief, from rage. She ran into the kitchen and came back with a pistol."

More fragments surfaced in David's mind: running, a woman's arms carrying him, the sharp report of gunshots. Multiple gunshots.

"She shot you," David said quietly. It wasn't a question. He had already been told this but hearing and taking it in are two different things.

"In the shoulder. The bullet went through and lodged against the bone." Miriam's good hand moved unconsciously to her damaged arm. "Daniel shot her twice before she could fire again."

Rivka leaned forward. "I had the engine running outside. When I heard the shooting, I moved to the back door as planned. We got you out of that house and into the truck while the neighbors were still figuring out what the noise was about."

More fragments surfaced in David's mind: running, a woman's arms carrying him, the sharp report of gunshots. Multiple gunshots.

"We got you to the truck," Rivka continued. "You wouldn't stop screaming. Not even when Dr. Blum tried to calm you."

"I dream about gunshots sometimes," David heard himself speak. "And someone is carrying me. Smell of gunpowder and fear. That was you?"

He'd meant to sound moved. Instead his voice came out academic. Detached.

Young Elsa, who had been listening with wide eyes, broke the tension. "So you were all heroes," she announced with the conviction of an eight-year-old. "Like in the stories."

Her innocent summary brought gentle laughter to the table.

"Not heroes," Rivka corrected, but her expression softened. "Just people doing what needed to be done."

David stood suddenly, wine glass in hand. The conversation around the table died. Faces turned toward him, expectant.

"When I went to Birkenau last year, I broke down. Complete psychotic episode. Heard voices, saw things no one else could see." The wine trembled slightly in his glass. "The doctors called it transgenerational trauma. Said I was channeling the experiences of those who died there." He looked around the table. "But it wasn't the dead I was connecting with. It was you."

The words sounded strange again in his ears. Everyone kept staring. The children busy with other things in the corner.

"You killed for me. People died violently so I could live. You carried that weight for thirty years while I grew up safe in England." His voice cracked slightly. "How do I thank you for that? How do I carry that knowledge?"

Wolf saved him. "*L'chaim*," the big man rumbled. To life.

"*L'chaim*," the table echoed.

"Well that was heavy as shit," Rivka muttered, just loud enough for him to hear. Her mouth quirked up. "Good speech though."

Through the remainder of the meal, the stories continued to unfold. The rescue team recounted other operations, other children saved, other families reunited. David learned that the six had continued their work for decades, though they spoke of it in careful terms.

As dessert was being served, Wolf tapped his glass for attention.

"Before the night ends, Miriam and I have something we wish to share with Fritz and Elsa." He nodded to his son, who disappeared inside briefly before returning with a large envelope.

Young David handed the envelope to David. "This is for you both," Wolf said formally.

David opened the envelope, withdrawing several legal documents. He scanned them, his expression shifting from confusion to shock. He handed them to Anna.

"A cottage," she read aloud. "Near Oxford."

Elsa made a small noise. "For us?"

Wolf nodded. "A small place. Three bedrooms, garden. Walking distance to David's college."

The papers moved to Elsa's hands. David glimpsed words like "deed" and "freehold."

"We can't," Fritz said automatically. "It's too much."

Miriam studied her wine glass. "We have been fortunate in our ventures over the years. You have nothing. Simple mathematics."

"But a house," Anna said quietly.

Miriam touched Fritz's wrist. "Not because you need charity. Because we need to know you're safe. Because David needs his family close." Her fingers tightened on his arm. "Because some debts can never be repaid, but we can try to balance the scales slightly."

Elsa's hands shook. "All these years. The foundation's help. The medications. The specialists. All you."

Miriam nodded once.

Fritz paused, searching for words. "We thought we were alone."

"Jews are never alone," Josef said from across the table. "We carry each other. Without that, what are we?"

Elsa reached for Miriam's hand. Connected. The two old women stayed like that, silent, connected by scarred hands across crystal and linen.

As the evening wound down, guests began to move around the garden in smaller conversations. Fritz cornered David by the dessert table.

"When you were born," he said without preamble, "your hair was so light it looked like honey in certain light. Your mother said you looked like an angel. I told her all babies look like angry potatoes." A ghost of a smile touched his lips. "She threw a shoe at me."

David felt something crack inside his chest.

"Your first steps were toward the radio. You loved music. Bach especially. Most babies want simple melodies. You wanted complexity." Fritz stared at his napkin. "When they took us to Birkenau, they ripped you from your mother's arms at the selection point. We thought they sent you directly to the gas chambers."

"But I survived," David said gently.

"You survived." Fritz nodded once, sharply. "We are making a new beginning now, yes? No pressure. No expectations. Just possibilities."

The old man looked smaller somehow. Vulnerable in a way that made David's throat hurt.

"I would like that," he said.

Fritz studied his face. "You have your mother's eyes. Her forehead. But your hands," he touched David's fingers briefly, "those are from me."

David fought sudden tears. Fritz pretended not to notice.

"My granddaughter tells me you play chess," the old man said. "Perhaps sometime we could play a game."

"I'd like that."

Fritz nodded. Satisfied with this small promise of future connection.

Later, after the girls were asleep in the guest apartment's second bedroom, David sat in the dark living room. Anna found him there.

"The girls are out cold," she said. "Elsa wants Fritz to teach her chess."

"He used to be ranked. Before the war. Almost made it to the master level."

"How do you know that?"

David frowned. "No idea. Something someone said, maybe."

Anna sat opposite him. Silence stretched between them, comfortable.

"Oxford," she said finally.

"Yeah."

"A cottage near the university."

"Yeah."

"Deed and keys from complete strangers who are not actually strangers, who have apparently been watching over your parents for thirty years."

"When you say it like that, it sounds insane."

"It is insane." Anna pulled her feet up under her. "Tomorrow we go back to Oxford. Back to your lectures and my research and school runs and grocery shopping. And what, we just fold in these people? These grandparents the girls never knew existed? These parents who've been dead to you your whole life?"

David had never loved her more than in that moment of perfect, pragmatic clarity.

452

"One day at a time," he said.

She snorted. "To recover from what?"

"Truth overdose."

Her laughter cut through the darkness. Sweet. Familiar. Real.

At the window, David watched the nighttime city breathe. Somewhere in that sprawl were the people who had killed for him. Carrying on with their lives as if tonight had been just another dinner party.

"Coming to bed?" Anna appeared in the bedroom doorway, wearing one of his t-shirts.

"In a minute."

She padded over in bare feet. Stood behind him. Not touching. Just there.

"What are you thinking?" she asked.

The question felt too large to answer properly. He settled for: "That I don't know who I am anymore."

"Same person you were yesterday," she said. "Just with more information."

He turned. "It's not that simple."

"No. But it's not as complicated as you're making it." She touched his face. "You're David. Oxford academic with a talent for bad puns and worse cooking. A Father who can't say no to ice cream before dinner. Husband who still leaves wet towels on the bed after eleven years of marriage."

His laugh surprised him. "You make me sound so ordinary."

"You are ordinary. That's the miracle, considering what you survived." Her hand slid to his chest. "Extraordinary things happened to you. Doesn't make you any less the man I married."

The clarity of her vision steadied him. Anna always saw through complications to essential truths.

"Oxford," he murmured.

"We'll figure it out."

"My parents."

"All of them. We'll figure that out too."

He nodded. Believed her.

Manhattan breathed around them, indifferent to revelations. Millions of lives unfolding in glass and steel while up here, a family cobbled itself together from pieces thirty years scattered.

"Come to bed," Anna said.

He followed her away from the city lights. Into whatever came next.

63

Departures and Decisions

The Feldman penthouse felt different in the morning light. Softer somehow. The rooftop garden that had seemed magical under evening stars now looked like what it was: an expensive attempt to bring nature to a concrete world. David stood at the kitchen window, watching Manhattan wake up fifteen stories below, while Anna made tea for a crowd that had multiplied overnight.

Fritz sat at the breakfast table in yesterday's clothes, studying a chess problem from the morning paper. His concentration was absolute, the kind of focus that shut out everything else. A survival skill, David realized. The ability to disappear into patterns and logic when the world became too much.

"Your move," the old man said without looking up.

David hadn't realized he was being invited to play. He slid into the opposite chair, studying the board Fritz had constructed with salt and pepper shakers, sugar cubes, and pieces of torn napkin.

"White or black?" David asked.

"You choose."

David moved a salt shaker forward. "Pawn to king four."

Fritz responded immediately, his pepper shaker meeting the challenge. They played in silence while the apartment filled with the sounds of family life. Anna directing the girls through breakfast routines. Elsa helping Miriam Feldman prepare coffee for twelve. Wolf on the telephone, speaking rapid German to someone about travel arrangements.

"You play like your mother," Fritz said after David sacrificed a sugar cube bishop. "She thought three moves ahead. I think five."

"Did you teach her?"

"She taught me. Said chess was like marriage. You had to protect your queen and sacrifice everything else." A ghost of a smile. "She usually won."

David moved his makeshift knight, a folded napkin that barely resembled anything equine. "What else haven't you told me?"

Fritz's hand paused over his next move. "Thirty years of life, David. We could talk until we're both dead and still have stories left."

"The important things."

"The important thing is that you grew up safe. That you became a good man. That you have children who laugh easily." Fritz captured David's knight with ruthless efficiency. "Everything else is just details."

But David caught something in the old man's voice. A weight behind the casual words.

"There's something else," David said.

Fritz studied the improvised chess board. "Your mother. Before they took us. She made me promise something."

The kitchen noise seemed to fade. David waited.

"She said if anything happened to her, if we were separated, I should tell you about the music box." Fritz's voice dropped to barely a whisper. "A little wooden box her father made. It played Brahms' lullaby. She said you loved it more than any toy."

David felt something shift in his chest. Not quite memory, but the shadow of one.

"It was in your crib when they came for us. You wouldn't let go of it, even when they ripped you from her arms." Fritz's eyes were distant, seeing something twenty-six years past. "She said if I ever found you, I should tell you about that music box. So you'd know she thought of you until the end."

"What happened to it?"

"Gone. Like everything else." Fritz moved his queen, a bottle cap, into attacking position. "But she wanted you to know it existed. That you were loved before you even understood what love meant."

David stared at the makeshift chess pieces, seeing them blur slightly. Somewhere in his mind, almost but not quite audible, he could hear the faint echo of a melody.

456

Anna appeared with fresh coffee, sensing the weight of the conversation. She kissed the top of David's head and retreated without a word.

"Checkmate," Fritz said gently.

David looked down at the board. His king, represented by a pen cap, was indeed trapped.

"I never saw it coming."

"The best moves are invisible until they're complete."

Harald and Margaret Rose arrived at ten-thirty, looking exactly like what they were: middle-class English people thrust into circumstances beyond their comprehension. Harald carried a worn leather briefcase that had seen thirty years of faculty meetings. Margaret wore a sensible wool coat and carried a handbag large enough to hold emergency supplies for any conceivable crisis.

David met them in the lobby, where they stood looking bewildered among the marble and brass of Manhattan wealth.

"Harold," David said, embracing the man who had taught him to ride a bicycle and helped with mathematics homework and attended every school play. "Margaret."

Margaret Rose had tears in her eyes before David finished speaking. "Oh, darling. Are you all right? Miriam's telegram was so mysterious. First class tickets, a car at Heathrow, then that lovely driver who wouldn't explain anything except that you needed us here urgently."

"Not urgently," David said. "But importantly. Very importantly."

In the elevator, Harold adjusted his glasses nervously. "David, what's this all about? Who is this Miriam person? And why does she have enough money to fly us first class and put us up in Manhattan?"

"Because," David said as the elevator climbed, "she's someone I want you to meet. Someone who's been part of my story longer than any of us realized."

The elevator opened onto the penthouse, and David led them into a room full of people. But before he could begin introductions, two small voices shrieked from across the room.

"Grandpa! Grandma!"

Eight-year-old Elsa and six-year-old Miriam launched themselves at Harold and Margaret with the uncomplicated joy of children who hadn't seen their grandparents in three weeks.

"Oh my dears," Margaret laughed, gathering both girls into her arms. "We've missed you terribly."

Anna appeared, smiling at the reunion. "They've been asking about you every day. But David, you didn't tell them Harold and Margaret were coming."

"I wanted it to be a surprise," David said. "For everyone."

Harold straightened up from hugging the girls, looking around the elegant penthouse with confusion. "David, what exactly is going on here? Who are all these people?"

But it was Fritz who made the difference. The old man appeared at Harold's elbow, his face showing a mixture of nervousness and profound gratitude.

"Mr. Rose," Fritz said in careful English. "I am Fritz Rosenberg. I believe you have been caring for my son."

Harold's handshake was firm despite his obvious confusion. "Twenty-six years. Since he was so tiny. But I'm sorry, I don't understand..."

"You raised him beautifully," Fritz said, his voice thick with emotion. "I can see this. A good man, a good father, a good husband. You gave him everything we could not."

The pieces began clicking into place for Harold. His face went pale. "You're... you're David's biological father?"

"Yes. This is my wife, Elsa." Fritz gestured to the small woman who approached hesitantly. "We are the people who lost him. You are the people who saved him."

Margaret stepped forward, her maternal instincts engaging immediately. "Oh my goodness. Oh my. You're alive. David always wondered, but we never knew..."

"We didn't know he was alive either," Elsa said quietly. "Until a few days ago, we thought our son had died at Birkenau."

The two women studied each other across thirty years of parallel motherhood. Margaret, who had dried tears and attended school concerts and taught driving lessons. Elsa, who had carried the memory of a stolen child through hell and survived.

"He was already a good child when he came to us," Margaret said softly. "Frightened, traumatized, but good. We just tried not to break what was already there."

"You succeeded beyond our wildest dreams," Elsa whispered. "Look at him. Look at his family. You gave him the life we couldn't."

"He has nightmares sometimes," Margaret said suddenly. "Even now, as an adult. He never remembers what they're about."

"Gunshots," Elsa said softly. "Running. Someone carrying him. The smell of fear."

Margaret nodded. "We never knew why."

"Now you do."

They stood in silence for a moment, two mothers who had shared the same child across an impossible divide.

"Thank you," Elsa whispered. "For keeping him safe. For making him happy."

Margaret's composure finally cracked. She reached for Elsa's twisted hands, and for a moment they held each other up across the wreckage of history.

Wolf clapped his hands for attention. "If I may interrupt this beautiful moment, we have practical matters to discuss."

The group gathered around the dining table, where Wolf had spread documents like a general planning a campaign.

"Fritz and Elsa will fly to London tomorrow," he announced. "I've arranged accommodations near Oxford while the cottage paperwork is completed."

Harold leaned forward. "This cottage business. David explained, but frankly, it sounds rather..."

"Overwhelming?" Wolf smiled. "It's meant to be practical, not overwhelming. A small place. Three bedrooms, garden, walking distance to the university. Nothing grand."

"But the cost..."

"Is irrelevant," Miriam said firmly. "We have resources. They have nothing. Mathematics is simple."

David watched Harold struggle with the concept of strangers providing houses for other strangers. The English mind couldn't quite process such direct action.

"There will be other support as needed," Wolf continued. "Medical care, English language tutoring for Elsa, whatever is required for adjustment."

"This is too much," Harold said, overwhelmed. "We don't understand. Who are you people? How do you have these resources?"

The question hung in the air.

"We are the people who found David," Miriam said simply. "Who brought him out of Germany. Who have been watching over his birth parents for thirty years, waiting for this moment."

Harold sat back, his face revealing the struggle to process such an enormous revelation. "You've been... watching over them? For thirty years?"

"Making sure they were safe. Making sure they were cared for. Making sure that if David ever came looking, they would be here to find."

Fritz nodded gravely. "We understand. You are David's family. That makes you our family too."

Harold looked around the room at these people who had orchestrated such an elaborate reunion, who had maintained such loyalty across decades. "I think," he said slowly, "we have a great deal to learn about each other."

"Yes," Fritz agreed. "We have time now. All the time in the world."

The practicalities took two hours to arrange. Flights, accommodations, contact information, emergency procedures. Wolf handled it all with the efficiency of someone who had been moving people across borders for decades.

At noon, the rescue team began their departures. Dr. Blum kissed both girls on the forehead and told them to study hard. Rivka shook hands with everyone except David, whom she hugged briefly and awkwardly.

"You turned out decent," she said gruffly. "Could have been worse."

Josef and Daniel left together, but not before Josef pulled David aside.

"Miriam will write to you," he said quietly. "About our ongoing research projects. Historical documentation. You'll understand what she means."

David nodded. "The work continues."

"Always. There are still questions to be answered. Still accounts to be settled." Josef's eyes were sharp behind his wire-rimmed glasses. "Someday, you might have questions of your own."

"What kind of questions?"

"The kind that can only be answered by action."

Before David could respond, Josef was gone.

Only Miriam remained for the final goodbye. She stood with David at the elevator while the others gathered luggage and organized children.

"This isn't really goodbye," she said. "I'll write. Carefully, but regularly."

"About historical research projects?"

Her smile was as sharp as winter. "Among other things. We're documenting some fascinating case studies. Late-stage Nazi administrative officials who escaped prosecution. Medical professionals who continued their research under assumed names. Academic contributors to racial theory now teaching in respected universities."

"Sounds like important work."

"Essential work. Someone has to ensure the historical record is complete." Her good hand touched his arm. "Someday, you might want to contribute to these studies yourself."

David felt something stir in his chest. Not quite desire, but the beginning of understanding.

"How would someone contribute?"

"By asking the right questions. By refusing to let the past remain buried." Her eyes held his. "By understanding that some debts can never be forgiven, only paid."

The elevator arrived. Miriam stepped inside, but held the door.

"Take care of them, David. Your parents, all of them. They've earned peace."

"What about you? Will you ever have peace?"

Miriam's smile was sad and terrible. "Our peace comes differently. One name at a time."

The doors closed, and she was gone.

That evening, David sat in his guest room while Anna packed their suitcases. Fritz and Elsa had retired early, exhausted by the emotional weight of reunion and the practical details of starting over. Harold and Margaret were in the building's library with the girls, probably trying to process everything they'd learned while helping with bedtime stories.

"You're quiet," Anna said, folding his shirts with mechanical precision.

"Thinking."

"About?"

David held up a piece of hotel stationary. His own handwriting, but the words felt foreign:

Miriam, Thank you for everything. I understand now what you've all sacrificed, what you've all become. I understand the weight you carry. I also understand that some questions can only be answered by action. When you think I'm ready, I want to help with your research projects. David

Anna stopped packing. "What's that?"

"A letter."

"To Miriam?"

"Yes."

Anna sat beside him on the bed, reading over his shoulder. When she finished, she was quiet for a long time.

"This isn't just about historical research, is it?" she said finally.

"No."

"They're hunting war criminals. The ones who escaped justice."

"Yes."

462

"And you want to help them."

David folded the letter carefully. "Six people risked everything to save me. Became killers to keep a promise to a dead woman. Spent thirty years carrying that weight so I could grow up safe and happy."

"That doesn't mean you owe them anything."

"Doesn't it?" David looked at her. "They showed me who I really am, Anna. Not just David Rose, comfortable academic with an interesting backstory. David Rosenberg, survivor, witness, son of the murdered. How do I live with that knowledge and do nothing?"

Anna was quiet, processing. Outside their window, Manhattan hummed with eight million lives, most of them unaware that fifteen floors above, a man was discovering the weight of his own history.

"The girls," she said finally.

"Will never know. This isn't about them."

"Your parents. All four of them."

"Will never know either. This is about me figuring out who I am and what I owe."

Anna lay back on the bed, staring at the ceiling. "When you put it like that, it sounds almost reasonable."

"Is it?"

"I don't know. Ask me in a year when you're writing coded letters about historical research projects."

David sealed the letter in an envelope. Tomorrow he would mail it from the airport, just before they flew back to Oxford, back to normal life, back to the ordinary world where tenure committees mattered more than Nazi hunters.

But tonight, he felt the beginning of something new. Not quite purpose, but the recognition that some debts could never be repaid, only honored through action.

Outside, Manhattan breathed through the darkness, indifferent to revelation. But in a guest room of the Feldman building, a man was learning that identity was not just about the past, but about what you chose to do with the future.

The letter sat on the nightstand, waiting for morning.

64

The Discovery

Aaron Levine had always known there were secrets in his grandfather's apartment. Benjamin had died three months ago at ninety-one, taking with him stories that Aaron had never quite managed to coax out during their weekly dinners. Now, standing in the cramped Upper West Side apartment that smelled of old books and stronger memories, Aaron felt the weight of those untold stories pressing down on him like dust.

The apartment was exactly as Benjamin had left it, preserved by Aaron's reluctance to disturb what felt like a shrine. Books in three languages lined every wall, their spines creating a patchwork of German, English, and Hebrew. Benjamin had been a meticulous man, a retired linguistics professor who had fled Berlin in 1938 with nothing but a doctorate and determination to survive. But he was found like so many others and sent to Birkenau.

Aaron had spent the morning sorting through papers: immigration documents, university records, a lifetime of careful documentation. Everything was organized, labeled, filed with the precision of a man who understood that paperwork could mean the difference between life and death. But it was the locked filing cabinet in the bedroom that had been haunting Aaron for weeks.

The key, when he finally found it taped beneath the bottom drawer of Benjamin's desk, was small and brass, worn smooth by decades of handling. Aaron held it for a long moment before walking to the bedroom, feeling as though he was crossing some invisible threshold.

The filing cabinet contained three folders, each labeled with a year: 1947, 1952, 1961. Aaron opened the first with trembling fingers.

The photographs were the first thing he saw. Black and white images of men in business suits, walking down city streets, sitting in

464

cafes, entering buildings. Surveillance photographs, taken with a telephoto lens from considerable distance. Each photo was annotated in Benjamin's careful handwriting with dates, times, and locations. New York, Toronto, Buenos Aires.

Aaron recognized none of the faces, but something about the methodical documentation made his skin crawl. These weren't family photos or travel memories. They were the work of someone watching, waiting, documenting.

The documents beneath the photographs were worse. Medical records written in German, bearing the letterhead of institutions Aaron had never heard of. Experimental data, subject numbers instead of names, clinical descriptions of procedures that made Aaron's stomach turn. And at the bottom of each page, the same signature: Dr. K. Keller.

Aaron sank into his grandfather's reading chair, the folder heavy in his hands. Benjamin had never spoken much about the war years, deflecting Aaron's academic curiosity with gentle changes of subject. "Some stories are better left buried," he would say, his eyes growing distant. "The living should concern themselves with living."

But these documents suggested Benjamin had been very much concerned with the past. The 1952 folder contained newspaper clippings about a fire in a Toronto boarding house. Three dead, including a German immigrant named Heinrich Mueller who had lived quietly in Canada for seven years. The 1961 folder held an obituary from a Buenos Aires newspaper, describing the tragic death of Dr. Klaus Brenner in what police called a robbery gone wrong.

Aaron found the connection in a manila envelope at the back of the cabinet. A list of names written in Benjamin's handwriting, each with a line drawn through it. Heinrich Mueller. Klaus Brenner. And at the bottom, still unmarked: Karl Keller, New York, New York.

The apartment felt smaller suddenly, the walls closing in with the weight of terrible understanding. Aaron's grandfather, the gentle professor who had taught him chess and told him stories about Berlin before the war, had been hunting Nazi war criminals. And if the pattern held, Karl Keller was still alive, somewhere in the city.

Aaron reached for his phone, then stopped. Who could he call? What would he say? That his grandfather, dead three months now, had been some kind of vigilante? That there might be evidence of crimes committed in the name of justice?

Instead, Aaron found himself at Benjamin's desk, opening his folders looking for this Karl Keller New York. The results were minimal: a small import business in Manhattan, a few business registrations, a man who seemed to have lived quietly and successfully in America for decades.

Aaron stared at the screen for a long time, thinking about the gentle man who had raised him after his parents died, who had never spoken of violence or hatred, who had seemed to embody everything good about survival. But the filing cabinet told a different story, one of patient hunting and methodical justice.

As the afternoon light faded through Benjamin's windows, Aaron made a decision that would change everything. He was going to find Karl Keller. Not to continue his grandfather's work (Aaron was a journalist, not a killer) but to understand it. To finally learn the stories Benjamin had taken to his grave.

He had no idea that in New York, six people were already watching Karl Keller very carefully. And that Aaron's investigation would soon become the most dangerous story he had ever tried to tell.

65

The Watchers

The coffee shop on Broadway had the kind of worn anonymity that made it perfect for watching people. Aaron had been there for three hours, nursing a series of increasingly cold cappuccinos while studying the import business across the street. Keller International Trading occupied the ground floor of a converted building in Midtown, its windows revealing a modest operation: a few desks, filing cabinets, and an elderly man with silver hair who moved with the careful precision of someone accustomed to routine.

Karl Keller looked nothing like a monster. At seventy-five, he was simply another well-dressed businessman in an expensive neighborhood, the kind of man who might discuss the weather with his doorman or leave generous tips at his regular lunch spot. Aaron had been watching him for two days, documenting his habits with the thoroughness that had made him a successful investigative journalist.

Keller arrived at 9 AM sharp, left for lunch at the same delicatessen every day at 12:30, and departed for home at precisely 6 PM. A life of comfortable routine, built on what Aaron was beginning to understand were the graves of children.

The medical records in Benjamin's files told a horrific story. Dr. Karl Keller had worked at Birkenau, conducting experiments on prisoners that served no medical purpose beyond satisfying scientific curiosity and Nazi ideology. Children had died under his care: not patients, but subjects. Test cases for procedures designed to break the human body in carefully documented ways.

Aaron was photographing Keller's building when he noticed the others.

A woman in her sixties, sitting on a bench across the street with a book she never seemed to read. An elderly man feeding pigeons who always managed to be in the vicinity when Keller left for lunch. A couple walking their dog at the same time every evening, their route perfectly timed to observe Keller's departure.

Aaron's journalist instincts kicked in. He was not the only one watching Karl Keller.

On his third day of surveillance, Aaron decided to follow the woman with the book. She led him through a maze of side streets to a small restaurant in the Village, where she met five other people around a corner table. Aaron took a seat at the bar, close enough to observe but far enough to avoid suspicion.

They were all elderly, probably in their sixties or seventies. Well-dressed, unremarkable, the kind of people who disappeared into any crowd. But there was something about the way they sat, the careful positioning that gave each of them a clear view of the entrance, that suggested these were not ordinary retirees meeting for dinner.

Aaron strained to catch fragments of their conversation, but they spoke quietly, occasionally lapsing into what sounded like German or Polish. The woman from the bench showed the others a small notebook, pointing to entries that made them nod grimly. When they finished eating, they left separately, at five-minute intervals, each taking a different route.

Aaron followed the last to leave, an elderly man with steel-gray hair and the bearing of someone accustomed to command. The man led him to a tailor shop in the Garment District, disappearing through a back entrance that Aaron noted carefully.

That night, in his hotel room, Aaron tried to make sense of what he was seeing. Six elderly people conducting surveillance on a Nazi war criminal. The same war criminal his grandfather had been tracking. The coincidence was too perfect to be accidental.

Aaron spent hours researching the others, using the facial recognition software his newspaper subscribed to and cross-referencing immigration records. Slowly, a pattern emerged. All six had arrived in the United States between 1946 and 1950. All had Eastern European surnames that suggested Jewish heritage. All had built successful, quiet lives in America.

And all of them, Aaron realized with growing certainty, were Holocaust survivors.

The next morning, Aaron made a decision that would have terrified the cautious journalist he had been a week ago. He was going to make contact. Not with Keller (not yet) but with the watchers. With the people who seemed to be carrying on his grandfather's work.

Aaron returned to the tailor shop, studying its exterior in the morning light. "Kraus & Son, Fine Tailoring" read the modest sign. Established 1951. The windows displayed suits that spoke of Old World craftsmanship and prices that suggested a discriminating clientele.

Aaron pushed open the door, setting off a small bell. The shop smelled of wool and pressing starch, bolts of fabric arranged with meticulous care. An elderly man emerged from the back room, tape measure draped around his neck like a badge of office.

"May I help you?"

"I hope so," Aaron said, his heart hammering against his ribs. "My name is Aaron Levine. I think you knew my grandfather, Benjamin."

The man went very still. For a long moment, the only sound was the ticking of an antique clock on the wall. When he spoke again, his voice carried traces of an accent that decades in America had not quite erased.

"I think you had better come into the back room, Mr. Levine."

Aaron followed him through a doorway concealed behind a curtain of fabric samples. The back room was larger than the shop itself, with chairs arranged in a circle and maps spread across a central table. The same maps Aaron had seen the group studying in the restaurant.

"Sit down," the man said. "My name is Daniel Kraus. And you, Mr. Levine, have stumbled into something much larger than you understand."

Aaron sat, trying to project confidence he didn't feel. "I know you're watching Karl Keller. I know my grandfather was doing the same thing before he died. I want to understand why."

Daniel studied Aaron's face with the intensity of someone accustomed to reading character from first impressions. "What do you know about your grandfather's war?"

"He was at Birkenau. He survived. He came to America and built a new life." Aaron paused. "And apparently, he spent decades hunting the people who had tried to kill him."

"Benjamin was a good man," Daniel said quietly. "A careful man. He understood that some debts can never be repaid, only collected."

"Are you going to kill Keller?"

The question hung in the air between them, dangerous and necessary. Daniel was quiet for a long time, weighing what to reveal to this stranger who carried his old friend's name.

"Justice, Mr. Levine, does not always wear a black robe and carry a gavel," Daniel said finally. "Sometimes it is an old man with a long memory and nothing left to lose."

Aaron felt the pieces clicking into place, the story he had been chasing finally taking shape. "How many others have there been?"

"Enough," Daniel replied. "Not enough."

The bell in the front shop chimed, and Daniel rose quickly. "You should leave. Through the back door. If you want to understand your grandfather's work, come back tomorrow evening at eight. Knock twice, then once, then twice again."

Aaron stood, his head spinning with questions and implications. "Will the others be here?"

Daniel's smile was sad and fierce. "Mr. Levine, after tomorrow evening, there will be no others. Only you, and the choice of whether to continue what Benjamin started."

Aaron left through the back alley, the weight of family legacy and moral complexity pressing down on him like the gray New York sky. He had come looking for answers about his grandfather's past. Instead, he had found a story that would either make his career or totally change his life.

He had no idea which he preferred.

66

The Revelation

Dr. Levi Blum's office overlooked Central Park from the seventh floor of a medical building on the Upper East Side that had seen better decades. Aaron sat in the reception area, studying the diplomas and certificates that lined the walls. Medical degree from the University of Berlin, 1936. Board certifications in psychiatry and neurology from New York institutions. A career spent healing minds damaged by trauma that most people could barely imagine.

Aaron had spent the morning researching each of the six people he'd observed watching Keller. Levi Blum had been the easiest to identify: a prominent psychiatrist who specialized in treating Holocaust survivors, author of three books on trauma recovery, a man whose professional life had been built around understanding the wounds that never fully healed.

What the official records didn't mention was that Dr. Blum had once been Berlin's leading neurosurgeon, a rising star in the medical community before the war destroyed everything. The torture and malnutrition of the camps had damaged his hands beyond repair, ending any possibility of returning to the delicate work of brain surgery.

"Mr. Levine?" A young receptionist appeared at the desk. "Dr. Blum will see you now."

Aaron followed her down a hallway lined with abstract paintings in soothing blues and greens. The office itself was warm and inviting, with leather chairs positioned to encourage conversation and shelves filled with books in multiple languages. Levi Blum sat behind a modest desk, reading through what appeared to be session notes.

He was smaller than Aaron had expected, with silver hair and intelligent eyes behind wire-rimmed glasses. When he looked up, Aaron saw recognition flicker across his features.

"You have your grandfather's eyes," Levi said, gesturing to one of the chairs. "Benjamin spoke of you often. He was very proud of your work as a journalist."

Aaron sat down, trying to process the casual confirmation of what he had suspected. "You knew him well?"

"We were friends for many years. We shared certain... interests." Levi closed the file on his desk and gave Aaron his full attention. "I assume you've found his records."

"Some of them." Aaron pulled out a photocopy of one of the medical documents from Benjamin's files. "Enough to understand what kind of man Karl Keller is."

Levi's expression darkened as he scanned the document. Even after decades of treating trauma, the clinical descriptions of Keller's experiments clearly affected him. "Where did you find this?"

"In my grandfather's apartment. Along with surveillance photos and newspaper clippings about some very convenient accidents." Aaron leaned forward. "Dr. Blum, I'm trying to understand what my grandfather was involved in."

"Benjamin was involved in justice, Mr. Levine. The kind that courts cannot provide and governments choose not to pursue."

Levi stood and walked to the window, looking out over Central Park where families were enjoying the autumn afternoon. "Do you know what it was like, those first years after the war? When we learned that men like Keller were living comfortable lives in America, Canada, Argentina? When we discovered that the world was more interested in forgetting than in remembering?"

Aaron waited, sensing that Levi was deciding how much to reveal.

"Benjamin and I met in 1949, at a conference for refugee resettlement. We were both trying to build new lives, to put the past behind us." Levi turned back to Aaron. "But the past has a way of demanding attention. When Benjamin showed me a photograph of Heinrich Mueller (Heinrich Mueller, who had personally selected Benjamin's sister for the gas chambers) walking freely through Toronto, eating ice cream with his Canadian wife... something broke inside both of us."

"So you killed him."

"We arranged for justice to be served," Levi corrected. "There is a difference, though I understand it may be difficult to see from the outside."

Aaron thought of the newspaper clipping about the boarding house fire, the obituary from Buenos Aires. "How many others have there been?"

"Seventeen, over thirty years. We are not random killers, Mr. Levine. Each target was carefully researched, thoroughly documented. Men who had committed crimes beyond imagination and escaped any earthly punishment."

Levi returned to his desk, pulling out a leather-bound journal. "Benjamin kept meticulous records. Names, dates, evidence. He wanted someone to know that these debts had been paid."

Aaron accepted the journal with trembling hands. Page after page of careful documentation: photographs, witness statements, historical records. Each entry ended with a date and a brief notation: "Justice served."

"Why are you telling me this?" Aaron asked.

"Because Benjamin believed you would understand. Because we are old, Mr. Levine, and the work is not finished." Levi's voice carried the weight of decades. "Karl Keller has lived thirty years longer than the children he tortured. That is thirty years too many."

Aaron closed the journal, his mind reeling with the implications. "You want me to join you."

"We want you to understand what your grandfather died believing: that some debts can only be paid in blood, and that forgetting to do that is the final victory of evil over good."

The office fell silent except for the distant sounds of traffic and children playing in Central Park. Aaron thought of his career, his reputation, the life he had built on the foundation of objective journalism and legal process. Then he thought of the medical records in Benjamin's files, the clinical descriptions of experiments performed on children who had died screaming in languages the doctor couldn't understand.

"If I wanted to stop you," Aaron said finally, "what would happen?"

Levi's smile was sad and knowing. "You would publish your story, expose our activities, perhaps save Karl Keller's life. And tomorrow, another Nazi war criminal would read about our group in the newspaper and disappear before justice could find him." He paused. "But you won't stop us, Mr. Levine."

"How can you be so certain?"

"Because you're Benjamin Levine's grandson. Because you've seen the evidence of what these men did. And because, deep down, you know that some crimes are so enormous that only permanent punishment can balance the scales."

Aaron stood to leave, the journal heavy in his hands. "What happens now?"

"Now you decide whether you're a journalist writing a story about us, or Benjamin's grandson continuing his work." Levi opened the door for him. "But decide quickly, Mr. Levine. We move against Keller in three days, and after that, it won't matter which choice you make."

Aaron left the medical building with his worldview fundamentally shattered. He had come seeking answers about his grandfather's past. Instead, he had found a moral complexity that his training as a journalist had never prepared him to navigate.

That evening, he sat in his hotel room staring at his grandfather's journal that Levi had given him, reading account after account of methodical justice served on men who had escaped every other form of accountability. And slowly, terrifyingly, Aaron began to understand that the story he had been chasing was no longer about his grandfather's secrets.

It was about what kind of man Aaron Levine was going to choose to become.

67

The Setup

Aaron spent the morning in reconnaissance, walking the tree-lined streets of the Upper East Side where Karl Keller had built his comfortable American life. The neighborhood spoke of money and discretion: the kind of place where a man could disappear into respectable anonymity, if that man had the right papers and enough time to perfect his new identity.

Keller's building was a converted brownstone with a doorman and security cameras, the kind of building that suggested success and stability. Aaron photographed it from multiple angles, documenting entrance points and sight lines with the thoroughness that had made him a successful investigative journalist.

Benjamin's letter, which he had read on the subway that morning, had been harder to process than Aaron anticipated. His grandfather's careful script describing the weight of necessary choices, the burden of memory, and the price of action. "If you are reading this," Benjamin had written, "then you have found them, and they have found you worthy. The circle closes, but the work continues."

Aaron spent the first day establishing patterns. Keller emerged from his building at 7:30 each morning, walked three blocks to a small café for coffee and a newspaper, then continued to his office at an import business he'd owned for twenty-five years. Lunch at the same delicatessen. Home by six. Predictable as clockwork, secure in the routine of a man who believed himself invisible.

On the second day, Aaron noticed them.

Two men in a black sedan, parked across from Keller's building. They changed shifts every six hours, professional surveillance that Aaron recognized from his own recent education. But their presence made no sense. If they were police or federal agents, why hadn't they moved already? If they were protecting Keller, why maintain such obvious distance?

Aaron photographed them from a coffee shop window, his journalist's instincts warring with his new operational training. Who else was hunting Karl Keller?

The answer came on the third day.

Aaron was positioned in a small park near Keller's office when he saw the exchange. One of the watchers approached a young man with a shaved head and visible tattoos, passing him an envelope. The conversation was brief, professional, ending with both men looking toward Keller's building.

Neo-Nazis. Aaron felt his stomach turn cold. They weren't hunting Keller; they were protecting him. Or perhaps preparing to move him before other hunters could reach him.

Aaron's carefully planned surveillance suddenly became urgent. He had to accelerate the timeline, get Keller isolated and vulnerable before these others acted. When he called Miriam from a payphone that evening, her response was immediate: "We'll handle the protection detail. You focus on getting him alone."

The group's methodical approach was a luxury they no longer had.

That evening, Aaron made his decision.

Keller lived alone in a converted brownstone on East 82nd Street, his apartment occupying the entire second floor. Aaron had observed enough to know the man's evening routine: dinner delivered from the same Italian restaurant, two glasses of wine, classical music until exactly ten o'clock. A life of careful, lonely precision.

Aaron rang the doorbell at 8:45, when Keller would be finishing his wine but not yet preparing for bed. Through the intercom, his voice was cultured, faintly accented despite decades of practice.

"Yes?"

"Mr. Keller? My name is Aaron Levine. I'm a journalist with the Times. I'm working on a story about postwar immigration, successful integration stories. I was hoping to speak with you about your experience coming to America."

A pause. Aaron could almost hear Keller's mental calculations, weighing curiosity against caution.

"It's rather late for an interview."

"I apologize for the hour. I'm only in the city briefly, and your story came so highly recommended. Perhaps just a few minutes? I understand you've built quite a successful business here."

Another pause, longer this time. Then the buzz of the door lock.

Aaron climbed the stairs slowly, his heart steady despite the magnitude of what he was doing. This wasn't the group's plan. This was something else entirely, something personal and immediate and necessary. The speed of his transformation from observer to participant surprised even him, but the moral clarity was absolute.

Keller opened his apartment door with a cautious smile, revealing a man in his seventies with silver hair and soft features that might once have been called kind. He wore an expensive cardigan and held a glass of red wine, every inch the successful immigrant businessman.

"Mr. Levine? Please, come in."

Aaron stepped into the apartment, noting the careful arrangement of furniture, the classical music playing softly from hidden speakers, the absence of personal photographs. A life curated for public consumption, with no visible connection to its dark foundations.

"Wine?" Keller asked, gesturing toward a leather chair.

"Thank you." Aaron accepted the glass, using the moment to study Keller's face, looking for traces of the young SS officer who had selected children for medical experiments. The man before him seemed so ordinary, so harmlessly elderly.

"So," Keller settled into his own chair, "what exactly would you like to know about my American success story?"

Aaron took a sip of wine, tasting something expensive and bitter. "Actually, Mr. Keller, I'd like to start with your German story. Specifically, your time at Birkenau."

The wineglass froze halfway to Keller's lips. His eyes, which had been merely curious, became suddenly sharp and evaluating. "I'm afraid I don't understand."

"Franz Klein," Aaron said quietly. "*Unterscharführer* Klein, who worked with Dr. Mengele selecting subjects for medical research. That Franz Klein."

Keller set down his wine glass with trembling fingers. For a long moment, the only sound was Mozart's Piano Concerto No. 21 playing softly in the background. When he finally spoke, his voice had lost its careful American modulation, revealing traces of the accent he'd spent decades burying.

"I don't know what you're talking about."

"The men watching your building would disagree," Aaron said calmly. "Black sedan, two shifts, been there for three days. They're not police, Mr. Klein. And they're not alone."

Keller's face went pale. "Who are you?"

"Someone who represents people with shared interests." Aaron leaned forward, his voice dropping to barely above a whisper. "People who understand that the past should stay buried, and that certain... inconvenient truths... need to be managed carefully."

Keller's eyes narrowed, studying Aaron's face for signs of deception. "What kind of people?"

"The kind who have been protecting assets like yourself for thirty years. The kind who have resources, connections, and a very strong interest in maintaining the status quo." Aaron gestured toward the window. "The kind who are very concerned about those watchers outside."

Keller stood abruptly, pacing to the window. He peered through the curtains, and Aaron knew he was looking for the black sedan. "What do you want?"

"The same thing you want. To keep you alive." Aaron joined him at the window. "Those men aren't here to protect you, Mr. Klein. They're here to clean up loose ends. Someone's decided you're a liability."

"That's impossible. I've been careful. I've never..."

"Never what? Never talked about the old days? Never kept souvenirs? Never contacted old friends?" Aaron let the implications sink in. "Someone knows who you are, and they've decided you know too much about other people who matter more than you do."

Keller sank into his chair, suddenly looking every one of his seventy-five years. "What are you proposing?"

"Relocation. New identity, new location, enough resources to live comfortably." Aaron sat across from him, projecting confidence he didn't entirely feel. "Our network has been helping people like you disappear when staying visible becomes... unhealthy."

"For a price."

"Information. Names, locations, details about others who might need our services." Aaron smiled coldly. "Think of it as a referral program."

Keller was quiet for several minutes, weighing his options. Aaron could see the calculation in his eyes: trust this stranger or face whatever the watchers had planned.

"How would this work?" Keller asked finally.

"Tomorrow night. A warehouse in the docks district. Neutral territory, secure location. You bring whatever you need to disappear: documents, money, information. We provide new papers and transportation." Aaron pulled out a business card with a phone number written on it. "Call this number at exactly 6 PM tomorrow to confirm. Come alone, and come ready to leave New York permanently."

Keller took the card, studying it as if it might reveal some hidden truth. "How do I know this isn't a trap?"

Aaron stood, finishing his wine. "Because if we wanted you dead, Mr. Klein, you'd already be dead. We're offering you what the men outside won't: a chance to keep living."

As Aaron reached the door, Keller called after him. "This network... How many people have you helped disappear?"

Aaron turned back with a smile that would have made Miriam proud. "Let's just say we have a perfect success rate. No one we've helped has ever been found."

The door closed behind him with a soft click, leaving Keller alone with his wine and his fear, and the promise of salvation that was actually a carefully crafted trap.

Aaron walked several blocks before stopping at a newsstand, his mind racing through what had just happened. He had looked a Nazi war criminal in the eye, lied to his face, and set him up for execution with a competence that should have frightened him. The journalist who had begun this investigation no longer existed, and the transformation had happened so quickly it left him dizzy.

He made his way back to Daniel's shop through the evening crowds, arriving just after 10 PM. The emergency protocol required two short knocks, two long, one short. Daniel answered within minutes, fully dressed despite the hour.

"This better be important," Daniel said, stepping aside to let Aaron enter.

"It is." Aaron followed him through the darkened shop to the back room, where Miriam and David were already waiting. They had been planning, he realized. Maps and documents covered the table, and both looked as if they hadn't slept.

"Tell us," Miriam said simply.

Aaron described the evening: the contact with Keller, the promise of salvation, the warehouse meeting. When he mentioned the surveillance team and their neo-Nazi connections, Miriam's expression darkened.

"Protection detail," she said grimly. "Someone's been keeping him safe."

"Not anymore," Aaron replied. "He's scared enough to trust strangers. He'll be at Pier 17 tomorrow night at nine, alone, carrying everything he needs to disappear."

David leaned forward. "And expecting help that will never come."

"Exactly." Aaron met his eyes. "We have one chance. If those watchers realize he's compromised, they'll move him before we can act."

Miriam studied the map of Manhattan's financial district, her finger tracing routes and escape paths. "Wolf can handle the protection detail with Josef. They've done this kind of work before." She looked at Aaron. "Daniel and Rivka can handle logistics afterward."

Aaron felt the weight of their attention, the final test of his commitment. "I set the trap. I want to see it sprung."

Miriam nodded slowly. "Then you and David will handle Keller. The rest of us will secure the perimeter and watch for complications." She looked around the table. "Thirty years of hunting, and it comes down to this. One last operation."

Aaron understood that he was witnessing the end of an era and the beginning of another. The torch was being passed in a darkened tailor shop at midnight, with maps of a warehouse district where justice would finally be served.

"Get some rest," Miriam said, beginning to fold the maps. "Tomorrow night, Franz Klein pays his debt."

68

Passing the Torch

The tailor shop felt different in darkness. Bolts of fabric became shadows, and the mannequins stood like silent witnesses to conversations that should never be overheard. Aaron arrived at exactly eight o'clock, his hand steady as he knocked twice, paused, then knocked once more, then twice again as Levi had instructed.

Daniel opened the door, studying Aaron's face before stepping aside. "Come in. Quickly."

The back room had been transformed. The work table was covered with maps, photographs, and documents. Aaron recognized some of his own surveillance photos of Karl Keller mixed among their materials. The six members of the group sat in a loose circle, with an empty chair clearly intended for him.

Miriam spoke first. "Dr. Blum says you want to help us more with Keller."

"I do." Aaron took the offered seat, aware that every eye in the room was evaluating him. "But I think I should understand what I'm volunteering for."

"Smart," Wolf said. "Your grandfather asked the same question thirty years ago."

Rivka opened a worn leather portfolio and withdrew a single sheet of paper, yellowed with age. "Benjamin's first assignment. A clerk named Heinrich Mueller who processed deportation orders in Krakow. Living quietly in Toronto under the name Henry Miller."

Aaron recognized his grandfather's handwriting in the margins. Notes about Miller's routine, his address, his daily habits. The methodical documentation of a man's final days.

"Benjamin tracked him for three weeks," Josef added. "Learned everything about his new life. His job at the bank, his Canadian wife, his Sunday dinners at the church he'd joined to blend in."

"What happened to him?" Aaron asked, though he already knew.

"Automobile accident," Levi said quietly. "Very unfortunate. Benjamin was quite shaken by it. Said he never imagined how it would feel to watch justice being served."

The room fell silent. Aaron understood he was being told more than just a story about his grandfather. He was being shown a mirror of his own future.

"We're getting old, Aaron," Miriam said finally. "Wolf's hands shake now when it's cold. Josef's hearing isn't what it was. My own reflexes..." She shrugged. "We've been doing this for thirty years. It's time."

Aaron felt the weight of the moment settling on his shoulders. "Time for what?"

"For the next generation to take over," David Rose said from across the circle. "They've been training me, slowly. Teaching me what I need to know. But one person can't do what six have been doing."

"You want me to replace my grandfather," Aaron said.

"We want you to surpass him," Miriam corrected. "You have advantages he never had. Professional research skills. Access to databases and records. A journalist's instincts for finding people who don't want to be found."

Aaron looked around the circle, seeing them differently now. Not as subjects for his investigation, but as mentors offering him an inheritance he had never expected.

"What would you need me to do?"

"For now?" Wolf reached into his jacket and withdrew a small camera. "We need current photographs of Keller's apartment building. Security arrangements, daily patterns, potential escape routes. Can you do that without arousing suspicion?"

Aaron took the camera, its weight solid and final in his hands. "When?"

"Tomorrow. His building is in the Upper East Side."

The moment stretched between them. Aaron realized this was his test. Not just surveillance, but complicity. The photographs would be used to plan Keller's death. By taking them, Aaron would become an accessory to murder.

Or to justice, depending on how you looked at it.

Aaron turned the camera over in his hands, feeling its weight. Such a small thing to carry such enormous consequences. "If I do this, if I take these photographs, there's no going back, is there?"

"No," Miriam said simply. "There never is."

Aaron thought of the children's faces in the files on Keller. Photographs from Mengele's experiments, before and after shots that showed the progression of unspeakable cruelties. He thought of his grandfather, sitting in this same kind of room thirty years ago, making the same choice.

"The world moved on," Aaron said quietly. "The trials ended, the camps became museums, and men like Keller got to live comfortable lives while their victims' families never got justice." He looked up at Miriam. "Someone has to remember. Someone has to act."

"Yes," she said. "Someone does."

Aaron slipped the camera into his jacket pocket. "I'll take the photographs. But I want to understand everything. Not just what we're doing, but how. Why these methods. Why now. If I'm going to inherit this responsibility, I need to know all of it."

David leaned forward. "It's not easy knowledge to carry."

"Neither was surviving the camps," Aaron replied, "but they did it. My grandfather did it. And now it's our turn."

The group exchanged glances, some unspoken communication passing between them. Levi nodded slightly to Miriam, who seemed to come to a decision.

"Very well," she said. "Josef, give him the Keller file. Everything we have." She turned back to Aaron. "When you return tomorrow evening, we'll begin your real education. David will help you understand the operational aspects. I'll teach you about selection criteria and risk assessment. The others will share their specialties."

Aaron felt the weight of the moment. He had walked into this room as a journalist investigating a story. He was leaving as something else entirely. A guardian of memory. An instrument of justice. A hunter.

"One more thing," Wolf said as Aaron stood to leave. "Your grandfather kept detailed records of every operation he assisted with. We have them, along with a letter he wrote for you. He always believed you might follow this path someday."

"He knew?"

"Benjamin was very observant," Levi said with a sad smile. "He saw something in you during your visits as a child. A sense of justice that wouldn't be satisfied with ordinary answers."

Aaron nodded, understanding that his entire life had been leading to this moment. The questions about his grandfather's past, the academic career studying Holocaust survivors, the restless feeling that important stories remained untold: all of it had been preparation for inheriting a mission he hadn't known existed.

"I'll return tomorrow evening," he said.

"No," Miriam corrected. "When you return, you'll come home. There will be no more phone calls, no more casual meetings. From now on, you're part of this family. And family takes care of family."

Aaron left through the back entrance, the camera heavy in his pocket and his grandfather's legacy heavy on his shoulders. Tomorrow he would take photographs that would help plan a man's death. In a matter of days, he would be participating in operations that would have horrified the journalist he'd been just a week ago. The transformation was happening faster than he'd imagined possible, but then again, some lessons couldn't wait for gradual acceptance.

The journalist in him should have been horrified.

Instead, he felt something like peace.

69

The Reckoning

The warehouse at Pier 17 smelled of salt water, rust, and thirty years of waiting. Aaron arrived first, at 8:15, carrying a canvas bag that clinked softly with each step. The space was vast and empty, with high windows that let in strips of orange light from the sodium lamps outside. Perfect for what needed to be done.

David appeared ten minutes later, moving through the shadows with the careful silence Wolf had taught him. He nodded to Aaron but said nothing. There was nothing left to say.

They worked methodically, setting up the space. Two chairs in the center, fifteen feet apart. A single work light positioned to illuminate the area without casting shadows. The canvas bag opened to reveal tools that had no names in polite society but served justice nonetheless.

At 8:45, the others arrived. Miriam, Wolf, Josef, Rivka, Daniel, and Levi took positions along the walls, becoming part of the darkness. Witnesses to what they could no longer do themselves. The guardians watching their successors take the oath.

"Wolf and Josef handled the protection detail an hour ago," Miriam said quietly. "They won't be interrupting us."

Aaron nodded, understanding without needing details. Some knowledge was better left unspoken.

"He'll come through the main entrance," Miriam continued. "Expecting salvation."

Aaron checked his watch. 8:58.

The sound of a car door slamming echoed across the empty pier. Footsteps on concrete, growing closer. Then the warehouse door opened, and Karl Keller stepped into the light, carrying a leather briefcase and wearing the expression of a man who believed rescue had arrived.

"Hello?" Keller called into the darkness. "I'm here for the meeting."

Aaron stepped into the circle of light, and Keller's face showed relief. "Mr. Levine. I wasn't certain you would come."

"We always keep our promises, Mr. Klein." Aaron gestured to one of the chairs. "Please, sit. We have much to discuss before we can proceed."

Keller hesitated, perhaps sensing something wrong in Aaron's tone, but fear of what waited outside overcame caution. He sat, placing the briefcase at his feet.

David emerged from the shadows, taking the second chair. Keller's eyes darted between them, confusion replacing relief.

"I thought there would be more of you," Keller said. "Papers, transportation..."

"There will be," Aaron replied. "But first, we need to verify your information. Thirty years is a long time to keep track of details."

Aaron pulled out a manila folder, opening it to reveal photographs. Children's faces, dozens of them, looking up from yellowed documentation. "Perhaps you could help us identify some of these subjects from your research at Birkenau."

Keller went very still. His eyes fixed on the photographs, and Aaron watched understanding dawn like a cold sunrise.

"You're not..." Keller began.

"No," David said quietly. "We're not here to help you disappear, Franz. We're here to make sure you never disappear again."

Keller started to rise, but Aaron's hand pressed down on his shoulder with surprising strength. "Sit. You've been sitting comfortably for thirty years while these children stayed forever young. You can sit a few minutes longer."

"Who are you people?"

"We are memory," Aaron said. "We're the promise that was made when six survivors walked out of Birkenau with blood on their hands and justice in their hearts."

From the darkness, Miriam's voice carried the weight of three decades. "We are the children you murdered, Franz. We are their parents and grandparents and the generations they never got to have. We are what comes after the world decides to forget."

Keller's breathing became rapid, panicked. He looked toward the door, calculating distance and odds.

"There's nowhere to run," David said. "Your protection detail won't be coming. We made sure of that."

Aaron opened the briefcase Keller had brought, revealing documents, cash, and a small journal bound in cracked leather. He flipped through pages covered in careful German script, notes about experiments and observations written in the same hand that had selected children for death.

"You kept records," Aaron said. "Even after all these years, you kept records."

"Evidence," Keller whispered. "Insurance. In case they ever came for me."

"They did come for you, Franz. We all did." Aaron closed the journal and looked directly into Keller's eyes. "Sarah Goldberg, age seven. You selected her for Dr. Mengele's temperature experiments. She died screaming your name."

Keller's face went white. "I was following orders. We were all following orders."

"Abram Goldman, age five," David continued, his voice steady as stone. "You chose him for surgical experiments without anesthesia. He lasted three days."

Aaron and David stood simultaneously, moving with choreographed precision. From the canvas bag, Aaron withdrew a syringe filled with clear liquid while David produced a length of rope.

"What are you doing?" Keller tried to stand but found David's hand on his shoulder, holding him down with gentle, inexorable pressure.

"Exactly what you did to them," Aaron said. "Except you'll have the courtesy of knowing why."

The injection was quick and professional. Keller's struggles became sluggish, then stopped altogether as the paralytic took effect. His eyes remained open, aware, terrified. Just like the children had been.

Aaron and David worked together, efficient and methodical. There was no anger, no passion, no dramatic speeches. Only the quiet administration of justice that had been thirty years in the making.

When it was finished, they stood over Karl Keller's body in the circle of light while the six survivors emerged from the shadows. The guardians of memory had passed their vigil to a new generation.

"It's done," Miriam said simply.

Aaron felt no satisfaction, no relief, no guilt. Only the certainty that the circle was complete and the work would continue. He was no longer a journalist. He was no longer Benjamin's grandson searching for answers about the past.

He was a hunter. And somewhere in the world, other monsters were sleeping peacefully in comfortable beds, believing themselves safe.

Not for much longer.

If you enjoyed this book you might want to give me some feedback or a review on Amazon. I truly hope you enjoyed it.

Gary H.

www.ingramcontent.com/pod-product-compliance
Lightning Source LLC
Chambersburg PA
CBHW061507020726
47502CB00006B/1963